D1624913

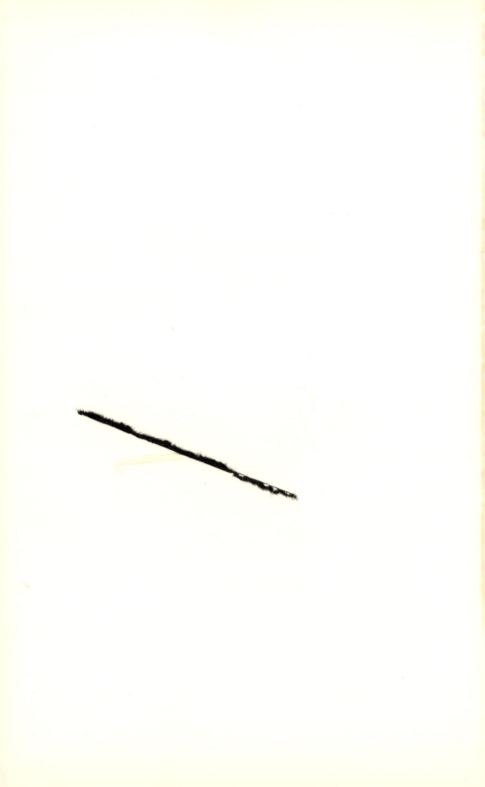

The Perfect Gift

Praise for the novels of
CHRISTINA SKYE

"A lively sensual Christmas story that features well-crafted characters, a sprinkle of humor, an intriguing plot, and a wonderfully misty Scottish setting."

Library Journal on *Season of Wishes*

"The hauntingly beautiful world of Draycott Abbey will totally seduce you."

Virginia Henley

"Complex and multi-faceted . . . Skye has written one finely crafted, very romantic love story."

Publishers Weekly on *Bride of the Mist*

"A guaranteed keeper that will be looked upon by future generations as classic literature."

Affaire de Coeur on *Bridge of Dreams*

Other Avon Books by
Christina Skye

BRIDE OF THE MIST

BRIDGE OF DREAMS

CHRISTMAS KNIGHT

HOUR OF THE ROSE

KEY TO FOREVER

SEASON OF WISHES

CHRISTINA SKYE

The Perfect Gift

AVON BOOKS ◆ NEW YORK

This is a work of fiction. Names, characters, places, and incidents either are the product of the author's imagination or are used fictitiously. Any resemblance to actual events, locales, organizations, or persons, living or dead, is entirely coincidental and beyond the intent of either the author or the publisher.

AVON BOOKS, INC.
1350 Avenue of the Americas
New York, New York 10019

Copyright © 1999 by Roberta Helmer
Excerpt from *Someday My Prince* copyright © 1999 by Christina Dodd
Excerpt from *Married in Haste* copyright © 1999 by Catherine Maxwell
Excerpt from *His Wicked Ways* copyright © 1999 by Sandra Kleinschmit
Excerpt from *The Perfect Gift* copyright © 1999 by Roberta Helmer
Excerpt from *Once and Forever* copyright © 1999 by Constance O'Day-Flannery
Excerpt from *The Proposition* copyright © 1999 by Judith Ivory
Inside cover author photo by Bill Morris Studio
Published by arrangement with the author

ISBN: 0-7394-0598-5

All rights reserved, which includes the right to reproduce this book or portions thereof in any form whatsoever except as provided by the U.S. Copyright Law. For information address Avon Books, Inc.

AVON TRADEMARK REG. U.S. PAT. OFF. AND IN OTHER COUNTRIES, MARCA REGIS-TRADA, HECHO EN U.S.A.

Printed in the U.S.A.

With warmest thanks
to all of the inspired booksellers
who keep the wheels humming,
the books moving,
and the stories flying off their shelves.

A special thanks to those guardian angels in human form: Carla Watland, Suzanne Barr, Daniel Garcia, Kathy Baker, Andrew Hobbs, Beth Anne Steckiel, Pat McGuiness, Becky Meehan, Debbie Neckel, Damita Lewis, Tanzy Cutter, Suzanne Coleburn, Jeannie Heikkala, Vicki Profitt, Kathy Hendrickson, Jolene Ehret, Lisa Clevenger, Mark Budrock, Mary Clare, Cindi Streicher, Jenny Jones, Jennifer Martin, Kathy Campbell, Terry Gowey, Mary Bullard, Merry Cutler, Annie Oakley, Jana Tomlinson, Tim Lowe, Mickey Mans, and Sharon Murphy.

You are all solid-gold wonderful!

The Perfect Gift

Chapter 1

Loch Maree, Scotland
Late autumn

THE FIRST SNOWFLAKES OF WINTER DANCED OVER SCOT-
land's green hills.

He stood on the high slope, knapsack on one shoulder
and gaunt face turned to the wind. The stony heights did
not deter him, nor did the chill of late October. He welcomed both wind and cold as the old friends they were.

His name was Jared Cameron MacNeill, and he had
come home to die.

It had seemed a good plan long months ago, when he'd
stood squinting at the beach beneath a baking Asian sun.
Now the Scotsman wasn't so sure.

His feet brushed the very edge of the cliff, where granite
fell away to cold air and biting wind. The seventh after
seven of his line, MacNeill felt his eyes glint with momentary pleasure at the sight of the mountains already snowcapped and bright in the gathering dawn. Then he turned
his face to the wind and forced all thought from his mind.
He simply felt.

How green the world seemed. How soft the heather.

Rounded slopes swelled from loch to bright loch. Even
the air was different here—light and sharp. Pungent with
peat and sea salt. The great loch had been home to his clan
for generations of gain and loss, warfare and peace. Now
Jared stared over the steep slopes, remembering tales of old
feats and dark blood rivalries. Though he had been gone

1

for six years, the brooding hills seemed unchanged. If only
the rest of his heritage were the same.

Don't look back.

Lines of exhaustion traced his lean cheeks, and his gray
eyes were empty of emotion. Perhaps he had felt too much,
crouched in the midnight streets of Rome, Bogotá, and
Kowloon. Or perhaps he had not felt enough. Not in the
ways that mattered.

Don't look back.

He stared at the rain-veiled peaks to the north.

Ben Slioch. The Fannich heights and remote Sgurr Mor
towering over the cold glass of Loch Fannich. Out to the
west An Teallach, bleak and dark, wrapped in perpetual
mists.

The names came to him in the old tongue, Gaelic learned
at his father's knee in rich phrases that rippled through his
mind like sunbeams off stormy water. The old sounds had
not changed, nor had the air. Every breath bit at his throat,
sharp with pine, peat, and the tang of the cold Atlantic.
Jared savored the memories as he looked down where blue
water clawed against the curving arms of ancient green hills
and golden bays.

Once again he remembered his brother's warning: *Don't
look back.*

Sound advice.

But it had come from a man who'd been too proud to
heed his own words. Jared wondered if it was pride that
had killed him.

Wind whipped at his long hair and lashed at his face as
Jared realized that he never should have returned to this
beautiful loch full of mystery and brooding silence. The
secluded hills held the bones of warriors and saints, and he
was neither. From here his journey led in only one direction.

His shoulders tensed beneath the folds of worn Hebri-
dean tweed. Even the wind could not shift the heavy
MacNeill tartan at his knees. He was the latest of his line
to stand on this high hill, the latest to watch the sun paint
tracks of gold over the great loch.

He would also be the last.

So be it.

A whine split the air at his elbow.

He ignored the shrill burst from the phone in his knapsack. He knew he should have left the cellular back in his car, but staying in touch was a habit hard to break. Nevertheless, his employers would soon learn to forget him, just as he meant to forget them. He closed his eyes at the thought, willing himself to ignore the shrill peals.

In a split second the Scotsman was carried back to a night two years before when his world had changed forever in a nightmare of heat and unrelenting pain. Trapped in a box in the stifling jungle, captive of a hostile government, he had discovered the boundaries of his own strength. Only through a miracle had he escaped dying from the nightly visits that had left his body bleeding and wracked with pain.

Don't ever look back.

Now he was home, and it was two months before Christmas, but what did that mean to him? His broad shoulders carried the marks of old wounds, and his heart carried a heavier weight than that. He had come to Scotland looking for some hint of home, only to find that the great loch and the high hills were no longer enough to soothe his soul.

Another peal jolted his reverie.

Jared smiled darkly. The careful men in careful suits would soon forget him. He was of no further use to them.

As the phone rang on, he turned to the west. Closer to the edge of the loch, he saw three laughing men load wooden crates onto a battered green lorry. A pair of schoolchildren chased a herd of wary sheep.

Something brushed his face. Early snow? Or was it regret?

The phone finally slid into silence. Perhaps they had finally accepted the resignation he'd left on their desks two days earlier. He could well imagine their shock.

What to do now? He supposed he should follow the weathered stone fence up to the house of his youth. *Taigh na Coille.* House in the woods.

But Jared found he hadn't the heart to see the gray stone walls or the tiny leaded windows. He certainly didn't want to walk among the old graves in the kirk. He would see them soon enough, and not as an idle guest. His visions since Thailand were clear in that respect. His death would come when he least expected it, walking beside a lichen-covered boulder beneath a tree with a broken branch.

The vision had come a dozen times since his return from Thailand. First the rock, then the tree, and then the feel of his own body slick with blood. Falling. Falling.

He was almost glad for the distraction when the phone jolted to life once again. His fingers locked on the cold base as anger flared in waves. "No more. It's *done*, damn it. Haven't you had enough of me?"

Silence hung. There was a low cough, partly lost in static. "Jared, is that you?"

He frowned at the sound. This was the last voice he wanted to hear, but old debts made this man impossible to ignore. "So it would seem."

"I suppose you didn't hear the calls. I've tried twelve times now. Not that anyone's counting." Nicholas Draycott sounded tired and worried. "Where in hell are you?"

"*Taigh na Coille*. Straight along Strath Bran and a right at Achnasheen."

"Come here for Christmas. We've got rooms and more at Draycott Abbey, and there will be no other visitors, so you needn't worry about tripping over anyone's feet. You can come and go at your pleasure."

"I've been there already, Nicholas. You and Kacey have done all that was possible—maybe even more. The rest is up to me."

"Damn it, man, you've got friends. Don't turn that hard Scottish back on us."

"I needed to come home. To watch the dawn and walk the Highlands." *One last time*, he thought.

"There's nothing for you there, Jared. Not now. Besides, I need you down here."

Jared would have laughed except the emotion was beyond him. "Need? You need what I *was*, Nicholas. Not what I am."

"I need both, you fool. Now get yourself down off that brooding hill. There's a car waiting for you in Kinlochewe."

"Why?"

"We'll talk when you get here to the abbey."

"No. I'm done with that work." *Or any other kind.*

"This is a personal favor I'm asking of you." Papers rattled, but they didn't quite cover Nicholas Draycott's curse. "Since it would be bad form for me to remind you who saw to your release from that hellhole in the jungle, I won't. I'll only say that I need you now."

"Just as a point of curiosity, do you ever take no for an answer?"

"Never."

Jared stared off to the west. The sun perched blood red over Gairloch, raising a blush over the distant curve of the sea. "I can well believe that. But with all due apologies, you'll have to this time."

"I'll come track you down, and I warn you I'll make it damned unpleasant. Remember, I know exactly what you're going through."

The sea churned. Jared remembered another place of darkness and pain and nights too deep for hope.

Forget the box. Forget Thailand, he thought tensely. But he couldn't. Maybe Nicholas Draycott realized that even better than he.

He cursed himself for his next question. "What is it this time?"

"A woman."

"Isn't it always?"

"She may be in great danger."

Something dug at Jared's chest. There were rules, and hurting a woman broke all of them. "Why?"

"Her father appears to have fallen in with the wrong sort."

"Let him help her."

"He disappeared about seven months ago, after an airplane crash in Northern Sumatra. He might have been carrying a fortune in historic jewels at the time."

To his irritation, Jared felt a pang of curiosity. "None of them were his own, I take it?"

"Most were from the Smithsonian, but a dozen or so were on loan from the royal family's private collection."

For a moment the world hazed black before Jared's eyes. Death was here, once again close enough to touch. Even the high glens and the silver lochs could not hold the darkness at bay. Perhaps death was the only constant in this bleak, chaotic world. "Why are you so interested in the daughter of a criminal?"

"A *possible* criminal," Nicholas corrected. "And no matter what the father did, he was brilliant, just as his daughter is. I want her here at the abbey for a project I'm planning."

"The daughter of a possible criminal? Bad choice, my friend."

"Too late. I've made up my mind."

"Then maybe you'll be lucky and she'll refuse. Either way, I can't help you, Nicholas."

"A very sophisticated set of criminals is involved, Jared. From what I've picked up in London, the matter goes far beyond simple theft."

What theft was ever simple? "Drug world involvement?" Jared's hands locked on the telephone. He knew better than most what rules that world played by. If drugs were involved, all the more reason to refuse his oldest friend, no matter the debt Jared owed him.

"Still too soon to say. If so, they're fishing far out of their usual waters. That's never a good sign."

"What do you expect of me? Surveillance and explosive work are what I know, Nicholas. Nothing of that sort appears to be involved here."

"I need your eyes, Jared. I need your hands, your reasoning power and that damnable Scottish tenacity. I'll need surveillance, too."

Frustration slammed down hard. "Sorry, but I can't."

"We'll discuss it when you get here. Kacey has stocked enough salmon for an army, and I've put away a stash of very fine single malt whisky. There'll be no more matchmaking, I promise you." There was a sound on the other end of the line. "Oh, yes, Genevieve has a gift for you."

Jared closed his eyes, remembering Nicholas's young daughter, full of life and a thousand questions. But he wanted nothing more to do with their smiling faces and caring eyes. Even the thought tied him up in knots. He wasn't fit for calm, polite society anymore, and he didn't want people to care for him. Normalcy terrified him. Maybe a year in a box did *that*, too.

Nicholas should understand, if anyone could. He had endured his own months of hell in Asia, captive at the hands of a crazed warlord flush with blood money from acres of opium fields. So why was he playing hardball now?

"I *can't*, Nicholas. You're not listening to me."

"Because I don't hear anything but rubbish. Kinlochewe, MacNeill." The twelfth viscount Draycott's voice was curt. "One hour. Look for the blue Rover."

The phone clicked dead.

Jared scowled at the handset. Damn the man. Damn a world where death struck with relentless frequency and absolutely no fairness.

Slowly he housed the phone and shouldered his knapsack, while the wind drove over the cliffs and seabirds soared above him, clumsy atop the churning silver loch.

Jared could picture Draycott Abbey clearly, the hereditary home of centuries of blue-blooded Draycotts with a legacy dating back to the age of William the Conqueror. The shadowed rooms were heavy with history and a tangible sense of magic. Jared had felt welcome there, even when he couldn't escape a twitching at his neck and the sense of shadows moving just beyond his vision.

Haunted, so it was said. Even Nicholas didn't deny the legend. Some even said that a surly Draycott ancestor still walked the parapets on moonless nights, warding off danger from his beloved granite walls.

Purest nonsense, of course. Had there been any ghosts wandering about the abbey, Jared would have seen them. But of course that was *one* secret even Nicholas didn't yet know.

Jared looked north to the snowcapped peaks, aware only of silence. A cold wind brushed his face like ghostly fingers.

He should have known that coming home would be a mistake. There was nothing to hold him here in this place of dead warriors and forgotten saints. He couldn't go back and he couldn't forget. The tension never seemed to leave him now.

Ah well, he might as well go and lend Nicholas a hand. After all, Jared had nothing else to do. Considering the clarity of his visions, he had time—and only time—to kill.

Draycott Abbey
Sussex, England
Two days later

The fire crackled softly, casting golden light over a row of Italian crystal paperweights and shelves filled with books. Jared waited, unmoving, while Nicholas Draycott paced before the study's high windows.

"Will you have a drink? There's sherry here, or I have whisky if you prefer."

"Neither, thanks." Jared waited in silent impatience for Nicholas to get down to business. He owed his friend that much.

Nicholas finally cleared his throat. "First of all, let me make one thing clear. This has got *nothing* to do with fame."

"What hasn't?"

"The Abbey Jewels collection."

Jared frowned. "Have I missed something? Are you and Kacey going into the necklace business?"

"Not bloody likely." Nicholas rubbed his jaw. "It's an idea Kacey and I have had for quite a while now. We want to re-create the pleasure that art has brought to us, and this seemed a good way to begin."

"By making jewelry?"

Nicholas shook his head impatiently. "What we have in mind is an international exhibition that would begin here at the abbey, then travel to a dozen venues in England and Europe. We want displays that show the history and the magic of metal and stone. We want cases that take a design apart, piece by piece and show how gold is etched and silver forged. We want photographs of emeralds *in situ* in Colombia and jadeite boulders from Afghanistan. Then we want to show how they are polished, studied, and shaped to final form. These things are part of our heritage, but they are also the heritage of the world. These skills should be shared, studied, and documented before they're lost to modern technology.'' He gave a low laugh. ''Does that sound pompous?''

Jared studied his friend over steepled fingers. ''It sounds like a remarkably good idea. But I still don't see how that involves me.''

''We've chosen our first artist. She's an expert in classical metalwork, and her skill is remarkable, especially in view of her age.''

Jared's eyes narrowed. ''And she also happens to be the daughter of a criminal.''

''A *possible* criminal. No charges were ever brought against her father.''

''Is she under criminal investigation?''

''Not at all.''

''Then what's the problem? Send out the invitations and get the exhibition on its way.''

Nicholas sighed. ''It's not quite that easy. For this project to succeed the way Kacey and I envision, we'll need support at the highest level, both culturally and politically. We've gotten commitments from the British Museum and several scholarly publications, and an American foundation has just given a sizeable pledge of support. Two museums in France have requested the show next year, and the royal family has indicated their interest in participation. Discreetly, of course.''

''Of course.''

''Which, as we both know, means multiple security clearances. To succeed, every aspect of the project will have to be high profile, since the art world can be damnably cutthroat. The scrutiny will be fierce, and once Maggie Kincade's connection to her father comes out—'' Nicholas made a tight sound of anger.

Jared could well imagine the result. But security was security, and there was no way Nicholas could hide the truth from the people who made a business of protecting England's public buildings and the safety of the royal family. ''What do you want of me?''

"Check her out. I'm very nearly certain that she had nothing to do with what happened, but if there's any hint of criminal involvement, or if she has knowledge about those missing gems . . ." He bit back an oath. "In that case, I want to know now, before things go any further."

"And if I find nothing?"

Nicholas picked up a vellum envelope from the desk beside him. "Then I want you to give her this. It's an invitation to present her designs here as the core of our first exhibition."

"And you trust me to make the decision about her innocence?"

"Without question." Nicholas held out a folder. "Here's a photograph and her address. I've also put in a background profile and your air ticket to New York."

"Rather presumptuous, aren't you?" Jared glared into the fire. "What makes you think I'll go?"

"Because you always pay what you consider to be your debts. You're insufferable about that streak of honor. I won't deny that this is important to Kacey and me, but you're entirely free to accept or decline as you choose. Of course, this will also make all the difference to Maggie Kincade's career."

"I'm not interested, Nicholas." Jared rose to his feet. "I can't afford to be."

"Why?"

Jared shoved his hands into his pockets, frowning. "I have my reasons."

"I'd like to hear them."

"Damn it, leave it alone." The words came out with suppressed violence.

"I would if I were anyone else. Or if *you* were anyone else. But as you know, it's a Draycott trait to be stubborn as sin itself, and I know you too well to be turned away by a little Scottish hostility."

Jared rubbed his wrists, remembering bamboo handcuffs and wet ropes. He drew a harsh breath. "I'm not the same, Nicholas. Thailand changed me."

"Changed you how?"

He wouldn't leave it alone, but Jared hadn't really expected that he would. Yet how did you begin to explain things from a nightmare, things that most people considered to be part of the twilight realm of science fiction?

Jared rubbed his wrists, choosing his words carefully. "It happened after one of the beatings. They cut a vein, and I bled for quite some time. No one came. It was night and I remember being cold—and then I remember being nothing at all."

Jared felt a glass pressed against his fingers. Frowning, he downed two inches of superb whisky. It might help him to complete the story he was about to tell. Then again, it might not.

"Go on."

"I died that night, Nicholas. No pulse, no heartbeat. I bled to death there on that cement floor and no one knew."

Dimly he heard the clink of ice and realized that Nicholas was downing his own drink. Perfectly understandable, since it wasn't a particularly pleasant thing to hear.

"God rot their callous souls." Nicholas touched his shoulder for a moment, and Jared managed—just barely—not to flinch from the contact.

Even in that brief moment of touch he sensed the weight of his friend's worry, which Nicholas had tried damnably hard to hide for weeks.

Jared closed his eyes, fighting the jolt of contact. Fighting the rush of bleak images. "You needn't worry about me so much."

"I don't—"

"Yes, you do. You're afraid I'll do something drastic, but you don't need to be."

Nicholas simply stared. "Have I ever implied such a thing?"

"No." That was exactly the problem, of course. "You don't have to say a word, Nicholas. One touch, one brush of the hand, and I know."

"What are you saying?"

"That I can feel things. Mostly by touch or the random brush of fingers. It began that night after I passed out. After I *died*," Jared said grimly. "When I came around, I was in a makeshift clinic bed with a chipped IV line in my arm, and I could sense emotions, unspoken thoughts. They were simply—*there*. Damned disconcerting, I don't need to tell you.''

Nicholas sank into a chair before the fire. ''Sweet God above, I had no idea. You seemed distant, aloof. Now I know why. Did you mention this new . . . ability in your debriefing in London?''

''Why should I? So they could use me as a new lab rat?''

''Perfectly understandable. I just wish you'd told me sooner, Jared. Not that it changes anything.''

''It changes *everything*. I'm barely fit to keep *myself* company, much less anyone else. Touching another person triggers an agony of chaotic images and emotions that get twisted up with my own until I doubt my own sanity. In short, I'm no good to you, Nicholas. Not for this project or anything else.''

''Why don't you let me be the judge of that?'' Nicholas hesitated, then held out his hand. There was a light of pure, devilish determination in his eyes.

Jared studied the outstretched fingers. Then, with a sigh, he gripped them with his own.

In that moment, Jared felt his friend's steely determination and unquestioning trust in his abilities. He also saw that Nicholas would never give up.

Jared frowned. ''It won't work, you know. I'll make a mistake or I'll offend someone. Maybe even you. How many of us can stand to have our minds picked clean by a stranger?''

''I'll take that chance.'' Nicholas pushed to his feet. ''Now I think you'd better go up and rest, because Kacey and Genevieve have something special planned tonight.''

''More card games?'' Jared gave a laugh that was slightly grim. ''It's getting hard to pretend that I don't know exactly what they have. Every time they touch me I can see, Nicholas.''

''Good lord, I had no idea.'' Nicholas gave a smile. ''A useful ability, however. It could save a person a great deal of money.''

''I'm serious, Nicholas. This is serious.''

''Of course it is. But sometimes it's better to laugh. Kacey taught me that.'' Nicholas stared at the framed photo of a woman with sunlight in her face and flowers braided into her long hair. ''Maybe if you're lucky, someone will teach you that, too. Now go and rest, because I'm not making your excuses tonight. Remember to study that file I gave you, too.''

''I believe I know how Captain Bligh's seamen felt two weeks out of Tahiti.''

''Trust me, my friend, you haven't seen anything yet.''

The moon hung like an icy sickle, stark above the black woods. Out beyond the Witch's Pool the wind rose in shrill lament.

The distant peal of bells rode the same current, sharp and sad over the rolling downs. Ten, eleven, twelve. And then once more, low and dim, more like a memory than any true stroke.

In its wake the lands of Draycott Abbey lay still. Asleep. Almost as if in hushed expectation.

Silence—and then something more. Something furtive that skirted the darkest of the night's shadows.

So it began, thought the figure motionless on the high parapet. In silence his tall form slid from behind a chimney of twisted tiles, settling into a slash of black velvet. Even the lace cuffs at his wrist were muted gray in the dappled shadows.

''Once more it begins,'' he whispered, eyes to the moat and the home wood beyond. But where?

The guardian ghost of Draycott Abbey frowned. His skills were good, far superior to those of any common mortal, but even he was not without his limits. He had met danger and faced violence many times, all in protection of his beloved abbey, but tonight the darkness held a scent of evil.

There was something almost familiar about the fear rippling along his spine. Something that felt very . . . old.

''Imagination,'' he said sharply. ''Too many nights of solitude.''

At his feet, a figure slid from the darkness, gray body

rising to keen amber eyes. A low meow drifted over the abbey's heights.

"So it calls to you too, my old friend? A stirring along the spine like whispers in a cold room?"

The cat curled around Adrian's booted feet, once and then again. His tail flicked sharply from side to side.

"Somewhere to the north?" Adrian turned to face the shadows beyond the moat, his face hard as the weathered granite at his feet. "You can sense it?"

The cat paced the roof and jumped to a sheer stone edge. There he stopped, his body frozen, just one more creature worked among the dozens of carvings.

"What sounds? I hear nothing." Adrian studied the patchwork of fields touched by moonlight. "It must be that feline imagination of yours."

Yet even as Adrian spoke, gossamer threads of sound drifted up to his ears. Haunting, they were. Sad.

And somehow familiar.

Adrian's strong hands closed. What trick was this? Who dared work such foul illusions *here*, in the heart of his beloved realm?

The cat's ears slid forward.

Adrian caught the thought before it was complete. "The piper? Of course I remember, but—"

This time the low notes were beyond ignoring. Faint and high, they crossed the black fields and soared to the abbey's cold roof.

Adrian listened, unmoving, his face like night itself. "If the man has come back, she will soon follow." The thought left him reeling. To remember now, after so long. To taste the old regret.

Dear God, he had failed her then and they all had paid the bitter price.

As if sensing his pain, the cat turned, amber eyes shot with specks of fire. His liquid meow touched Adrian's mind like warm fingers.

"Thank you, my friend." His voice was not steady for all his efforts. Grimly, the abbey ghost paced to the parapet's edge and stared down sixty feet and more to the shimmering line of the moat. For the first time he allowed himself to remember in full clarity, despite the pain it brought.

By the stone wall the pair had met. In a past nearly too dim to recall, fate had cast their lives together. By the bright roses they had laughed and bent to their first sweet kiss. And there by the roses Adrian had failed them. Never mind that he'd had a different name then, a different form. His guilt was exactly the same.

Pain wrapped about his heart. So much sadness. So much he would prefer not to remember. The old betrayals had never healed.

And now they were coming back to his haunted abbey, back to the dangers that had stalked them centuries before.

The knowledge fell like the weight of the house itself, crushing down upon his shoulders. He could not fail them again. This much Adrian knew.

Gradually, he grew aware of a shape at his hand. Blinking, he looked down to keen eyes and sleek gray fur. ''So you see it all again, too. How they met. How their laughter rang over the green lawns, then stilled to far more than laughter. And I should have known they would find joy in each other. He wooed her with his music and with his smile he broached her heart. Damnation, I should have guessed what would happen before it was too late . . .''

The cat brushed hard against his tense fingers. The movement brought Adrian back to the chill night and the faint thread of sound from the north.

''Yes, we shall watch. Together as always, Gideon. Perhaps, with God's help this time, we shall not detect the madman's coils too late . . .''

Together they stood, two shapes that might have been stone or yet no more than the fabric of shadows. The haunting strain of the pipes rose around them, no more real than any other part of the abbey's magic.

And all the while something far more dangerous waited in the restless night.

Chapter 2

New York City
Late October

MAGGIE KINCADE CRADLED A FACETED 8 CARAT BURMA ruby. Holding her breath, she nudged the blood-red brilliant into a hand-cut bezel of pure silver.

Then she stood back. And smiled.

Perfect.

She ignored the knotted muscles at her neck. With luck, the piece would be gone within the week, the first of a dozen designs already commissioned by clients for Christmas gifts. Taking commissions required the skill of a master and the patience of a saint, but Maggie thrived on the constant challenge. Now, with a positive cash flow, she could finally fill her depleted inventory.

Patience, she thought. Her mother had always warned her that success came in its own time and its own way, and for Maggie the process was far too slow. After two years as a freelance jewelry designer, she had acquired a loyal following but not nearly enough clients for the dreams she confided to no one.

And dream, she did. Of sculpted ivory and hammered gold. Of emeralds dangling from fine hand-pulled silver chains. Maybe even a school to train a new generation of artists in shaping precious metal. And of course her own showroom, its windows filled with braided silver and etched gold. One day sunlight would gleam off an elegant door with a brass sign that announced: *M. E. Kincade, gold-smith. Fine jewelry by design.*

Her fingers tightened on the ruby. *And what if you fail, Maggie Kincade? What happens then?*

The silver bezel gleamed, tossing back the image of her face, with a mouth that was too wide. Maggie wondered if anyone else noticed the circles beneath her eyes formed by long nights of worry.

She jumped at the shrill peal of her phone, muttering as she nearly dropped the ruby. For long heartbeats she stared at the phone and thought about letting it ring. She was tired of the questions, tired of the intrusions. Finally habit won out over self-preservation. "Yes?"

"Okay, a little bird tells me you have two men in there and they've been there since last night."

Maggie smiled at that familiar, smoky voice belonging to her cousin Chessa. Both of her cousins possessed the scary ability to call whenever anything important was going on in Maggie's life. No doubt in an earlier age Chessa and Faith Kincade would have been burned as witches, but thankfully those days had passed.

Last year Faith had moved to England, where she was designing accurate period gardens, while Chessa managed a small, elegant shop in New York's fashionable Soho. There she showcased her striking fabric designs, along with Maggie's jewelry. And Chessa never let a day go by without checking on her younger cousin.

"Who told?"

"Hey, I never divulge my sources. But trust me, they're good."

"What two men?"

"Oh, no one important. Maybe it was Mel Gibson and Harrison Ford."

Maggie stared at her ruby with a grin. "Haven't seen either of them for days."

"Oh, yeah? How many days?"

"Three or four at least." Maggie's eyes glinted. "A woman needs *some* time to rest."

"Jeez, Mag, you never could share, even when you were a whining five-year-old in pigtails. First the Barbie Dolls, now you hold out on me with Indiana Jones. It's criminal.''

As usual, her outrageous cousin managed to make Maggie laugh, and laughter had been a rare commodity in Maggie's life over the last seven months. ''I'll be sure to tell Indy that you're interested. His people will get in touch with your people.''

''Yeah, yeah, they all say that.'' Somewhere a sewing machine hammered like distant artillery and fabric rustled. Probably silk, Maggie thought.

Chessa Kincade sniffed loudly. ''You working?''

''Finishing a necklace.''

''Hmm.'' The sewing noises grew quieter. Maggie heard the sound of a door closing. ''Are you okay, Mag?''

''I'm fine, Chessa.'' Maggie avoided the calendar on the opposite wall and the date circled in red crayon. She ignored the ache in her neck and the two deep welts on the inside of her palm. ''Life is just perfect.''

''You sound distracted.''

Maggie ran a hand through the chaos of her hair. ''Of course I'm distracted. I was *trying* to work.''

Nails clicked lightly on the other end of the line. ''How long has it been since you ate?''

''A meal, you mean?'' Maggie frowned. There had been a banana at dawn as sunlight burned over her wooden floor. Maybe a handful of nuts and a cup of tea as the morning light faded into afternoon. The truth was, she never had been too good with eating. Snacks were taken on the run, and nourishment often came in the form of a powdered shake while she bent over a sheet of 24K gold or a flawless Siberian diamond. When she was caught up in a design, Maggie never thought of food—or anything else.

Chessa sniffed. ''I thought so. I'll be right over.''

The phone went dead.

Maggie stiffened as a furry brown shape raced under her worktable, skirted a wan asparagus fern, and vanished into the cracked brick wall. Not the *mouse* again.

Somewhere outside a truck backfired. A taxi driver screamed profanities in a foreign tongue. *Another glamorous day in Manhattan*, Maggie thought.

She sank into the room's only chair and cradled the ruby,

shaky with the exhaustion that always struck at the end of a project. Only then did the strain of hours of painfully detailed work hit her. But the result was always worth the discomfort.

Right now the polished stone gleamed in her fingers, hints of pink, gold, and blue dancing with life in the focused light. The facets were clear, and the bezel curved flawlessly to cradle the ruby. Now came the final step.

Moving to her worktable, Maggie eased the stone onto a choker of hammered silver set with inlaid gold. Then she smiled slowly.

Sensuous. Simple. Absolutely stunning. All the hallmarks of a Kincade design.

The choker was striking enough to make her forget the street horns, the unpaid bills, and the headache building behind her eyelids. But there was something Maggie couldn't possibly forget. She looked past the decorated Christmas tree, a gift from Chessa meant to conjure up a magic mood for the designs Maggie had to complete before Christmas. Above the tree hung a calendar full of moody Scottish lochs and imposing granite castles. But it was the circled date that caught Maggie's eye.

Seven months since she'd lost her father. Silly to feel a sharp pang, she told herself. Silly to care so much.

Carefully she set the completed choker in her steel display case underneath a row of faceted white Siberian diamonds that winked with cold, almost unnatural perfection. They were not Maggie's favorite stones, but her father had loved their clarity. Despite her financial straits, she refused to sell them, keeping them as a link to the father she had always loved but had never come close to understanding. Daniel Kincade had been a master at his craft with an artistic vision that was legendary. No client ever walked away unsatisfied with his work.

And Maggie still missed him as much as if he'd been gone only a few hours.

She touched one of the diamonds, remembering how he'd taught her to shape a bezel or polish a newly cut gem. She had listened in rapt silence, absorbing every word, and now that classical training was part of the foundation that allowed her absolute control over an array of difficult, costly materials. No one else had had Daniel Kincade's ability to identify obscure stones and coax fire out of their unpolished surfaces. With unerring genius and a flare for the dramatic, he had made his reputation on three continents. After twenty years of designing, he had earned the right to name his price and choose his clients among the world's richest and most knowledgeable collectors.

Until the day he hadn't come back.

Seven months, Maggie thought. Seven months of wondering if Daniel Kincade was truly dead. Seven months of wondering if he could possibly have committed the robbery the police claimed he had.

Maggie sighed. Her shoulder ached, but her heart ached far worse.

When did the pain finally ebb? When would she stop expecting him to shove open the door, his arms weighted down with gifts from a dozen far-flung countries?

She pushed back the curtain and stared out at the late afternoon traffic. The facts weren't much help. Not much of her father's body had been found after the small plane he was riding in went down over the jungles of Northern Sumatra. Among the tangle of bones, torn metal, and seared bits of clothing, the searchers had turned up three teeth that matched his dental records. They'd turned up his passport, too. The embassy had sent it back to her, blackened by flames and sheared almost in two. Then they had closed the case, officially declaring him dead.

Intellectually, Maggie agreed with them. But the heart, a daughter's grieving heart, was a different matter entirely. She'd never quite accepted the reality that he was dead.

Had he lost consciousness before the fire took hold, or had he suffered the agonizing knowledge of his death, watching the ground slam toward him?

Seven months.

Something struck her window. Maggie spun around, arms tensed as a rain of gravel hammered at the glass. *Forget it*, she told herself sharply. This was the city that never slept. She was just experiencing her normal jitters after five days of work on a demanding design.

She shoved back a strand of cinammon-colored hair and swept her snub-nosed pliers and wire cutters back into their neat drawers as the floor shook.

A few seconds later she felt another tremor, courtesy of a blasting cap set by the workmen demolishing the town house next to her loft building. She barely managed to grab a pair of pink pearls as they careened across her worktable from the force of a third impact. With luck, the building would be razed before she lost her sanity along with her remaining stock of gems.

Silence fell, thick and blessed. Then a board creaked outside in the hall just beyond her door.

Maggie spun tensely, her heart racing. Probably another TV cameraman or a tabloid reporter trying to sniff out news of her father. Jewel thieves made for good audience demographics, she had learned. She was lunging for her heaviest metal shears when the door snapped open.

"Relax, Mag. Drop the shears and I promise not to skewer you with a chopstick."

"Chessa?"

"A good thing you gave me a key." Laughter sailed out of the shadows. "Hey, I said I'd be right over. It's not Indiana Jones, but who else is going to take care of you when you forget to eat?"

Slender and vibrant, Chessa Kincade sailed through the room like a whirlwind, immaculate in black velvet and a tapestry vest that looked two centuries old—and was actually even older. Fashion had been in her blood ever since she had sewed her first French seam at the age of six. She was still sewing perfect seams, though now she worked in crepe and duppioni silk instead of worn muslin.

"God, you look a wreck." Chessa frowned at her cousin. "Don't you *ever* sleep?"

"I had a silver design class last night. The students wanted to try etching and we ran over."

"How long over?"

"About four hours, but you should have seen what they made. They're showing real promise, Chessa, and their energy is astounding."

"It's the teacher I worry about, not the students. Crazy

woman." Chessa gracefully pushed back one full sleeve and slung down two large bags, still managing to look elegant in her exquisitely fitted linen poet's shirt and soft black velvet jeans. She moved like a model—which she had been until her love of restoring medieval tapestries had branched out into a line of fine period lingerie, which she wore at every possible opportunity, fully aware that no one modeled her clothing as well as she did.

Small wonder Maggie felt like a frump whenever they were together.

Maggie's fashion sense was limited to gems and precious metals. She didn't even own a slip. Jeans were her fashion staple, since she could never find anything off the rack to suit her gangly frame.

"First we eat." Chessa dropped a monstrous leather satchel onto the room's only chair, then turned imperiously. In seconds she had Maggie's worktable covered with boxes of obscure vegetables and handmade sauces with exotic, smoky smells.

"But my silver—"

"Forget your silver. *Eat*."

Chessa shoved a pair of chopsticks into her hand, and Maggie knew better than to argue. Her cousin was a virago with the face of a Botticelli angel. Besides, the food smelled wonderful. She sniffed, trying to identify the mix of spices. "Hunanese?"

Chessa sighed. "Thai. If you'd pay the slightest attention, you'd know I gave up Hunanese food months ago. Too many additives. Have some tea."

Maggie sniffed suspiciously at the dusky brew. "I hope this isn't more of that milk thistle poison you brought last time."

"That *poison*, as you term it, clears out your liver like nothing else on this planet."

"I think I'll stay toxic," Maggie muttered.

"Not if I can help it. Try some of this."

Maggie sipped carefully. "What's in it?"

"Gingko leaves, ginseng, and roasted barley. Great for mental acuity." Chessa's lips curved. "Even better for your love life."

What love life? Maggie thought. These days she was running on energy and blind obsession. All she had was her teaching, her design work, and an unending stream of visions that pulled her from sleep with dreams of inlaid amber and platinum-wrapped jade.

But not for much longer. Without professional backing there would be no more stones and no more sheets of precious metal. What Maggie needed was a patron with deep pockets and permanent gallery space to showcase her line, first in New York, and then across the country. After that, she dreamed of setting up a small craft school where rigorous classical techniques would be combined with cutting-edge design concepts.

More dreams.

Chessa's eyes were dark with concern. "How long since you ate a complete meal? By that, I mean something more than tea and a handful of nuts."

Maggie frowned. "Yesterday morning. Or maybe last night. I don't remember."

"You're a disgrace to the Kincade name. People will think that we starve you."

Maggie started to protest, caught between humor and exasperation. Then she saw the look on her cousin's face.

Chessa was standing very still, staring at her in the single pool of light from the work lamp. "Oh, Mag, I forgot. It's his anniversary, isn't it? October 12, seven months to the day that your father disappeared."

Maggie felt something press at her eyes. "It doesn't matter. He's gone, and I'm an idiot to keep hoping otherwise." She swallowed, wondering why the cold, hard facts made no difference. If only she'd had a chance to say good-bye, the way she had during her mother's lingering bout with cancer. Maybe if Maggie had told her father how much he'd mattered to her, the pain wouldn't be so sharp now.

Chessa slid her arms around Maggie's stiff shoulders. "Of course it's not stupid. He was your *father*. It's perfectly right that you should remember him and grieve in your way. Forget what I said, Mag. I'm being a complete idiot, as usual."

Maggie's hands clenched and unclenched. She didn't

want to remember, but she did. "It's the uncertainty, I think. I was too late to talk to him at the gate, and there was only time to see him wave. I never dreamed that he wouldn't come back. Even now when I hear a sound in the hall, I expect him to bang open the door, unannounced, the way he always liked to arrive." She tried to swallow the low whimper, the long ache of loneliness and loss.

"He shouldn't have rushed off," Chessa said fiercely. "I know you don't want to hear it, but he left you in the lurch." Her hands tightened. "He was good at that."

"No more arguments, Chessa. Not today."

Chessa scanned her face. "There's something else, isn't there?"

Maggie shoved her fists into her pockets, frowning.

"You can't possibly hope to lie to me, Mag. Let's have it. *All* of it."

"It's bills." Maggie drew a raw breath. "Bills and bills and bills. Thousands of dollars that my father owed. I don't know how I'm going to pay them off." She sank into the rickety steel chair and stared blindly out the window while rush hour traffic screamed along Houston Street.

"How bad is it?"

"He owed money to two auction houses in Paris and a diamond wholesaler in California. I've already had three calls this morning from a customs broker at the airport who says he hasn't been paid for almost a year and he's going to send *men* after me. Unpleasant men with accents. I feel like an extra in a bad John Travolta movie." Maggie tried to smile and failed completely. "Then there are the reporters. They've been staking out the building, following me home and ringing the bell at all hours of the night. They won't give up on a chance at a story about the notorious jeweler turned cold-blooded thief—at least that's *their* slant on things. But I can manage the reporters. It's the bills I'm worried about. I don't have that kind of money."

"There's only one thing to do." Chessa tapped a manicured nail against her jaw and smiled slowly. "You pay them."

"*How?* I'm barely getting by, considering the bleedingly high cost of materials."

At that moment the buzzer rang shrilly. Maggie peered through the peephole and frowned, her body stiff with tension.

"Ms. Kincade? Margaret Kincade?"

Maggie didn't move. "Why?"

"I have a delivery of roses here. Invoice says they're for a Margaret Kincade."

"Roses?" Chessa hissed. "Open the door."

"I didn't order any flowers," Maggie said tightly.

"Must be a gift," the man outside said. "Look, lady, I'm just making the delivery here, and I need a signature to—"

"Go away," Maggie said. "Ms. Kincade's not here and we both know that you're not from any florist shop. And you're not going to get any more pictures—not today or any other day. Not after the lies that you people keep printing." Her voice was harsh with anger and pain.

"Come on, open up, Ms. Kincade. Just for a few questions. We want to know why your father disappeared—and what happened to those stolen gems."

"Go away."

Maggie closed her eyes and sank back against the wall. There had already been two reporters at her buzzer that morning. One had assured her he had dry cleaning to deliver, and the other swore he was collecting for UNICEF. Would they ever leave her alone?

A string of curses drifted past the heavy metal door frame, and she straightened her shoulders. "If one more reporter tries that, I'm going to use my blowtorch on his face."

"Great idea. It will make a lovely human interest piece for the front page. *Jeweler rearranges reporter's cheeks*," Chessa said calmly.

"Don't you ever get upset?"

"Life's too short to get upset."

"I hate it," Maggie muttered. "They follow me, they phone me, they harass me."

"Face it, love, you're news. *Big* news. That makes you a prime target. You have to admit that the publicity has brought us a herd of new customers."

"To gawk. To gossip. Not to buy."

"They will. We've got exceptional merchandise, and they won't find it anywhere else in New York. They'll come back," Chessa said confidently. "And then they'll buy, trust me."

"It might be too late. I won't have any more designs, not with my inventory liquidated to pay bills."

Chessa frowned. "There has to be a way."

"You think I should sell my body on Ninth Avenue? I doubt I'd have any takers."

"You've got those boxes in the safe deposit. You told me your father had been putting away some special stones as his personal stock for future designs. They'll help you pay his bills."

"By selling his inventory?" Maggie pushed to her feet and paced the room with sudden, raw energy. "I couldn't. They were his favorite gems, the most beautiful stones he'd saved from years of searching. I can't—"

"You can." Chessa gripped her arm and pulled her to a halt. "You *must*. He's gone, love. All he's left you is a mountain of debts. Selling his private collection of stones is your only way out."

Maggie opened her mouth to protest, then closed it again. Chessa was right, she realized numbly. At the moment, her father's unsold inventory was her only marketable asset. It would have to go. All of it.

She rubbed a hand along her neck, wincing as she brushed a hard knot of muscles. "I took a piece to Michaelson today. You know how he is, all oily politeness and eyes like a predator."

"What did he say?"

" 'Lovely.' 'Flawless.' Then the snake offered me a pittance. I would have laughed if I hadn't been so insulted."

Chessa's eyes took on an edge of cold determination. "He scented blood. It happens all the time. What you need is drama, excitement. Presentation is everything in business, as I've been forever trying to tell you."

"I don't do drama. That's your department."

"You do now. Mystery and elegance, too. You'll soon have Michaelson and everyone else eating out of your hand.

You've got the stones.'' She draped a cut velvet scarf over Maggie's shoulders, nodding slowly. ''And I've got the perfect plan.''

The next morning at eleven, three black limousines blocked the curb outside Chessa's fashionable shop on Broome Street. Inside, sunlight filtered over antique carpets and polished wood shelves that resembled the private rooms of a very fine English country house.

But *this* country house had satin camisoles and lace peignoirs draped over the heirloom chairs. Potted dwarf palms cleverly focused the eye on a hanging display of handmade lace dressing gowns that would caress a woman's skin and leave a man in a state of acute discomfort.

Nearby, a pair of Chessa's sensuous camisoles framed a mahogany desk with the jewelry that had earned Maggie a fervent following.

But none of the three men pacing in the elegant room was looking for lingerie. They glanced up irritably as Chessa sailed in, elegant in a crimson velvet sheath and strappy velvet high-heels.

Maggie blinked as she recognized three of New York's most prominent jewelers in the same room. All wore Armani, and their watches alone could have paid the shop's rent for about a decade.

The closest man raised a manicured hand. The Rolex on his wrist flashed imperiously. ''We've been waiting for a half hour. Why did you call us?''

''Because, gentlemen, you are about to receive the offer of this or any other lifetime.'' Chessa moved past them with all the grace of the fashion runways she had dominated for ten years. She knew how to command attention and she did it now, pulling them after her into the curtained area reserved for important customers.

''What offer? My wife has all the lingerie she needs, Ms. Kincade. And I'm *not* in the market for jewelry,'' he said flatly. ''I buy in volume and all my sources are abroad.''

''You must be James Michaelson. I know your shop on Sixty-first Street.'' Chessa eyed the two other men. ''Mr. Antonio. Mr. Dussaint. You both design from scratch, I believe. But to do that you need quality materials. Unusual stones like tanzanite, Siberian diamonds. South Sea black pearls.''

The Belgian, Dussaint, frowned. "You have such sources?''

Maggie listened from behind the curtain, her hands clenched. They might not go for this. On the other hand, she knew exactly how persuasive Chessa could be. And if Chessa could convince the three men to stay long enough to see what Maggie had to show them . . .

Chessa swirled in a blur of crimson. "By that you mean gems. Possibly a set of matched rubies formerly the property of a European royal family. Or maybe even some chatoyant sapphires.''

The Belgian stroked his Hermès tie and leaned forward. "Show us.''

"Patience, gentlemen. Patience.'' With an easy elegance, Chessa gestured them to the three chairs arranged at the far wall, then drew a bottle from a silver server. "Taittinger for each of you.'' She filled three crystal goblets in turn, making the most of every second of expectation. "A little something to set the mood.''

Beyond the curtain Maggie stood in an agony of uncertainty, expecting them to march out at any second.

Then the Belgian chuckled with reluctant admiration. "A fine stock, Ms. Kincade. And now that we are properly interested, perhaps you will show us these items. You said they had something to do with Daniel Kincade?'' There was an edge to his voice.

Chessa merely smiled. "It happens that his personal collection of fine stones is available for sale. Since you three gentlemen have unquestionable taste, you have been chosen to receive the first opportunity to bid.''

"Kincade had nothing. I've seen the papers. He took everything with him when he disappeared. I haven't got time for this nonsense.'' But Michaelson stopped cold as Maggie strode from behind the curtain. She wore a satin sheath of pure black, one of Chessa's finest creations. At her shoulders was a black cashmere shawl, which she slowly pulled away to reveal a simple but blindingly sensuous choker studded with two hundred diamonds and a fine single teardrop pendant at the center.

"My God, it's the Solitaire," Michaelson breathed. "Kincade said he'd never finish it. I asked him a dozen times and he always put me off." He blinked at the necklace, then stared sternly at Maggie. "How did you get that?"

"He gave it to me," Maggie said calmly. "I designed it with him and I helped him set most of the stones. It was the last piece we worked on together."

The jeweler's eyes widened. His gaze swept the elegant dress and returned to the amazing curve of flashing fire at her neck. He nodded slowly. "I know your work, Ms. Kincade. It's quite impressive for someone so young. You have all your father's technique, and the Solitaire is beyond description. I had no idea it was finished."

Maggie didn't tell him that she had finished the necklace by herself in the months since her father's disappearance. "One of you will leave here today with the Solitaire." Her voice was full and confident now. She had no doubt that her father's jewels would sell themselves to these men who recognized superior quality when they saw it. "We'll open at two hundred and fifty thousand dollars." As she spoke she ran her fingers over the shining platinum-set design, which glowed with cold white sparks against her skin.

"It's mine," the Belgian muttered. "I'll give you two hundred and eighty."

"Three hundred," Michaelson snapped. "And a certified check on your desk before the close of the business day."

The other jeweler put down his champagne with a snap, not to be outdone. "I say three hundred and fifty."

Maggie turned, letting the recessed lights play over the exquisite white diamonds. "You're looking at ninety-three point seven six carats, gentlemen. All highest grade matched fancies."

"Four hundred," the Belgian muttered, determined not to be outbid.

Maggie ran a hand lovingly over the white gems and smiled.

The Belgian shifted forward in his chair, determination

in his set features. "Damn it, make that four hundred and twenty."

Inside the quiet shop, Jared MacNeill moved from glass case to glass case, studying the silver and cut stones.

A young woman in unadorned black merino wool offered him an appreciative smile. "May I help you?"

Jared decided her spiky purple hair wasn't as odd as he'd first thought. "I hope so. I'm looking for a gift."

"For a friend?" She gave a small, knowing smile.

Jared hid a scowl. How in the hell had he gotten pulled into this? He was surrounded by night dresses and a lace camisole with satin flowers set in very suggestive locations, but he couldn't leave yet. He had caught enough of the conversation in the next room to realize there was a private auction going on.

Why would Maggie Kincade sell her father's personal inventory? As a jeweler she could have used the stones for her own work. As a daughter she would have held on to the pieces for their sentimental value.

Jared inched closer to the drawn curtain as the bidding continued in swift, heated waves. At this rate she'd be a very wealthy woman. She wouldn't have the slightest interest in the hard work necessary to complete two dozen pieces for Nicholas's first Abbey Jewels exhibition. She wouldn't need the strain of traveling and giving dozens of interviews.

And that would leave Nicholas and Kacey crushed, Jared knew.

The saleswoman cleared her throat. "Would you call her a close friend?"

What was that supposed to mean? Did they sleep together? "She's the wife of a very old acquaintance." He pointed to a pair of intricate plaited silver hoops, then decided Kacey could use something to go with the earrings. "Maybe the bracelet in the corner, too."

The woman with the purple hair made an approving sound as she lifted out a curve of sensuous silver inlaid with a dozen gold birds in flight. Kacey would love it, but she loved everything that bore M. E. Kincade's hallmark.

Kacey had been the first to spot the unique designs in twisted wire and layered metals, and then Nicholas had stumbled upon the architectural pieces, carefully cut to fit together like designs in a puzzle.

Jared studied the small example before him. Gold rectangles captured every detail of a soaring cathedral, complete with cabochon gemstones for windows, doors that opened and closed, and a polished obsidian roof.

"I'll take that one also." Jared heard the excited voices in the neighboring room, where a new piece was being shown. As the curtain shifted, he saw Maggie Kincade turn slowly, the Solitaire necklace now exchanged for a sleek platinum chain capped with two large black pearls.

His eyes narrowed. She was unforgettable, just like her designs. Deceptively simple, and dangerously sensuous.

He hadn't expected to enjoy looking at jewelry. He certainly hadn't expected to feel a vicious stab of desire at the sight of her tall body poured into that flowing column of black silk.

Her voice drifted through the open curtain. "The black pearls come from a private source in Japan, part of the imperial collection since the Tokugawa period. They were sold to my father only five years ago."

Jared's eyes narrowed as new bids came in eager waves. The woman could have sold them sawdust at this point.

"Will that be all for you, sir?"

He blinked to see the young saleswoman holding out an elegant set of wrapped boxes. It was too soon for him to leave. He needed more answers. "Maybe something in lace," he murmured.

"What size is the lady?"

"Size?"

"Six? An eight perhaps?"

Jared ran a hand through his dark hair. "She's not very big. Normal size," he said vaguely. "About this tall." He raised a hand to his collarbone.

The saleswoman was obviously used to male vagueness about lingerie sizes. "About my height, would you say?"

"More or less."

"Her bust size?"

How was he supposed to know a thing like that? "Don't you have something that would fit anyone?" he asked helplessly.

"I might have something in the back." She tapped her cheek for a moment, then vanished through a door framed by topiary trees.

Jared inched closer, only to frown as Maggie Kincade backed out through the curtain. Her head was bent, and the silk of her dress whispered. He stared at the line of her shoulders, feeling his body tighten as if in the presence of a sensitive explosive device.

She was shoving at her neck, head down and muttering, and her next step brought her flat against Jared's chest. The contact caught him without warning, twisting deep, slamming right into his heart.

Nerves snapped.

Muscles tightened all over his chest, in crushing awareness of the soft outlines of her body. She smelled like sunshine, and her thoughts were full of color. They flooded through him, rich and sensuous, a storm of silver, platinum, and polished rubies.

It took him an infinity to remember where he was and how to breathe.

Work, he told himself.

A professional request from a friend.

Somehow the explanation didn't make her thoughts stop humming or her soft perfume any less elusive.

With fierce effort, Jared dragged himself out of the quicksilver race of her mind. He was still struggling to regain his control when she spun around, flushing. "Sorry, I didn't see you there."

He couldn't seem to speak. Time slowed down, captured in the sparkle of her eyes and the extraordinary necklace she wore.

"It's this necklace. Something's wrong with the wretched clasp."

The necklace, remember? Answer her, fool.

Jared drew a breath and pointed to the strand of hair twisted around her pavé diamond clasp. "You're caught."

"Blast. No wonder it won't budge."

"Perhaps I can help you."

Her eyes narrowed. "You're a jeweler?"

"Hardly." Jared gestured to her neck. "But I think I can manage to unfree a knot or two. May I?"

He had the sense of sudden stillness, as if she had gathered herself tightly away from all intrusion or observation. And in that place of utter stillness, she watched him, asking silent questions and measuring whether he was friend or foe.

He could feel her wariness as she bit her lip, staring at his face.

And then she nodded.

"I'll try not to make this too painful," He smiled, skimming her shoulder and easing one finger beneath the captive strand. Her perfumed hair shifted, then curled about his hand, binding his fingers with its warmth.

Jared grimaced at the contact, unable to fight the immediate pull of her thoughts.

Excitement. Sheer, heart-pounding anxiety.

The silence seemed to tighten, separating them from the muttered bids and the noisy world outside. Jared didn't move, didn't speak, painfully aware of the brush of her hair, the sunlight on her shoulder, the curve of her cheek.

Then her wariness slammed through the link. She was measuring him, assessing him as an enemy. Or as a hostile reporter, he realized.

It took but a few instants of contact for him to register a dozen things about Maggie Kincade, including her pride and her temper. Beneath them lay a relentless curiosity.

That curiosity was turned on him now.

"I think you've done it." She made a breathless sound and started to pull away, her thigh brushing his hip. Jared frowned as desire jolted viciously through him.

But the knotted hair held firm.

"Not quite," he muttered. His fingers met her skin, and the link flared anew.

The air seemed to thicken. He tried to breathe, overwhelmed by a wrenching impression of skin and clamoring nerves as she broadcast her sudden awareness of his own body.

Curious. Surprised by the keen sensual pleasure of his fingers.

The force of her thoughts made Jared's fingers lock up. Before he knew it, the clasp had slipped free. He bent closer, only to be distracted by the tiny silver mark at the top of her shoulder. "You've got a scar." He knew enough not to touch it. Contact now would be death to his control.

"A pair of metal shears fell on me the first day in design school." She gave a low laugh. "It wasn't exactly an auspicious start."

And then in spite of his caution, Jared traced the silver mark with his fingers—and grimaced as desire jolted through him again.

Down boy, he thought grimly. She was just a client. There was no excuse for what he was feeling. He stepped away. "There. I think that should take care of the problem."

She turned and gave him a quizzical smile. "Thank you, Mr. . . ."

"MacNeill. Jared MacNeill."

"I'm going to have to change this clasp." Her voice was muffled as she straightened the sleek chain at her neck link by link. "I want the things I sell to be perfect."

"Nothing's perfect." The words came out more harshly than he'd intended. Maybe because it was suddenly difficult to stand close and not touch her. Or maybe it was because he was fighting an urge to slide his lips over that silver mark at her shoulder, then work his way slowly upward.

Insane. Absolutely insane.

But Jared could sense the imagination and the passion she held for her work. They fascinated him. *She* fascinated him.

And the way she filled out that silk dress should have been illegal.

Her eyes narrowed. "If you actually believe that, you must be very bored."

"I'm not bored now."

She tilted her head. "No?"

The stillness was there again, but now Jared sensed it

came only through great force of will. She was measuring him again, making checks on an invisible list.

She gave a little shrug and turned away. "I thought Karen was out here."

"She went looking for something in the back." Jared studied the platinum hoops at her neck and the black pearls nestled between her breasts. She looked very cool in all that jewelry. He hardly qualified as an expert, but he was certain the pearls alone were worth a small fortune. "Your necklace is lovely."

"Thank you." She didn't smile as her hand slid restlessly along the chain, and Jared saw that her fingers weren't entirely steady.

So his first assessment had been off. Maggie Kincade only appeared cool, he realized. At close quarters he couldn't miss the wistfulness that had crept into her eyes when she'd touched the necklace. He had the sudden impression of a restless flame trapped beneath glass, and he wondered what it would take for a man to slip beneath that careful, guarded surface of hers.

She would be as complex as her designs, he suspected. Sharp edges and hidden warmth, with nothing quite what it appeared. Revealed slowly, piece by piece and layer by layer, she would be a puzzle a man could spend years trying to solve.

And touching that wonderful mouth of hers would be like lingering over sweet, ripe fruit.

"Here you are, sir. This should fit any size."

Jared blinked at the saleswoman holding out a silk shawl filled with delicate floral designs.

"That one's Chinese. The embroidery squares date back to the mid-nineteenth century."

It took Jared several ragged heartbeats to assimilate what Maggie was saying. "Silk." He tried to nod astutely. "Chinese, you say."

He didn't take his gaze from her face. There was a deep watchfulness about her now as she stared back at him.

"Did you want to look at something else?"

At you. For about twenty years. Preferably without silk or anything else on that amazing body. He cleared his throat. "No, this will be fine. Could I have it wrapped?"

"Certainly. Karen will help you." She smoothed back her hair and took a deep breath, as if preparing for a difficult encounter. "I'd better go. I hope you find something perfect after all." Her lips curved. "It would serve you right."

"Maybe I have."

Turning in a swirl of black satin as a voice called loudly from the next room, she didn't hear his soft words. "Is the necklace for sale?" Jared blurted, driven to speak to her again so he could watch emotions spin and dance over that vibrant face.

Her hand brushed her neck. "I'm sorry, but it's just been sold."

"A pity. It's simple, but very powerful. I suppose the greatest beauty usually is," he said.

His gaze shifted, brushing her shoulders. He saw a faint wave of color fill her cheeks. He was glad for that. It meant he wasn't the only one feeling uncomfortable in the encounter.

She raised her chin. "You're staring."

"Most men would."

More color washed her face. She wasn't accustomed to male attention, Jared realized. For some obscure reason the thought pleased him deeply.

"Do you make a practice of buying gifts for one woman while you stare at another one?"

"The gifts are for a friend. Just a friend."

Her beautiful mouth thinned. "Of course she is."

"Why would I lie?"

"I haven't the faintest idea." She shrugged. "But most men do."

Time stood still. As her perfume drifted, Jared felt heat claw up through his chest. When had he last felt this jolting, almost painful awareness? Why now, for a woman he barely knew?

Jared was still searching for an answer when he felt a draft at his back. The bell above the door tinkled sharply as a man in a rumpled raincoat pushed inside.

Then Maggie Kincade gave a gasp of surprise as a camera whirred off half a dozen shots, capturing her gown, her necklace, and her momentary expression of panic.

Chapter 3

WITHOUT THINKING, JARED MOVED IN FRONT OF MAGGIE, blocking her with his body. "I suggest you stop."

"Out of the way, pal. *She's* the one I want. Ms. Kincade, what about that necklace you're wearing? Did your father leave it for you? If so, how do you know those aren't some of the gems that were—"

Stolen.

Even before the word was finished, Jared's hand was curled around the man's neck. "You're not listening. Ms. Kincade is busy."

The reporter squared his shoulders. "Who says?"

"Irrelevant. Because you're just about to leave."

"Like hell." The camera fell and the man's fists leveled. "What makes you think I give a rat's ass what *you* have to say, pal?"

Jared dodged the first swing easily, then sidestepped and caught the reporter in a chest lock. Without a word, he shoved the sputtering man outside, then closed the etched glass door in his face. The man glared through the glass, raised his camera, then muttered a crude phrase, which he emphasized with a noisy ball of spit at the door frame.

Fury burned a red swath through Jared's mind as he went in pursuit. Maggie's hand touched his shoulder, stopping him.

"Don't."

Blocked by layers of fabric, he felt only the indirect contact of her fingers. For a blinding instant he had an urgent need to touch her, to cradle her cheek and trace the curve of her neck so he could read her with all the fierce intimacy of his gift.

It seemed to take forever before he mastered the urge, and the struggle left his voice harder than he intended. "Why not? The bloody fool ought to clean your doorway on his hands and knees."

"I like the image." She gave a crooked smile. "But he's not worth your time. None of them are."

"They do this often?" Jared stood very still, hating the idea that this happened to her on a regular basis.

"Often enough. It's better not to provoke them. Like most hive creatures, they behave badly when you stir them up." There was bitterness in her voice, a bitterness that Jared understood well.

"Then maybe you need an exterminator." He remembered his own awkward fight through a crowd of jostling reporters upon his return from Thailand. At least the government had run interference for him, but Maggie Kincade appeared to have no one to help her. "You should hire a guard," he said tightly.

"We've been considering the idea."

Jared watched the reporter make a rude gesture, then amble back across the street. "Someone who could break their cameras as well as their smug faces."

A half-smile curved her lips. "The idea has definite attractions, but no." She gave a small shrug. "It would only lead to more trouble. They never give up." Someone called her name from the other side of the velvet curtain. "I'd better go. But thanks for caring. It's very kind of you."

"No." Jared searched her face. Once again he had the sense of a bright, restless flame caught behind glass. One day the flame would flare up, sharp and bright, and he envied the man who was there to warm himself at that fire when it happened.

"I'm not kind," he murmured. "Quite the opposite. I enjoyed helping you and that's why I did it." To his shock he realized his hand was rising to her cheek. What was *wrong* with him? She was business, purely business, no matter what odd fantasies were stealing into his mind.

Friend or not, Nicholas would frown on Jared's personal involvement with Maggie Kincade.

Again color flared in her face, this time washing all the way to her chest. Jared's body answered with another savage kick of desire.

She took a step back. "I'm sorry about the necklace."

"Don't be. It's probably beyond my price anyway. I can only envy those pearls."

"Envy?" She looked confused.

He stared at the shadowed area between her breasts where the pearls lay cradled by warm, silken skin.

Her breath caught. The pearls rose and fell sharply with the sudden movement of her chest. The air between them seemed to grow heavy, to vibrate with unformed questions and unspoken possibilities.

"I'd better go." She didn't move.

"That's probably a good idea." He continued to stare at her.

"Maggie, is anything wrong?" A woman's head appeared at the curtain, eyes narrowed with interest.

"Just another reporter, Chessa. He's gone now." She looked at Jared. "Thank you again for your help."

He gave a shrug that could have meant anything or nothing at all.

"Karen will finish with your gifts."

"Of course." Jared managed to make his voice flat and impersonal. Purely business, he told himself. Or it should have been.

But he didn't turn away until the curtain blocked his last sight of her. Even then her subtle perfume lingered to tease his senses, an unusual blend of cinnamon and roses that was as complex as the woman who wore it.

Jared realized his breath was coming fast, and his body was a hell of a lot tighter than when he'd walked in. Maybe it was the intimacy of the small room, filled with frothy lingerie meant to inflame a man's imagination. But Jared knew that wasn't the real answer. His reaction was to Maggie Kincade. Because of the vulnerability he had seen in her eyes and the passion he had sensed in the restless colors of her keen mind.

He studied the room, trying to focus in the wake of her departure. *Stop dreaming and work*, he told himself tensely. Nicholas had every right to want answers before he extended an invitation, and Jared was determined to get them. From what he had seen so far, Maggie Kincade had no hidden contact with her father or anyone who might have been an associate of his. Nor was she consorting with criminals and living a life of splendor on ill-gotten gains.

Jared ran down a mental list of the jewels that Daniel Kincade was suspected of stealing. There had been no black pearls among them.

Of course, this could all be part of a cold, detailed plan. She could be biding her time until the attention died, but Jared didn't think so. The woman who'd stood frozen and speechless in the glare of a photographer's flash had been stunned and anything but ruthless.

After today's sale, she could count herself a very wealthy woman. She had every reason to shun publicity. Maybe Nicholas's offer wouldn't interest her at all.

There was only one way to find out.

The Cantonese restaurant was packed solid, every seat jammed with students, tourists, and regular lunchtime visitors. Maggie ignored the growl of her stomach as she slid into a spot beside Chessa. "How much?"

Chessa gave her a radiant smile. "Nine hundred seventeen," she intoned. "Thousand," she added.

Maggie stared at her hands, outstretched on the table. "I can't believe it. That much in just two hours?" She took a ragged breath, her nerves tight. Purely the aftereffects of the sale, she thought. It had nothing at all to do with the man she had met in the shop that morning. There was no earthly reason why she should keep remembering his slow smile and the play of his hands on her neck. And it had to be her imagination that his hand had been moving toward her cheek. After all, there was no *possible* chance she'd ever see him again.

He had left with his purchases and that was that. Probably married anyway, Maggie thought.

She finally managed to force him out of her mind.

"Thanks, Chessa. We actually did it," she whispered.

"Not we. *You* did it," her cousin said.

"It's enough. I can pay all the bills. I might even have something left for a new platinum shipment."

"You're damned right you will," Chessa said angrily. "You're keeping aside *whatever* you need for your new designs. You have to work, Maggie, and work takes quality materials. Your father meant some of those stones for *you*, remember?"

"I don't know what he meant for me. It's not as if we talked about what would happen when he died." Sighing, Maggie shoved a tangle of hair from her forehead as she sat back against the thick banquette. She had changed from Chessa's gown into her usual clothes, comfortable jeans and a deep gray turtleneck that set off the warm highlights of her hair. Her only adornment was an intricate torque of silver and twisted gold, one of her first projects in design school. Even then the Celtic influence had been at work on her imagination.

Lost in thought, Maggie didn't notice the assessing glances of a pair of passing men. Had she seen, she would have put it down to curiosity and nothing more. "I remember. But the bills come first, Chessa."

"I wish your father had thought that way."

"He tried to." Maggie shrugged. "He just didn't have a business mind." She gave a low laugh. "Not that I do either, but I'm trying."

Chessa toyed with her enameled tea cup. "Just remember that those debts were your father's, not *yours*. Pay the bills and use what's left over for your own design work."

Maggie picked up a menu, well aware that her cousin never gave up an argument. "Let's order. I'm ravenous." She was feeling far too happy to argue, and she meant to savor the feeling as long as it lasted. "How about fried dumplings?"

"Promise me, Maggie. Tell me you'll spend something on yourself, blast it."

Maggie lowered the menu. "Please, Chessa. I'll do whatever has to be done, but I'll do it in my own way."

"But there's no need. I'm sure if I spoke to my father, he would loan you enough to—"

"You've loaned me too much already. I don't know when I can pay it back."

"You're family. You don't *have* to pay it back. Now stop before you make me really angry." Abruptly she turned, darting a glance over her shoulder.

"What's wrong?"

"I'm not sure," Chessa said after a moment. "I'll be right back. Order for me, will you? Black bean soup and fried dumplings."

Then she was gone.

One table over, Jared was perusing the handwritten menu. He blinked as a woman in black velvet jeans slid into the seat beside him. She wore a tapestry coat, and her dark hair spilled in waves over her shoulders. The woman from the lingerie shop, he realized.

"All right, damn it, who *are* you?"

His brow rose. "I beg your pardon?"

"Forget the innocent routine. I saw you talking to Maggie in the shop this morning. Now, two hours later, you're seated right here behind us. Since I've never believed in coincidences, I want to know why you're here."

Jared took his time in answering. Nicholas's instructions had been clear, and it was time to follow them. "I had a very good reason for being in your shop today."

Chessa's eyes narrowed. "Does this reason have anything to do with Maggie?"

"Yes, it does."

She sat back with a muffled oath. "I *knew* it. You're a reporter, aren't you? Another bloated worm crawling around in search of a story."

Jared steepled his fingers. "I didn't say I was a reporter."

"Then what *are* you?"

The question lingered. Jared frowned as he saw Maggie Kincade slip out of her seat and come toward them. She looked, he decided, even better in jeans than she had in black silk. Soft denim hugged those endless legs in a way that made tension fist at his chest and work downward. He dragged his eyes away, up to the simple curve of hammered silver at her neck. The intricate inlay work and sensuous lines of the design left no doubt that it was from Maggie's own hand. Like her, it was simple, yet tantalizing. The combination did sharp things to Jared's pulse.

"Chessa, what's going on?" Maggie's eyes widened when she saw Jared. "Why are *you* here?"

"I think you'd better sit down," he said.

"Me? Why?"

"Because I have some news for you, Ms. Kincade." He saw her sudden pallor and read its source. "It's not bad news."

"Is there any other kind?" She sank into a seat beside her cousin. "Let's have it."

"He's been following you, Mag. He doesn't look like a stalker." Chessa eyed Jared suspiciously. "Then again, who's to say? But if you're not a reporter or a stalker, what are you? And you'd better not tell me you're from the IRS, coming to claim your cut already."

"Ah, that would be your tax people, I believe." Jared gave a faint smile. "Not bloody likely."

"You're Scottish, aren't you?" Maggie restlessly straightened a pair of chopsticks, then folded and unfolded a napkin. The frown between her eyes deepened.

"That I am. You have a good ear, since I've lost most of my accent." Five years in Asia and two decades spent crisscrossing the globe for his father's military postings had done that.

And then a year in a box as a political "guest" of the government of Myanmar had left him barely able to speak at all.

"Are you from Christie's in London?" Maggie said tightly. "Did my father owe you money, too?" There was a harrowed look in her eyes now.

That confirmed the reason for her morning auction. So her father had left more loose ends than was generally known, Jared thought. "No, I'm not from Christie's, and your father didn't owe me money."

"Then why—"

The restaurant owner appeared with a tureen of steaming soup. He set it down before Jared with a flourish and a flood of staccato Cantonese. Then he eyed the two new arrivals.

Jared nodded. "Yes, we're together. We'll need two more bowls, Mr. Wong."

Maggie watched the restaurant owner move off in search of more utensils. "You've been here before?"

"A few times this week. The food is very good."

"And you speak Chinese?"

Jared nodded. He didn't mention that he also spoke German, Gaelic, and backstreet Thai.

"Forget the soup, Professor." Chessa eyed him with cold suspicion. "What do you want with my cousin?"

"This." He slid a heavy vellum envelope across the table. Light glinted off the embossed gold coronet flanked by two dragons.

Maggie frowned as Jared centered the envelope before her. Then her body went absolutely still. But now he realized that apparent calm of hers concealed a restless flow of emotion straining to break free.

With the right man she would succeed, he thought. With the right man there would be no need for protection or pretenses. Of course, *he* wasn't the right man—not for Maggie Kincade or for any other woman. Not after Thailand.

"It's for you," he said. "Open it."

"Draycott Abbey." Chessa frowned as she read the elegant printing. "It must be about that design competition you entered in the spring."

Maggie cradled the envelope uncertainly. "Do you know Lord Draycott?"

"Very well." Jared's face betrayed nothing.

The necklace glinted as she turned to measure him. Sunlight cast amber sparks through her tousled hair, and in her casual gray turtleneck she looked all of eighteen, rather than a woman tackling hard, painful problems. But Jared, of all people, knew just how deceptive appearances could be.

"And you came all the way to New York to give this to me?"

"It wasn't far out of my way," he lied smoothly. Nicholas had insisted on that story. He hadn't wanted her to feel pressured or overwhelmed by his offer.

Jared wasn't entirely surprised to hear Chessa Kincade's snort of disbelief. "You just happened to be in New York? Maybe you were in the market for some lingerie?"

Maggie touched Chessa's arm. "He could be telling the truth."

"Why don't you open the envelope and find out, Ms. Kincade?"

Her eyes darkened, the smoky blue of a loch at dawn. He liked the way she gently traced the embossed coronet on the envelope, as if taking precise calculations of her future and its possibilities. In fact, looking at her was becoming downright addictive, Jared thought.

"I'm not sure I want to open it." She gave an unsteady laugh. "I might not be able to recognize good news anymore."

"It's like riding a bicycle. I'm told one never forgets."

"I never was much good at bicycles either." She toyed with the envelope, frowning. "I'll open it later."

Jared sat back slowly. He hadn't expected to care about the outcome. He wasn't prepared to feel personally involved in the results of Nicholas's decision. But like it or not, he was. Three days of secretly watching Maggie Kincade struggle to knit together the torn pieces of her life had left him with an intense and very personal interest.

He froze, trying to block a flow of impressions as her foot brushed his under the table. But he could no more resist reading her than he could cease to breathe. At the surface lay wariness, followed by curiosity and a needle-sharp intelligence. Below that lay the hard-won pride that kept her from revealing any of those things. She wouldn't be an easy person to understand. Winning her trust would be harder still. So why did he care about doing either?

From the start he'd had reservations about her selection for the exhibition, mostly from a security standpoint. Now that he had observed Maggie Kincade for three days, he was coming to believe that Nicholas was dead on target. Her work was a striking mix of unexpected textures and classical techniques, fascinating even to an outsider like himself. She succeeded because she was passionate about her work and ruthless in the demands she made on herself. He had even watched her from the back of a busy classroom one night, where she was surrounded by the students who clearly adored her.

But Jared had also picked up traces of the darker side of Maggie Kincade. She was on edge, struggling to deal with the loss of her father and the unanswered questions left by his disappearance. Until those questions were resolved, her father's notoriety was her notoriety, shadowing everything she did. Jared was certain that her selection would create a security nightmare once the British tabloids got wind of Nicholas's plans.

Which they would do any day.

Still, the choice belonged to Nicholas. Jared was simply the messenger, though that role had had its pleasant moments.

"Come on, Mag. Open the cursed thing before I suffer cardiac arrest," Chessa muttered. She turned as two men pushed beneath the beaded curtain just inside the restaurant's front door. "Oh, no. More reporters. Those two were at the shop yesterday asking questions."

Jared reached across the table. For the space of a heartbeat his hand covered Maggie's. It took more effort than he'd imagined not to react at the hot flare of contact.

Honor, he reminded himself. People were entitled to their secrets, no matter how complicated or painful.

"Go on." He rose to his feet with a grim smile. "The corridor will take you straight to the kitchen. There's a door to the street."

Maggie's hands clenched. "Why are you doing this?"

"Call it a favor. Or call it repayment for a very pleasant day." His voice hardened as the two men gestured and went for their cameras.

"But it's not your problem. *I'm* not your problem." She stood unmoving, all tension and indecision. The curve of silver at her neck rose and fell jerkily with each breath. "And they might hurt you. Two men decked Chessa's brother last week when he wouldn't get out of their way."

Jared's smile was slow and very cold. "They won't deck me."

She stared at his broad shoulders. "No, I suppose not. But I still don't see why you're making this your business."

The hell of it was, Jared didn't know either. He told himself the question was irrelevant. "You underestimate yourself, Ms. Kincade. Now *go*."

"He's right, Mag. Come on."

"Stop!" the man in front barked. "They're going out the back. Get the camera, damn it!"

Jared produced a very pleasant smile as he heard Maggie and her cousin slip from the banquette and scramble toward the kitchen. He was still smiling when his arm rose and the first camera hit the floor, reduced to twisted metal and shattered glass beneath his foot.

"Are you nuts? We're the *press*. You can't do that."

"As a matter of fact, I can." Suddenly Jared was back in Thailand, hearing the thud of bamboo on human flesh. He felt the blind fury of being hounded, prodded, and tormented because of the color of his skin and words on his passport. As a captive in box number 225, he had reached out from his prison, aching to touch fresh air and silence. Through the rusted metal bars he had caught a gust of night air, rich with jasmine and a hint of orchids.

Neither could hide the stench of sweat and fear.

When his hands had clenched on the rusty bars, he'd felt the trickle of blood. Then he'd heard the sharp stamp of feet. They'd come ahead of schedule. Hands on the bars— key in the lock. Taunts in a foreign tongue.

Then the bamboo.

That night he had been almost too tired to fight. He'd almost forgotten what he was fighting for, but he had not turned away. There had been no mercy in the face before him. No weakness in the hands that gripped the length of bamboo with its point of rough metal. When the questions came in an angry staccato of Thai, Chinese, and perfect English, he had given them the silence they hated.

So the bamboo fell. And fell. And fell.

He had made no sound. The act had cost him dearly, but irritating his attackers was his only pleasure. After an hour, he had prayed for death, but they wouldn't even give him that.

Fighting the pain, he'd thought of stars: Vega. Sirius. Altair. As the torment broke over him, he tried to remember the stars shimmering in the loch where he had grown up. The memories were all that had kept him from screaming, until the darkness finally enfolded his tortured body.

The man in box number 225 had known what it was like to give up hope, but Jared wasn't going to let Maggie Kincade come close to knowing that kind of despair.

"Wise guy, are ya? Let's see how you like this, pal."

Jared moved first. He put his whole weight into the punch and enjoyed the feeling of his fist as it struck the cursing, ruddy face below a pair of hard, furtive eyes.

Some favors were definitely more pleasant than others, he decided.

Maggie's heart was still pounding as she pushed open the door to her apartment, the vellum envelope with the gold coronet clutched in her hands. "Did you see that, Chessa? He broke both their cameras."

"That's not all he broke, and he didn't even raise a sweat. Incredible physique." Chessa tossed down her coat, smiling at the memory. "I think I could almost like the guy after all." Abruptly she rounded on Maggie. "Now open the bloody thing. And don't tell me you don't know what I'm talking about."

Maggie stared at the heavy envelope. She had submitted two samples of her work months ago as part of her application for an international jewelry exhibition sponsored by the twelfth Lord Draycott and his American wife. After weeks of waiting and worrying, she had forgotten all about the submission.

Now she regretted the impulse to submit her designs. She'd had too much failure lately, and she didn't need any more. "Don't get excited. They're probably telling me to not give up my day job. Politely worded, of course. The English are good at that."

"Why would they send a messenger to tell you that?" Chessa countered.

Light played over the Christmas tree in the corner as
Maggie tore open the envelope and tried to pull out the
single heavy sheet, but failed. *Get a grip,* she told herself,
remembering the hard mouth and the dark hair that had
brushed against broad shoulders.

He'd had gentle hands. Old eyes.

But Maggie didn't want to remember. She didn't want
to feel this coiling heat or gnawing curiosity. She definitely
didn't want to owe a stranger for any favors, no matter how
much she had needed his help.

Lamplight struck the golden coronet. And what if she
had won? How would she feel to see her designs in platinum and gold resting among heirloom hallmarked silver
and historic gems in cases that bore the dignified Draycott
crest?

Only heaven. Only a chance at dizzying professional success and recognition by the finest craftsmen and goldsmiths
in all of Europe, along with the support of one of the oldest
collecting families in England.

From what Maggie had read of the viscount's plans, the
Abbey Jewels would soon become one of Europe's most
publicized exhibitions, including a year's endowed residence and financial backing while she completed her port-
folio of designs. She would revel in the teaching and
education projects that the viscount had outlined, along
with some restoration work.

Chessa's arm wrapped around her. "Well, what does it
say?"

"They can't possibly want me." Maggie touched the
cool vellum, remembering years of hopes and dreams. "No
one else sees the things I see, Chessa. How old and new
can be matched. How metal can flow and bend."

Chessa shoved her down into the chair. "Just open the
wretched thing. I may collapse any second, and I understand that Dr. Welby doesn't make house calls anymore."

Maggie touched the tiny gold letters. She tried not to
care, tried not to hope, but her throat tightened. *I won't lose
this chance*, she said fiercely. Something slammed down
hard into her chest. *I can't.*

She tore open the sheet and felt the envelope drop to her

feet. The mouse peeked out at her from its hole, squeaking softly.

"Tell me this instant, Margaret Elizabeth Kincade," Chessa hissed.

Maggie swallowed hard. "I'm in," she whispered. "I'm *in*. I'm going to England, Chessa. I'm invited to have my designs shown exclusively at Draycott Abbey and selected venues throughout Europe. After that comes a year in residence as a teacher at the craft museum Lord Draycott has just endowed in Sussex."

Her cousin's crow of delight was almost drowned out by the blare of horns from the street below, followed by the scream of the buzzer. *More reporters?*

"You're getting out of this hole tonight," Chessa said flatly. "We have work to do."

Maggie barely heard. She was *in*. She was going to England. She still couldn't grasp the reality of the news.

"How long before you leave?"

"Leave?"

"For England," Chessa said impatiently.

Maggie squinted down at the invitation. "Three weeks, I think."

"Three *weeks*?" Chessa swirled, a mad blur of silk and fine tapestry. "You'll need shoes, dresses, gloves—"

"I already have gloves."

Chessa sniffed. "Leather and heavy duty canvas *aren't* what I had in mind. After all, there will be parties. Openings. Formal evenings in those big, stuffy English conservatories." She tapped her cheek. "Lingerie, too. I bet you don't even *own* a pair of panty hose," she muttered in disgust.

"I wear pants," Maggie said defensively. "And I like my style just fine."

"What style? You're a sixties throwback, pure and simple. I bet you don't even know what a foundation garment looks like."

"Does a soldering vest count?"

Chessa rolled her exquisite eyes skyward. "Bless her father, for she knows not how she has sinned." She caught Maggie's arm and tugged her toward the single cramped bedroom, her face militant. "Go pack because you're coming home with me tonight. First, we're going to celebrate your acceptance letter with Veuve Cliquot at Henri's then a long, leisurely dinner at Le Cirque. The best table, of course."

"But we don't have reservations . . ."

Her cousin gave a smug smile. "As if Vincenzo would dream of seating me anywhere but the best spot."

"What if there are reporters?"

"Vincenzo hires men to take care of things like that. Big, nasty men with bulges beneath their specially cut Armani jackets." She looked assessingly at Maggie. "Tomorrow we do clothes. I have a wonderful ensemble of hand-rolled French silk that will be perfect on you."

"But I—"

Chessa raced into full gear, ticking off items on an imaginary list. "Half-slip, garters, and camisole. Then we add real silk stockings—the *only* kind to have, believe me. Men just adore it when you roll them off slowly. I'll bet that man in the restaurant knows everything there is to know about silk stockings." Her eyes darkened. "And the perfect way to take them off. Did you see how he looked at you?"

"What do you mean?"

Chessa snorted in disgust. "Of course you didn't. You never do." She tapped her jaw. "Well, it wouldn't bother *me* to find out more about him." Her eyes gleamed for a moment, then refocused. "But back to business. "I'll take care of the clothes. I *suppose* we can leave the jewelry to you." She dodged the pillow Maggie flung through the air. "Just a joke, idiot. I wouldn't dream of cramping your style when it comes to jewelry. There you're an undisputed genius." She frowned at her cousin's tangled cinnamon curls. "But we have some *serious* work ahead of us with your hair."

Maggie crossed her arms militantly. "Forget it, Chessa, I'm *not* cutting my hair. No way."

Chessa didn't even hear. "How long did you say we have?"

"Three weeks."

"Miracles have happened in less, I suppose. I'll say a

few prayers.'' She took Maggie's arm in a firm grip. ''On the way, we'll stop at a little place I know on First Avenue. They have the most *incredible* handmade Italian shoes. . . .''

In a few minutes Maggie had gathered her most valuable gems and metals in a special aluminum carrying case, along with pliers and shears, in case inspiration struck in the night. Then she turned and surveyed the shadows. The room was dingy, no doubt about it. There were no bookcases. No flowers or comfortable chairs.

It was a place to work and nothing more. A place where she passed time twisting silver and spinning dreams, until she had a real workshop of her own full of glinting spirals and stars slanting across fine chains of hand-twisted gold.

She put her last wedge of cheese down for the mouse.

''We'll call Faith from my apartment and bring her up to speed. Then I want you to try on this fabulous shantung sheath. It will fit you like a second skin. I think my gold sandals might even work with it.''

Caught between smiles and exasperation, Maggie started to protest, but Chessa was already striding to the door, tossing on her long coat.

Suddenly there was magic in the air. Light played over the tiny Christmas tree and set the needles dancing. A lace angel dangled from its string beside a cat with a bright red Santa hat.

And this was her gift, Maggie thought, cradling her vellum envelope, suddenly giddy as she felt the grains of one life sliding away while another life began. She smiled at the first dig of pleasure, the first kick of excitement. Where would it all end?

As she followed Chessa to the door, neither one saw the shadow slipping along the back fire escape.

Chapter 4

London
Three weeks later

CAR HORNS SCREAMED ALONG BOND STREET. ANGELS spread fluffy wings above cases bright with Christmas treasures. Men in wool hats sold roasted chestnuts from smoking metal stalls, and ornamented trees flashed in bright shop windows.

Maggie barely noticed.

The man was watching her again. Oh, he was careful about it. Discreet in that amazing way the English had. A flicker here, a short study there.

She crossed the street, moving briskly, then stopped for a glance in a window. He was twenty feet behind her, speaking on a cellular phone. And he was *definitely* watching her.

Maggie surveyed the street. Two cafés. A bookstore and a jewelry shop. Her body was tense as she pushed open the door to the jewelers. And in that moment she almost forgot her pursuer in the glitter of diamonds and pink pearls and star sapphires. The cameos arranged on an elegant cushion of black velvet immediately caught her eye. Several were rose, and some were blue. All were sculpted with the fine hand of a master.

Maggie frowned as she heard the door to the shop open and the bell tinkle behind her. She managed not to turn, despite the burning sense that she was once more under scrutiny.

"Something is wrong with the cameo, madam?" The graying jeweler crossed behind the counter and looked at her anxiously.

"No, it's beautiful, but I prefer that pale cream intaglio. The woman and child are exquisite and the cutter's flair shows best with no distracting color. It's brilliant work."

The jeweler nodded, approving her choice. "My thoughts exactly. So many want new colors, new styles. The classical is so soon forgotten." He shook his head in resignation. "Where money goes, the artists must follow."

"Not all artists," Maggie said firmly. "And no one could possibly improve on this. The look on the mother's face is pure emotion." She cupped the beautiful oval of a woman holding a young child. It was nineteenth-century Italian, very beautiful and very expensive. "Is it by one of the Saulinis?" This pair of sculptors, father and son, had excelled at meticulous detail. Maggie had seen examples of their work, but had never touched one.

"So it is. I was fortunate to acquire it in Florence last year. You would like the piece perhaps?"

In the excitement of her discovery, Maggie forgot about the man who had been watching her. Her mind grappled with a dozen design ideas: a platinum choker or gold braid. Perhaps a simple knotted satin cord.

She took another glance at the discreet price tag. Steep, but worth every pence. Especially for a real Saulini cameo. "Fine. I'll take it."

"My compliments. You have excellent taste." The stranger she'd forgotten in her excitement spoke from behind her.

Maggie stiffened as he crossed the room and admired her cameo.

"I couldn't help but notice. It's a lovely piece."

His eyes were harder up close, and she noticed there were little streaks of gray at his temples. "Yes, it is," she said stiffly.

He smiled, slightly uncertain. "Forgive my question, but I'm certain that I recognize you."

Maggie shook her head, already turning away. She refused to believe that he could be a reporter, although she'd heard gambits like this before. Why did she never seem to

have Chessa's ready quip or Faith's brash bravado, the
throwaway line that turned intrusive questions into good-
tempered camaraderie? "You're wrong. We haven't met."

She turned her back stiffly as the jeweler returned with
her receipt. Then the old man smiled broadly at the
stranger. "So nice to see you again, my lord. Give my
regards to your wife if you will."

Lord?

The man beside her thrust out his hand, smiling apolo-
getically. "I should have introduced myself immediately.
I'm Nicholas Draycott, and I'm quite certain that you're
Margaret Elizabeth Kincade, though the photo you sent
with your jewelry designs doesn't do you justice."

Maggie swallowed. *He* was the twelfth viscount Draycott? At least that explained why he had been following
her. But she'd pictured someone balding and overweight,
with red cheeks and faded tweeds covered with dog hairs.

He cleared his throat. "Sorry if I'm not what you expected."

"My mistake. But call me Maggie. All my friends do."

"Maggie, it is. When did you arrive? Our meeting isn't
until Thursday."

"I had some things to do before we met, and I didn't
want to miss the Etruscan exhibit at the British Museum.
Then when I saw the cameos outside, I couldn't resist coming in for a look." She decided not to mention that she had
put him down as a Lothario on the prowl.

"Perfectly understandable. My wife and I succumb to
temptation here far too often." He chuckled softly. "Sa-
muels makes it impossible to say no to his private treasures."

"One tries for quality, my lord." The jeweler turned
away to aid a matron agonizing over a choker of matched
pink pearls that was worth a small fortune.

"My wife will be delighted to meet you. We both loved
your design of the abalone swans set in etched silver. As a
matter of fact, she should be home now, if you can spare
an hour. And since you're here I think we should talk about
some ideas I've had for the displays. After that we can

make arrangements to get you down to the abbey and see the layouts first hand.''

Maggie swallowed, feeling a bit overwhelmed. She was intensely conscious of her well-worn blue jeans and plain white shirt. His wife would be exquisite in vintage Chanel, no doubt. Someone beautiful and exceedingly aloof.

All the old, painful shyness hit Maggie in a rush. ''Oh, I couldn't possibly visit today. I'm not dressed, and I'm sure your wife won't want to—''

''I insist,'' Nicholas said firmly, taking both her package and her arm. Somehow Maggie was out on Regent Street before she knew it. ''Kacey will never forgive me if I let you get away. Besides, we're just around the corner.''

Maggie followed, each step awkward and self-conscious. There was no polite way to escape him now. All Chessa's fine dresses were packed in her single bag, along with the clever high-heeled sandals and elegant pumps. Today Maggie had dressed solely for herself in worn jeans, plain white T-shirt, and a simple white shirt. Her sole adornment was a beaten silver necklace inset with a single chip diamond.

''I don't think this is such a good idea.''

Nicholas smiled broadly as they rounded the corner to a street of quiet town houses. ''You're probably right. I warn you, my wife will covet that necklace you're wearing.''

He was just being polite, Maggie thought. Hammered silver didn't exactly go with vintage Chanel.

''Here we are.'' Maggie caught a breath as Nicholas pushed open the door. Blue shutters covered the tall windows. The tiny courtyard was explosively green, rimmed by rows of climbing rose vines.

Inside, the house held a delicate scent of lavender and pine needles. A set of white doves decorated the long marble mantel, nesting above sprays of holly and tartan ribbons. Even the shadows seemed warm and full of peace.

''Kacey, I'm back. I've brought someone to see you,'' the viscount called. ''Ms. Kincade has arrived early, it seems.''

Maggie's heart sank at the sound of a door opening up the stairs. No doubt Lady Draycott would be tiny and exquisite. Probably color coordinated in perfect heirloom pearls and a cashmere sweater set. Or maybe a museum-quality designer suit.

A door slammed.

Maggie gawked at the figure flying down the steps. There was nothing stiff or formal about her. Her hands were streaked with oil paint, and her blond hair spilled about her shoulders, shoulders covered by a simple white T-shirt over a pair of worn blue jeans.

"You're here already?" Kacey Draycott's green eyes glinted with good humor as she studied her newest visitor. "I must say, I appreciate your taste in high couture, Ms. Kincade. But I won't shake your hand because I'm up to my elbows in oil paint."

"My wife is restoring a Whistler *Nocturne* from the Tate Gallery. Otherwise we wouldn't have been in town today." Nicholas's voice was warm with pride, almost as warm as the heat that filled his eyes when he looked at his wife. He held open the door to a sitting room where sunlight spilled over bright chintz armchairs. A pair of fine rosewood end tables was covered by a dozen stuffed bears in bright tartan jackets. Children's books were piled beneath a fig tree decorated with tiny white lights. There was beauty but no formality to the room, and Maggie felt her awkwardness begin to ebb.

Almost immediately a black-clad figure appeared with a tea service balanced on a lacquer tray.

"Ah, Marston, come and meet our new artist. Ms. Kincade has just arrived from the States."

The butler bowed slightly. "I found your inlay work to be most extraordinary, Ms. Kincade. Do you use flux or solder for your joinings?"

Maggie blinked. "Both. It's more whim than technique, I suppose. If I went by the book, there would be no room for inspiration."

"Perfectly understandable." As the butler arranged the tray, Maggie saw that in addition to his very correct dark suit he was wearing neon orange running shoes. "And inspiration is all, is it not?"

"For me, it is. You've done metalwork before?" Somehow it seemed hard to imagine that proper English butler handling a blowtorch.

"A bit here and there. I'm nowhere near your league, I'm afraid." Marston arranged the linen napkins expertly, then straightened. "There is a caller for you, my lord." He hesitated for a moment. "The gentleman is in the study. I believe he was hoping for your swift return."

Nicholas looked at Kacey, who made a brushing gesture with her hand. "Go away, love. This will give me a chance to corner Ms. Kincade about that necklace she's wearing. I'm under strict orders to buy something of Ms. Kincade's for Kara MacKinnon. Otherwise she'll never speak to me again."

"Not *the* Kara Fitzgerald MacKinnon of Dunraven Castle?" Maggie frowned. "The editor of *New Bride* magazine?"

"One and the same," Nicholas chuckled as he headed to the door. "She and my wife have become thick as thieves. But Kacey can tell you about that better than I." He appeared slightly distracted.

Kacey Draycott poured a cup of tea as the door closed behind her husband. When she handed the cup to Maggie, a carved pendant slid from beneath her shirt.

Maggie drew a sharp breath. "That's lovely work."

Kacey stroked the intricately carved oval of rare lavender jadeite. "It was a gift from Nicholas on our first wedding anniversary, and I seldom take it off. He told me it was very old."

Maggie studied the design of entwined dragons. "From the carving style, I'd say it's about sixteenth century. And the stone is genuine jadeite, Burmese, no doubt. The best always is. You don't see that shade of lavender very often today."

Kacey caressed the smooth stone. "Sometimes I could almost swear I feel the other women who've worn this piece, along with their joy and pain. It actually feels warm against my skin."

"Good jade always does. The ancient Chinese believed that jade protects better than any medicine. Poisoned food was even supposed to crack a jade dish, which made it a handy stone for suspicious emperors worried about a possible assassination. In fact, my father always said . . ." Maggie stopped, then drew a level breath. "My father was an expert in jades as well as faceted gems. He could have told you what hill village your piece was mined in and probably the name of the court carver who sculpted it. There wasn't much he didn't know about fine period stones, from Han jade to old mine diamonds."

"Daniel Kincade, your father," Kacey said matter-of-factly.

Maggie nodded, already steeling herself for the questions to come.

"My mother had a pair of his earrings, pink diamonds on tiny silver chains. She never had more compliments than when she wore them." Kacey hesitated. "I'm . . . sorry about what happened."

Maggie tried not to remember the incessant ringing of the doorbell in the house above the Hudson. Day after day the restless reporters had gathered for a glimpse of her, like wolves to the kill. What better sport than to stalk the daughter of the jewel king who had tried to cheat two governments out of a fortune in uncut gems?

"Just for the record, my father didn't steal *anything*. They said he'd been given those stones to cut and polish, and instead he'd stolen them, but it just isn't true. He *couldn't* have done a thing like that."

Kacey met her gaze with unflinching honesty. "Just for the record, we don't believe the story either, so you can put that concern out of your head."

"You don't understand." Maggie's palms were damp, her heart racing. "My presence at the abbey will be a problem for you, considering the scandal." She shoved back her hair. "You might soon regret choosing me."

Kacey's smile was gentle, but chiding. "A little scandal is the *last* thing Nicholas and I are worried about, Ms. Kincade. We've had our share of pushy reporters here and at the abbey. In fact, you might say that a scandal first brought us together." She sat down gracefully and filled her own cup. "Did you ever find out what happened to your father?"

"I tried, but things were complicated. All I got was the official government report that his plane went down after he had fled to avoid arrest. But my father would *never* have done something like that. I even sent an investigator to Sumatra, and his report was unequivocal. There was no sign that my father had lived through the crash. There was also no sign of any stolen gems."

Maggie's voice trailed away. Her father had left chaos in his wake. Even now she hated to think of those nightmare months.

"His death must have been a terrible shock."

"I'm beginning to get over it. But I can't help wondering why you're willing to give me a chance. Given the accusations, most people wouldn't be so generous."

"Your talent is genuine and very rare, Ms. Kincade, and you've never been accused of anything. It would be criminal if we *didn't* give you a chance. My husband and I both agree about that. Your artistic skills are extraordinary, but rarer still is your gift as a passionate, enthusiastic teacher. We'll need all of those skills if our craft program here is to succeed the way we hope. There will also be some restoration work involved as part of the show. Not many people could carry out all three."

Maggie sat very still, stunned by the calm generosity in Kacey Draycott's face. "The media won't forget. They'll have a field day once they know why I'm here. 'Swindler's daughter at historic abbey—another robbery in store.' That sort of thing."

"Just you let me deal with the press," Nicholas said calmly from the doorway. "I have more than a little experience with reporters and their tricks. All you have to do is marshal your inspiration. I'd like to include a display of an old necklace we dug up recently in the wine cellar. Judging by the cloth wrapping, it has to be at least several hundred years old. I think it would be fascinating to show how you determine the date of the piece and how you will go about restoring it."

Maggie nodded slowly. "I saw the sketches you faxed me in New York before I left. Replacing the silver should be no problem, but if the stones are nicked, they'll require refaceting, and you may lose some of the original material.''

''You're the expert. I'm sure you'll retain as much as possible. When can you have a look? I'd like to see how you show the stages of repair work.''

Maggie thought of the crowded two days she had planned. First the British Museum, then a stop at the Tower Jewel House. After that she wanted to visit one of her father's old friends, provided she could track him down. ''Perhaps this weekend?''

Nicholas hesitated. ''Frankly, I was hoping to have your input on the display cases as soon as possible. The builders are backed up right now, but the sooner they have designs in hand, the better.''

He was right of course. Even settled at the abbey, Maggie could still get back to London on the weekends for her museum visits. ''I'll be happy to take a look. Is it far to the abbey?''

''Only a few hours by car.''

''I don't have a rental car.'' Maggie frowned. ''Is there a train available?''

''I have a much better idea. I have a friend who's headed there today to finish some work on our new security system. I'm sure he'd be more than happy to drive you down and show you around. I'll be following tomorrow with the final sketches from the display company, and we can go over them together while we look at some sample cases already set up at the abbey.'' A figure moved across the front corridor, suitcase in hand. ''It appears that my friend is ready to leave right now. A bit of a restless nature, I'm afraid. Stop pacing and come in here,'' Nicholas called.

Maggie stared at the tall man who put down his suitcase by the door. The force of recognition felt like a fist to her chest. There were lines at his eyes that hadn't been visible in New York. She wondered if he'd been sleeping well.

Her muscles tightened painfully. *''You?''*

''Jared MacNeill. I'm afraid we never met properly before.''

Maggie held out her hand. ''Maggie Kincade. You do security work?''

"Among other things." He stared at her outstretched hand, unmoving, then finally offered his own. Maggie could have sworn that his jaw tightened as they touched.

When he gently released her hand, there was something distracted, almost grim, in his expression. "You've accepted Nicholas's offer, I take it?"

Maggie nodded, wondering why the room suddenly seemed too small, too short of air, almost as if this cool Scotsman had claimed every bit of space with the simple power of his presence. She couldn't seem to pull her gaze from the small cut on his jaw. "Did a reporter do that?"

He fingered the fading pink welt. "This? Just a scratch, I promise you."

A scratch that must have hurt like blazes when it was fresh, Maggie thought. "Did you tell Lord Draycott what happened? I want to be sure he knows what to expect."

"He knows." Jared flashed a glance at his host. "He's had his own share of squabbles with Fleet Street. I think he actually enjoys a good brawl now and again."

"Don't demolish my reputation so soon, Jared. I meant to convince Ms. Kincade that I was a proper British lord before I ruined her good opinion with the truth."

"Perish the thought." Kacey Draycott rose and straightened her husband's tie. "There's nothing proper about you, and thank heaven for it." Their lips met, lingered.

Jared hid a smile. "If you two can manage to tear yourself away for a few more minutes, we'll say good-bye. I'll take Ms. Kincade by her hotel and collect her bags on the way. We'll stop for dinner at the Mermaid in Rye, and we should be at the abbey before eight." He looked at Maggie. "Assuming that's acceptable to you?"

"I did have some appointments to make in London, but I suppose there's nothing that can't wait." Maggie had the sensation that she was politely but firmly being taken into charge, and she wasn't entirely certain she liked it. Still, she had accepted Nicholas's offer, and there was no reason she shouldn't get right to work.

"Perfect." The viscount rubbed his jaw. "The abbey will suit you, Ms. Kincade. It's very quiet there, and Jared will show you where everything is, since he'll be staying over tonight as well.''

"At the abbey?" Maggie stiffened. "But . . ."

Jared's brow rose. "Is that a problem? If so, I can put up at the hotel in Alfriston.''

His calm answer made Maggie feel foolish for her momentary discomfort. Clearly this was not the sort of man to take advantage of the situation. The awkwardness was all in her own mind. "No, of course not.''

"Then it's settled. I wish I could travel down with you two, but I've business to finish tomorrow morning. Marston is traveling down later tonight anyway, and he'll see that you're comfortable.''

A *butler* waiting on her? "There's really no need for that.''

"Marston wouldn't hear of anything else. Full protocol for our first resident artist, you understand. As for myself, let's just say that I'm selfish," Nicholas added, a hard glint in his eyes. "I'm rather looking forward to a bit of scandal.''

The uniformed officer made a crisp figure as he stood rigid, staring out at the gleaming dome of St. Paul's. He did not care for uncertainty, and he deplored errors of any sort. Unfortunately, the world was full of both.

"Ms. Kincade has arrived in London?''

"Yesterday, sir.''

He frowned, nudging a row of books on the side table into a perfectly straight line. "Any sign of contact with her father since her arrival?''

"None.''

The officer's frown grew deeper. "What about those pictures from Asia?''

"Details are expected tomorrow.''

"Of course.'' He steepled his fingers, watching sunlight strike the bright golden dome before his window. "Just the same, stay on top of it. I don't need to remind you how important this is. And keep your men well back in their surveillance. I want no indication that she's being watched, understand?''

When the door closed softly, he was still standing at the window, his shoulders rigid bars of black against the streaming afternoon sunlight.

Chapter 5

Less than half an hour later, Maggie's bags were stowed in Jared's trunk and they were weaving through late afternoon traffic on the M25 headed southeast. A light layer of clouds touched the small villages, occasionally veiling the road, making Maggie glad that someone else was handling the wheel.

The Scotsman seemed to enjoy the challenge.

"Nice car." Maggie brushed the gleaming console of burled wood. "Old, isn't it?"

"A Triumph. My father's car once. An eternal annoyance, but I can't imagine driving anything else."

Maggie watched his strong hands ease the car into a turn, then whip past a truck laden with freshly cut fir trees.

"It doesn't bother you, I hope?"

She blinked, realizing she had been staring at his powerful fingers and remembering how he had tackled the two reporters in the Chinese restaurant. "Does what bother me?"

"My driving." He gave her a quick, measuring glance. For some reason it left her pulse thready. "Does it bother you?"

Forget his hands, Maggie thought irritably. *Forget all about him.* "Not at all. I've been known to push the pedal myself sometimes. There's nothing like a quiet lane in autumn with leaves skittering up as you feather the motor right to the edge."

"Now that's something I'd enjoy seeing."

"Really? Most men I know go pale at the thought of a

woman at the wheel. For some strange reason they seem to consider driving well a sex-linked trait, purely male.'' Maggie settled back against the soft leather. ''What about you, Mr. MacNeill?''

''Call me Jared. And no—I enjoy watching a good driver at the wheel, whether male or female.'' He turned, his eyes narrowed. ''Maybe you'd like to try your hand right now.''

''Drive on the wrong side of the road?'' Maggie gave a short laugh. ''Not a chance. I may be reckless where speed is concerned, but I'm not entirely without sanity.''

''You've got good reflexes. You'd do.''

His low, murmured words sent blood skimming to Maggie's face. ''Why do you say that? You know nothing at all about me.''

''You might be surprised.'' He smiled at some private image. ''Nicholas makes his decisions carefully, you see.''

''You talked about me?'' Her hands tightened as she considered what might have been said.

''Nothing personal. Mostly we discussed the plans for this project of his. It's intensely important to both him and Kacey. They feel it's a responsibility to pass on the legacy that they have been lucky enough to enjoy.''

''Not many people in their position would be so passionate—or so generous.''

He downshifted smoothly, passing a dairy truck, then shot her a quick glance. ''For what it's worth, I think he made the right choice.''

The words sent an odd heat curling through her chest. Not that *his* opinion mattered, Maggie thought hastily. A plume of clouds drifted over the trees, plunging them into a tunnel of gray. ''I hope he doesn't have reason to regret his choice.'' Her hands opened on the smooth leather seat. ''Reporters on both sides of the Atlantic seem to have long memories.''

''Let Nicholas deal with that.''

''I suppose I'll have to.'' She studied him curiously. ''Have you known him long?''

Jared's eyes were unreadable as he peered through the drifting fingers of mist. ''Over fifteen years. Sometimes it seems like yesterday. At other times, it seems like a few lifetimes.''

He seemed reluctant to say more, and Maggie didn't push him. Instead she settled back and watched stone fences race past in a blur, hiding estates that probably dated back to the age of Cromwell or before.

History was different here, she thought. A few decades meant nothing in the grand parade of British events, measured out against wars and revolts and famines. Even the youngest village in this part of the country had to be six or seven hundred years old.

''Something amusing out there?''

''The fences. The houses. The *age* of everything.'' She ran a hand through her hair and shrugged. ''I'm beginning to feel very, very young.''

''I suspect you're old enough.''

''For what?''

His lips curved slightly. ''For anything you want. Age is largely a state of mind, after all.''

''My father always said that.'' She glimpsed a quiet town square where a decorated fir tree held place of honor before a church with half timbered walls. ''He almost made me believe it.''

''Almost?''

Maggie shivered, suddenly aware that the temperature had dropped sharply since they'd left London. She didn't want to talk about her father. ''I try. Sometimes I slip.''

''Maybe we all do.'' He nudged on the heater. ''Why don't you get some rest? There's a blanket behind you if you need it, and we have another hour before we reach Rye. I'll be sure to wake you.''

Maggie snuggled beneath the heavy tartan throw pulled from the narrow seat behind her. With the motor purring in her ears, she closed her eyes, enjoying the sensation of speed, of flying through a corridor of trees toward some shadowy mystery she couldn't yet fathom.

But for some reason she didn't understand, the journey felt intensely . . . familiar.

*   *   *

Midnight.

Snow on a cold road. Wind that snapped the holly and jerked the twisted boughs of hazel.

'Twas a night for mischief and harm, had she but noticed. Yet the slender woman in gray worsted saw nothing save the rutted road before her as she tugged at her cloak, willing the miles before her to close.

But they did not. The road snaked ahead, twisting and dark. Too late the full sense of her danger became clear.

She'd been a fool to sneak from the abbey against her father's will—and even more of a fool to attempt to return alone across the windswept downs.

Well she knew of the smugglers who plied their desperate trade from here south to the white chalk coast. But until now she had never thought they could do her a scrap of harm.

Until now . . .

Behind her the wind growled, tossing up dirt and pebbles. Her vision blurred as she tugged her old cloak tighter and prayed she would soon be safe at the abbey with the leaded casement windows locked and barred against the wind growling off the channel.

A branch sailed past, striking her shoulder, but she pushed on over the dark rise. Brambles tugged at her long skirts, making her fight for every step. She had an hour more before the abbey's high walls came into sight. And another quarter hour's walk through the home wood after that . . .

And all for what?

Jewels. An hour of forbidden study with a master goldsmith from Amsterdam. But no jewels were worth this sort of danger.

The pounding of hoofbeats came in a sudden lull of the wind. Low and fast, they raced from the north. What traveler would be abroad on such a moonless night?

No casual traveler. Someone on a darker mission, a hunter in search of prey.

The hooves drummed close behind her now. Refusing to give way to panic, she caught up her dusty skirts and plunged into the deepest heart of the thicket, where no horse would dare to travel.

And no grim rider.

It was but a minute's work to sweep her cloak over her head and sink down within the spikes. And there she waited, watching the dark road that led from Alfriston's sleepy lanes.

In the end, they came not from Alfriston nor from the lonely coast. Over the downs they rode, across the barren hills dotted with skeletal trees. There were four men and four horses and they traveled at the gallop, like riders who knew well their way and equally well their prey.

Probably after a rich coach and a Londoner with gold sovereigns hidden within Moroccan leather panels. Not for someone like her. Her hands locked, trembling at her waist. Even if they looked, surely they would not see her here among the dark brambles.

The wind rose shrill over the low hills, carrying the rough end of a shout and words she did not understand.

In a sickening jolt of clarity, she realized these faceless men had but one prey.

Draycott's daughter.

She curled into a tighter ball, certain now that she was hidden by the black branches. The horses neighed and plunged to a halt but a yard before her.

No move to betray her hiding place, she thought desperately. No small sound or yet a single breath. Wind-tossed sand and dry, broken gorse tickled her nose and burned her eyes. Still she did not move.

Slowly the brambles parted. A silver foil probed the branches. Her cloak was picked up and sent flying, like great black crow's wings carried on the wind.

She huddled amid the dead boughs, revealed now, but never would she stoop to show her fear. Highborn, she was, carrying the blood of kings, and her pride was bred to nerve and bone. Daughter of a viscount. Keeper of England's finest old abbey, though she cared little for the titles.

"Out with you!" The words were harsh with foreign tones.

She glared. She locked her body in angry protest. Move she would not.

"Hast you ears? Come out or you'll touch this fine steel."

Trembling, tossed between fury and terror, she rose from her bower, her hair spilling moon-silver about her shoulders. "And you shall hang from a high rope, coward. My father will see to it—you and all the miserable dogs that bark at your feet."

A flash of bright cloth. The drum of a curse in a tongue far older than Norman French or Saxon English.

The foil rose to probe her shoulder. There it remained with silent, capable menace.

She gave no thought to fear. Not to fear had she been bred, a Draycott daughter.

"If it's gold and treasures you seek, then great fools you are. I've nothing of worth for you. No sovereigns, no trinkets. Not even a simple crucifix of sandalwood or ivory."

The foil brushed back one silver-pale strand. Tall and unsmiling, the leader of the band moved close, grimmest of the four. "Naught of treasure, you say?" His laugh was hard as Sussex iron forged by night on the dark hills. "Naught of worth?" His laughter churned above the wind, setting the horses to a restless dance. "But I have you, *my bonny lass. You with hands of silver and fingers of magic. 'Tis* yourself *I'll take to ride before me this night."*

They knew *she thought wildly. Her name. Her family. Every detail about her.*

She struggled to understand, to shape some angry defense. But there was no time. Cold ropes covered her wrists and a smoky length of rough wool bound her arms.

"I'll fight you. You'll rue the day you swept me to your saddle," she shrieked. "You'll never hold me. Not you or any other!"

And then the patterned wool blocked her mouth. She was tossed up before the leader's saddle, caught like a chicken trussed as the grim band pounded north by night, just as they had come.

*   *   *

Panic swept through her.

Rain tinged the cold air and ropes bit at her wrists as she threw herself from the terror and the darkness, a scream on her lips. "Never! You'll not hold me. Neither you," she gasped, "nor any other!"

Outside the window, oak trees rustled in a gentle wind and clouds sailed like stately galleons across the sky. No storm. No rain.

A dream.

She sat up slowly. Only a dream, Maggie told herself, trying to fight the tremors at her chest.

A motor sputtered to silence. Hard hands touched her face briefly, then pulled away.

"Maggie, what is it?"

For a moment she had the oddest sense of another face and another night. Of horses wild before the wind and wool that smelled of peat and heather.

She looked down, frowning at her fingers buried in the folds of the old tartan. No doubt that had been the source of her fears and foolish dreaming. Just a piece of cloth that had triggered some imagined scene from history.

"Maggie?" Jared touched her chin, and his eyes seemed to darken at the slight contact. "What's amiss then?"

For an instant, another world was before her. Enormous and complete it hung, vibrating in the rough slide of his voice.

Then it vanished. And she was Maggie, only Maggie. And he was but Jared—powerful, inscrutable.

She swallowed. "It was a—dream. Just a dream."

"You screamed. You nearly put your fist through the window."

"I told you it was just a *dream*." She stared at the tartan, then wadded it up and shoved it behind her. "You didn't have to stop."

"I preferred that to us landing in a ditch."

"Well, I'm over it now, whatever it was, so we'd better go." She couldn't bear being close to him, feeling the hard scrutiny of his eyes. "How much farther is it?"

"About twenty minutes. But we'll stop for dinner in Rye first."

Maggie sat back stiffly. "It's kind of you to ask, but would you mind if we forgo dinner? The jet lag must have caught up with me, because I'm suddenly exhausted. All I want to do is curl up in a warm bed."

After a slight hesitation, he nodded. The motor sputtered, then purred back to life.

Maggie turned away, avoiding his keen eyes, uncomfortably aware of his concern and the nearness of their bodies even as she told herself she was nothing of the sort.

"Tell me who called." Kacey Draycott studied her husband's tense face in the shadows that filled the quiet study. A clock ticked softly beside a wreath of holly and painted gilt apples. In the two hours since Jared and Maggie Kincade's departure, there had been four phone calls.

Nicholas frowned, facing the window. "Someone in Whitehall."

"There's something wrong. That's why you wanted Maggie at the abbey so soon."

"Never could fool you, could I? Not even that first day in the stables when I was so certain *you* were a reporter."

Kacey touched his shoulder. "Don't try to change the subject, my love. It involves Maggie, doesn't it?"

After long seconds, the viscount nodded. "There's been some news of Daniel Kincade. . . ."

"Maggie's father?"

Nicholas nodded. "A routine surveillance camera in the Singapore airport turned up the picture of someone who looked damned similar. The same thing happened in Sri Lanka, near an outbound flight to England."

"What are you saying, Nicholas?"

He took a hard breath. "That Maggie's father might not be dead after all. And it is entirely possible that he's headed toward London as we speak."

Chapter 6

MAGGIE STARED UP AT THE ABBEY'S GREAT GRAY WALLS, stark in the darkness.

Moonlight dusted the high parapets and glinted over hundreds of tiny mullioned windows. *Maybe you should pinch yourself*, she thought wryly. *Or maybe you should just sit back and enjoy the ride.*

There was only one problem: Maggie had never been one for sitting back and enjoying anything. Life had taught her that pleasures were usually short and generally jerked away just when you started to enjoy them. Now she stayed on her guard, watching and seldom committing herself.

It was safer that way.

Jared took the bags from the car as she turned to sit on a jagged boulder that overlooked the sweep of the moat and the dark woods beyond. Against her better judgment, she relaxed, letting the beauty of the night slip into her soul. "Exactly how old is the abbey?"

"A Norman ancestor first claimed these hills through a grant from William himself. Since then a Draycott has always held this quiet corner of England for King and Crown." The Scotsman's lips curved. "Of course there *was* that period when the house fell into the hands of a zealous religious order that required a strict vow of silence. The only sounds to be heard here then were tolling bells."

"I wondered if it had actually been an abbey."

"Absolutely. The monks were hard workers and built all the high, vaulted ceilings you see through the house. The current structure was completed around 1255. Cromwell's men were all set to demolish it four centuries later, but one of Nicholas's wily ancestors managed to convince them that it was a bad idea. In the 1790s more reconstruction was begun." Moonlight played over Jared's face as he studied the imposing walls. "It truly is an amazing place. Three wars have been planned here. Four American presidents have stayed here. Two British monarchs have honeymooned here." Mist trailed across the parapets, flowing white around the shapes of carved animals.

"I'm impressed." Maggie looked up at the dark walls. "There's probably even a ghost or two hovering around the back corridors."

"So it has been said."

A cold wind played over her neck. "You're kidding." She studied his face uncertainly. "Aren't you?"

"I'm afraid not. Actually, he's seen on quite a regular basis by visiting tourists. But you're shivering. Let's get you inside."

Maggie didn't move. She fancied she could feel those ghosts now, lingering around her. In the same way, she could feel the love of generations of Draycotts who had cared for this beautiful old structure.

Too much imagination, she decided.

She should have been delirious with happiness, but she wasn't. As usual, the nagging uncertainty had returned. Soon she would have to smile and perform, digging deep and remembering a thousand details that her father had taught her. Perfection was expected of Daniel Kincade's only child.

Did she have it in her?

Maggie watched a pair of swans glide over the moat's restless currents. She had a centuries-old necklace to repair using authentic period materials. Then she had to diagram the process exactly, explaining each step in terms that any amateur could understand. That was daunting enough. After that came the task of completing her own designs for the Abbey Jewels collection.

No, she wasn't smug or delirious; she was terrified.

But she straightened her shoulders and studied the trees beyond her. She *would* succeed with her newest designs.

She already had two works in mind, the first a delicate silver tree inset with pavé diamond fruit, the other a moat of bronze carrying swans of hammered platinum. Even now the graceful shapes whispered softly, beckoning her to begin the painstaking work of construction.

Jared put down the last of the suitcases. "Is something wrong?"

"Not really." She crossed her arms, shivering as tendrils of mist brushed the moat. "I was just thinking of two designs I have planned. Already I can see a dozen more. There really must be some kind of magic at work in this place."

"Everyone who comes here says that." Jared studied the distant trees, gray with mist. "And yet everyone feels the magic in a different way."

"What about you?"

He shrugged. "All the usual, I'm afraid. Grand mental panoramas of knights on horseback and arrogant statesmen who struggled to hold this place of beauty and keep its future safe." He gave a dry laugh. "Everyone experiences a different vision of the abbey's past, and some people seem to be affected more deeply than others. I'll give you the grand tour tomorrow if you like, but I think we'd better go inside now." He studied the dark slope of the woods, then turned south to the curving gravel drive.

"Did you see something out there?"

He shook his head. "Only shadows. Are you certain you aren't hungry? I can produce a tolerable omelet when required."

"There's no need." Maggie stifled a yawn. "Sleep is number one on my list of priorities at the moment." She pushed to her feet. "Tomorrow I might take you up on that offer, however."

She held out her hands, framing a bar of moonlight. There was something strangely personal about the silence that wound through the darkness now. Nothing moved in the woods, and even the air was still. Almost as if the house was waiting for her.

The hair prickled at Maggie's neck. For the space of a heartbeat she had the disorienting feeling that she had been here before, on a night when the moon slid low and darkness reigned at the dead of midwinter.

In that cold moment of awareness, Maggie felt the shadows press close.

Almost like memories.

And that's about as idiotic as it gets, she thought angrily.

Mist touched her face. Overhead a layer of clouds ran before the icy curve of the moon. Jared picked up the suitcases and Maggie followed, almost without conscious thought. They climbed slowly, crossing the broad steps scattered with the first dead leaves of winter. As Jared pushed open the oak door, Maggie fought the uncomfortable sensation that someone—or something—was watching them.

Draycott Abbey lay still in the moonlight. Its stone towers and twisting chimneys rose dark as dreams atop the Sussex hills.

Up on a small balcony, Jared stood watching a pair of swans crisscross the moat. He knew he should fall into bed and try for a few hours of sleep. The house was utterly quiet now, and the light in Maggie Kincade's room had gone off hours ago.

At the mere thought of her, his body tightened with acute awareness. He remembered the smell of her perfume in the car and her restless, broken breathing. Then her terror as she'd flung out her arms in sleep, nearly catapulting them into a ditch.

He hadn't accepted her answers in the car or her attempts at calm. She had looked sheet-white in the moonlight and shaken to the core.

Her emotional well-being is hardly your problem, he told himself. But his painful awareness of her was. The prickling sensitivity that had caught him by surprise in New York had become worse. He could sense her presence and her mood across a noisy room in a way that was becoming damned uncomfortable. Even a chance brush of their fingers left him sweaty, his heart kicking in his chest.

Since his return from Thailand he'd tried to control these unwanted forays into other people's thoughts. This was different. Nothing matched what he felt around Maggie Kincade. The closest comparison was a sheet of wind driving straight off the sea and knocking him broadside.

Ever since their departure from London, he had been asking himself why. Had he met her somewhere before, perhaps in a museum or a quiet shop when she'd visited England? Had some previous encounter triggered this damnable sense of familiarity he had about her?

Impossible. Had he met her before he would have remembered every detail, every gesture on that expressive face.

His fingers closed over the chill curves of the wrought iron balcony. The why of it didn't matter. All that mattered was this electric awareness that surfaced all too often, slowing his responses and shattering his ability to assess threats. Jared knew just how dangerous that could be.

He paced restlessly, watching a bar of moonlight brush the flagstones while his mind worked through details of the upgrade to be finished on Nicholas's security systems. He couldn't afford to be restless, and he definitely couldn't afford to be careless.

Jared had learned that lesson well at the ultra-secret SAS explosives school in Norfolk when a fellow soldier had been torn apart by the blast from a device that was supposedly disarmed and absolutely safe. He had learned another rule there, equally important: *You only get one chance.*

Jared had blown his chance somewhere on a jungle hillside in Asia. He had died there with his blood slipping to a cold cement floor. In the normal course of things, he would have stayed dead, but he hadn't. And the price of his return was a gift that was fast becoming a curse.

Moonlight broke over the restless water circling the abbey's lawns. As Jared stared down, he wondered how the proud walls would look in spring, wreathed in bright roses and warm sunlight.

The odd thing was that part of him already knew the answer, though he'd spent no other season within the abbey's weathered walls. Yet somehow he saw how roses would climb and twist, clustered over the gray stone.

His mouth tightened. He was losing his edge. Too much imagination played havoc with a man's coordination and decision-making abilities, making him useless in a threat. He'd tried to tell Nicholas this a dozen times, but his friend had refused to listen. That kind of loyalty could get someone killed.

His body tensed as he revisited the dark alleys and cold nights of his past. He had faced more anger and despair than most men. One by one, he had fought down his enemies and conquered his regrets. But this sense of limbo he had felt since Thailand was a special kind of hell, and waiting was all he had left since he had glimpsed the manner and place of his own death.

It was moments like this, past midnight in the ragged hours of night, that the man from box 225 yearned for the brush of soft hands and the gentle glide of a woman's hungry skin. If he were very lucky, maybe even with a woman of passion and curiosity like Maggie Kincade. In their heated joining he might have found some semblance of peace.

But the peace wouldn't endure, he thought grimly. And he had never been a man to settle for pretense or empty fantasy.

So his bed went unshared and his pain went unassuaged. If he muttered or twisted in the night, there was no one else to hear, which was probably just as well.

He smiled wryly at the moon hanging over the gatehouse. Since his return, he'd learned to be versatile in his methods of physical distraction. A ten-mile run over steep, wooded slopes worked fairly well, but a predawn plunge in the abbey's icy, spring-fed moat worked better still.

For the moment he decided to forget about female company and check the e-mail messages waiting for him on his laptop. Moving inside, he scrolled through a half dozen messages for products he didn't need from companies he didn't know. There was nothing of any importance waiting for him.

With a yawn, he flicked off his laptop and heard a woman's silky voice purr goodnight. The sound file was a little joke from his computer-genius friend, who had assured Jared that the voice belonged to a sedate grandmother of six in rural Indiana. The knowledge did nothing to dim the effect of her smoky farewell.

Jared settled back in a deep wing chair beside the French doors overlooking the south lawn. Tomorrow he planned to finish testing the upgrades he'd made to the abbey's south wall security. With luck the whole process should require no more than several hours, in spite of the minor bugs he had discovered in the program. If he was very lucky, he'd also manage to be out of sight whenever Maggie Kincade was present.

Frowning, he picked up the latest techno-thriller, hoping it might ease him down into sleep. His gaze narrowed on the slouching figure on the jacket flap, a writer who supposedly captured the gritty reality of post–cold war Asia. The truth, Jared knew, was a lot more boring—and far more inhuman than any best-seller.

The man from box 225 understood that better than anyone.

Still, a diversion was a diversion. He flipped on a single desk lamp and settled back, book in hand, only to feel a ripple of uneasiness. Mist drifted past the window as he rubbed the knotted muscles at his neck and told himself there was no reason for wariness. The abbey's security was running perfectly, and no alarms had been triggered. This tickle between his shoulder blades had to be pure imagination.

Shaking his head, Jared plowed into the story. After three pages, his vision darkened and the book fell forgotten at his feet. As he plummeted into the cold tunnels of sleep, his heart pounding, he was gripped by a pain that felt as old as the unsmiling Draycott ancestor in the portrait that hung above his head.

His fists clenched.

A dream, Jared told himself. Nothing more.

Just another bloody incomprehensible dream . . .

Moonlight.
Cold wind on a lonely cliff. Rain that slammed over rutted roads and danger that hung like a silent, twisting noose.

He had only until dawn to find her. After that she would be lost to him—and to everyone else who loved her.

He ran through trees, feeling the slap of cold boughs against his face and chest. Panting, half lost, he was. Half blind. Completely sick at the certainty of her loss.

He should have sensed her desperate plan at once. When she'd come to his bed, he should have known it was a ploy. Tying her to the great oak posts would have kept her from her reckless plan.

A plan meant to save him.

Worry gnawed at his chest. His dirk dug into his hip, and somewhere in the darkness came the stamp of feet. A musket discharged with sullen fury.

His hand clenched at the woman's cry, off to the north.

The woman he had vowed to cherish and protect.

His fault.

All his fault.

Desperate to find her, he ran through the skeletal trees, heedless of safety or sense, falling straight into the trap that they had laid for him . . .

Jared awoke to a silent house and pain drumming in his head. No horses stamped in the courtyard, and no screams filled the chill hour before dawn.

With a curse, he rose, fighting away the ragged edges of sleep. Was it the cry of a bird that had woken him or the mist that whispered against the window? Or was it simply the unconscious knowledge of the woman who slept only a few rooms away?

Outside, the moon hung in fragments, caught between the arms of skeletal trees, which seemed to shift and move as if in a foreign landscape.

Probably another bloody dream, Jared told himself. Exactly like the ones that had begun in that cramped box dug into the jungle slope.

He was scanning two files that Nicholas had left for him when a beeper sounded on his laptop. He frowned as he saw a message flicker onto the screen. He began to type his reply, only to catch a hint of movement down on the lawn near the moat.

Make that someone, he thought grimly, seeing the flicker of pale clothing. The hour was far too early for lost hikers or innocent tourists, and hard experience had taught Jared to be suspicious. Quickly, he pulled on worn jeans and soft-soled shoes. Next thing he knew, he would hear the distant chime of church bells while the notorious abbey ghost shimmered into view beside the gatehouse, all rustling lace and hideous laughter. At least that was what a dozen tourists swore they had seen.

Jared didn't believe a word of the tales. Had there been any ghosts at the abbey, he would have sensed them before this.

At the window he froze.

A woman stood by the moat, dressed all in white.

A muscle tightened at Jared's neck. *Maggie Kincade.*

Why was she jaunting through the woods in the dead of night? And why was she wearing what appeared to be a nightgown?

There was an odd, dreamy quality to her movements that made him frown. Neither that nor her presence outside made any kind of sense.

A ribbon of mist curled up the hill, adding a layer of unreality to the night. He ran for the door . . . and stopped cold as a wisp of sound drifted through his head, hauntingly sad. Like faint music it echoed from his balcony in teasing waves, now clear, now gone.

A piper here at Draycott Abbey? What mad prank was this?

Irritation and something darker lengthened his stride as he pounded down the abbey's shadowed corridors. At the outside door cold air struck his face, and once again he heard the faint trill of music.

But now the woman in white was gone.

Chapter 7

JARED WORKED HIS WAY ACROSS THE DARK LAWNS, DOWN through the whispering trees, and there he finally found her. She wasn't crouched near the north wing, trying to pry open a window. Nor was she razoring out a square of glass to force the lock on a quiet rear door.

She was sitting on the edge of the stone bridge.

Just sitting.

Smiling, while her legs dangled and she traced invisible patterns over the old stone. Jared stared at her. ''Maggie?'' he called.

No answer.

Maybe she hadn't heard him. Maybe she was drunk. Maybe she was restless and had come outside for some fresh air.

All the way to the moat? And she didn't look drunk. She looked for all the world like she was playing a quiet game, waiting for a lost friend to appear.

Jared plunged down the hillside, frowning as he drew closer. Her bearing seemed wrong. Even her face seemed different here in the moonlight and mist.

Younger.

Excited.

Then the soft white gown moved, skimming her breasts and leaving his stomach twisted in a vicious knot of naked awareness. He hadn't been intimate with a woman in months—he hadn't wanted to be. He'd had no inclination for the agonizing link of raw emotions that such a contact would have forced upon him.

So why did desire lash out now? Why did he feel her with every nerve in his body?

The whole scenario was ludicrous, entirely impossible. Then Jared remembered that Draycott Abbey had a reputation for bringing the impossible to life.

Her mouth swept into a quick smile as he approached. Her head tilted, and her laughter rippled like morning sunlight.

The sound chilled him. It was too young, too innocent. What in God's name was happening? "Maggie?"

As before, there was no answer. He stared, suddenly cold, feeling the ground turn to foam beneath him.

Moonlight touched the long sleeves of her simple white gown with silver as she rose to her feet. Her full breasts rose and fell, each high curve outlined clearly through the soft fabric of her gown.

Jared's jaw clenched at the sight. "Why don't you answer me?"

Her head cocked. White and silent, poised at the top of the bridge, she was a study in innocence.

"Well?"

A frown marred the pale beauty of her face. She shifted from side to side, and the dry leaves in her hands fell like scattered rose petals.

"Answer me." Exhaustion made his voice harsh. "Say something, damn it."

Her fingers plucked at the folds of the cambric gown. "My lord? Do you finally come for me now, after all these months of silence?"

There was a sweetness to her voice that fit perfectly with the surreal atmosphere of the night. She might almost have been a child—if Jared could have ignored the full curves and dark, enticing hollows beneath her thin gown.

Which he bloody well couldn't. No man could have.

His muscles locked in aching awareness. "Get down or you'll be hurt."

But she only leaned forward, smiling. "Nay, my lord. Come, catch me here as you were wont to do." Her hands stretched toward him. "Unless the fine ladies at court now hold all your regard."

"Stop," Jared hissed, realizing she meant to fall and let him catch her. But it was too late. She moved toward the edge of the stone bridge and stepped off.

He caught her with a jolt of pain, cursing as they toppled onto the damp earth, barely missing the moat. Jared rolled sideways and pinned her beneath him.

Softness anchored him at hip and chest, tightening his throat, while the intimate contact slammed his body to full arousal. She was strong for a woman, her muscles trim but defined by hours of work at shaping and cutting metal. But it was the force of the link between them that left Jared weak as he plunged into the chaotic images of her mind. She was still asleep, he realized. And in her dreams, she seemed to recognize him.

Not as he looked now, but with a different face and different garb.

What in the name of heaven did it mean?

He pulled away, afraid to touch her longer. "What are you about, woman?"

She stared up at him, puzzled. "Why so cold, my lord? You were not so harsh when last we parted here on the bridge." Her chin rose. " 'Tis the court which is to blame, I trow. The Queen and her ways make you frown most ill."

Court? What was she talking about?

"Do not measure me so bitterly." Her fingers opened, tracing his cheek, and Jared felt the touch race through a hundred searing nerve ends.

"I don't. I'm simply trying to understand you."

She sighed. "My father gave up long ago. Now court holds him in its thrall, too. He has forgotten my very existence."

"Damn it, what are you talking about?"

Her palm gently covered his mouth. "Have I done aught to offend? Has cook's fare been ill? If so, I will tend it with my own hand." Then her cheeks filled with sudden color. "Perhaps my doublet and hose displease you."

Her words made the tiny hairs rise along Jared's neck. *Doublet and hose?*

"Enough," he growled, fighting the spell of her odd

speech and the soft perfume that drifted from her skin. "What are you doing out here, Maggie?"

"Maggie? I know no Maggie."

"*You* are Maggie."

Jared could have sworn there was genuine confusion in her face. "Nay, not I."

He gripped her hand and pulled her to her feet. "You're coming inside and no more discussion."

"As you will, my lord. And would you choose for me to share your bed—"

Bed?

Jared froze, every muscle tense. "What are you talking about?"

"As your wife, it is only meet and proper." Her voice fell. "Unless you find me repellent and not to your liking."

"No, damn it, of course I don't find you repellent. That is, I don't find you any way at all." He jammed hard fingers through his hair. How had he gotten into this bloody argument? There was no wife lurking in his past. He had made damned sure that no one was entangled with him. Not wife, or mistress, or any other partner.

She looked at him, all innocence, her eyes overflowing with adulation and love.

Was she a lunatic?

With a curse he turned, half-shoving her up the rocky slope toward the house. "Fine," he muttered. "If your name *isn't* Maggie, tell me what it is."

She stumbled over a rocky outcrop. "My name? You must know it full well by now. It has been four years since we met, my lord."

"Stop calling me that."

"Very well, my—" She caught back the phrase just in time. "I am Gwynna. You took me as your wife."

"I *have* no wife, damn it."

She spun about, her eyes huge and wild. "You were never wont to be so cruel, my lord. Cold and distant, but never knowingly to deal such pain. You know full well that we *were* wed."

Jared watched a tear creep down her cheek. He clenched

his hands against a restless urge to pull her close and trace that salty path with his mouth. Somehow he seemed to know exactly how she would taste, how she would feel against his painfully hardening body. Madness or not, the image enflamed him until thought and breath seemed impossible.

In his turmoil, he almost missed the first faint probing. It came weblike at his back, slow and tentative. Jared stiffened as the touch grew sharper.

Someone was behind them, out in the darkness. Watching.

Again the feeling came, light and subtle, like the brush of searching fingers. Some new infrared tracking device? If so, Jared had never felt such contact before.

Gripping her arm, he pulled her back into the shadows. "Why—"

"*Quiet.*"

To her credit, she caught his urgency and fell silent beside him. Overhead the leaves stirred in a wild dance that set shadows flickering over the cold slopes.

He tried to ignore the restless network of her thoughts and the warm pressure of her body, while he focused on the threat behind them. Somewhere to the north a bird shot from the dense foliage.

"Stay down," he ordered, pulling her toward the dense trees behind the stables. With luck and careful movements, they might avoid being seen. But first they had a rugged, stony slope to traverse. "No noise." Jared pointed up to the abbey, visible through the trees. "We'll head up the back way."

Her brow creased. " 'Tis a sort of game you wish to play?"

Jared didn't have time to argue or explain. He had to get them inside. "Just keep quiet and stay close."

Grimly, he tugged her forward, keeping to the mottled edge of shadows. The first yards were slow but manageable, and then the slope pitched sharply, rising to a tangle of rocks.

"Go ahead of me," he whispered, gripping her waist and pushing her forward. He stiffened at the contact, struck by the rush of her fear and confusion. Yet again he glimpsed his face as she saw him.

Wrong, he thought. All wrong. A different face with longer hair and younger, happier eyes. The face of a stranger.

But Jared had no time now to ponder the image. As soon as he could, he released her, gasping as the contact broke. To his relief she moved ahead without further prodding. Her steps were surprisingly nimble, as if she had taken this route before, but Jared was certain that *he* had not brought Maggie here.

Two yards. Three. Four.

Abruptly he felt the probing return. So they'd been spotted, their passage marked. Long nights in dangerous places had taught him to expect the worst, and he did that now. Body tense, he shoved Maggie directly in front of him, shielding her from a laser sight or the bullets that might target them at any second.

The night lay silent from moat to maze. Not even the wind stirred now.

Jared stared back into the darkness, watching for movement. A hint of light flickered briefly beyond the moat, then winked out. They had fifteen more yards, give or take, and she seemed to be struggling for breath.

He caught her as she slipped on a bare piece of granite and grimaced as her fear surfaced in his mind. "Stay to the right," he whispered. "There's no clear footing if you—"

Too late. His words were lost beneath her cry of panic as she lost her balance and plunged forward in a blur of white, striking the naked stone.

The prickle at Jared's neck sharpened to a stab. Her cry had been unmistakable in the silence. They were in immediate danger, and he had to get her up and moving.

He cradled her face and cursed to see blood matting her hair and cheek. He prayed that she hadn't broken any bones. "Hang on," he whispered. "I'm going to carry you."

She whimpered as he swung her up over his shoulder and bent into a crouch for the last punishing climb across the rocks. As soon as they reached level ground, he sprinted for the sanctuary of the stables. His back was tight as he negotiated the final yards of damp grass. If they were targeted, the bullets would come now in their final window of exposure.

He felt something heavy and cold gather in the darkness behind them. He gripped Maggie tightly, then crouched to make the smallest target. Down the hill on the south slope of the abbey, he heard the crack of twigs as he reached the haven of the stables. Abruptly the movements ceased. There was no sound then, no sign that there had been any pursuit. But Jared felt the cold rage that exploded out at them from the darkness.

It was almost worse than any bullet.

Maggie was sheet-white and bleeding as he set her carefully on an antique velvet sofa in Nicholas's office. He stroked her cheek, again struck by what felt like swirling mist.

Out cold, he realized.

Panting, he ran to check the security cameras on the far wall. All appeared to be operating normally, and no alarms had been triggered, inside or out.

What in the hell was going on?

Turning, he studied the woman on the sofa, frowning at the dark blood streaking her temple. ''Maggie, can you hear me?''

His hands weren't entirely steady as he moistened a towel with water and probed the angry welt. She winced, twisting restlessly at his touch. Gently, he cleaned away the blood, relieved when he found that the jagged gash was not deep. Jared's medical knowledge was limited to basic field first aid, but he suspected the wound would heal without stitches. It was the impact of the fall that worried him. The sooner she woke up the better.

Pulling a first aid kit from Nicholas's desk, he layered a generous amount of antibiotic cream over the wound, then stood up slowly. ''Damn it, Maggie, wake *up*.''

She twisted beside him, flinging one arm out in panic just as she had done in the car. When he tried to hold her still, her fists tightened, flailing wildly at his chest.

Jared cursed as she caught his chin in a point-blank blow. "Stop fighting me."

Her eyes opened, glazed with pain. "You'll find naught here," she whispered. "He has gone, and what you seek has gone with him."

"Who? Who are you talking about?"

Her eyes seemed to glaze over. She struggled wildly, and then went very still. After a moment she looked down, touching her dress, the sofa, her hands. And then she turned her head to stare at him.

Jared watched confusion slowly inch into recognition.

"Jared?"

"Right here."

"I—I don't understand. Why are *you* here? I was in bed asleep and then—"

"And then what?"

"I don't know. I think I heard a sound at the window. Or maybe it was the telephone."

"It wasn't the phone," he said grimly. "You were outside, Maggie. I found you down by the moat." He decided not to mention his icy sense of pursuit. He didn't entirely understand it himself.

"Outside?" She stared at him in disbelief. "That's impossible." She tried to laugh, but the sound trailed away. "You're serious, aren't you?"

"Dead serious." So was whoever had watched them.

She brushed her forehead and gasped as her fingers came away streaked with blood. "Why is there blood in my hair? What happened?"

"You tell me."

She closed her eyes. "I . . . don't remember. I was asleep and then I was here with you."

"Think," Jared said tightly. "Something must have made you go outside."

"I don't *know*. Didn't you hear me?" She tried to stand up and winced at the movement.

Her color fluctuated, and fresh blood appeared on her forehead. Arguing would get them nowhere. Grimly, he eased her back against the sofa. "Stop fighting me."

"I didn't leave the abbey. I couldn't have." Maggie

winced as a trail of blood slid onto her cheek. "I don't even know my way, remember? Why don't you believe me?"

"Because I was there, Maggie. I saw you."

Jared released her with a grimace. His stomach was twisted into knots, and his mind seemed unable to function. Though their contact was broken, he still felt the stabbing pain of her wound. He also realized that Maggie had no memory at all of being outside.

No one could lie that well, not through the link. Which left Jared right back where they'd started.

He ran a hand through his hair and decided that putting a few feet between them would be a damned good idea, although he was beginning to wonder if simple distance would help.

Before he could move, Maggie lunged unsteadily to her feet, color flooding into her face. "Why are you saying these things?"

At least she was fully awake now. Unlike before, she seemed perfectly rational. "Because I have to. I saw you, Maggie. Someone else was there, watching us from the woods. Now why don't you stop arguing, sit down, and help me with some answers."

"I don't want to sit down." She put a hand to her head, her voice trembling. "What you're telling me is impossible."

"I only wish it were." Jared's eyes narrowed. "You're bleeding again."

"I can handle a little blood. What I can't handle is more of these ridiculous stories."

"Someone was out there, Maggie. I saw his movement in the trees."

"Why? Why would someone hide there to watch us?" Suddenly her body stiffened. "You think this is . . . because of my father."

"I didn't say that."

"You didn't have to," she muttered. "You've got 'suspicious' written all over your face." She caught a jerky breath. "I want to leave."

"You're in no condition to go anywhere."

Her face went paler still. "You can't keep me here. I've done nothing wrong."

Jared's eyes narrowed. There was one way to find some answers.

His jaw clenched. Touching her would tell him what he needed to know. Before this, he had been too distracted to know what to look for, but now he would be controlled and prepared. Of course the process would also leave him drained, but it was a price he'd have to pay.

He took a step toward her.

"What are you doing?" There was a broken note of panic in her voice.

She slipped behind a heavy end table, and Jared followed. The contact would be painful, but if she was a threat to Nicholas, Jared had to find out now. He feinted left, then caught her shoulder as she spun in the opposite direction. When his fingers locked on her arm, the link instantly throbbed to life.

Fear. Confusion. Searing anger.

"Stop," she gasped, trying to pull free.

"I'm afraid I can't. Not just yet." He stilled his breath, focusing deep and fighting his way past shadowy barriers of fear and uncertainty. The heart, he thought. The heart never lied.

"Why? Tell me what's happening."

"I can't, damn it. I don't understand myself," he said grimly. "But I will."

Then Jared opened his hands with icy precision and slid one palm slowly over her chest.

Chapter 8

"STOP."

She trembled as she spoke.

Jared tried to ignore the sound, willing her not to move. He needed only a few seconds of direct contact now.

His hand slid lower, rising and falling with each tug of her breath. There was no time for argument. He had to know exactly what Maggie remembered of her time outside, and if she had any clue to who had been watching them.

He closed his eyes, trying not to feel her softness beneath his fingers, trying not to notice her trembling or how much her warmth was affecting him.

No excuse for making it personal, fool. But suddenly Jared couldn't seem to do anything else.

She twisted against him, her hip jammed against his taut thigh. He grimaced, trying to ignore his body's instant response, then moved his palm between her breasts and watched her face as his fingers opened gently over her heart.

Panic. Confusion.

In a rush, the thoughts and feelings battered him, but he held her still, forcing his way ever deeper into her mind. He needed all her secrets, no matter what they hid.

Cursing, he tightened his focus. Burning shapes took form—designs for platinum and beaten gold so sharp that his breath caught at their clarity.

So *this* was what Maggie Kincade saw when she worked. He hadn't realized that images could be so compelling. Half lost now, he slid through the restless tides of her mind, caught by sunlight on a metal disk and sparks thrown from a newly polished ruby.

So simple, he thought. And yet so hard to reach. There were dozens of designs now, each more striking than the last. Years of work were held there.

He pushed deeper. *Fury. Awe at the abbey around her. Leaden exhaustion.*

Jared winced as the pain throbbing at her forehead shot through him. The gash was hurting her badly, but he couldn't afford to spare her.

Or himself.

His fingers tightened. "Have you ever been to the abbey before?"

She blinked at him. "No, of course not."

The truth.

"Have you ever wandered off like this before, without any memory of it?"

"I don't *know*."

Again the truth.

"Do you know who was watching us?"

"I have no idea what you're talking about." Her breath came in ragged puffs, and Jared touched her confusion, knowing it was utterly real.

Looking down, he saw her body strain. His hand was open, wrapped around the soft folds of her gown. He was shaking, sweating, fighting to keep his balance.

How had things raced out of control so fast? Second by second she was dragging him deeper, capturing him with the dance of her mind even as her warm skin seduced his painfully aroused body.

No excuse, he told himself.

And no excuse for this damnable feeling of complete *familiarity* about her.

"Have we ever met before?" He hadn't meant to ask, but somehow the question slipped out. Maybe this was the source of what he was feeling. Maybe she had some slight, fragmented memory of him from sometime long before.

"In New York." She took an angry, shaken breath. "Why are you asking these things?"

"Before New York."

"No. *No.*"

Absolutely true. Damn it, what was she doing to him? Why couldn't he pull his mind free of hers?

He forced his fingers from her gown, sweating. Immediately she lurched away with a gasp. But distance made no difference. Every curve was imprinted on Jared's brain. Every cell of his body carried the scent of her perfume and the feel of her skin.

He took a hard breath. "I'm sorry for that. There were things that I needed to know."

"Like what? Whether you enjoyed touching me? Whether I frighten easily?"

Blood oozed from the wound on her forehead. "I won't do it again," he muttered. There was no need. All he had to do now was calm her down.

She backed toward the door, swaying. "And you think I'd believe you *now*?"

"You must."

"Not a chance." She took another jerky step, struck a lamp, and watched the brass frame clang to the floor. "You can't push me around. You're no better than those reporters in New York. At least they were *honest* about what they wanted."

"You don't understand." Of course she didn't, and there was no way in hell he could begin to explain.

"I don't want to understand." Her voice was strained, almost hoarse now.

"You have to try, Maggie."

She covered her ears with trembling fingers. "Stop saying my name like that, as if you knew me well. As if we were old friends—or something more."

So she'd heard it in his voice. Maybe she'd even felt the same hints of recognition that he had. "Listen to me."

"No. All I want to do is get away. This house—you—I can't stay here. Something's wrong, terribly wrong."

Jared's eyes narrowed. "How do you expect to leave it when you can barely walk?"

"I'll manage," she rasped. "Having a car crash would

be a lot more pleasant than staying here.'' She turned wildly. A pile of books toppled to the floor.

"Maggie, stop.'' Jared strode after her. "I can't let you go.''

"And you can't keep me, either.'' She backed another foot toward the door, clearly distraught. "I don't remember, do you hear? Nothing about what happened tonight.'' Her fingers dug at her head. "When I try, there's only . . . shadows. Then crushing pain.''

"I'm not going to hurt you.'' Jared took another step.

"No?'' She laughed tightly. "What do you call what you just did?'' Her ankle struck the corner of an end table, and Jared snagged a priceless blue-and-white Ming vase before it toppled to its ruin on the floor.

The doorway was just behind her.

She saw her chance and lunged, gasping, but Jared managed to catch her shoulders, then turn and pin her against his chest.

Heat.

God, the sweet searing heat of her. The joy of simply holding her. He could barely breathe with the force of it— and with the painful sense of recognition that followed.

Beside them a row of Venetian glass paperweights exploded over the floor in a cloud of glittering fragments. Dimly, Jared heard wind snap at the windows, banging the fragile colored panes. The very stones of the abbey seemed to shake in their distress.

"Broken,'' Maggie whispered. "All of them broken.'' She shoved at his chest. "What's happening to me?''

"To us,'' he said harshly, his hands spanning her shoulders. She felt perfect, he thought. As if she belonged right there, nestled at his chest.

He wanted to feel her this way often. He wanted to guard and protect her always.

Madness.

She swayed, and his arms tightened. Slowly, he drew her head against his chest, knowing it would make the pain lessen. She was dizzy, exhausted, but she still didn't back down an inch. She only raised her head and studied him as if through a long, blurred tunnel. "Why won't you let me go?" And then her eyes closed.

He didn't answer. God help him, he *couldn't* answer.

He didn't want to let her go, not ever again. His jaw clenched as he had a sharp impression of horses at the gallop and the clamor of soldiers. Almost like a memory, he thought. As if once before he'd let her go, and something terrible had happened.

There was only one thought in his mind as he carried her up the shadowed stairs to her room. He could not let her be harmed again.

The moat shimmered. Clouds veiled the moon.

Virgo rising.

Saturn trine Uranus.

The walls of high stone groaned softly, heavy with centuries of memory and travail. Quiet yet not quiet, they waited, never impatient. Never forgetting.

Somewhere in the night came the low peal of distant bells as Jared settled Maggie in her bed beneath a sea of damask covers. Her eyes were closed, and she did not see how he straightened the white linen pillows and spread another blanket across her body. And when he was finished, something held him still, too deep for naming. The play of moonlight on her hair, perhaps, or simple curiosity to watch her vibrant features relaxed in sleep.

By the bed he stood, drinking in the sight of her, a man too long cheated of beauty and wonder. Moonlight left his face in shadow, gaunt cheeks a reminder of nights of hell, nights of pain in a box.

He wouldn't think of that now. Now was for wonder and imagining. Dear God, he thought, how beautiful she was. How lost in sleep with one hand curved against her cheek and her hair spread wild upon her pillow.

Desire wrenched at his chest, silent as dreams too long buried. Heat flared as he saw the etched line of her cheek and the outline of one silken thigh.

He should go. There would be no peace here in watching and wanting.

And yet he stayed, caught by magic. Wishing that for one night he might be a different man.

A hero with happier eyes and a soul that did not bear the weight of sadness.

Jared stiffened, struck with the sudden sense that they were not alone. Energy rippled—perhaps even an intelligence that he could not define. He scanned the room, frowning at the velvet curtains, the small gilt mirror, the roses in a silver vase. Suddenly he smelled roses everywhere, rich and glorious, perfuming every corner of the room. It was an illusion, he knew, but one just as real as any other part of the night's magic.

He should turn away. He should return to his work, to finish scanning the three new files from Nicholas and try to sleep.

He did none of those things.

The magic held him. And yes, the wanting.

Too aware, too restless for sleep, he stood in a bar of moonlight and watched her. Wanted her. When she twisted against the pillow, he ignored all reason and smoothed a strand from her cheek, shuddering as the contact sent him down to meet the racing pattern of her dreams. They were fleet, filled with colors and yearning, images that left her harrowed, breathless, caught by trailing sadness.

For dreams, they felt very old.

Jared stiffened when she shoved back blankets and linen, rose warily to her feet.

"Maggie?" he whispered.

She did not turn, did not hear, framed in moonlight and entirely unaware that he stood mere feet away. Somewhere a bird cried a shrill lament, and Jared felt the skin pull taut, prickling across his shoulders.

Dreamlike, she reached for the table beside the bed and cradled her hands around emptiness. Empty still, her fingers rose, as if to lift a candle high. Her white gown flashed as she padded barefoot to the door, eased it open, and listened intently, each movement filled with caution.

Jared followed her down the hall and along the spiral stairs to the great front hall, where she stopped, head cocked to listen. Satisfied, she crept along the wall to the rear corridor.

Where was she going now?

The thick oak door to the cellar loomed in the shadows. She made a ghostlike movement as if to set a candle on the floor, then shoved at the door. Frowning, she put her shoulder to the wood, surprised that it did not move.

What purpose could she have here?

His only answer was the sight of her digging at the outline of the heavy door, almost as if searching for a lock or knob that did not exist.

Jared inched closer. Curious to see what she would do next, he slid back the shiny new high-tech bolt and pushed open the heavy, climate-controlled door. Shadows stretched before them, covering the broad stone steps spiraling down to the wine vaults, part of the abbey's original foundation. Instantly she plunged ahead, oblivious to the shadows, with the sure step of someone who knew the passage well. But how was that possible?

Jared followed her down, flicking on a switch as he passed. Light poured over damp stone walls lined with rack after rack of dusty, priceless bottles. At the foot of the stairs she stopped. Her head cocked, and then she sank to her knees by the dusty stone, carefully tracing each hand-hewn block.

Almost as if she was looking for a particular one.

Enough, Jared thought, as confusion gave way to full-blown irritation. If this was a trick, it made no sense at all.

He was within a breath of telling her so when she gave a low sigh of discovery. Oblivious to dust and cold, she sank flat beside the wall and dug at a pale square gleaming in the overhead light.

The mortar was fresh, he saw, as was the line of four granite stones. Woodshavings dotted the floor beside deep ridges, and nearby tracks had been cut out by some heavy machine. And that, Jared decided, made no more sense than anything else in this silent, trancelike episode.

But Maggie seemed more determined than ever, digging blindly at the stone and caking her fingers with grime and dust that could have been a century old.

"Stop, Maggie."

Still she crouched, dragging her fingers along the sharp rock and keening softly. Now Jared saw the silent tears that mottled her cheeks and dotted the dust while tremors rocked her shoulders. Last of all he saw the dark stains on her palms where the sharp granite had cut deep welts.

"Gone," she whispered, sliding to the floor like a puppet whose strings had been cut. "Every jewel. But who knew of this place? Who dared to watch me even here?"

She rocked back and forth, speaking in broken whispers, hands to her head. Now blood joined the tears on her cheeks, and Jared could bear no more.

She was still whispering as he raised her to his chest.

And she was still entirely oblivious to his presence as he again carried her back up the cold steps to her room.

This time Jared had no thought of leaving.

Carefully he cleaned her face and settled her back into bed, then turned to scan the room. The couch would do well enough for a man who had learned to accept mud and cold cement at his back and beatings every night.

The moon was sinking now. Silver light dusted the floor as he tugged off his shirt and slowly stretched his long frame on the velvet cushions. He still had no explanation for Maggie's somnambulist wandering. His only hope was that Nicholas could provide some clue to the desperate, dreamlike search he had witnessed.

Until then, she wouldn't leave his sight for a second.

Outside the moat shimmered, and clouds veiled the moon.

Virgo rising.

Saturn trine Uranus.

Chapter 9

SUNLIGHT BRUSHED THE ROOM. SOMEWHERE A BIRD SANG with noisy abandon.

Morning, Maggie thought. If there were birds and sun, it was probably time to wake up. She opened one eye and peered over her pillow at the bright room where light flashed off gilt mirrors and crystal vases. She stretched, then caught herself with a wince.

Not good. Her whole body ached, as if she'd had an argument with a truck and lost. For some reason the soles of her feet felt tender, and she couldn't seem to focus.

She touched the embroidered linen pillowcase, then traced the heavy damask coverlet. She was in one of the most beautiful bedrooms she'd ever seen in the most impressive house she'd ever visited, and she felt as if she was recovering from a grade-A hangover, even though she never drank.

Actually, Maggie couldn't remember *what* she'd done before her disturbing discussion with Jared. Even those details were blurred. Oddly, she didn't remember climbing the stairs or getting into bed. She didn't even remember putting on a nightgown.

She frowned down at the covers, searched for a moment, then gave a soft sigh of relief when she touched a flowing white gown. Now the problem was why she didn't remember putting it on.

That particular mystery could wait, she decided. First she wanted a hot bath, some steaming English tea, and—

Her body went rigid.

First she wanted to know whose naked chest was stretched out over the sofa a few feet from her bed.

A man. Definitely a man, judging by the tight, sculpted muscles untouched by the crumpled sheet that had just fallen to the floor.

Maggie took a jerky breath. So what if there was a man in her room? So what if he had nice—okay, *extraordinary*—thighs and a face that ought to be outlawed?

She sat up with a jerk.

A face like Jared MacNeill's.

Maggie bit back a groan as pain lasered across her forehead. Her knees felt tender, too, along with her fingers. What was Jared doing in her room, gorgeous, half naked, and entirely asleep?

She closed her eyes, struggling to clear her tangled thoughts. She was mature. She'd seen men in various states of undress.

So maybe none of them had looked half as good as he did. Maggie admitted that she'd never seen a stomach like that—washboard flat and rock hard. So what if soft black hair dusted his skin right down to the opening of his worn jeans? So what if they were stretched taut and fit him like a second skin?

She sank down with a soft, strangling sound as Jared turned restlessly to his side, straining the already deep opening of the jeans even wider.

The man was built, Maggie thought, closing her eyes on a reedy sigh. No male should look that good. It was downright indecent.

Not that she was going to look at him again. Or allow that gorgeous stomach to throw her off stride. She was going to slide out of bed, clear her ragged thoughts under a nice pounding shower, then confront him calmly about what had happened last night and why he was sleeping in her room.

Calmly, she thought. *Very* calmly.

Her hands were sweating as she eased back the covers, and she was fairly certain someone could have heard her heart pounding in the next county. So much for calm.

Thankfully, her uninvited guest appeared to be oblivious.

She lowered one foot to the floor, shimmied out from beneath the covers, and stood up slowly. Holding her breath, she took a careful step away from the bed.

No sound behind her. So far so good.

Slowly, she thought, keeping to the balls of her feet. Only another yard or so to go.

Linen whispered. Maggie nearly screamed at the sound of Jared clearing his throat.

"You dropped this, I think." He was right behind her, holding out the white cambric belt of her gown.

Maggie thought she'd probably dropped ten years of her life, too. She straightened her shoulders. "Thanks. I was just going to—dress."

Calm, she told herself.

Mature.

"You probably want to do the same." She gave him a sidelong glance and nearly swallowed her tongue.

The jeans rode even lower now, wedged over muscle and a dusting of darker hair beneath that hard, lean waist. She could see the outline of his thighs clearly, and she could also see a firm, very suggestive ridge of male muscle beneath the taut zipper.

Her face flared red. So much for calm and mature. "I'd better go. I need to clean up—that is, to think."

To breathe, she thought wildly. When had all the air been sucked out of the room?

"Maybe we should talk first," he said in that voice that made her think of aged whisky.

"Talk about what?"

"About last night."

Her gaze snapped to his face. "Last night?" Blast it, why was she blushing? His hair fell over his forehead, and faint stubble covered his cheeks. He looked focused, dangerous, and sexy as hell. "What about last night?" she squeaked.

"Don't you remember?" His gray eyes locked in hard, and Maggie had an uncomfortable sensation that they were stripping off three layers of skin and reading every secret corner of her whole life.

"Of course I remember." She swallowed. "We came

inside. You showed me to my room, and then I went to sleep. End of story.''

His eyes narrowed. ''Not quite.''

Maggie didn't much care for the lurid possibilities that shot into her mind. After all, they were two reasonably sane adults involved in a cultural project of key importance. He couldn't have—she *wouldn't* have—

''What happened?'' she demanded.

His dark brow slanted up. ''You don't remember.''

Don't look down, she thought. *Forget about his chest and keep your eyes on his face.* On that hard mouth. On those stubbled cheeks and smoky eyes that wouldn't seem to let her go. ''Obviously not, or I wouldn't ask.''

Maggie knew she had to get a grip. And any minute now she would—just as soon as the room stopped spinning and she remembered how to breathe. ''Why don't you put on a shirt or something?'' she said irritably.

''I think we should talk first.''

''I'll talk a whole lot better when you're dressed,'' she snapped. ''After all, we're complete strangers. Well, *almost* complete strangers.''

He didn't move. ''Something happened last night, Maggie.'' His jaw hardened. ''It might be very important.''

''What do you mean, 'happened'?''

''Just what I said. When you woke up—'' He jammed his fingers through his hair. ''Did you feel different in any way?''

''Other than the sensation that a truck had run over me, no.'' She saw him shoot a look at the rumpled covers on the bed. ''Now wait just a minute.'' She might be fuzzy-headed and exhausted, but there were *some* things a woman didn't forget, and spending a night wrapped in Jared MacNeill's arms would have to top the list. ''I slept here. You slept there.'' She hesitated. ''Didn't you?''

''Close enough.'' He turned to pace.

''What do you mean, 'close enough'?'' She told her heart to stop jackknifing toward her stomach. ''Did we or didn't we?''

His eyes narrowed. ''We didn't sleep together, if that's what you mean.''

Thank God.

Maggie hid her relief with a broad shrug. "So what seems to be the problem?"

"The rest of what happened last night," he muttered.

Maggie had a sudden suspicion she wasn't going to like what came next. All the more reason to take time to clear her head first. "Look, I'm sure it's very interesting, but I really want to clean up first." She frowned. "I feel dusty for some reason, and I have a headache that won't quit." She had a sudden, blurred impression of darkness and the whisper of the moat. Then pounding feet—followed by sharp pain.

None of it made any sense.

"Why don't we talk about this in half an hour? I'll finish dressing, then come find you downstairs." She put her hand on his arm in a gesture of reassurance. "There's no reason to worry about a little—"

Blood.

Maggie froze.

There were dark streaks on her right hand and a thick layer of grime beneath her fingers. Blood covered the ragged edge of one cuff.

"What . . . happened?"

"I think," Jared said slowly, "that you had better sit down."

Maggie didn't want to sit down. Calm seemed entirely out of the question, along with mature and confident. Confusion was tying knots in her stomach. "I think you'd better start explaining."

"I was trying to—as much as I could, at least."

"Start with the blood," she said hoarsely. Confusion was racing into panic, and she didn't like the feeling. She had never lost consciousness before, and she couldn't bear the thought of gaping holes in her memory. How did a person simply lose whole minutes out of his life?

"You fell when we were coming inside." He started to say more and then stopped.

"But I *didn't* go outside. Not last night, not with you or anyone else. I've told you that already."

"Then why are your feet dusty?"

"No way." She balanced and raised one foot.

Dirt. Just like he'd said.

Calm down, she thought. There had to be some reasonable explanation. "So the floor is dusty in here."

"Marston has his staff clean with the fury of zealots. He can spot a dust mote at sixty paces."

Maggie shook her head, fighting a wave of dizziness. "No."

"Every word is true."

"You're *lying*. You have to be." She gripped her robe, suddenly aware that her fingers were trembling. "Why are you making these things up?"

"You're shivering. Sit down." Jared pulled a blanket from the bed and draped it around her shoulders.

"Don't touch me," she hissed. "For your information, I have never experienced memory losses, hallucinations, or temporary bouts of insanity."

"Maggie, I wasn't implying that—"

"Weren't you?" She charged on angrily. "Just because I'm an artist, that doesn't make me irrational."

"Don't you think I know that?" Jared took a step forward, and Maggie shoved one hand against his chest, stopping him. The air shimmered, tight with tension, and she could have sworn that he flinched before he stepped away from her.

"Don't come any closer," she said tightly.

"Do you honestly believe that I would harm you?" A muscle clenched and unclenched at his jaw.

"I'm not sure what I believe. All I know is that there's blood on my hands and welts on my feet and I have no idea how they got there."

"You walked in your sleep last night."

Maggie simply stared at him. "That's impossible."

"Unusual, not impossible. And I know it happened because I followed you."

Maggie's throat was dry and achy, and there was pressure building sharply behind her eyelids. I don't believe you."

She turned away from the window, unable to face the golden beauty of the abbey in the streaming sunlight.

Something nagged at her consciousness, disturbing but too faint to pinpoint. Could he possibly be telling the truth?

No, it was impossible.

"I'm sorry if I upset you."

"This has nothing to do with *you*." *A lie*, a voice whispered. It had everything to do with this hard-faced man with the deep, lilting voice. "I have to go. I can't stay here."

He started to grip her arm, then jammed his fists into his pockets instead. Maggie looked away, trying to ignore how the movement strained the worn denim even tighter.

"I'm afraid there's something more that you need to know. When this project began, I told Nicholas not to get involved with you. If I'd had my way you would never have come here."

Maggie spun around, white-faced. "I won't listen to this."

"You have to listen. That was *then*, Maggie. Nicholas chose to ignore my reservations, and he was right to."

"Don't overwhelm me with praise," she said bitterly.

"I can't afford to be emotional. I'm being paid very well to ensure the security and success of the Draycott exhibition. You—and concerns about your father—present a major problem in that area."

"My father? Don't tell me this is more old accusations."

"Not old accusations. I'm talking about new developments as of one week ago." Something flickered in his eyes. Maggie thought for a moment it might have been compassion.

She didn't want his compassion. "More thefts laid at my father's door? My father was a genius, but even *he* couldn't steal gems from beyond the grave."

"Not from beyond the grave," Jared said. "Your father isn't dead. He was sighted last week boarding a flight in Singapore. An airport security camera caught him on film."

Maggie could only stare at him in shock. "I refuse to listen to this. My father is dead, Mr. MacNeill. *Dead.* He died seven months ago in Northern Sumatra."

"That's what the reports say."

"His plane went down over heavy jungle. The trackers found widespread wreckage that contained two burned skeletons, a handful of blackened gems, and my father's passport.'' Maggie felt a cold weight at her chest, where each detail was carved into her still grieving heart.

''The reports say that too. Did it ever strike you as odd that his passport would survive intact?''

''No.''

''The crash could have been staged, and your father was most likely nowhere near the plane when it went down. Then he—or someone else—planted the passport where it would be found afterward, along with an inferior set of gems to give the whole thing the ring of authenticity.''

''That's entirely ridiculous.''

''Is it? Who identified the wreckage? Not regular consular staff.''

''I don't remember.''

''I do. I checked to confirm it. The man was with the DEA.''

''DEA. That's—''

Jared answered for her. ''American Drug Enforcement Administration. You will agree that body verification of random crash victims hardly falls under their usual job description.''

Fury left Maggie's chest heaving. ''Are you saying my father was running *drugs*?''

''Not at all. But someone might have thought he was.''

Maggie had thought she was too scarred to feel any more pain from accusations about her father. Now she realized she'd been wrong. ''You're either crazy or very sick.'' She started to brush past him, only to feel his fingers lock around her wrist.

''I'm neither. And it's time you stopped running from the truth.''

She stared at his fingers on her hand, her pulse racing. ''Let me go,'' she whispered.

''In a moment,'' he said harshly. ''After I explain something else. This exhibition is intensely important to Nicholas and Kacey. It will involve priceless objects of personal and historical importance, since Draycott Abbey's history is also the history of England. The opening ceremonies will be attended by a half dozen members of the royal family.

Nicholas hasn't the right to take chances with security, not under those circumstances.''

''My father is dead, Mr. MacNeill.'' Maggie looked away, blinking. ''He has been dead for almost a year, no matter what rumors you may have heard.''

''More than rumors.''

Maggie laughed raggedly. ''Do you think you're the first one to tell me that he was sighted in Java or Borneo or sipping a dry martini in Macao? You're not. There have been a dozen rumors. I even sent my own investigator to Asia, but every lead came back empty. And they all—'' Her voice broke. *Hurt*, she finished silently.

His fingers tightened on her arm. ''Maggie—''

She jerked away. ''I don't need your help or your compassion, Mr. MacNeill. My father is dead, and I'm finally beginning to accept that. To me he was nothing but perfect. Nothing but wonderful and brilliant and demanding. He loved his work with a passion. A man like you wouldn't understand that.''

Something moved in his eyes—dark, almost sad. ''Stones don't make for comfortable friends. It sounds like a damned uncomfortable way for a lonely girl to grow up.''

How had he known that she was lonely? Maggie hid her shock, struck as before by the sense that he was probing her deepest secrets. ''Who said I was lonely?''

''A lucky guess,'' he murmured. ''What shall I tell Nicholas?'' His eyes narrowed. ''Is the exhibition off?''

The thought stabbed deep. Maggie *wanted* this exhibition, yearned for it with every atom of her being, but too many questions had been raised for her to charge ahead blindly. She couldn't accept the shattering possibility that her father was alive and that he had lied to her, betraying her completely. The mere thought left her bleeding inside, caught in a devastating sense of loss. ''Tell Lord Draycott that I need some time to think.''

''Do your thinking here.''

''I can't.'' Maggie frowned. ''There's something overpowering about this place. Haunting, beautiful, but overpowering.'' She drew a jerky breath, studying her grimy fingers. ''Even now I have wisps of dreams. Faint images that come and go. It's not a pleasant feeling, I assure you.''

"We'll go out to the moat and retrace your steps. Maybe it will help you to remember.''

For a moment Maggie was tempted to stay, to work things out as he'd suggested, step by step. But the pressure at her chest was building, bringing a sense of suffocating panic. *"No.* I'm leaving as soon as I dress. Don't even think about trying to stop me.'' She studied his harsh features, unable to judge whether it was anger or concern that flared in his eyes.

"Very well. I'll tell Nicholas what you said.''

"And you won't try to stop me?''

He shook his head slowly. "No. I'll arrange for a driver and car to take you back to London. I'm assuming that you won't care to accept a ride from me,'' he added grimly.

Maggie flushed. "I would prefer it that way, yes.''

"That much is fairly obvious. But you're making a mistake.''

"It won't be the first time.'' Maggie looked down at her crumpled sash, then set it carefully on the bed. Maybe this was all a dream. After a shower everything might snap back into focus and the world would begin to make sense again.

But maybe not. Perhaps her world would never be calm and focused again.

"Good-bye, Mr. MacNeill.'' She was glad that her voice sounded steady, calm, as she walked away from him, very careful not to look back.

Jared watched her cross the room and close the door. Water hissed, then rose to a roar, drumming in the shower.

He hadn't needed contact to see how badly his words had upset her. Even a blind man could have sensed her turmoil over her father, and how it hurt to balance that concern against a driving desire to be part of Nicholas's exhibition. But Maggie Kincade wasn't one to accept things halfway.

That meant more questions for which there weren't answers. It meant time for her to come to her own decisions. Jared could admire that kind of stubborn pride if it didn't make things so bloody complicated.

Meanwhile, he had promised not to try to hold her here, and he wouldn't. But he hadn't promised not to follow her or be concerned about her.

Now he was going to dog her every step until he had some answers of his own.

It was a long, silent drive back to London.

Maggie was relieved when Jared stayed true to his word, not trying to keep her at the abbey. As she watched the trees blur outside the car window, she told herself she simply needed distance and clarity. No problem in her life had ever left her so confused, battered at the very core of her identity.

But few people had lost a father, only to find him again.

Mile after mile, she replayed the jagged pieces of her conversation with Jared, each time drawing back from the terrible possibility that his story could be true. She was white and shaken by the time she reached London and sank down on the narrow bed in her cramped hotel room.

If her father really *was* alive, she would have to face that fact and all its painful ramifications. She would have to rethink every word he had said and every promise he had made, then decide exactly what role he could hold in her life.

The pain cut her like a knife.

How could he have betrayed her?

She drew up her knees, fighting back a broken sob while tears came, hot and swift. Her body was numb and she realized she was shaking. There was no more fighting the possibility. The news could be true. Probably *was* true.

Maggie locked her hands over her chest. ''Daddy, how could you?''

She had loved him, trusted him.

Idolized him beyond words.

''Dear God, how could you? . . .''

Chapter 10

NICHOLAS WAS PACING THE MORNING ROOM WHEN JARED arrived in London. He looked every bit as haggard as Jared felt.

"I don't like it. She shouldn't be out of your sight, Jared. Not after what happened."

"I've got a friend watching her for the moment. I arranged for him to drive her back to London. She'll be safe."

"Tell me again what happened."

Jared crossed his arms tensely. "Hell if I know. One minute she was asleep, and the next I saw her walking beside the moat."

"But why?"

Jared shrugged. "She didn't even know her real name. She might have been sleepwalking, but that doesn't explain the other differences. Her voice, her gestures. She was like a stranger."

"I don't understand."

"I don't either." Jared strode to the window, watching sunlight brush the courtyard. "There was something odd about her demeanor, Nicholas. Almost childlike. I'm not sure I can explain it, since everything happened so fast. I also know that someone was out there watching us."

Nicholas frowned. "You *felt* it?"

"Without a hint of doubt."

"I'd like to think it was a coincidence, but I don't. Did you pick up anything else?"

Jared shrugged. "Rage. Not much beyond that."

"I won't go back on this invitation, Jared. No matter what her father was accused of." He rubbed his neck. "Despite what's happening, I mean for everything to go ahead on schedule. But to do that I'm going to need your help."

"Are you certain this is what you want?" Jared felt a nagging sense of inevitability as he stood by the window, staring across the flagstones.

Almost as if he'd stood here exactly like this before.

As if he'd waited and worried while sunlight touched the neighboring roofs.

"I'm certain."

"In that case, there's one more thing you should know. Late last night Maggie walked down to the wine cellar. Sleepwalking, I'd call it. She crouched by the bottom step and dug at the stones, dug until there was blood on her hands. I noticed there was a fresh patch of mortar there, but you didn't tell me why."

Nicholas's face paled visibly. "The bottom step? Good God, that's where we found the necklace when we were drilling holes for more electric lines."

"Maybe you mentioned it to her."

"Absolutely not. No one but Kacey, the workman, and myself knew where that necklace was hidden." Nicholas sank into a chair and rubbed his forehead. "I'm beginning to feel like Alice in Wonderland."

"She mentioned a name, too. Glenda—or maybe it was Glenna."

Nicholas turned slowly. "Could it have been Gwynna?"

"I suppose so. There was something odd about her voice, and I didn't understand everything she said. Why?"

Nicholas's face was shuttered. "I'll have to check some old records."

"For what?"

"For a list of births and deaths at the abbey. You see, Gwynna happens to be a very old Draycott family name, and I'm getting a bad feeling about all this." Nicholas drew a hard breath. "Stay close to her, Jared. Stay very, very close."

*   *   *

On a Thursday afternoon at four o'clock the British Museum's jewelry exhibit was nearly empty. A few Japanese tourists wandered past a set of early Celtic torques, but otherwise the gallery was quiet.

Maggie was hunched over a sketch pad, her thoughts afire. Her pencil raced, capturing delicate spirals of wire decorated with turquoise and pearls. Gold leaves rose against a cutwork sun, and a new moon hung below, shimmering in hammered silver over platinum.

Second by second the pages hissed past.

When Maggie finally sat back, her fingers were numb, but she had a notebook full of exciting ideas. Only then did she permit herself to wonder when she would use them.

A long and sleepless night had convinced her there were serious reasons to reconsider Nicholas Draycott's offer. In everything but her creative vision, Maggie had forced herself to become a creature of firm practicality. She allowed herself no self-indulgent fantasies of white knights and overnight successes. But Draycott Abbey had changed that. The haunting house had touched her deeply, disturbed her, drawn her in with an almost seductive sense of—

Familiarity.

If that wasn't enough of a problem, she had to consider that her father might still be alive. The possibility left her in turmoil. Maggie wasn't sure she could face the knowledge of her father's betrayal. No child could.

She closed her notebook with a snap. Shadows touched the high windows, and daylight was fading. She ought to leave for her final appointment, then grab something to eat on the way back to her grimy hotel room.

But she made no move to leave. Around her sunlight glinted on glass cases, reflecting a thousand years of magic created by nameless artisans who had left behind only their silent genius.

One day, perhaps in some far century, her own work might glitter on a translucent, high-tech museum case. Or maybe not.

A shadow fell across her sketchbook.

"Nice use of line."

Maggie blinked, looking up into the light. Her fingers

tightened when she saw Jared leaning against a marble column. He looked more formal today, clad in a tweed jacket in muted colors of the North Sea. His hands were shoved deep in his pockets, and his eyes looked too sharp, as if he hadn't slept well.

Only fair, she thought bitterly. He had seen that her own sleep was fitful and short.

But she wasn't interested in *anything* about Jared MacNeill. She couldn't afford to be.

She gathered her pencils with cool precision and rose to her feet.

"No need to leave on my account."

"I was finished anyway."

He moved to block her way. "We need to talk, Maggie."

"Do we? I think talking is the last thing we need to do." Frowning, she tried to push past, but he caught her arm and held her still.

His fingers were callused, almost as hard as his eyes. It struck Maggie that he moved with a controlled intensity that hadn't been evident at the abbey. He also seemed restive, as if something held him on the very edge of control.

She glared down at his hand. "Let me go," she said in a flat voice, angry at the heat of his fingers and the immediate flare of sensual awareness his touch provoked.

"Nicholas Draycott says you've created a whole new life for a dying form of early European metal inlay."

"So?"

"If you're that good, you should stay, Maggie."

Her fingers clenched on her notebook. "I haven't decided what to do."

"You don't look like someone who gives in to fear and runs away."

"What would you know about fear or running away?"

"More than you might imagine. Why don't you talk instead of running?"

She strained impatiently at his hand. "I don't need to talk, I need to think. Alone," she added tightly.

"Something happened to you at the abbey. Something made you walk down to the moat in the darkness. You can't ignore that."

"I don't remember going outside." But Maggie did remember the sight of him in the morning stretched out on the couch in his jeans. The image made her whole body tighten. "Now I'd like to leave."

"Come back with me," he said gently. "Today. Right now. Whatever is wrong, we'll find it."

"Good-bye, Mr. MacNeill."

A muscle bunched at his jaw, and he pulled out a cellular phone. "Call Nicholas," he ordered softly. "If you won't talk to me, talk to him."

Maggie frowned, watching him stab in a series of numbers.

He listened for a moment, his hand tight around the phone. "Kacey? Oh, he's not there? Then perhaps you'd speak with Ms. Kincade. Assure her that I'm neither trying to browbeat her nor hustle her into my bed. I'm simply trying to act in her best interests." He held out the phone to Maggie, who gripped it reluctantly.

"Ms. Kincade?"

"Yes, I'm here."

"I'm afraid Nicholas had to go out a few minutes ago, but I'll have him phone you tonight. Meanwhile, I hope you'll listen to what Jared has to say."

Maggie drew a deep breath. "This exhibition meant everything to me. It would be heaven to take part, especially since you and Nicholas have been so generous. But something terribly odd happened yesterday at the abbey, and even now I can't remember clearly."

"I'm sure that there's an explanation. We can help you find it."

Maggie gripped the phone. Why did they have to be so nice? It would only make her decision that much harder. "I need some time to think. I can't do that at the abbey. I'm sorry, but that's how it has to be."

Frowning, Jared took the phone. "Thanks, Kacey. I'll ring Nicholas back later." He turned, studying the quiet room. "I'd rather go someplace private to talk."

"Here or nothing." Maggie crossed her arms. "You have exactly three minutes."

"In that case, I think you should see this." He drew a

sheet of paper from the pocket of his jacket.

Maggie frowned down at a grainy photograph of a crowded room with palm trees just outside the windows. A man sat on a bench, one hand shading his face. The features were blurred and his cheeks were gaunt, but there was something familiar about his eyes.

Her gaze flashed to Jared's face. "Where did you get this?"

"A source in British intelligence forwarded it to Nicholas. They want to be certain he understands what kind of ride he's in for," Jared added grimly.

It could be her father, Maggie admitted. The eyes were right. So was the proud tilt to the man's jaw. But she was not going to reveal that possibility to Jared, not without firm evidence.

"It will take more than one out-of-focus photo to convince me of your wild story." She shoved the glossy paper back into his hand, wanting to be rid of it. "And now if you will excuse me, I have a research appointment upstairs in European metalwork. After that, I have plans for dinner."

Jared scowled as he stalked down the granite steps. He was furious inside—furious at his lapse of control and the silent bond that was fast growing.

Maggie Kincade was stubborn, but he'd dealt with stubborn subjects before. She was angry, but she had every reason to be, given the photograph he'd handed her.

Neither of those things explained why Jared had behaved like a rank amateur, allowing his control to shred until he felt a personal attachment.

He remembered how she'd looked sketching in the corner. Her focus had been absolute. An explosion wouldn't have shaken her from those drawings. Her sure confidence and unconscious grace had intrigued him.

Then she'd looked up. Pale cheeks. Smoky blue eyes. A long cool mouth the color of ripe raspberries. A mouth that a man would dream about with the kind of dreams that left his sheets tangled and the blankets stripped free.

The desire had come then, fierce and sudden. He hadn't

felt that kind of hunger for months, yet each time he looked at her, the intensity of his feelings grew.

There had been other women, of course. Some had even lasted through his traveling and long absences. But none had ever shaken him so quickly or completely.

And then she'd made that bloody crack about him not understanding emotion or passion. . . .

He swore softly as he watched traffic snarl toward Great Russell Street. Perhaps she was right. Emotion had never been his strong suit. Nor had trust.

He halted beneath the front portico, where a side corridor gave him a clear view of the doorway to the museum offices. Maggie would have to use that door to leave.

Jared glanced at his watch. The museum closed in an hour. That would give him just enough time to check any new information.

When Maggie came out, he would be waiting.

She felt him even before she saw him. He was standing just beyond the museum's front steps, a tall column of shadow against the gathering twilight.

She didn't slow her steps or turn her head as she passed. "Go away."

He moved out of the gloom, slipping into pace beside her. "You aren't going to ask me about the photograph?"

"Obviously, a fake. That's easy enough to manage in this day and age with digital equipment."

"You're very certain about things, aren't you?"

"Listen, Mr.—"

"Jared."

"MacNeill," she finished coldly. "Let's get one thing clear. You know *nothing* about me, and that's the way it's going to stay."

"Why does talking about your father frighten you?"

Maggie managed to keep her voice steady. "Forget the cheap psychology. It's not going to work any more than your questions. If Nicholas Draycott wants to talk to me about the exhibition, fine. All he has to do is call. But pressure won't make me arrive at a decision any faster, I assure you. Meanwhile, this conversation is closed."

"He says you're good, Maggie. He doesn't want you to lose this chance." Jared gave her an assessing glance. "But maybe you're afraid of succeeding. Maybe you're looking for an excuse to bow out before things get rough."

"Things have been rough before. It took years of gashed fingers and burned skin to learn what I do. Now I worry about real things that I can taste and touch, not about fantasies in an old house with too many shadows. Not about grainy photographs which are probably fakes."

"If that man is your father, why didn't he appear before now?"

"My father is dead."

"Ask yourself this, Maggie. Was he afraid of something? If so, you might be in a great deal of danger yourself." His hand closed over her shoulder as she tried to push past him. "There are a dozen more pictures where that one came from. Are you afraid of seeing them, too?"

"I'm not afraid of solid evidence. You have yet to show me anything close. Now unless you move out of my way, I'm going to call to that nice policeman who's sauntering toward us and tell him you're harassing me."

"There's no law against talking to a beautiful woman on a lovely night."

"Accosting. Stalking. That won't sound good in court." Maggie turned as the policeman drew within earshot. "Excuse me, Officer, but I'm looking for Picadilly Circus. Can you give me directions?"

"Certainly, miss. But you're 'eaded dead wrong. What you want is to be 'eaded north, then make a sharp right just beyond the park. Watch for the Santa and reindeer. They're plenty hard to miss."

As Maggie listened, she covertly checked the spot where Jared MacNeill had stood.

Empty. Apparently, the threat had worked.

And what if what he told her was true? What if her father was in some kind of danger?

Christmas tree lights flashed in the distance, and the smoke of roasting chestnuts drifted through the air. Maggie pulled up her collar against the wind and took a deep breath. If her father was alive, he *would* contact her. She refused to believe that anything could sever the blood ties and affection of a lifetime.

But as she crossed Jermyn Street and headed north, Maggie couldn't shake a sense of uneasiness.

Nor could she shake the lingering impression that someone was watching her.

Chapter 11

TWO CHINESE STONE LIONS STILL GUARDED THE SMALL town house attached to the shop of Anders von Leiden. Maggie paused at the foot of the steep steps. Had it actually been ten years since she had stood here?

She should have come to visit sooner, but there had been too many easy excuses to avoid seeing a man who could evoke so many bittersweet memories of her father. He had been her father's best friend, one of the few professionals who had Daniel Kincade's unqualified respect. When Maggie had finally written, there had been no answer.

If what Jared had told her was true, Anders would have some clue. There was no one her father would have contacted sooner.

She rang the front buzzer framed by a pair of coiling brass serpents. The sound echoed hollowly, but there were no footsteps.

Maybe her father's friend had moved. Or maybe he was gone, too. Ten years might have taken their toll on the craggy-faced Dutchman. Maggie rang again, and once more there was no answer.

She turned, her eyes bleak as she made her way back to the street.

Then the small barred window was thrown open. "We are closed for the night. We will open tomorrow at ten. You will please to come back at that hour."

Maggie recognized the gruff voice. She spun around to smile at the man in the worn satin smoking jacket. "You would turn away the daughter of an old friend, Anders?"

The old man went very still behind the ornate metal bars. "What friend is this?"

"The man who forged the brass lantern by your door. The man who taught you to facet your first ruby."

His voice caught audibly. "Margaret?"

Time seemed to freeze, heavy with tension and memories. She heard the sound of locks being thrown.

"Maggie, is that you?"

He descended awkwardly, arms outstretched. He seemed very pale and far older than she had remembered, but that might have been the effect of the full beard he now sported. "Is this possible? Little Maggie Kincade, all grown up?"

His arms engulfed her. He locked her tight, rich with the smell of pipe smoke and oranges. His quilted silk jacket was smooth and cool beneath her cheek, just as her father's had once been.

Maggie blinked back tears, caught in a wave of bittersweet memories.

"In the flesh." She pulled away to study his face. "Mostly grown up, anyway. Depending on who you ask."

Shadows veiled his hollow cheeks, and he seemed to have trouble speaking. "Very grown up. Taller than I am now. But there is regret in those lovely eyes. Pain, too, I think." He cleared his throat brusquely. "Too much emotion for an old man. So now you turn up on my doorstep without a single word."

"I meant to phone. Somehow the calls never got made."

"As stubborn as your father, I see this. Kincade to the toes, you are."

She gave a crooked smile. "I can always leave if you want me to."

"And let you out of my clutches? Unthinkable. You must come in at once." Cane in hand, he guided her awkwardly up the enclosed staircase and through a door to his private flat. "My Annie would love to see how you have grown. She always said you would stand fine and tall."

"Is she here?"

"Alas, no. Annie is gone from me these six years."

"I'm so sorry, Anders. I didn't know."

"It was better, no? Her heart gave up before my Annie

did, but she was tired.'' He flipped on a light, and an amber glow lit walls filled with books.

He straightened his shoulders. ''Enough of this gloomy talk. Tonight we celebrate, no? You will take some very fine sherry.'' The warmth seemed to surround her, infectious as his mood. For a moment it almost seemed to Maggie that she had come home after months of wandering. ''And now you will tell me everything.'' His eyes narrowed suddenly. ''You do not come with a man? If so, I will certainly toss him from the roof of St. Paul's.''

Maggie laughed tightly. ''Not a man.''

''It is good. You must save your fire for work, Maggie. You have the hands of an angel, you know. Just like your father. Maybe you are even better than the Daniel I knew,'' he said gravely. ''Now you will drink my sherry and we will talk.''

Maggie looked back as he closed the door behind her.

Outside rain drummed at the pavement, and it might only have been her imagination that something moved in the shadows across the street.

The Dutchman's house hadn't changed a bit since Maggie's last visit. Bookcases still lined the walls, and fine medieval tapestries still glowed above the stone fireplace. There was a cozy, lived-in sense about the small room. The tiny lights strung along the stone mantel gave a hint of cheer to a tree made of sculpted malachite.

''So, you come to London for the exhibition at Draycott Abbey.''

''How did you know that?''

The old man slapped his big hands together. ''Me? I know any news about jewels and about you, Ms. Margaret Kincade. I make it my business, no? Lord Draycott is a man well respected.'' He nodded briskly. ''Very proud you make me.''

''Don't be.'' Maggie frowned at her sherry. ''I might have to bow out.''

''Why is this?'' He paced anxiously. ''You are chosen, yet you can tell him no?''

''I have my reasons.''

"None that have sense, I think."

"I need time to think things through, Uncle Anders."

He sank slowly into the faded chair before the fire. "Is good to hear that old name. I remember the last time you come here, all knees and pigtails. You love my Celtic silver, remember?"

Maggie thought of that magic month she had spent with her father in London, poking through hoards of uncut gemstones. They had argued endlessly about proper faceting styles and new polishing materials. The visit had sealed her fate, for she could think of no other life but jewelry design after that. "I remember. I still like Celtic silver, too, though I'm doing my own designs now."

"Show me," the old man commanded.

"They're . . . more modern, Uncle Anders. My own style. You probably won't care for them."

"Leave an old man to make his own decisions, please."

Maggie pulled a small leather case from her handbag and set it on the cherry table before the fire, suddenly uncertain. Her father had died when she was just starting to experiment with free-form work and mixed metal inlays. In a way, showing these things to Anders was almost as difficult as braving her father's hypercritical eye.

"So this is your best?"

Maggie nodded tensely, waiting for his reaction.

He sat forward, studying the complex silver inlays arrayed on black velvet.

With careful fingers, he raised a brooch containing five pieces of polished turquoise. "Chinese turquoise. African, too, I think. And this one is from your Albuquerque, no? The Kingman mine, it is called?"

Maggie nodded. "I wanted to show the variety in the stone colors—how different hues could still work together."

"Most interesting." He pulled a jeweler's loupe from his pocket and studied the stones. "It is your polishing, too?"

"Everything."

"Hmmmm. Chip solder. You have much patience to position your pieces. Not so many work stones this way now."

Maggie held her breath, once again an awkward girl of fifteen on fire with her first taste of traditional craftsmanship. She could almost feel the ghosts of frowning goldsmiths in the room with her.

Finally the Dutchman sat back. "Is good," he said at last. "Nice technique and a most unusual sense of line. It is European but with just enough of your brash American flair."

Before he could say more, metal crashed loudly in the street, followed by the crack of gravel striking the front windows.

"What was *that*?"

He shrugged. "Just the young animals who look for fun. Nothing else they have to do at night." He shook his head. "After a while, I learn not to hear them."

"Have they bothered you, Uncle Anders? If so, you must call the police."

"There is no need, my Maggie. They make noise but nothing more. I can still use my fists well." His eyes hardened behind his thick glasses. "And I have a weapon in a drawer if I should need it."

"But—"

"No buts, please. Tell me instead about this way you layer your metals. It is most intriguing."

Rain tapped at the windows as one topic led to another and the hours passed in laughter and noisy argument. When Maggie looked up, she was shocked to see it was well past midnight. "I shouldn't have stayed so long. You must be exhausted."

"Nonsense. Seeing you is a pleasure not to be denied an old man."

She hid a yawn. "Really, I should go."

"Very well, but I drive you. And first, I show you something." Cane in hand, he moved to his desk and searched through small boxes tied with plain white string. Finally he dug out a small velvet bag and spilled a dozen colored gems onto the table before Maggie.

They glinted fiercely, an icy rainbow of color.

Silently she studied the bright, faceted stones.

"Well?"

It was a test, she realized. Ruby, emerald, and luminous tanzanite. Pretty, valuable, but in no way unique. What did the shrewd old dealer expect her to see?

She drew out her loupe above the ruby. "No inclusions. Very bright. In fact—" She stopped, looked twice to be sure of the pattern she had just noticed. "Is this some new kind of faceting?"

The Dutchman's face was unreadable. "You tell me."

Maggie turned the stone. "Something's wrong here. The crown has been cut through and there are tiny fractures on two sides." She dropped the loupe into her hand, suddenly angry. "An insult to good stones. Who would do this?"

"Someone with plenty more where those come from," the old man said softly. His fingers closed on the velvet bag.

"I don't understand."

"All are this way, fractured and marred. And yet they are worth a nice amount if perfect. Odd, no?"

"Where did you find them?"

"Here and there, from different people at different times, for this world of ours is a small one, my Maggie. If a good stone is cut in Sydney, we hear of it in London. If a fine Siberian diamond is shattered in Hong Kong, we hear of that, too. But this—" He took an angry breath. "This clumsiness is without excuse. One does not cut without skill." He picked up the single emerald, frowning. "But I ask myself if there is a thread."

"What kind of thread?" Maggie sat forward tensely.

"Your father is working on something when he disappears. He calls me in Amsterdam, you see. Very excited, almost like a boy, he tells me I am to prepare for champagne and a night at the Ritz, all to be his gift. And then the next week . . ." His hand shook as it closed over the brilliant stone. "The next week he is gone."

"And you think there could be some connection?"

The old man shrugged. "One wonders, that is all. He tells you nothing about this project?"

Maggie frowned, trying to remember. Her father had always had some new scheme in his head. Work was his greatest pleasure, and he had dedicated himself to it completely. Some might even say obsessively. Because Maggie shared his passion, she had never resented the hours of distracted silence and meticulous tinkering.

"He seemed excited about something. I remember we were to meet in New York the next month and he hinted that I would be surprised. But there was nothing specific. You know how secretive he could be."

Anders laughed dryly. "Always a man with his secrets. And no one else asks you about this?"

"No."

"Ah well, then it is of no matter." He swept the stones back into their bag, then pulled a flat leather case from the same drawer. "This one is for you, my Maggie." Inside glittered a ring set with three exquisite colored diamonds. "It was your mother's. Daniel asked me to reset the stones in platinum. He tells me it is a gift for you. But I could not find you to send it. Now, you are here and grown and it should be yours."

Tears blurred Maggie's vision as she stared at the facets of pink, palest blue, and faint green. For *her*?

The stones warmed between her fingers, almost as if her father's touch still lingered, and she held her breath at the sharp sense of his presence. His gift. So he hadn't forgotten her. And he *had* meant to come back.

A car horn blared, and the moment was shattered.

"Enough of this sad reminiscing." Anders cleared his throat loudly. "Finish your sherry, then I take you to your hotel. But you will be careful with this ring, no? Very valuable. Better you show it to no one."

Maggie slid her father's ring into her handbag, then moved to the window. Streaks of rain glittered against the night like the tracks of shattered diamonds. She shivered, unable to delay her next question any longer. This was the one man who might be able to give her answers.

"What if we're all wrong? What if—" She swallowed hard. "What if my father is alive?"

The Dutchman tapped to her side. "What question is this?"

"The question of someone who's had too little sleep. Maybe someone who's just a little scared." Outside, blurred against the driving rain, a traffic light changed from green to blood-red.

"Someone is telling you this? Someone makes you believe Daniel is still alive?"

Maggie heard the anger and disbelief in his voice. "No, not that. It was just a wild thought that came to me."

He cupped her chin carefully. "You are certain of this, my Maggie? No friend can say such a thing. Do not listen to those who are not friends."

"I know," she said wearily. "Forget I mentioned it."

"Come." He replaced his satin jacket with a warm wool blazer, then searched about for a pair of glasses. "Now I drive and I tell you how first I meet your father. You know this?"

She shook her head.

"It is a rainy night almost forty years ago."

"He told me you met in Morocco."

"He lies as usual. No, it is Paris. Most definitely Paris. The rain comes down in sheets and I see your father by the Seine. He is standing on the bank at midnight, an empty bottle of Veuve Cliquot at his shivering feet." The old man chuckled. "And he is stark naked, you understand."

All through the drive across London, Maggie laughed at the convoluted antics of the two incorrigible men. She was still laughing when Anders stopped across the street from her hotel. "Thank you for everything."

He raised a dismissing hand. "Is nothing."

"Save Friday for me. I expect you to show me all the shops."

"And which shops would those be?"

Maggie grinned. "The ones with back rooms where men like you and my father found all the really good stones."

"Who knows better than I?" He winked broadly. "Now go, go. To sleep with you, my dear. It is too late." He wagged his finger. "No parties, remember. No wild dancing. Most of all, no men or your work suffers. I am like a father now, and this I do not permit."

Maggie was still chuckling as she watched his car disappear down the street. Through Anders, she had glimpsed an entirely new side to her father. She had never imagined him capable of wild escapades and reckless gaiety, until now. Yet there was a bittersweet quality to the discovery. She could only wonder why Daniel Kincade had never revealed that side of himself to his own family.

She turned up the collar of her coat, feeling wind whip at her face. At least the rain had stopped. Otherwise, she'd be soaked before she reached the hotel's front steps.

Maggie heard a soft cough. Out of the shadows a car inched up beside her.

Suddenly the street was too quiet, too empty. Before she could pull back, the door jerked open and she was caught tight. She searched vainly for someone to help her as cold fingers ground down over her mouth.

Then she was dragged back into the shadows.

Chapter 12

TWISTING RIGHT TO LEFT.

Grappling madly, fighting the relentless hold.

Nothing worked.

Maggie shoved blindly against the cold hands. Her foot hit a broken cobblestone, and she was flung sideways, slammed against a wooden barrier at one edge of the silent street.

Cold eyes glittered behind a black wool ski mask. The man's open palm moved along her hips. ''What's in that bag of yours?''

Maggie thought of the ring that Anders had just given her. There was no way she would let her father's last gift be taken from her like this.

''I've got credit cards—money. I'll get them,'' she said breathlessly.

He made a hard, mocking sound. The wooden barrier dug into Maggie's back, and she felt the sweat on his palms.

She wanted to scream. She wanted to dig her fingers into his eyes. Yet she waited, knowing she would have only one chance to catch him off guard.

She sank slightly to one side while he ransacked her handbag. At the same time she eased her hand into her deep pocket.

Loupe. Maglite. Polishing cloth.

Then she felt the cold metal outline of her air canister. A full dose would blind him, at least temporarily. Silently she eased the metal tube into her palm.

He clamped his hand over her mouth, and the sight of her pale face seemed to excite him. "What I want is money." His eyes narrowed. "Or maybe something else . . ."

Panic broke over her as she tried to speak against the suffocating pressure of his hand.

He laughed softly. "Frightened, are you? Good. We're just getting started here, love. It's only the two of us now." He shoved her flat against the wooden barrier, his hand still locked over her mouth.

Then she felt him move behind her.

Down went her heel, grinding into his instep. Wrestling the air canister from her pocket, she aimed it point-blank at his eyes.

The force of the first spray sent him backwards, cursing and digging at his face. Maggie fled in the only direction open to her, toward a mound of broken flagstones that bordered a twisting alley. Beyond lay light, noise, and the traffic of a broader avenue. Her heart pounded in a sick rush as she lurched away from the hoarse curses and falling stones.

He was coming.

Desperately she veered toward a row of cement reinforcements before a wall of dirt. She pitched to her knees, then scrambled to her feet, clawing at paving stones and gravel as she fought her way toward the far side of the alley.

Then he was behind her.

He jerked her against the grimy brick wall, away from any hint of light. His breath was hot and sharp on her face as the knifepoint settled at her neck, then slowly pressed deeper, drawing blood. Through a wave of pain she heard him laugh.

His eyes glinted behind the mask, seized with hot, flickering excitement.

He didn't want her money. He didn't want credit cards or her passport. His hand moved over her wrist, then twisted sharply. Maggie gasped at the sudden wrenching pain.

"Fine little hands, so nice to touch. So easy to break."

His mouth settled at her ear. "What would you do to make me stop? Say what you'd do, love. Maybe I'll stop now, while you're still pretty."

She wouldn't answer. He was toying with her, baiting her.

He dug at her body, and her father's ring spilled onto the ground. "Diamonds?" The man froze, staring at the muted glint against the gloom. "What other surprises are you hiding?"

A newspaper fluttered up the alley, and somewhere behind them a car horn blared twice. Her captor swung about with a curse, giving her time to recover her ring.

The movement was enough to bring Maggie within reach of an acetylene torch balanced on a sawhorse with the remains of a workman's lunch. She grabbed the cold metal, raising it with a shaking hand, and the torch flared to life in a blue roar of heat. "Stay back," she said hoarsely, rage beating down her terror. "This flame burns at about 500 degrees. It will sear the skin off your face in seconds."

He stopped, but only for a moment, circling slowly to her left. "Clever woman. But you can't hope to get past me, now can you?"

In her hands the torch hissed, and the flame flickered sharply.

The cold eyes narrowed behind the mask. "Losing fuel. Too bad for you."

Maggie's hands tightened. He was right. She had at most a few more seconds. With a wild heave, she hurled the canister at his face, then ducked through a narrow hole in the wooden barrier.

She was nearly through when his hands circled her ankle. Maggie cried out as his nails dug into her skin with cruel force.

Over the thunder of her heart she heard the crack of cobblestones. Wind rushed past her face, and suddenly her foot was free. A shout echoed dimly as she scrambled forward into the darkness.

Only then did she see her attacker twist against the wooden wall, moonlight playing over his black mask as a second figure crouched on the rutted earth.

Her attacker struck the wall and swayed.

Maggie watched, dazed, while the figure in black was tossed across the paving stones, then heaved facedown against the dirt, where he lay gasping and twitching.

A step behind her.

A hand at her back.

Then Jared's familiar voice with its low, rolling accents of the north. "So here I find you," he muttered. "Sweet Lord, I thought I'd never track you down."

"You followed me?"

"I was at the hotel waiting for you to cross the street. Then you disappeared."

She felt an overpowering urge to lean on those strong shoulders and hold on tight, but she fought it down.

He touched her hair gently. "Okay?"

When she nodded, he swept up her bag and slid it over her shoulder. "How did you hold him off?"

"With a discarded acetylene torch. I threatened to burn off his face if he touched me again."

"We'd better get him to the police," Jared said grimly. "Then I'll be wanting to ask him a few questions myself." He raised Maggie's face to the dim, filtered light, and his voice tightened. "Did he hurt you?"

"He scared a good ten years off my life. Otherwise, no."

"Fortunate for him or I wouldn't let him forget it." The look on his face made Maggie certain he meant exactly what he said. "Come on."

As Jared turned back to the face of the alley, a car loomed into view, blocking their exit. "Better not risk that way out," he said tightly. "We'll have to go across."

"What about him?" Maggie frowned at the motionless man on the damp earth.

"We'll send an official car around once we're clear. Right now I don't like the feel of things." He pulled her up a slippery slope of mud and broken roof tiles, his face grim as they passed her attacker.

Maggie guessed Jared hated the idea of leaving him behind. She wasn't thrilled about it herself.

A dozen paces brought them to a barrier of discarded

truck tires. "Hurry," he said. "There will be more of them back that way."

"How do you know that?"

"Call it a hunch." They were at the far edge of the alley. The dim border of a streetlight cast jagged shadows over the ground.

Tiles clattered behind them, and they turned to see Maggie's attacker stumbling back toward the alley and the waiting car.

"Jared, he's—"

Her sentence was drowned out by the roar of a motor. The car backed up sharply and a door slammed.

Then they were left alone in the night.

Maggie's hands shook. Her knees were bleeding, and the gash on her throat burned. Suddenly the enormity of her danger struck home. She stood rooted to the cold pavement, staring blindly at the mouth of the alley. She might have cried here, bled here. *Died* here.

If not for Jared.

Something that had been drifting at the edge of her mind swam into sickening focus. Something she had barely heard in her terror. A word her attacker had muttered in the darkness.

Her name.

Dear God, had the man whispered "Maggie" just before he'd pressed his knife against her throat?

Jared's hands slid around her shoulders. "What is it?"

She bit back the words she'd been about to say. There was no reason to make things more complicated. In her confusion and panic, she must have misunderstood that single, muttered word.

She managed a low laugh. "Nothing that a long, hot bath won't cure."

He stared at her in silence, eyes narrowed. Then he pulled her toward the bright lights beyond the alley. "That can be arranged, I believe."

Maggie didn't ask how or when. Suddenly she didn't care where he took her, as long as it was away from this place. Her mind shut down, frozen and insensible.

Yet even then a sense of violation persisted, making her stare into every shadowed doorway.

Maggie opened her eyes to the slap of water and a wall of unrelenting black. Memory returned at the same moment as wakefulness, and she sat forward with a gasp, only to relax at the feel of Jared's shoulder against hers.

His hand settled impersonally on her shoulder. "Relax."

Maggie felt a pitch and roll beneath her feet and realized they were rocking up and down. "I must have dozed off." She peered out at the darkness. "Where in the world are we?"

"Someplace safe."

Light flickered through a wall of trees. "Not the abbey, surely."

"Closer. My place on the Thames."

"An odd place for a home."

A lonely place too, she decided as a steel-and-glass structure loomed out of the trailing mist. Was home a rundown warehouse in sore need of paint?

Only up close did she see that the building had signs of recent renovation. The metal doors were new, and the cement steps from the narrow wooden dock were freshly painted.

"Do you always come and go by boat?"

"Mostly." He laughed shortly. "Nothing better to keep persistent salespeople from the door."

"And everyone else, I imagine."

"I manage to find company when I need it."

The door opened with a well-oiled hiss, and he steered her through a narrow corridor of steel girders. They climbed two flights before he keyed a number into what appeared to be a high-tech security keypad and pushed open a metal door.

Maggie had a sudden impression of red and black against walls of brushed steel. In the sudden glare of overhead lights she saw towering squares of white with slashing brushwork of almost Oriental simplicity. "Are these yours?"

"A friend made them."

With a hushed sound of surprise, Maggie moved closer, reaching out to the rich, textured paper bordered by a frame of exquisite silk tapestry.

"Careful. That one is still drying."

Maggie turned slowly. "They're *yours*, aren't they?"

He shrugged. "Maybe."

Maggie watched him slide a kettle of water onto a gleaming electric cooktop, then flick on a laptop computer perched nearby on a granite countertop. There was competence in every movement, just as there was competence in the hands that had laid paint in such slashing, beautiful lines of color.

The pictures were good, Maggie thought. In fact, they were marvelous. But she still couldn't believe that *he* had painted them.

Her gaze was captured by a long gash of crimson and black. Mountains in mist? A river twisting through low hills? "Where have you exhibited?"

"Nowhere. Nicholas keeps trying to harass me into a show, but I'm not interested."

"You should be. They're—well, *marvelous* comes to mind."

He set two stoneware mugs on the counter as the kettle began to hum. "Not interested. I paint for myself and no one else. If some musty critic started in on me, I'd probably shoot him in the head."

Maggie started to argue but was distracted by a glimpse of the far wall. Hinged cabinets of intricately inlaid cherry framed floor-to-ceiling windows before an unbroken expanse of night sky and restless water. "It's . . . beautiful," she said softly.

"I like looking out at the water. It invariably seems to put things into perspective." He offered her a steaming cup. "I hope you like tea with your brandy."

"Strong, is it?"

"Fair warning."

Maggie took a sip, coughed, and was glad he'd given her advance notice. The hot mixture seared her throat but created a very pleasant afterburn.

"Why don't you get some rest? The guest room is across

the hall.'' Jared was already bent over the humming screen fast filling with animated images. They appeared to be some sort of architectural designs.

She looked closer, only to find his hands closing over her shoulder.

''I can't see? Don't tell me it's top secret.''

He turned her around and aimed her toward the first door beyond the kitchen. ''The guest room's that way. You'll find extra towels in the bathroom and whatever else you need in the closet.''

Maggie realized he hadn't chuckled at her comment. He was serious about the screen contents' being secret. At that moment she realized how little she knew about the man who had just rescued her.

Distant thunder.

Rain pattering on the window.

The sound of horses at the gallop and angry, shouting voices.

Can't stay.

Have to leave. Not too late—please, not too late, too late.

Maggie sat up with a start, a cry on her lips and fear clawing at her chest. Nothing moved around her and the night was silent, save for the slap of water and the distant rumble of a foghorn. As memory returned, she lay back. Her legs were twisted in a blanket, and one hand was trapped in the sleeve of the oversized pajamas she'd found in Jared's closet.

No wonder she felt suffocated. With a shaky laugh, she eased free and padded to the window.

The view was beautiful, a swirl of black and pearl gray. It had to be nearly dawn, judging by the light just beginning to touch the horizon where the river snaked east. Maggie could understand why Jared loved this place. There was an unbroken serenity in being surrounded by such water views.

Idly she checked the bookshelves. Computer books by the dozens. An original play script with notes of Olivier and Leigh performing *Macbeth.* Sun Tzu's *Art of War* in Chinese with an English translation and scribbled comments in the margin.

She stopped at a highlighted phrase.

All warfare is based on deception.

Frowning, Maggie moved to the broad table running along the window, where half a dozen canvases were turned to face the wall. Works in progress.

She itched to look, but the artist in her balked. Looking unasked would be an unforgivable violation. A studio was not just where your hands worked, but where your soul worked. Curious or not, Maggie had no right to peek without an express invitation.

Still, it was strange to think of the man with the hard jaw and the careful eyes as an artist capable of the emotion she'd seen captured on those great, flaring canvases.

She peered along the corridor to the kitchen, where a single light burned above the cooktop. Jared was asleep beside the computer, his head on his arms and cold electric light flickering over his face. His shirt was open and he was barefoot, long legs encased in frayed, well-worn denims. He looked exhausted, Maggie thought. Yet even in sleep there was a power to his body that made it hard for her to look away.

An odd heat filled her face. She tried to pull her gaze from the long lean legs and the open button at his waistband. There was no reason to stare. There was no reason for her pulse to spike and her body to feel heavy with sensual awareness. He was just a man and she had seen men before, hadn't she?

None like this one, a voice whispered.

Abruptly a phone rang softly down the hall.

Maggie hesitated, waiting for Jared to wake. When he gave no sign of hearing, she padded down the hall and picked up the receiver warily. "Hel-lo?"

"Jared?" A woman's voice poured silkily over the line. "I tried your main number and only got your machine. Why didn't you call?"

Maggie stared at the receiver.

"Jared, are you *there*?" Petulance warred with the warmth in the unknown voice. "No, don't answer. Let me apologize first. I was—well, completely off the other night. You have your job and I understood how it would be. But

I'm lonely, so come over, won't you? It's so lovely and warm here in bed.'' Sheets rustled softly. ''And there's nothing but me. I want you in the most appalling way, Jared.''

Maggie swallowed. What should she say?

''Jared, why don't you *answer* me?''

Maggie took a deep breath. ''This is Mr. MacNeill's answering service. I'm afraid he is unavailable right now, but I will see that he gets your message. What name shall I give Mr. MacNeill, please?''

''To hell with my name.'' The woman muttered something else, hot and unrepeatable, then slammed down the phone.

No, it wasn't the sort of message you could leave with a third party.

Maggie wandered back to bed, only to toss restlessly. Her smile faded in a sizzle of jealousy at the thought of Jared wrapped in warm sheets with another woman. Some instinct told her he would be a masterful lover, as careful in pleasure as he was with the other details in his life. He would be a man who took time with a woman, overwhelming her with his intensity and his control.

The thought left her cheeks flaming.

Not with *her*, he wouldn't. She didn't know the man well enough to be jealous, and she wasn't ever going to.

But her hand rose to her mouth, retracing a faint thread of memory.

Then with a hiss of anger, Maggie mounded her pillows over her head and closed her eyes.

Maggie woke up to bright sunlight.

Outside, the river was a road of beaten silver banked by dark trees. She was still absorbing the beauty when she heard the pad of feet and a knock at the door.

''Awake yet?'' Jared was wearing the same soft jeans, but now a dark sweater hugged his chest.

''Possibly. It depends on that lovely smell.''

''Coffee. Eggs. Fresh scones.''

''Don't tell me you *cook*.''

His brow arched. ''Pure self-defense. Chasing people

through dark alleys always leaves me with an appetite. Now up with you or everything will be ruined.''

Maggie fought back a wary smile as she tugged on a robe that was miles too big and padded into the kitchen. Jared set a full plate before her, then sat back to watch.

She paused with a fork halfway to her mouth, oddly disturbed by his scrutiny. It was almost as if he was trying to slip past skin and bone to find the heart of her. "You aren't eating?''

"I've already eaten.'' His eyes narrowed. "Did you sleep well?''

"Umm.''

"Is that a yes or a no?''

"It's an umm.''

He studied her over the rim of his teacup. "Have any memories surfaced?''

The question left a hollow tug at her chest. For a little while she had managed to forget the abbey and its shadows, along with her concern for her father. "None.''

"They'll come.''

"I almost hope they don't.'' Maggie suppressed a shudder. "What about the man in the alley?''

"I've notified the police. Without a license plate or a clear description, I'm afraid there's not much they can do.'' He reached out and brushed a crumb gently from her cheek. "Let me worry about it. There's more when you finish that.''

Maggie felt the feather-light touch of his fingers like a jolt of direct current. For a moment the room seemed to shift, oak beams and shadow instead of a sleek, contemporary kitchen.

She was relieved when he pulled away. She took a bite of the omelette and sighed in pure satisfaction. "I need to leave soon. I have two shops to visit on Brompton Road this morning.''

"Fine. I'll pick you up afterward.''

"You've been very nice, but that's not necessary.''

"Five o'clock. The Ritz. I'm taking you to dinner,'' he said firmly.

Maggie frowned and pushed away her plate. He was

crowding her again, overwhelming her. "I've got other plans."

"Cancel them."

"No." She didn't stop to consider, sweeping to her feet. The man was too sharp, too cool. Any more contact would throw her off balance entirely. "I said I *can't*."

"Then afterwards. The Ritz lobby at seven."

She sighed. "No."

"One way or another, I'm going to see you home safely tonight."

Maggie glared, taking in the firm set of his jaw. "Are all Scotsmen this obstinate?"

"No." A smile lurked in his eyes. "Some are worse."

"I give up. But make it eight instead."

He took her hand as she rose, his eyes watchful. "Be careful today."

"I always am."

His fingers closed, tracing slow circles over her wrist, and she felt electricity dive straight down her spine. She didn't like this shivery feeling that came with every movement of his hands. Even worse was the way his eyes narrowed, as if he could see exactly the effect he was having on her.

And was enjoying it.

"It might be worth it, you know."

"What?"

"Letting go, just once. Putting down that prickly guard of yours while you stop looking for shadows. Maybe you could even try trusting someone for a change. People do that on occasion."

He wasn't cocky now, Maggie saw. He wasn't even calm. There was a fine edge of tension to each word, and banked desire shimmered in his eyes. His fingers moved slowly over her palm, and she felt her hand open unconsciously at his touch. When had a simple meal become such a dangerous thing?

Maggie closed her eyes and pulled free. "Not me. When you let go, you get burned, MacNeill. And I have enough adventure in my life."

"Maybe not," he said. "Maybe neither of us does. It

might be one hell of an adventure to find out.'' He watched her rise, the intensity of his gaze almost painful.

Maggie made her decision as she went off to dress. She owed Jared MacNeill for her rescue, but she wanted no more involvement. Balancing her life was hard enough, and she couldn't afford any personal entanglements.

So she had absolutely no intention of being anywhere near the Ritz lobby tonight, not at seven or eight or any other hour.

Chapter 13

AT TEN MINUTES TO EIGHT JARED PULLED HIS TRIUMPH into an empty spot near the Ritz and strode inside. Maggie was nowhere in sight. He'd suspected she might not show, of course, and had taken precautions.

After a quick conversation with the maitre d', he flipped on his phone and drummed his fingers on a polished table-top.

"Mac, is that you?" his friend Izzy answered promptly.

"Afraid so. Where is she?"

"Staring at the jewelry window outside Harrod's, look-ing like someone with all the time in the world."

Jared said something low and graphic in Gaelic.

He'd been right. She'd had no intention of meeting him tonight. "Any sign that she's being followed, Izzy?"

"None that I've picked up, but I've been mostly in the car. If you want, I'll circle the block and then go in on foot to check."

"Don't bother. Just keep on her. I'll be by as soon as I can cut through traffic."

Less than ten minutes later, Jared moved up silently be-side Maggie. She was peering through a window at a neck-lace of matched black pearls set in braided platinum. "Making your Christmas list early?"

She spun around, one hand to her chest. Her gaze locked on his formal white shirt and black evening jacket. "What are *you* doing here? You're supposed to be—"

"At the Ritz?" he finished calmly. "So I was, until you failed to arrive."

"How did you know I was here?"

"I had you watched."

"You did *what*?" Her face flushed bright pink.

Jared took her arm and pulled her down the street, blandly ignoring the interested looks from a pair of passing men in homburgs.

"Just what do you think you're doing?"

"Taking you to dinner. Unless my information is wrong, you haven't eaten since breakfast. I expect you must be ravenous after visiting four jewelry shops, two museums, and a dozen bookstores."

"You had no right to have me watched . . ." Her voice faded in a sputter.

"There's no need to hiss. You've got to eat, and I'm prepared to take you. How about Hunanese?"

"I wouldn't eat with you for all the tea in China." She wrenched away. "What makes you think you can follow people around, poke into their lives and then swoop down like some hawk to force them to your bidding?"

"It's dinner, Maggie, not a lifestyle change."

Or was it? Jared thought. Did trust come so hard with her that a simple dinner invitation became a major assault?

"I can't imagine what she sees in you."

Jared frowned. "Who?"

"Your woman friend with the purring voice. She phoned last night while you were asleep. It seems that she was verrrry lonely. She wanted your company—in bed."

Jessica had phoned again? Jared tried to hide his irritation. She had been after him for three months, since they'd been introduced at a party given by one of Nicholas's friends. She still refused to accept that Jared wasn't interested.

"She's not my woman friend."

"No?" She shrugged, but Jared saw a glint of irritation in her eyes. "I suppose complete strangers call you in the middle of the night and offer you their bodies."

"One can wish."

Maggie spun away, muttering. "I don't need a watchdog. I just want to be left alone."

"That won't be possible."

"What happened last night was a random crime. It had nothing to do with me or my father."

He waited, saying nothing.

"But you still don't believe that, do you?"

"In my experience, coincidence doesn't exist," he said grimly.

"Was following me Nicholas Draycott's idea or yours?"

"Both."

"In that case, you both can—"

She was about to say more when a garbage can clattered down the narrow drive, barely missing her feet. Seconds later a black shape shot through the darkness, yelping wildly.

Maggie froze. "If that was an overfed English rat, I don't want to know."

"Not many rats that I know yelp. It was a dog, I think." Jared studied the gaunt shape cowering inches away.

The dog stiffened, growling softly as another can rattled over the drive. Behind the clanging metal a trio of young boys swaggered into view.

"'Ere, where'd the brute get off to?" one demanded, scowling at Jared.

"Haven't seen it."

"No? Then what d' ye call that mangy bag of skin pressed against yer feet?" The tallest boy, probably all of sixteen, made a quick, poking stab with a stick pulled from beneath one arm. "'E's my bleedin' dog. Going 'ome with me, so 'e is."

Jared caught the stick and sent it flying. "The dog stays here," he snapped. "He's frightened and he's shivering and I expect he's tired of your bullying."

"'Ere now, yer can't do that. Property's property, ain't it?"

Behind Jared the puppy flattened his ears and eased backward, trembling.

"This 'property' appears to have different ideas." Gently, Jared picked up the trembling animal and his eyes turned very hard. "Now push off before I take a stick to you, the way you've done to this little fellow."

The boys looked at the dog, then looked at Jared's broad shoulders, then set off toward the street.

Silence fell. The dog yipped happily, shoving a wet nose into Jared's face.

He winced. "Probably has fleas and worse."

The thin body lurched enthusiastically.

"What's your name, then?"

A quick bark. More wild wriggling.

"I guess that leaves the name up to me. What a mess you are." Jared chuckled, scratching the small, alert head. "You look like a cross between a fox and a mongoose. I shudder to think what your parents were."

Small, pointed ears flopped forward, and the puppy lunged for Jared's bow tie, covering it with saliva.

"I can see I'm rapidly going to regret this."

Maggie laughed. "I think he's cute. All that hair goes so *well* with your evening jacket. So does the puppy saliva." She smiled smugly. "And since you can hardly take him to dinner, I'll find my own way back to the hotel."

Jared frowned at her over the mass of wriggling fur. "Hold him for a moment, will you? I think he's caught."

"Do you really expect me to fall for that?" Maggie shook her head. "Not on your life. Enjoy your meal and your new friend."

"I'm serious. It's his paw." Jared stared down in disgust. "Somehow he's managed to get twisted in my shirt."

As Maggie reluctantly bent closer, the dog yelped. Ears flattened back, he struggled, clearly in pain. "Poor thing. Come to Maggie, then, and let the mean old man tug you free."

Jared ignored her jibe, gently probing to find the little paw, now solidly thrust between the studs on his evening shirt. With every movement the dog whined pathetically. "They must have hurt him," he said harshly.

"I think he's bleeding. There's something dark on your shirt, and he doesn't seem to want me to touch his neck." Vainly she tried to hold the mass of struggling fur, then thrust the puppy back to Jared. "Just tell me where he's caught."

"Fourth one down, I think."

Maggie stared at the white shirt beneath the struggling fur and counted downward. She had half an idea to leave now, while Jared was so distracted.

But with a resigned sigh she went to work, one hand sliding beneath the restless animal while she searched for the first button. A moment later Maggie found they weren't buttons at all, but impossible little circles caught through the tightest of holes. "What *are* these things, anyway?" she muttered, bent over Jared and trying to avoid the yelping puppy.

"They're studs."

Studs. It figured.

"I'm afraid they're going to be tight."

"You can say that again." Twice her fingers slipped free, and the wriggling paws didn't help a bit.

Maggie bit her lip. The last thing she wanted was to cause the poor creature any more pain. "Hold him tighter, and back over there beside that light post so I can see what I'm doing."

They must be a sight, she thought, following Jared with one hand wedged beneath his shirt.

A middle-aged couple strolled past. Their eyes widened, registering sharp disapproval. "Can we get this done before anyone else wanders by?" she muttered. "What will they think?"

"That they've just interrupted the prelude to a steamy evening," Jared said calmly. "And that I am a *very* lucky man."

"Because I'm tearing off your shirt in lust?"

"Something like that." Jared raised his arm, pulling the crisp white fabric tighter across his lean chest. "Tear away."

The trouble, Maggie decided, was that the shirt was cut too well and she had no room to maneuver. And the real trouble, she decided a moment later, was that he was too warm, too hard, too muscled beneath her fingers.

Heat flared over her face. She frowned, trying to keep her thoughts on the job, on anything but that expanse of male chest. She finally managed to grip one metal circle and rip it free to the puppy's excited barking.

"One down, three to go."

"I only hope he's housebroken," Jared muttered.

Maggie's gaze swung up in shock. "He hasn't—"

"Not yet, but I wouldn't put it past the wretch. Hurry, can't you?"

Another stud tore free, giving Maggie room to shove her whole hand under the shirt. She thought she saw Jared's jaw tense as she brushed his ribs.

Warm skin.

Hard, shifting muscle.

She closed her mind down hard, telling herself she felt nothing, wanted nothing. There was no reason for this swift, hot awareness of his body. "There's some sort of string here. I think it's wrapped around his paw."

"I thought it was something like that."

The dog's wild movements appeared to have shredded one edge of Jared's cummerbund, leaving the creature trapped tighter than ever.

"Did you find it?" There was something odd and distant about his voice.

Maggie tugged hard, following the thread lower until it vanished.

Right beneath his waistband.

"I can't," she snapped.

"Why not?"

"It's gone beneath your—your clothes," she said in a strangled voice.

Increasingly restless, the dog lurched wildly up at Jared's face, only to collapse with a shiver of pain.

"You'll have to, I'm afraid. Much more of this and he'll hurt himself badly. I can't say it's pleasant for me either," he added hoarsely.

Maggie shot a glance at his face, trying to read the expression in his eyes.

He raised his arms higher. "Just have at it, will you? The dog and I will both survive somehow." He muttered a low phrase of Gaelic as her fingers edged down toward his waist. "At least I hope so."

In a blur of embarrassment, Maggie found the waistband and followed the heavy thread lower. "It's caught."

"I *know* that."

"No, it's caught lower. On your . . . on one of those button things." She bit her lip. Trust him not to have a zipper like any *normal* man. "Give me the dog and you finish it."

Jared shifted the restless, frightened animal toward her and was rewarded with a low howl and a burst of kicking limbs. He muttered a graphic curse. "No good. You'll have to do it. Just think of me as another insensate diamond that you're mounting." His mouth twitched. "No pun intended."

Maggie closed her eyes and searched lower, tracing that hard, flat stomach. *Don't think about it*, she thought angrily. Don't remember how he looked with his jeans half open.

She stiffened as she found the damnable thread . . . and something else that was clearly outlined against her fingers. Her gaze snapped to his face.

"What's wrong?"

"You—it—"

His eyes were very dark. "Of course I am. You can't probe at me with those amazing hands of yours and not expect a reaction," he said flatly. "You'd have a dead man twitching."

Amazing hands?

She stared at the ground, her breath coming hot and fast. "Look, I can't do it." She spoke in a rush, wishing she were anywhere else. Why did it matter so much? Why couldn't she just smile and be blasé, as either of her worldly cousins would have done?

Because she'd never been good with blasé. In fact, she'd never been good with much of anything except her cold gems and glittering metals.

"I can't," she said raggedly.

Jared freed one hand, touching her face gently. "Hard going, is it?"

She nodded, eyes lowered. "Look, I'm not—oh, I'm not the one for this, Jared."

His soft laugh feathered over her cheek. "I wondered when you would get around to using my first name. Considering where your hand is, it seems about time."

She had expected mockery and irritation in his face. Instead she found eyes that crinkled with quiet sympathy. She stared back, oddly moved by the laughter lurking in his face.

Surprised most of all that the gentle laughter seemed for himself as much as her.

"Why don't we muddle through this together? Try to forget I'm even here."

Right, Maggie thought. As if she could forget that warm chest and all those warm, rigid muscles.

He cleared his throat. "Anytime would be good."

"It might hurt."

"My dear girl, it already does. Worse than you can imagine," he said dryly, his lips twisting in a crooked smile as he raised the struggling puppy once more. "I'm at your mercy."

A smile tugged at her lips. How could she refuse when he was being so damnably *nice* about all this? The man could be almost pleasant when he tried.

She closed her eyes, wedging her hand lower, beyond the trembling paw and the stiff waistband, trying vainly to ignore the interesting textures of soft cotton and harder outlines beneath. Cheeks hot, she eased her hand deeper into the encasing fabric.

Almost there. One more good tug . . .

Maggie gnawed anxiously at her lip. "Jared, this is it. Pulling might hurt."

No answer.

She was bent on one knee before him, searching madly. Her head rose at his silence. "Are you . . ."

"It would be very good if you could finish the job," he said, his voice low and gravelly.

She heard the tension and the tight edge of control.

Ignoring everything else, she twisted and pulled. To her infinite relief, the threads unraveled and tore free, accompanied by the puppy's wild barking.

"It's all over." Maggie surged to her feet, her cheeks burning.

His eyes were closed tight.

"Jared? Did I—are you . . ."

"Alive. Barely. One day I'll probably thank you for a

most intriguing experience. But not just now.'' Stiffly, he tucked the dog under one arm and took her hand with the other. ''I doubt that I will ever think about shirt studs in the same way ever again,'' he muttered.

Chapter 14

"HE NEEDS TO GO OUT." THEY WERE ON THE FRINGE OF Chelsea. The wind was rising, and dry leaves skittered over the front window.

"Out?" Jared frowned down at the puppy wriggling with distress in Maggie's hands.

"You know—*out*. At least I think so. I've never had a dog."

A pet had never been a possibility while she was growing up. Her mother had been too frail, too nervous, to have an animal underfoot. Later, when Maggie was on her own, there had never seemed time for a pet with all her other responsibilities.

"Out it is." Jared pulled to a halt beside a straggly field bordering a construction project and opened his door. "Off with you, Max, and don't be long."

Maggie hid a smile. "Max?"

"Short for Maximilian. Something tells me he'll grow into the name."

Maggie watched the puppy trot off to explore a mound of dirt, yipping happily. "You're not going to give him away, are you? To one of those terrible . . . farms?"

"Why do you ask?" There was something guarded in his voice.

"Because in a way he's my responsibility." She crossed her arms and looked away. "I can't just let him be shoved into a cage somewhere."

He angled her face back to his. "What kind of monster do you take me for?"

Maggie shrugged, trying to ignore the touch of his hard fingers. "The usual kind. Someone with no time and a dozen pressing responsibilities. In fact, you'd have every reason not to keep him." Her voice was shaky, but she refused to believe that it had anything to do with the way Jared was caressing the corner of her mouth. "And I wish you'd stop that."

"This?" His thumb spanned the curve of her lower lip.

"*That*." Her voice wasn't half as annoyed as she would have liked.

"Illogical creature."

She stiffened. "What's *that* supposed to mean?"

"You refuse to think of poor old Max stuck in a cage. Then you do the very same thing to yourself."

"I do not." Maggie glared at him. "I can relax when I want to. I know how to have fun. As a matter of fact, I have *lots* of fun." Sometimes she did, anyway. "And for your information, I'm perfectly relaxed." She saw his slow grin. "*What?*"

"If you're so relaxed, why are your knuckles white where you're gripping the armrest?"

She frowned. "It's just a thing I do with my hands. Habit."

"And that would also explain why your foot has been tapping out Morse code against the door for the last five minutes."

"My foot?" She stared at the offending body part and flushed when she realized it was true. Why did he get to her this way?

"It doesn't mean a thing." She swallowed. "Isn't that dog done yet?"

Jared slid a strand of hair behind her ear. "Max is doing fine. It's you I'm worried about, Maggie." His hand drifted over her cheek and down her jaw. "Very relaxed. Any more relaxed and you'll dislocate your jaw."

"Don't worry about me. I'm fine." Dimly, she heard her foot tapping again.

"Too late. Somehow I've gotten used to worrying about you. Heaven knows why, since you fight me every second."

"I'm not fighting, I'm discussing. That's what mature adults do." Even as she spoke, Maggie had a strange urge to lean closer and find out if his mouth felt as good as it looked.

"Adults can do other things."

There was a smoky edge to his voice. Maggie wasn't going to ask, truly she wasn't. The words just slipped out. "What other things?"

His lips curved. "This," he whispered, skimming her neck slowly with his knuckles. "Or this."

He bent closer.

Maggie swallowed. He was going to kiss her.

To her horror she wanted to be kissed. She wanted to feel his hands in her hair and the play of his hard mouth. What was wrong with her?

She sat stiffly, her pulse unruly and her skin hot. His lips brushed hers, feather-light, and she felt the curve of his smile.

"Relax." He cupped her chin. "I'm not planning to bite."

Relax? She might just as well try to fly. She could barely breathe, and all thought was unraveling. The problem, she decided, was that the man could kiss.

Really kiss.

She'd expected shock and wariness when his mouth feathered down over hers. Instead there was heat and slow, building sweetness. He didn't rush; he didn't push. He simply savored—and invited her to savor in turn.

It was a devastating combination, and somewhere amid the swirl of need and wonder she forgot to be wary. She opened her mouth to his gentle pressure and sighed as his tongue skimmed over hers, adding another texture of pleasure to the shimmering layers of need.

More, she thought. And she could have sworn that he cursed in the same moment the thought flashed through her mind. Her heart was pounding. She wanted to lean closer, exploring the textures of his mouth.

Suddenly Maggie went still, very still. The need rose, too sharp now. Letting down her guard simply wasn't an option, not with a complicated man like this. Not with the chaos of sensations she was feeling.

Her hands locked on his chest. She tried to forget how he'd felt, all warm skin and restless muscle. "Jared?"

"Mmmmm."

"I think—we'd better talk."

He pulled away. Slowly his fingers rose, curling in the wild tangle of her hair. And then he looked at her, simply looked, breathing hard. "God."

"What?" she whispered.

"You. That." He took a long breath. "*That*."

She fought back a rush of pleasure at the sight of him, just as tense and confounded as she was. At least both of them were suffering. "You mean that simple little kiss?"

"That—whatever you want to call it—was neither simple nor little." He frowned. "Not unless kissing usually separates the top layer of skin from your scalp," he muttered.

Maggie would have laughed if she'd been calmer. Slowly her fingers opened over his smooth black lapels, which now wore a fine sheen of puppy hairs. "So you felt it too?"

"Like a tank blast." He looked angry and baffled. "It ought to be illegal." He shook his head. "You're fine to look at, Maggie. Braw shape. Wonderful legs."

Wonderful legs? When had he seen her legs?

"A grand mouth," he added hoarsely.

Her heart hammered. He thought that? Why hadn't he said so?

"But I wouldn't have touched you if I'd realized it would be so damned dangerous."

"Me?" An odd lump settled in the center of her throat. "Dangerous?"

"Oh, yes. The genius with platinum and white diamonds. The woman with the reckless laugh and the wild hair that I just can't seem to keep my hands out of." A pulse raced at his jaw as he pulled her back toward him. "And I'm going to do it all again."

So he did.

Maggie shivered, caught in a flood of heat as her body shifted to almost painful awareness everywhere their skin met. Suddenly she wanted her hands under all those stiff clothes so she could feel his smooth, powerful muscles again. "Max," she said desperately. "We've got to—"

"Max is in puppy heaven," Jared muttered. "It's *you* that you should be worrying about."

She heard his exasperation and his challenge. 'Is that so? I don't think that—"

"Don't think." This time when he kissed her, she was ready—or she tried to be. Eyes open, she watched his head descend, certain that watching would take away the shivery click of synapses and nerve ends before her mind shot off into a sensual haze.

Watching didn't help. Her eyes blurred, and most of her brain seemed to dissolve when he slid his arm behind her and drew her onto his lap. With a soft oath he brought his mouth to hers, not light but urgent now. Taking, then taking again. Searching for answers, just as hungry as she was.

She gave a low sound of surprise, her hands tightening on his jacket, her body instantly, shockingly awake.

Wanting him. Wanting heat and skin. She knew she would find pleasure in both with this man. Maggie had never fantasized like this before, never imagined in such hot graphic detail. She felt reckless, giddy, almost as if she was coming home to someplace she'd long forgotten.

"Maggie, I want you."

"Yes. Do." Her arms slid around his neck. Her head fell back as he rained kisses blindly along her neck. "Please."

"Please what?"

"Everything. Now," she said, lips to his.

"God." His mouth took hers in sudden urgency. His hands were unsteady when he found the hem of her sweater and covered her waist, climbed, then spanned the warm curves of her breasts while she whispered his name.

He stopped, his breath coming hard. "Maggie, tell me if—"

"Yes." Equally breathless, she shifted, wanting skin and warmth and this amazing, mind-jolting touch. "I do."

He watched her face as he trapped the pale curves and traced the dark, tight crests barely restrained beneath wispy lace.

His eyes narrowed. Lace fell away so that she filled his hands. Then he found her with lip and tongue, driving her need to a madness, making her shudder when his mouth locked hard, exploring her with rough, demanding strokes.

She should have been frightened, but she wasn't. There was too much pleasure. And with it came the sudden sense that this was somehow familiar, that she had known just such a touch long before.

The awareness grew, taking on an intensity that bordered on pain. His breath stirred the hair on her cheek, and she smelled his heady mix of scents, cinnamon and cold wind and man. Maggie knew exactly where they were headed and didn't care. Common sense was gone, replaced by dizzy discovery. They were tangled like teenagers in a car on a public street, she thought wildly. She barely knew him and she still wasn't sure she liked him.

None of that mattered.

How could it when he seemed to know everything about her? He had awakened something dangerous within, something lost. In his hands she'd become a stranger, impetuous and unrecognizable.

She might have heard the sigh of the wind. She might have only imagined the angry ring of horse hooves on dark, frozen earth and voices in a night without stars. Maggie frowned as wisps of dreams teased the edges of her mind. She fought to hold the drifting images, but they slid away like restless mist.

Only then did she realize that Jared's hands were tensed. He was smoothing down her sweater. She heard his low Gaelic muttering as he slid back from her.

He'd stopped. Stopped cold. And why should she be surprised?

Another rout for Maggie, she thought. *Another crash and burn. Well, she would take it like a man.*

She tried to pull away. Instead, he caught her, watched her, one hand rising to her tousled hair. And then he smiled, a slow crooked curve of cheek and lip that melted ten years from his face and demanded an answering smile from her.

"My sainted Gran had a word for a lass like you, Maggie Kincade."

"Oh? And what was that?" Her voice was far too shaky.

"Bonny. A sharp tongue she had, and everyone in the glen feared her wrath. A grand old thing she was. I wish you two could have met, for she'd have chuckled at that hair of yours. It's the same wild color as her own."

"Oh." Even as she spoke, Maggie felt the tension in his thighs and the hard line of his aroused body. He had wanted her, and he wanted her still. Yet he had pulled away.

Maggie stared up at him in confusion, feeling her cheeks go hot. "You stopped."

He nodded.

"I . . . suppose there is a reason. Maybe you didn't care for what you were feeling."

"Does it feel that way?"

She moved and felt the lie of her words. "I suppose sometimes that just happens." She gnawed at her lip. "Hormones. Stress. Like temporary insanity."

He caught her shoulder, scowling. "What happened can't be put down as insanity, temporary or any other sort."

"Nothing personal. It's just—I don't do this." *Never before. Why only with this quiet, brooding stranger?*

"And you think I do?" he asked with sudden anger.

She shrugged. "No more than another man. Blame it on chromosomes." She looked down. "And I *don't* have amazing hands," she said unsteadily, feeling a strange urge to cry.

"That you do, and I'll have no more arguing the point." His voice tightened. "It would be far too pleasant to make up after. We're going somewhere to talk, Maggie. Right now. But we'll do it in a brightly lit room with a table between us, or I can't vouch for my good sense."

"Talk?" She couldn't accept the enormity of what she had felt, was still feeling. "I don't think I want to talk."

"Too bad." Turning, Jared surveyed the darkness. "Max? Where has that wretched dog gone now?" There was no answering yelp. "I suppose I'll have to go find him."

She hesitated. "Jared?"

"Yes?"

"I'm sorry for what I said. I know you'd never drop Max at some horrible dog warehouse."

"If he keeps dribbling saliva over me, I might change my mind." After a swift touch to her cheek, he opened the door and strode over the mounded earth, calling loudly for Max.

A muffled yelp drifted from somewhere behind a low hill, and the puppy shot into view, filthy with dust and dry leaves, ecstatically happy.

"Come here, you brute. Heel."

In answer, the puppy flattened, rolling playfully in the dirt.

Jared rolled his eyes. Maggie thought he might have muttered something about finding a farm after all. She was smiling when the dog bounded to his feet and raced off over the field.

"He thinks it's a game." Grumbling, Jared started after him.

"I'm coming too." Maggie was determined not to miss the sight of six feet, four inches of Scottish manhood brought low by eight pounds of mischievous puppy.

"I don't promise that there won't be blood shed," Jared muttered darkly. "Of course it will probably be my own."

A low rumble drifted over the mounded dirt. Jared turned, studying the far edge of the field. "Come on," he ordered grimly.

"But this is private property. We can't just—"

"We can and will." Jared lunged, catching Max on the top of a muddy mound. He gripped the dog firmly beneath one arm and pulled Maggie behind him.

"What's wrong?"

Jared looked north, where a row of half-finished town houses glinted like metal skeletons in a single broken streetlight. "Just keep up."

The shadows deepened, lapping at Maggie like chill memories. "If I'd known I was getting involved with James Bond, I would have run in the other direction."

"As I recall, you tried."

"Very funny, tough guy, but for *your* information—"

"Be quiet," he said urgently. His hands clamped down

on hers as he studied the swaying shadows. "Someone's out there."

"Right. Like I'm going to fall for that one."

Max yipped restlessly.

"Hush, Max." Jared sank down behind a pile of rubble, with Maggie in tow. "He's just beyond the guard's box. Watch the door about waist high, and you'll see a hint of movement."

"Probably a bird. Or maybe a stray cat. Do we really have to squat here in the dirt while some poor scruffy animal . . ." Her voice trailed away.

Darkness shifted again. Movement disturbed the shadows.

"See him?" Jared's voice came low at her ear.

Maggie swallowed hard. "By the iron fence?"

"He's wearing black, staying slow, but he's there. Keep low."

Out of the corner of her eye Maggie caught another hint of movement.

"He must have followed us out of London," Jared said grimly. "If I hadn't been so bloody distracted with finding out how you taste, I'd have noticed him sooner."

"What do we do now?"

With a metallic clang, a backhoe heaved to life near a pile of wooden shutters, then slowly pivoted. The big rubber tires bit into the dirt and surged forward.

"Jared?"

He was busy scanning the high stone fence to their left. "Yes?"

The backhoe spat loudly, and a plume of smoke drifted toward them. "It looks as if we're about to have company."

Jared slid Max beneath his jacket and buttoned it firmly. "That should hold him. Let's go."

Maggie scrambled after him. "You know, there *could* be a perfectly normal explanation for all this," she muttered. "The driver could be putting in some harmless overtime."

"Even my old deaf aunt wouldn't believe that piece of nonsense."

Gasping, Maggie crossed a mound of bricks and slid into

a ditch ankle-high with water and a cement pipe running across the far side. Something moved near her foot. She didn't want to think about what. ''Remind me to wear paratrooper's boots the next time I go anywhere with you.''

Oily smoke filled her lungs as the backhoe's lights flashed on. For a second Maggie was frozen by the blinding glare. Then Jared tugged her out into the middle of the ditch, while icy water swirled past her knees.

Teeth chattering, she plowed through the heaving murk. ''What are you doing *now*?''

''First we tried hide-and-seek.'' Frowning, Jared scanned the black mouth of the drainpipe. ''Now we're going to play boot camp.''

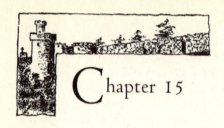

Chapter 15

"YOU MEAN CRAWL?" MAGGIE'S VOICE BROKE. *"IN there?"*

"That's the plan."

"Oh, no, you don't. There's no *way* you're going to get me in there. Not with snakes and rats and heaven knows what else." She cast a desperate glance over her shoulder, praying she'd been right about the innocence of the driver.

But the black shape was still coming.

"It's this or the backhoe," Jared said, pulling her in behind him.

Light flared over them. Glancing back, Maggie saw a figure hunched behind the wheel. The ground began to vibrate, shock waves traveling through the cold cement at her back. There was no more question of a mistake, she admitted, as Jared tugged her forward into the darkness.

The pipe shook once and began to rise. She felt Jared's hard shoulder brace hers.

"We're moving," she said hoarsely.

"He must have wedged the teeth beneath the mouth of the pipe." Jared staggered backward as the cement floor shook, then tilted sharply. "The great bloody fool." He found a metal bar protruding from the wall of the pipe and gripped it tightly. "Grab my waist."

Maggie gasped as she was tossed against him. She heard the puppy yip. "If I die in here, I'm going to murder you, MacNeill. Both Max and I will."

His hands closed on her waist, pulling her closer, and Maggie was infinitely thankful for his strength as the cement rocked sharply, tossing them about like matchsticks.

"Any other great plans?" she said through gritted teeth, as she struggled to stay upright.

"One." Jared twisted, scanning the mouth of the pipe. "We jump."

"We *what*?" Fear jangled Maggie's nerves, but there was no time to protest. She was already hurtling toward the far end of the pipe, Jared's body wedged protectively beneath her. Her shoulder struck the rough cement, rocked her sideways, and then Jared pulled her into a roll just before he struck the ground, protecting her and the puppy.

"Run," he ordered, scrambling to his feet and tugging her over the rutted soil.

Maggie followed, ignoring the stabbing pain in her right arm. Acrid smoke filled her lungs. She was only dimly aware of Jared, charging on toward the empty guardhouse while the ground rumbled behind them, dirt and debris heaving free in the backhoe's wake.

Jared yanked her over a hill of cobblestones. "Almost— there."

"Almost *where*?" she panted.

"Here." Metal groaned as Jared scrambled onto the ragged seat of a rusting forklift. He pulled her in front of him, wedged between his thighs and a row of gears.

Maggie bit back hysterical laughter. They were going into some crazy automotive duel, *mano a mano*? "Jared, I don't think this is such a good idea."

"You have something better in mind?"

"Well, no—"

"Then hold on, because we're moving." He twisted, and the huge forklift lumbered forward. The two machines circled clumsily, and there was no question that their unknown pursuer meant them serious harm as the backhoe turned sharply, its metal jaws snapping.

Pebbles flew past Maggie's head as they veered uphill toward a makeshift metal guardhouse.

"Hold on. We're going to see if anyone's in there."

They lurched over the ground, with the backhoe gaining steadily. All Maggie could hear was the whine of the motor beneath her feet and the panicked race of her own pulse. She wasn't ready to die. She had two emeralds she'd promised to Chessa for a pair of heart-stopping earrings. She had her rent to pay, her library books to return, her yearly dental checkup to finish.

Only now it looked as if someone was determined to see her grounded permanently, and Jared's suspicions about her father were starting to seem less fantastic.

Something smashed against the vehicle's metal arms, breaking her grim reverie. They slammed into the guard-house, banging open the door, and Maggie winced as a flashlight beam struck her face.

A burly figure in a khaki uniform stalked through the open door. "What in bloody hell's going on here?"

Jared managed to turn the forklift and pull to a halt. "We need your help."

"That's quite enough nonsense from you lot. Burglary. Destruction of property." The guard waved a heavy, military-issue flashlight. "You won't be treated kindly for that."

Jared swung to the ground. "You should be following the man in that backhoe."

"Now is that a fact?"

"I'm certain the Metropolitan Police will want a word with him."

The guard shoved his hands on his hips. "And just where would that man be?"

"Behind us."

"An inventive story, so it is, except there's no one at all behind you two."

Maggie turned. To her shock the pitted earth behind them was empty. The backhoe stood dark and unmoving beside the cement pipe.

"But he was *there*," she rasped. "He tried to run us down."

"A fine tale, miss. You can tell the nice constables all about it."

Even as the watchman spoke, two police cars roared into the open yard, sirens wailing.

"Just what I always wanted to do," Maggie muttered. "Spend a night in a cold, crowded London jail cell. You

really know how to show a girl a good time, MacNeill.''
Too bad he wasn't anywhere close to hear her.

Maggie stared at a pair of constables doing what appeared to be exquisitely boring paperwork. Her shoulder ached, and her tongue felt like shoe leather. The cup of tea she'd just been given could have eaten through carbon steel.

But she was lucky to be unharmed. If Jared hadn't been so sharp-witted, they might be decorating the pavement in that new housing tract. Meanwhile, their pursuer had slipped away without a trace. After their protests, the two officers had searched the field, coming up with nothing.

Maggie knew there was no possibility of coincidence now. Someone wanted her badly frightened—or worse. She sank back in the metal chair and tried to think, but her questions only seemed to bring more questions.

She gave a prayer of thanks at the sight of Lord Draycott striding toward the narrow desk and the constable in charge. Behind the viscount, a gaunt man with white hair and military bearing moved quietly across to Jared. Despite her own exhaustion, Maggie noticed Jared's restless pacing and the tension in his shoulders.

Two hours of confinement had left him broody and crackling with barely contained frustration. He was a man who liked control and order. He would hate being caught unprepared almost as much as he hated the knowledge that their pursuer had escaped without a trace. Maggie had a fairly good idea how he was berating himself right now.

But there was more than anger in his tense body. Something was wrong, Maggie realized.

Behind her the door creaked open.

''You're free to go, miss.'' A female officer in a starched uniform held out Maggie's handbag. ''And here's someone who's been missing you.'' With the slightest curve of her lips, the officer slid the yipping puppy into Maggie's arms.

''Poor Max.''

''Poor, nothing. The brute nearly took off my thumb. Still, a bit of milk and a bone should soon put him to rights. And a bath wouldn't hurt.''

Maggie felt a rush of pleasure as the cold, wet nose

pressed against her neck. She looked up to see Nicholas Draycott, worry in his eyes and lines of strain cutting into his forehead. "What a night. How are you holding up?"

"Other than the fact that my stockings are history and I probably look like a zombie, I'm fine. So is Max, here." She gave a crooked smile. "Jared doesn't look so good though. Thanks for coming down to bail us out."

"Actually, Jared had that fairly well in hand. I'm merely here to lend moral support."

"Fools," Jared muttered as he crossed the room. "They still don't believe anyone else was there. Do we need pictures to convince them?" He lifted Max from Maggie's arms and shook his head as the puppy nuzzled his neck. "Down, you filthy creature." Stroking Max's head, Jared strode off to confer once more with the man at the constable's desk.

Maggie watched the white-haired man sit down next to Jared. "He's someone important, isn't he?"

Nicholas said nothing.

"You're not going to tell me?"

"All I can say is that your father's disappearance left unanswered questions, and your encounter tonight seems to have reopened most of them."

"So this is about *me?*"

"You are part of it."

"They still didn't find the driver?"

"I'm afraid he made a clean escape during all the fuss. Very professional."

"What about the security guard? He saw no one?"

"Only you two." Nicholas rubbed his neck, frowning. "Unfortunately, he's a family man with eight years on the job. The police are inclined to believe him."

Maggie fought her anger. "Someone had to be driving that backhoe. When he lifted the pipe he could have killed us. How do they explain that?"

Nicholas watched Jared arguing with one of the constables. "The construction people say that they've been having trouble with that particular backhoe. Lights shorting out, motor stalling—that sort of thing."

"The last I heard, motors didn't start themselves."

"You know that and I know that. Unfortunately, there is little more we can do without concrete evidence."

"Would a videotape of Jared and me being flattened by a backhoe do well enough?"

Nicholas looked grim. "Jared and I will see that doesn't happen."

Maggie shoved her hands deep into her pockets, hating the fear stabbing at her chest. "How can we be sure this has anything to do with my father? Jared was there, too. Maybe this man had some old grudge and I just happened to get in the way. I wouldn't be surprised if Jared MacNeill has a whole address book full of people who'd like to run him over with a backhoe."

Nicholas's frown grew. "What makes you say that?"

"Something in his face. He's always watching other people and scanning the street as if he's waiting for something to happen. Something bad."

"A good description." Nicholas smiled grimly. "He'd be irritated as hell to be caught so accurately."

"You didn't answer my question. Why are you convinced that this has to do with my father?"

"Information to that effect has been received. A government investigation has been initiated." He looked down with distaste at the cup of cold tea in his hands.

"Initiated by whom?"

"I can't answer that."

"Then tell me about Jared. Who is he?" Maggie felt an odd tightening in her throat. "*What* is he?"

The cup tipped. "He's someone who wants to help. We both are." Nicholas nodded his head slightly as the man with white hair strode past, his bearing erect and military.

"I'm starting to wonder if staying in London is a good idea. New York was noisy, but at least demented strangers weren't trying to run me down with backhoes."

"Don't you want to catch this man?"

Maggie gnawed at her lip. "I have no evidence to show that my father is not dead, Lord Draycott. For me that's all that matters. I think it might be best for everyone if I leave."

Nicholas watched the man with white hair hand a card

to the overweight officer at the outer door. "If you left England now, it might be . . . misconstrued."

Maggie stiffened. "Misconstrued how?"

"As you know when your father disappeared, a fortune in gems went missing. Some of those gems were on loan from your government, but some were part of a traveling collection taken from the royal family's own vaults. I think you can understand why there is still a feverish curiosity about where those stones ended up."

"So it all goes back to the missing jewels. Funny how my father always turns up as the villain." Maggie rubbed her throbbing forehead. Her shoulder was on fire, and she was on the edge of complete exhaustion. "There's no point in discussing it. I want to go back to my hotel. That is, if I'm *allowed*. Or am I still being held for attempted theft of a rusting forklift truck?"

"You're free." Jared appeared beside her, his eyes dark and angry. "We both are."

"I suppose I should be glad for small favors," Maggie said. She had to fight the urge to brush Jared's cheek. He looked edgy, his nerves stretched taut.

Jared slid a strand of hair from her shoulder. "Nicholas is right, however. Leaving England now wouldn't be the wisest idea."

"What do you mean?"

Jared glanced at Nicholas.

"Marston is expecting you."

"Fine. We'll leave as soon as she checks out of the hotel." Jared gave a distracted look at Max, who was once again drooling on his bow tie. "Down, Max."

Maggie didn't move. She wasn't a puppy or a chess piece to be pushed around on a board, no matter *how* nicely they might arrange it. "Go back to the abbey?"

Nicholas cleared his throat. "Think it through. Whoever was driving that backhoe is still wandering free. If you're staying at Draycott Abbey, it will be a great deal harder for him to get at you."

Something cold skittered over Maggie's neck. "*No.* Not there."

"It's not open for discussion," Jared said flatly. "I'm

taking you back for your clothes, and then we're leaving.''

He looked tired, Maggie thought. Worse than tired. His face was pale and drawn, and he moved restlessly with every breath, almost as if he was struggling to keep his control.

Maggie started to protest, then gave up. For the moment, she could see no choice but to do exactly what they said. Even if going back to those tall granite walls was nearly as frightening as being pursued by the backhoe.

''Nice hotel.'' Jared studied the plaster dangling from the elevator ceiling. ''Great atmosphere.''

A section of the elevator door was missing, and Maggie watched in sickening fascination as the floors lurched past, inches away. She was nearly dead on her feet, and spurts of color kept blurring her vision.

Jared, on the other hand, seemed to look more composed and controlled with every passing second. In fact, it was downright galling how good he looked with his evening jacket slung over one shoulder and Max snoring comfortably under his arm.

Not that she was going to think about Jared MacNeill in any *personal* sense, Maggie thought quickly. Things were already too complicated. She didn't need any additional entanglements.

The elevator rumbled to a halt at the sixth floor, and Jared heaved open the door. The hallway was dark, lit by a single grimy lamp. He eased Max closer and took a protective grip on her arm. ''Stay behind me.''

''I'll do nothing of the sort,'' Maggie said. ''This isn't a dark alley, and I highly doubt that a team of wild-eyed assassins is going to jump us between here and my room.'' Punchy with exhaustion, she dug in the mud-spattered pocket of her handbag for the room key and stumbled, landing on a shoe that was missing its heel.

''Steady.'' Jared grasped her elbow. ''Better?''

''Just perfect. Actually, I enjoy being pursued and arrested. All in all, it's been a fascinating evening.''

His fingers opened over her wrist. ''I'm serious. How are you holding up?''

Maggie blinked, suddenly struck by the odd sensation that he was . . . reading her somehow. Or at least trying to.

Which made about as much sense as the idea that her father was still alive, or that someone had decided to come after her for the missing jewels.

She pulled away and jammed her key into the lock. "There's nothing wrong that a hot shower and a decent night's sleep won't cure." The door opened with a creak. "In fact, I intend to take care of both just as soon as I—"

She stopped, frozen.

One by one, tiny details began to sink in.

Her closet door wasn't quite closed, and her hairbrush had been moved. The phone directory on her desk was face up, instead of facedown as she'd left it.

Fear rocked her in cold, swift waves. "It can't be."

"What is it, Maggie?"

"The room. Everything's wrong. He must have been here, too."

Chapter 16

JARED MEASURED THE ROOM QUICKLY, EXPERTLY, AS IF assessing a threat. As he did, he stepped in front of Maggie. *To protect me*, she thought. *Using his own body as a shield.* Dear God, what had she gotten into?

"Why do you say everything's wrong?"

"Someone's been here." Maggie swallowed hard. "In my closet. In my clothes."

He pulled her against his shoulder, and Maggie was glad for the reassuring warmth of his body, even for the sleeping presence of Max.

"Are you certain?" He stared at the small room. "Nothing looks out of place to me."

Maggie closed her hands together. "Recognizing patterns is my profession, remember? I happen to have something the experts call spatial memory."

"Which means?"

"When I see an arrangement of objects, I remember them in perfect detail. Trust me, someone's been here."

"Is anything missing?" Jared asked grimly.

"I'll have to check."

He moved silently in front of her. "Let me have a look at the bathroom first."

This time Maggie didn't protest his interference.

He emerged moments later, shaking his head. "No sign of anyone there. What about your clothes?"

A quick check of the warped oak veneer dresser revealed that her stockings were neatly folded, but not in the order she had left them. Anyone else wouldn't have noticed. She ran a hand over her lingerie and frowned. The lacy camisole had been moved, along with a matching slip.

For a moment she couldn't speak, swept with panic. She felt trapped, violated by the hands of a stranger. "He—he's been in here, too."

"I'll help you pack," Jared said grimly. "We're leaving right now."

Maggie didn't bother to argue. Suddenly it didn't matter where she went as long as it was away from this place.

"What about your tools and jewelry materials? You must have some valuable things with you."

She drew a shaky breath. "Not here. I—I didn't like the look of the clerk on duty."

"Who, Don Juan with the greasy tie?"

She managed a shaky laugh. "That's the one. I have a small work case here, but I took all my stones to a local bank and rented a short-term box. I only kept my wire and a few tools."

"Good. We'll collect the rest tomorrow." He pulled a suitcase from the closet and began slipping clothes from their hangers, while she opened a drawer and tossed a stack of lacy underclothes into the open suitcase.

On top of the stack went Maggie's last three pair of stockings. "Chessa will murder me if I ruin all her work."

"Chessa?" He was nearly done with the closet.

"My cousin. You met her in New York. Fashion image expert *extraordinaire*." Her lips curved in a rueful smile. "Whether I like it or not."

"I wouldn't think you'd need any assistance with your image." There was a rough note in his voice. Maggie turned to find him staring at her.

Like a man having hungry thoughts.

She cleared her throat. "A compliment? Don't shake your reputation now. I might faint." She tried to laugh—and failed.

"I never pretended not to be interested, Maggie. I'm not that good of an actor."

Heat curled into her face. In spite of her exhaustion, in spite of the night's pursuit and her recent intruder, she felt a melting sensation somewhere in the pit of her stomach. "Just what are you trying to say?"

He closed the suitcase with a snap. "I'm simply stating the obvious." There was a harsh edge to his voice.

"It wasn't obvious to me."

"So now you know. Does it bother you?"

"I'll tell you after I've slept for twenty-four hours and I have at least a few brain cells firing again."

"Sometimes thinking doesn't help," Jared said. He put something into her hand. "Here, you dropped this."

It was one of Chessa's creations, a long wisp of lace and crepe in a gray-blue shade that matched Maggie's eyes. Jared studied the fragile fabric. "I'd be seriously appreciative if you wore that for me sometime."

Maggie wasn't used to men who were so direct. The men she knew would have hinted and alluded. Not that approach or technique would have made any difference. She simply wasn't in search of a relationship, Maggie told herself.

But when she looked into Jared MacNeill's eyes, something stirred inside her, making her pulse jolt. Maybe what she felt were dreams, newly roused after long, empty years.

They walked outside in silence, Jared gripping her suitcase. A chill wind slashed down the street while the moon came and went behind pale, boiling clouds.

Jared turned up Maggie's collar, then studied the sky. "Do you believe in magic?"

"That depends."

"On what?"

She hunched her shoulders against the cutting wind. "On whether there's a full moon and whether the air is filled with the scent of roses."

"Yes on both accounts. The last roses of summer are in bloom in the abbey conservatory. They're said to be the most beautiful of all."

"In that case, the answer is yes."

She thought he would chuckle or sneer. Instead, his eyes narrowed. Something flared in those twilight depths. "That makes two of us. And since we're being honest . . ." Slowly, his hands opened on her shoulders, protective and something more. "I want you, Maggie. I didn't expect it and I don't know where it will take us, but you need to know.''

She swallowed, fire in her face, fire in her blood. She was suddenly conscious of every move of his body. ''Jared, I—''

''Don't answer. I don't need an answer.'' His hand smoothed her cheek, feathered her hair. ''At least not yet, I don't.''

Jared drove fast and well, while Max lay dead to the world at Maggie's feet.

''Rather a tight fit?'' Her pulse skipped as her thigh brushed his beside the gearshift.

''No one's ever complained about it before,'' Jared said calmly.

No, Maggie figured they wouldn't. Not a woman anyway. It was too intense to ride low with the motor throbbing and the dark miles sliding past. ''No one?'' She couldn't resist the challenge.

''Actually there was one. She complained about the lack of maneuvering space, as I recall. The gearshift cramped her style, she said.''

Maggie had a sharp image of restless hands and heated limbs. Both left the quick flare of jealousy. ''Is that so?'' she said sweetly. ''I'm sure you managed handily in spite of all obstacles.''

He chuckled softly. ''Jealous?''

''Not a chance, MacNeill.''

''I do like that steel in your voice, Maggie.''

''Sure you do. But you didn't answer my question. Did you . . . score? I believe that's the word you men use?''

His hand curved down over hers. ''I don't. And the answer to your question is no. I didn't. We didn't. Sometimes trying to get someplace can be a lot more fun than actually arriving.''

Heat arrowed through her chest. More images swept into her mind, sharp and tormenting. Getting someplace with this man would be more than she could handle, Maggie sensed. He was too smart. Too calm. Too damned self-controlled.

She seemed to be just the opposite.

The challenge slipped from her lips before she knew it. "Wanna see if you've lost your touch?" She listened to her husky voice, hearing it almost as a stranger's. Even that realization didn't make her stop.

He slowed, then pulled into a grassy curve bordered by a high hedgerow. Between them the motor purred. "I'm not clear about the question," he said roughly. "What exactly are you offering?"

Maggie knew. She wanted to see him restless, confused. Hungry . . . *for her.* She decided she was entitled, considering he had already made her feel all those things.

She clicked her tongue. "Bad response, MacNeill. You know what they say—if you have to ask, you can't afford it."

Moonlight touched the hard angle of his jaw. He anchored her chin and then slowly traced the curve of her lower lip.

Maggie realized that she was trembling and her silly challenge had just become something dangerous.

"You're trembling." Jared's voice was husky.

"So?" There was little hope of hiding the fact while his hand anchored her face and his thumb explored her lips. "Does it matter?"

"I'm not sure." His fingers slid into her hair. "Do you tremble like this often?"

"Maybe."

He tilted her head until moonlight poured like liquid over the curve of her cheek. "Lying isn't your style, Maggie," he whispered.

"What makes you think—"

"Because you're bad at it. Because you freeze up when a man like the Don Juan in your hotel gives you a suggestive glance. You're interested, and that frightens you because you're not used to being interested."

Maggie swallowed hard. How did he read her this way? In twenty-five years no one had ever seen through her defenses half so well. They were still practically strangers, for heaven's sake.

"Do you do card tricks along with your mind-reading act, Maestro?"

"You might be surprised." There was an odd tension in his voice as he twined his fingers around a strand of her hair.

She waited for him to pull her closer. To tilt her head back and plant a pulse-wrenching kiss on her mouth. Her heart foundered as she felt the hard flex of his thighs slanting against hers.

He did neither, simply watching her.

"It might be damned interesting to find out just how big this car is. How it handles under . . . close quarters. With the right person, the performance statistics might be awesome."

Maggie stiffened. "But I'm *not* the right person, is that it?" She felt a stab of pain. Until that instant she hadn't realized how everything had blown out of proportion, which only showed what a fool she was. She shoved his hand away with jerky fingers. "Well excuse the hell out of me. So sorry if I don't fit your *statistics* for the perfect partner."

"You're not listening, Maggie." He caught her arm. "There are two of us here, remember? I'm as wrong for you as any man alive. Even if I weren't, there would still be the question of timing, which is definitely bad."

She glared at his shadowed face, trying to decide if this was solid gold diplomacy or something he actually believed.

"Instead of arguing, why don't you try trusting me instead?"

"Stop *doing* that."

"What?"

"Reaching out. Probing my mind. Pulling out things I haven't said."

"You think I'm a mind reader?" he asked gravely.

"I think you're something. I just don't have a name for it yet."

"I hope it will be mentionable in mixed company."

Don't count on it, Maggie thought, turning to stare out at trees lit by restless moonlight. How could she have let herself become so involved after a few hours? Was she completely losing her mind?

"Get some rest."

As if she could sleep with his thigh brushing hers every few seconds.

As if she could ignore her erratic pulse every time a curve brought her body against his. There was no *way* she could relax with his shoulder jammed against her in the narrow seat.

Maggie stifled a yawn. Her eyes closed. While the motor purred in her ears, she sank down into sleep, dimly aware that Jared was saying something in Gaelic. Low tones, rolling and rich. Sounds that might have led men into war or counseled mothers on their loss of a braw son.

For no reason she could name, they sounded familiar. . . .

They rode through the night and far into gray morning. She was past noticing time or location, cramped before her captor in a tight, uncomfortable ball. When the horses finally slowed, hard hands pulled her down onto the ground.

She swayed to her knees, but shoved away those who tried to help her. "Remove this cloth from my eyes. Or are you too much cowards to let a woman see your faces?"

She heard the pace of restless feet and low muttering. Something brushed her cheek and she flinched.

" 'Tis no weapon I hold. Drink, my lady. We've but a brief rest, then we're back to the road."

Pride warred with common sense—and pride lost. She swallowed, choking on the raw spirits that burned down her throat. "Do you think to turn my wits to mush with your vile drinks?"

"No hope of that, though it might be better for us all. You may pace freely now and ease your legs until we remount."

"Where do you take me, to some enemy of my father's? Have they promised you gold for me?"

There was no answer save the sigh of the wind.

"There will be no gold, you fool. My father will trade not a ha'penny for my release," she said with weary bitterness. 'Twas a son her father had prayed for, not a lone

sniveling daughter, and he had made those feelings clear every day since her birth.

What fools these men, to expect gold coins or treasures in trade for her freedom. Her father might even offer a prayer of thanks to be relieved of the daughter he had never wanted.

A stubborn, ill-graced daughter at that, one who would rather study the shaping of gold than the art of needlework, as any normal female ought.

Thinking of her father hardened her resolve. "Have you no tongue?"

"Aye, a tongue I have. And also the wit to know when best to keep that tongue between my teeth. He'll have my skin for a saddle if aught of harm comes to you. 'Tis time to remount," the man added flatly.

He? The question rang through Gwynna's head as she fought the hands that trapped her shoulders. Then she was shoved back onto the weary horse, and there was no hope of escape.

Who commanded these men? Who had laid down the conditions for her capture?

She was glad for the rag that hid her bitter tears as they took to the muddy road once more.

Headed north where steep hills lay veiled in heather.

Maggie sat up slowly. Somewhere a motor sputtered to silence while her heart pumped. "Don't tell me I almost put my fist through the windshield again?"

"Close."

She looked down. Her fingers were buried in the folds of his old tartan. Jared must have placed it over her. Just a worn piece of cloth, but again she had the sensation of another world. Another set of hopes and dreams.

She swallowed. "It was just another . . . dream." She shoved the tartan behind her. Jared hiked Max against his chest. "Do you make a habit of fighting in your sleep?"

"I don't know."

Silence hung. "Did . . . your partners never tell you?"

There had been few enough of them, Maggie thought,

and discussing her dreams hadn't been part of the late-night conversations.

She looked away. Remembering left her too hollow inside. "Not that I recall." She wasn't about to discuss her sexual history with anyone, even with Jared.

Especially with Jared.

"Can we go on now?"

He didn't move.

"Or is this interrogation part of your *official* duties as my keeper?"

"I'm not your keeper, Maggie."

"No? You could have fooled me." A fragment of memory surfaced from her dreams, making her shiver.

Jared studied her face. "If you ever want to talk—"

"I won't."

"—then I'll be here to listen," he finished.

He was cool, detached, and she hated him for it. She didn't want to lay her dreams and sorrows bare for him or anyone else to see. "I'll remember that. *Now* can we go, if you are *quite* finished?"

"I'm finished," he said softly. "For now."

He settled Max back on the floor at Maggie's feet. The motor coughed, then fell into a low purr, and Maggie felt a wave of relief when they began to move.

She closed her eyes, refusing to think about her strange dreams. Fighting a yawn, she snuggled back down in the seat and tried not to remember.

Or to dream.

"Maggie, wake up."

A hand shook her knee.

"Go 'way. Not asleep," she mumbled, jerking awake to darkness. She peered outside, seeing nothing. "Where are we?"

"Almost at the abbey." Jared's voice was grim.

"That's good, isn't it?"

"It would be if there weren't a car parked just in front of the drive."

She made out the unbroken sweep of trees. "I don't see anyone."

"His lights are off."

"Then how did you see him?"

"Just an instinct." And a decade of experience in the world's worst places, Jared thought. He knew that stabbing pull at his neck well, since it had saved his skin more than once. It was far more than vague instinct that had brought him to a halt just before reaching the abbey. Just as certainly, he couldn't tell Maggie that.

Even now he could sense her mind at work sorting possibilities, snapping puzzle pieces into place. It was fascinating to touch that restless intelligence, and Jared knew he had already been drawn in far deeper than he intended.

"You think that's . . . *him*? The man from London?"

Her voice was steady, but he could feel her fear. And he refused to lie to her. "It might be. I'm taking no chances."

She gnawed at her lip. Calculating again. "Is there any other way in?"

"Nothing I could manage without four-wheel drive. Definitely not at night."

"So what happens now?"

"A little check."

"But—"

"Hold Max." The night was cool and silent around them as Jared got out of the car.

"I'm *definitely* going to bring combat boots the next time I go anywhere with you," Maggie grumbled.

"There's no need for boots. Right here is where you stay, Princess."

"I'm no princess."

He touched her chin slowly. "Maybe that's for the prince to decide."

"Newsflash, MacNeill: there *are* no princes. There are only princesses with bad eyesight and frogs who are excellent at concealing the extent of their imperfections."

He held her a moment longer than necessary—and a hell of a lot longer than he should have. "We're going to have to work on that pessimism of yours," he said roughly. "Now sit and don't move. Not for anyone or anything, understand? Not until I get back. And keep Max reasonably quiet.''

"All right, but I still don't understand why—''

The car door gently closed, and the leaves parted.

Maggie realized she was talking to empty space.

Chapter 17

IT WAS ALL TOO FAMILIAR, JARED THOUGHT GRIMLY. Damn it, how had he gotten back into the work that had nearly killed him?

Because a friend needed a favor, and you don't refuse a friend.

Especially not if he's the man who saved your life.

He hugged the ground, silent and wary. His old skills were coming back, along with the biting adrenaline high. He wished he didn't remember the sensation so well.

At least tonight he brought certain new skills to the table, skills that most people would deny even existed.

Jared took a deep breath and listened to the night.

Listened.

Became one of the silent night creatures.

To his left, a wary rabbit slid back into its narrow burrow. To his right, an owl clung to a high branch, implacable and patient with the certainty that comes only with great age and many kills.

Jared felt their presence—just as he stretched his senses to find the man sitting behind the wheel of the car parked beyond the narrow stone bridge. Jared heard him curse, shove open the car door, then glance at his watch.

Moonlight struck the outline of his badge.

Or what was meant to look like a badge.

Jared crept closer, one more shadow in the restless night. When the officer lit a cigarette, light brushed his face briefly.

In silence Jared worked his way behind a hedge, where

he was close enough to scan the license plate.

2A61D.

He memorized the string, then inched toward the far door. Somewhere the owl hooted, sighting his prey. For a split second Jared felt the keen eyes move through the forest and then the great wings opening. Higher, flushed with killing instinct, the great bird soared, then dropped down, talons bared to cleave cold space.

A strike. Claws thrusting deep into fur and quivering muscle.

Jared imagined each detail as he crouched unmoving by the unmarked police car.

He looked down and realized his fingers were buried in the soft earth. His back and shoulders were taut, and his pulse hammered in his ears. With angry determination, he focused on the job before him.

Across the clearing the officer dropped his cigarette and ground it out beneath his boot. Jared realized he would get no more information here. He was melting back into the night by the time the policeman turned back to his lonely post.

Maggie peered into the darkness. Wind touched the bushes and sighed through the high hedges. Somewhere a bird called shrilly. But there was no sign of Jared.

Where in heaven's name *was* he?

It had to have been twenty minutes since he'd left. Maybe even more. She tried not to conjure up images of danger. After all, the night was quiet and this was a peaceful English road, not some powder-keg war zone in a third world dictatorship.

She bent her head to Max's warm face. "It's safe, isn't it, Max? I'm just a big fool to sit here worrying." The puppy gave her a forceful lick and shook his stubby tail.

Right, she thought. That's just what she'd said before the backhoe came careening out of the night and before she noticed her room had been searched. And if nothing was wrong, why didn't Jared come back?

When a hand closed over her leg, she almost screamed.

Branches brushed her face as a figure crawled close and crouched down beside her.

"J-jared, is that you?"

"You were expecting someone else?"

Relief flared at the sound of that rough whisper. "What took you so long?"

"I had to answer some questions. I told you to wait in the car."

"I was restless. Is it . . . *him*?"

"Not unless he's a better actor than I thought."

Maggie's breath slid out in a hiss of relief. "Thank God."

"You're shivering."

"C-cold." A lie, of course. She'd been terrified. Too busy painting bleak 3-D scenarios of what could have happened to him.

"Come here." He eased her against his chest and pulled the fallen tartan around her shoulders. Even then she couldn't relax, and her hands were locked to fists.

"Talk to me, Maggie." He ran his fingers along her cheek. "Where are all those inventive insults when I need them?"

She drew a jerky breath. "I'm fine, okay? J-just fine. And I wasn't worried. Not a bit. Not even when you took forever and I saw an owl fly right over my head and you *didn't* come back." With a choked sound she turned, her gaze locked on his face. "I thought he'd found you. I thought you'd never come back." Slowly her hands rose. "I thought . . ." Her hands slid against his chest, shaking hard.

"I'm here. I came." Jared felt her touch sizzle like live electricity. Through her open hands came the churning storm of her fear in cold, smoky waves.

Strange how often emotions could be reduced to strong colors. And right now those colors were all over him, radiant as living things.

He frowned. Damned if he was going to slip any deeper into her feelings. The intensity of touch always left him drained, exhausted, and tonight for some reason it was far worse.

Because this was Maggie, because she turned him inside out in spite of all his noble resolutions.

He forced his mind back, focusing on the moving world around them. Restless trees. Damp earth. Wind from the east with a hint of coming rain. *Don't slip into her mind, fool. Don't give in to temptation and ride down deep, no matter how much you want to find out how many other men there have been and how they hurt her.*

"Jared, what is it? What's wrong?" She was very still, staring at him, one palm open against his chest. That simple touch was enough to hold him in torment while her thoughts blazed naked through his head.

"Jared?"

The touch was burning him, twisting him inside out. He had to force his jaw to move. "Wrong?"

"You weren't moving, almost not breathing. Are you sick?"

Sick. How he wished it were so simple. Then a simple prescription could return his life to order. No more brushing against strangers in a crowded room and feeling the agonizing slam of their chaotic thoughts. No more sensing what people would say before they said it.

Focus. Remember all the ways you've learned to control this thing you do.

He took a hard breath and let it out slowly.

"I'm not sick." Not in a way she or any doctor would recognize.

"Then what's wrong? If it's not the man from London out there, we're safe, aren't we?"

He looked at the shadows dappling her smooth cheeks. Without even trying, he read the fear that climbed in her chest.

Fear of losing *him.*

With a silent curse he twisted away, forcing the contact closed. He had no right to jaunt through her mind and pick up secrets. Some things were still sacred.

At least they should be.

"Jared?"

"I want to be sure it's not someone else sent to harm you," he said tightly. "A few calls should do exactly that."

He pulled at his back pocket and activated a small cellular phone.

"Are you calling the police?"

"Someone better."

"Lord Draycott, you mean?"

"No."

Static hummed, and then a groggy voice answered. "Do you have the faintest idea what time it is, Jared?"

Jared muffled a chuckle. "All too well. Sorry to rouse you, Izzy, but I need some answers."

Instantly his friend's sleepy tone vanished. "What kind of system? Corporate, private, or institution?"

"Institution. I need an auto plate verified."

"Give me a few seconds to get inside."

"No traces, remember?"

The man on the other end sniffed. "As if I ever leave traces." A keyboard clicked swiftly. "What's the number?"

Jared repeated the string he had memorized.

At the other end of the line Jared's friend made a swift set of entries, then gave a low whistle. "You neglected to mention that this is an official plate."

"How official?" Jared asked quietly.

"Sussex Police Force. You know they have secure systems."

"That should slow you down for all of about three minutes."

With a soft laugh, Izzy clicked out a new string of entries. "Code is only as good as its designers. And it happens that I know most of them. Late at night at a software trade show people talk. There's an irresistible urge to brag about a recent bit of genius in a new code string. And with a little nudging . . ." His breath caught, and a delighted chuckle drifted over the line. "Bingo, we're in. Now let's see what's here. Two vehicles out for repair. Four registered for transfer. Here's the active list. No. No. No. No." More clicking. "Got it. Registered for official use."

"Any internal list to show the current driver?"

Fingers tapped. "Tonight must be your lucky night, Mac. It's registered to a Detective-Sergeant Wakeford."

"First name?"

"Adam."

"Thanks, Izzy. That's all I need for now, along with the main switchboard number."

"I won't even think of asking why. Here it is."

Jared scrawled down the number, smiling faintly. "Get some sleep, Izzy. I'll talk to you in the morning."

"It already *is* the morning," his friend muttered before ringing off.

"What was that all about?" Maggie whispered.

"The vehicle on the road is officially registered to the Sussex Police Force. That much checks out. Now we determine if it's where it should be. And with the right person."

"You think the officer might be some kind of imposter?" Jared could sense her shaping questions and inching away from the dark possibilities that came as answers.

"It's possible. Until I've ruled out the possibility, we're staying right here."

He waited for her to protest, but this time she was silent. She looked off to the north, where the dark towers of the abbey were visible against the greater blackness of the sky. "You're right. I only wish you weren't."

He put his hand on her cheek. "I wish I weren't too."

He pulled away before her emotions registered too clearly, and then he dialed a new number. Static gave way to a precise male voice.

"Sussex Police."

"I would like to report a suspicious automobile parked on my property."

"Name and location?" The question was clearly routine.

"Lord Draycott. The driver and car are parked at the end of my drive here at Draycott Abbey."

There was a momentary hesitation. Papers shuffled. "Are you calling from the property right now, Lord Draycott?"

"I am."

"Would you please identify the license plate of the vehicle in question?"

Jared repeated the string he had given to Izzy.

"I see." The officer cleared his throat. "As it happens

that is one of our cars, Lord Draycott. After your earlier request for a police presence, we sent a man over immediately.''

Jared sat back slowly. ''My . . . earlier request.'' He took a short breath, thinking hard. ''That was most prompt of you. I confess, you've caught me off guard. I'm very sorry to have troubled you.''

''Nothing to worry about, my lord. Anything else I can do for you?''

''I have two guests coming in tonight. In fact they should be arriving any moment. I'd appreciate it if you'd pass their names on to your officer: Jared MacNeill and Margaret Kincade. Do you have that?''

''I'll radio the information through right now. Wouldn't want any false arrests.''

''Absolutely not.'' Once in a night was more than enough, Jared thought irritably. ''By the way, I'd like the name of your man on duty. Just to thank him properly.''

''Detective-Sergeant Adam Wakeford. Let us know if you have any more problems, my lord.''

''Indeed, I shall. Good night to you.''

Jared rang off, staring out into the rushing darkness. There was no possibility that Nicholas Draycott had called for police presence, without notifying Jared first. He would phone Nicholas in London later to be sure, but Jared had no doubt that someone had set up this little scenario as a warning—and a demonstration of exactly how clever and well informed he was. No doubt it was their friend from London, once again proving he could stay a step ahead in the twisted game he had initiated.

Jared closed the cellular phone and shoved it back into his pocket. Suddenly the night's silence had turned threatening.

''He checked out?'' Maggie wiggled closer. ''Is it okay to go inside now?''

There was a leaf dangling from her hair, and her eyes were huge. Jared felt a wave of anger tear through him. He had underestimated their enemy back in London, but he would not make the same mistake again. ''He checked out perfectly.''

"But why is the police car here?"

"It seems Nicholas called him."

Maggie frowned. "And he didn't tell you? That doesn't sound like something he would do."

She was too sharp, Jared thought. "He probably tried to call, but the phone was out of range. It happens quite often, I'm afraid."

She looked down at her locked hands. "I . . . see."

She didn't believe him. Jared could feel the tension emanating from her, half hidden beneath her exhaustion.

He turned away, careful not to touch her again. He didn't want to feel her thoughts. Right now he didn't even want to feel his own.

Detective-Sergeant Adam Wakeford was young and tired. He lurched from his car as Jared eased up the drive toward the bridge. One hand locked anxiously on his belt as Jared rolled down his window.

"Officer Wakeford, I believe?"

"That's correct. And you would be whom?"

"Jared MacNeill. This is Ms. Kincade. Lord Draycott phoned for you to expect us."

Some of the stiffness left the officer's shoulders. He peered briefly inside the car, then nodded. "Go right on up, Mr. MacNeill. It's all quiet out here. No sign of any trouble tonight." He stifled a yawn, clearly irritated at a useless assignment.

Jared wished he felt half so confident. He maneuvered the long, twisting drive, remembering other nights and other visits to the grand old abbey.

Quiet dawns. Lazy afternoons of silence spent trying to recuperate after Thailand.

He looked at Maggie, who was bravely struggling to keep her eyes open. "Right now all you have to do is fall into bed and sleep until you feel like waking. I'll bring up your bags."

"Sounds like heaven to me," she mumbled, hiding a yawn.

They stopped before the weathered granite walls of the

gatehouse. Moonlight dusted the windows and lay like snow across the quiet courtyard.

Maggie looked behind her. ''Fortunately, there don't appear to be any madmen in backhoes jolting up the drive.'' She opened her door and started toward the house, one bag under her arm.

''I'll take that,'' Jared muttered, shifting Max.

''Thank you, Jared. Right now I'm too tired to fight.'' She frowned. ''But I do want the truth. So maybe in the morning you'll tell me the *real* reason that police car was waiting down by the bridge.''

Chapter 18

DAMASK ROSES IN CUT CRYSTAL VASES.

What appeared to be genuine Constable landscapes on the wall by the French doors.

Maggie took a long, slow breath. ''Looks like you're not in Kansas anymore,'' she whispered to an empty room. She was edgy and she could have told herself it was from the emotional backlash of the last two nights, but Maggie knew the source lay in this ancient home, in the aura that clung to every corner and casement. Even a person with no imagination could feel the weight of history in rooms where kings had plotted and wars had been launched. Here long generations of Draycotts must have dabbled in court intrigues from rooms with secret tunnels for swift escapes.

Maggie sank slowly back into the antique poster bed. Draycott Abbey was still powerfully compelling, but so far there had been no more strange lapses of awareness.

So far.

Wind brushed her neck, and she turned to see a sleek form pacing over the floor. The gray cat moved with regal poise, his amber eyes keen and unblinking.

''I hope I'm not taking your room.'' Here in the abbey's unbroken stillness, it seemed perfectly normal to speak to a cat. ''Where did you come from, by the way?'' As if in answer, the French door creaked open, pale curtains floating out in a ripple of cold air from the balcony.

The cat stopped beside the bed and stared up at Maggie, almost as if waiting for an invitation.

"Be my guest."

The bright eyes blinked. Ears back, the creature jumped onto the silk coverlet, circled once, then sank into a ball.

As a rule, Maggie wasn't a cat lover, but there was something different about this one. Like the rest of the great house, he seemed keen. Still. Waiting . . .

All of which was clearly impossible. She had simply gone too long without a decent rest, and her nerves were in a state of meltdown. That was the only sensible explanation for this odd fantasy she was weaving about a simple cat.

Except that looking into those unblinking amber eyes, Maggie had the definite impression this was far *more* than a simple cat.

She turned as Jared appeared at the door, barefoot and minus his jacket. To Maggie's disgust he looked good enough to eat.

"I see you've met the abbey's real lord and master."

"The cat? He certainly does make himself at home. I hope this wasn't his room."

"Every room at the abbey is his, according to Nicholas and Kacey. Good thing I left Max back in my room. I've had enough excitement for one night." He bent to the bed. "Yes, my big friend, you're special and you know it, don't you?"

Gray ears perked forward. A long, liquid meow rippled through the room as Jared worked a hand over the intelligent head.

"I didn't even hear him come in." Maggie studied the French doors, still rocking in the wind. "I suppose one of the latches came loose."

"I'll check for you." Jared just kept petting.

Maggie crossed her arms. "So."

No answer.

"Was there something you needed to see me about?"

"Nothing in particular. Just to see if you needed anything."

"I'll be fine." She studied the gleaming silk walls. "But there's a sort of feeling here. Something I can't put my finger on."

"Welcome to the club." Jared pushed to his feet with silent grace. "The more you see of the abbey, the tighter it will hold you. No one ever understands all its secrets, not even Nicholas."

Maggie's brow rose. "You don't have to do the haunted manor routine with me."

"I'm not." His voice was dead sober.

"Whispers in the corridors? I didn't like it here before, but that had nothing to do with ghosts or strange lights in deserted wings."

His eyes narrowed. "What did it have to do with?"

She locked her arms across her chest. "Too much beauty. Too much mood and history, I suppose." She gave a crooked grin. "I'm an artist. Things like that are supposed to set me off."

"Still no memories?"

Maggie shook her head. Some part of her hoped that lost chunk of memories stayed buried.

"After a while, you might change your mind about this house." Jared moved to the open balcony doors and peered out into the darkness, then closed the doors and latched them securely. "Most people come to love it here." He turned, studying the cat on Maggie's bed. "So are you staying or going, my friend?"

The cat's tail flicked once. He looked from Jared to Maggie, and she could have sworn those keen unblinking eyes were searching for the answer to questions she couldn't even imagine.

As Jared closed the door with the cat close behind him, Maggie heard faint bells echo over the dark hills. For some reason the sound made her uneasy.

It took longer than it should have to quiet her mind and slip free of the house's spell. As she eased down into sleep, Maggie swore to control her restless imagination. There would be no more dreams of flying horses against a wild sky.

Muttering softly, Jared bent forward and tapped a command on his keyboard. In disbelief he watched the screen flicker as this query, like all his others, brought no answer.

All official accounts declared Daniel Kincade dead of an air mishap over Sumatra, and nothing had changed to call that statement into question. There were no secret financial transactions, no pending legal actions, and no covert attempts to tap into the savings account he had left for his now-deceased wife.

All was as it should be, at least on the surface.

But Jared had never settled for surface appearances or easy answers, though on occasion that particular trait had nearly gotten him killed.

Beside him the gray cat purred companionably and rubbed his head against the edge of the flickering screen.

"No luck. The bloody man is either truly dead or he's a genius at burying himself deep. And his daughter can be almost as irritating." *But far more intriguing, especially when her eyes flash and her laughter fills a room like sunlight.*

The cat gave a low purr, his tail flicking from side to side. Jared slid his hand over the sleek fur.

"I know. She also twists me up in knots every time I touch her." He remembered Maggie's face when he'd kissed her in the car and the hot, sweet storm of her desire. His body responded instantly to the memories.

But thinking of Maggie made him remember the father who had almost certainly betrayed her by feigning his death.

"Damn it, *nobody's* that good. If he's alive there's got to be a record of him somewhere and a base for his movements." Experience had taught Jared that no one lived without resources. If Daniel Kincade was alive, he needed financial assets and human help, and both of those could be traced.

He tapped the keys again, using the passwords to a secure government database, the gift of a high ministry official who owed him a favor for rescuing his son from a messy political situation in Thailand. Once again Jared found no trace of Daniel Kincade.

Finally he sprawled back against the couch and nudged the knotted muscles in his neck. Tomorrow he would see what Izzy could do. Just possibly he had missed something in his search. If so, Izzy would spot the mistake instantly.

Jared closed his eyes, one hand on his neck, the other on the cat curled at his side. As always, the abbey left his senses humming. With each creak of the stairs and sigh of the wind against a leaded window, he imagined pacing feet and restless spirits from a distant age.

Warriors and poets.

Statesmen and fools.

They had all walked the abbey's silent halls. Even now their secrets lived on, part of the heart of this magnificent old house.

At his side the computer screen flickered to life. Deep in restless dreams, Jared did not see. Only the great cat saw, amber eyes unblinking on the night.

Over the downs came the faint peal of church bells, low and sad. The sound made the cat ease to his paws and stare intently out into the darkness.

He came as he always did, in a flutter of white lace and black satin while light swirled above the abbey's restless moat.

As the figure gathered shape and form, the scent of roses grew, dense and sweet. Wind swayed the branches climbing over the weathered granite and brushed at the tall French doors.

Adrian Draycott studied his lace-clad arms, then smoothed his waistcoat of black satin. In full, imposing form he paced the balcony.

The clouds shifted. A single beam of moonlight touched the abbey, glinting over the rippling waters of the moat. Somewhere a night creature cried, low and shrill.

The abbey ghost raised his head, waiting. Listening.

Behind him the glass doors opened, and a gray form ghosted onto the balcony.

"So there you are, Gideon. Is aught amiss inside?"

The cat meowed once, eyes alert.

"Asleep, is he? Hardly surprising, given the sort of night they've both endured." He rubbed his jaw, white lace agleam. "His sight has grown since last he walked these halls. I only wonder that he cannot feel it himself."

In one powerful movement, the cat leaped to the ornate grill atop the balcony.

Adrian Draycott, the deceased eighth viscount Draycott, smiled at his companion. "Because he is distracted, you say. When did a beautiful woman ever fail to distract a mortal man?"

The cat's tail flicked.

"History between them? Far too much, I fear." The abbey ghost stared out over the moat into the black woods to the north. "They would both feel that past now, Gideon. If only they allowed it."

A meow drifted from the scrolled balcony edge.

"You propose that I should stir those memories? You know the price of interference, my friend. It is nothing to be undertaken lightly—alive or dead."

Light seemed to flicker deep within the cat's amber eyes.

"I know well that she already remembers. Aye, but see what pain it brings her. And her pain becomes my pain."

The abbey ghost stood rigid, elegant as his priceless portrait standing at the foot of the Long Gallery. He leaned close to the balcony, his face as weathered and cold as the granite walls of the house he had loved so much in mortal life—and even more in death.

Suddenly his hands tightened. "Do you feel it, Gideon? Out there past the Witch's Pool?"

The cat paced along the balcony until he flanked the ghostly viscount. His ears slanted forward.

"Danger," Adrian whispered. "Always it comes. Old debts must ever be repaid, I fear."

The cat meowed softly, shoving against Adrian's fist.

"Let them try, by heaven. Let them seek an entrance. They'll rue the cold midnight that they attempt it, as I live and breathe."

The cat stirred softly on the rail. Beside him Adrian drew a slow breath, then laughed grimly. "As usual, you are entirely correct, my old friend. I neither live nor breathe. But my power of protection remains. Whoever watches in the night will find their dark games more difficult than they imagine."

He toyed with the lace at one cuff.

"Yes, perhaps some interference is in order. Nothing crude, of course. Perhaps . . . a dream or two." A smile touched his arrogant mouth. "As I recall, the dreams worked well enough before, when that fellow Dickens came to visit. In the height of winter it was."

The cat's tail flicked from side to side.

"Of course I remember it was your idea. Yet in three nights he envisioned the greatest story of his career, and he had you to thank for it. I did think the summoning of Christmas Future was a stroke of true genius on my part, however."

Though the abbey ghost chuckled softly at his recollection, the tension did not leave his tall form. He could stir a dream or part a drawn curtain without the slightest strain, but he knew with cold certainty that more would be required of him than dreams or legerdemain.

In dreams it had begun, Adrian thought, and in dreams it would end. For once again the old treachery was upon them. But perhaps in dreams two stubborn people would find the peace an earlier age had denied them. Unmoving, he studied the ripples of the moat, seeking the restless patterns of the future that lay before them all.

Beneath his hand the cat stirred.

Adrian sighed. Like the dreams, hate did not die. Old betrayals ran before them now—just as they had long ago.

Maybe he could send them away. The woman already felt the chill of the past within these walls, and the Scotsman would be easier to touch than she, for the sight burned in his blood. Yes, he could try, Adrian thought.

Wind scoured the courtyard, tossing dry leaves against the gray walls. Anger filled the air, heavy and churning while Adrian Draycott stood caught in his tangled planning.

And all the while the whisper of betrayal rode the cold wind. Already Adrian knew it was too late. They could not leave—not in time.

Lace rippled. Satin gleamed, though the moon locked behind banked clouds. A bell rang once, low and sad.

And then the balcony above the moat was empty.

Chapter 19

WARMTH POURED ACROSS MAGGIE'S FACE. WITH A SIGH she snuggled deeper into the cool sheets.

The smell of roses filled the air.

Roses?

One eye blinked open. A crystal vase with red blooms gleamed on the side table. Maggie heard the soft trill of birdsong beyond the sun-kissed French doors, where water murmured, swept in restless patterns against banks of green.

Draycott Abbey. A place of magic and secrets.

As she sat up slowly, images darted like small, quick fish. For a moment there was cold wind with the smell of peat smoke locked in fine old wool.

Just a dream, she thought irritably, tugging on her long robe. One of Chessa's creations, its shimmering satin was dotted with handpainted designs of whimsical moons and clouds. Chessa's taste was excellent, and Maggie knew that the rich peach hue sent a glow through her skin, setting off her caramel-colored hair. The heavy silk lay warm against her skin, like a lover's kiss.

Like a lover.

The memory of Jared's touch flashed in her mind. His tension after their arrest. His icy calm during the drive from her hotel.

The heat of his hands when he had touched her in the cramped car.

With a low, angry sound, Maggie shoved away the memories. She wasn't looking for a fling, and she certainly wasn't looking for a long-term relationship. Work was all that mattered in her life now.

Not men. Not sex, no matter how original or intoxicating.

Muffling an oath, she slid from the bed and was relieved that a quick shower did wonders for clearing the last fragments of her restless dreams. She slid a brush through her hair and tugged on one of Chessa's soft, clinging sweaters with a matching skirt of pale gray cashmere, then went in search of her tool case.

Last night the intricate scrollwork on the leaded windows had left her imagination racing, and she wanted to try a new design in silver wire against hammered gold. Inside it she would center a single cabochon aquamarine. Or maybe one perfect black pearl.

Maggie went very still as she studied her small metal case with its neat rows of tools and wire. Something was wrong. Just as in her hotel room, something had been moved.

Slowly she ran her fingers over the dozen narrow compartments.

Silver alloy. Pliers. Wire. Cross-lock tweezers.

Her breath caught. The wire was upside down, her tweezers had been shifted, and the silver alloy was in the wrong compartment.

Someone had touched her case. While she'd slept, someone had slipped inside, invading her privacy. She locked her fists, fighting a wave of panic. Who had come into her room? How had he breached all the abbey's defenses?

Then Maggie saw a ragged edge of white shoved beneath her flat-nose pliers. With trembling fingers, she slid the folded envelope free.

And read the single word scrawled in bold black letters. *Her* name.

No figment of her imagination now. No dream or illusion. Inside the envelope she found her camisole, one she realized had been missing from her hotel dresser. The lace was crumpled, as if hard fingers had molded and stretched it with violent strength.

She swayed, catching herself against the tall oak armoire, and then fought back a whimper of shock and anger.

He was *here.*

He was watching her, toying with her, feeding her fear until he chose to reveal himself and his twisted plans.

"Jared," she whispered, arms locked tight. "I need you."

The bedroom was in shadow. Jared lay twisted in the sheets, one arm slanting from the bed. Max was sprawled on his chest, a small dark clump who produced periodic soft snores.

At any other time Maggie would have laughed at the sight of the two of them, but not now. *"Jared."*

His powerful shoulders snapped upward, and Max slid onto the pillow, still snoring.

"Maggie?" Jared sat up, frowning. "What's happened?"

She held out the envelope with shaky fingers, fighting to keep her voice steady. "He was here, Jared. Last night. He came into my room while I slept."

"Who?"

"Read it."

Jared shoved a hand through his hair and twisted the sheet around his waist. Dimly Maggie realized there was probably nothing beneath it except solid muscle.

His fingers locked with hers as he pulled her down beside him on the bed. "Relax and then tell me where you found it." Every word was slow, thoughtful, calm.

So calm that Maggie wanted to scream or curse or shake him. "I found it—" She took a hard breath. "I found it with my tools. This was inside the envelope." She tossed the crumpled camisole down onto the bed and turned away, feeling sick and violated.

Feeling like a victim, which made her angriest of all. "He . . . touched it. You can see how it's pulled out of shape." Her voice shook. "He did those things as a message. It was some kind of sick warning to me."

Jared ran a hand over her arm and she felt the play of his skin, warm with sleep. Then she closed her eyes as his arms enfolded her.

"He was h-here, Jared. Somehow he got inside."

"I don't think so. I think he left that envelope in your hotel room, Maggie. Did you check your case yesterday?"

"I looked inside quickly. I suppose this letter might have been shoved beneath a sheet of metal. I wasn't really thinking. All I wanted to do was leave after I realized he'd been there."

His fingers eased through her hair.

"It *is* a warning, isn't it? He's trying to frighten me."

"Maybe." Jared's jaw clenched as he studied the crumpled camisole. "Or maybe it's a warning to us. Either way, I don't like it." He dropped the lacy fabric. "If you don't feel safe here, I can make other arrangements."

She stared at him. "What kind of other arrangements?"

"Someplace completely anonymous. Team protection if you want it."

"Would that make me any safer? Can you guarantee that?"

He muttered softly and stood up, tucking the sheet firmly at his hips. "No."

He was all muscle and tan skin where the white fabric stopped. Maggie saw his shoulders flex as he stood stiff and angry before her. She realized then that all his cool logic had been an act. Inside he was fighting a silent, white-hot anger.

Somehow that made her feel slightly better.

"I'm frightened." She balled the camisole between her fists. "I still don't believe my father is alive, but I've got to be sure. You and Nicholas were right about that. So I'm staying. If this lunatic can find me here, he'll surely find me somewhere else." With an angry sound she threw the camisole down onto the bed, where it unrolled slowly, dangling along the edge of one pillow and hanging from one torn, violated seam. "He's *not* going to win."

"No, he's not." Jared lifted the envelope by one corner and slid it into a manila folder on his dresser.

"For prints?"

"If we're lucky. Paper isn't the friendliest medium. I'll need to dust your tool case too. But even if something does show up. . . ." He frowned down at the sheet. "I'd better dress."

"Wait. Tell me what you were going to say."

His eyes narrowed. "Even if we're lucky enough to pull a decent print or two, I have a feeling we'll find nothing on our man."

"You mean he's a professional. He has ways to see he's not identified."

"That's my guess."

"Then how can he be *stopped*?"

A muscle flashed at Jared's jaw. "There are ways, Maggie, but it will take time. Are you prepared for that? Can you stay steady when you know he's out there waiting, hoping one of us will make a slip?"

"Whatever it takes, I'll do it. I have no choice. This madman might know something about my father and how he died. Maybe he was involved." She turned sharply, bracing one hand against the window, envisioning ugly scenarios that might have culminated in her father's death.

Across the room, Jared stood motionless, watching her body stiffen. He had a raw urge to pull her into his arms and slip his hands into the warm tangle of her hair. He wanted to feel her sigh as his mouth opened over hers. Then he wanted to drop his sheet, tug her back on the bed and find out what it took to make her arch against him with wild pleasure.

But it didn't require a man of his keen insights to know that the time was impossibly wrong for mindless sex, no matter how intoxicating. She was confused and she was in danger. Right now her mind was three thousand miles away, lost in a restless green jungle dotted by scraps of blackened, twisted metal while she searched for answers that had pained her for months.

She wasn't a quitter and she wasn't a coward. She desperately wanted to close the door on her sad past, but she needed solid reasons.

Jared couldn't give her the reasons she wanted. Daniel Kincade's recent sighting in Asia brought too many questions back into sharp focus. Contact with the rumpled camisole had generated no spark of energy, and Jared suspected their enemy had worn gloves, like a true professional. But if Maggie needed answers, he would find them. He would walk through fire for her and open his mind, no matter the cost to himself.

Because there was always a cost.

Sunlight touched her hair, a dozen shades of gold and chestnut. Jared turned away, afraid he would give in to the temptation to probe the swift, restless flow of her thoughts. With her, only *her*, the temptation was almost beyond resisting.

"No matter what happens, I want to thank you. This isn't your fight." She spoke unsteadily from the window, her back turned. Jared saw her hand slip over one cheek.

He made a tight, angry sound. "Maggie, you don't have to—"

"Yes, I do. I know there will be risks, Jared. I don't know what my father did to make these people so determined, but I owe it to us both to find out. It's not your fight, though. You have every right to walk away now before you're dragged in any deeper."

"That changed last night when that damned backhoe came after us."

She turned slowly, and sunlight poured over her face. "Are you sure?" For the first time Jared noticed the fine lines around her eyes. "I need to know what I'm getting into, Jared. Most of all, I need to know who I can count on if things get worse."

They will. Hard experience had taught Jared that. But he was in, regardless of what threat came next. The fingerprints on her tool case, or the lack of them, would be a clear clue. If their pursuer was a professional, there would be no hint of a print anywhere on the metal. Worse yet, a print might lead them to a dead end, such as an American senator, a French general, or a college professor who had been dead for twenty years.

Laughing at them. Playing with them. Showing them just how good he was.

"You can still leave," she whispered.

"Yes, I can. So could you. I doubt it would be a success for either of us. That's the sort of people we are."

She made a tight gesture with one hand. "I don't want to owe you, Jared. It's not something I do well. My father left me nothing but debts—financial and emotional.'' Hèr hands locked, twisting restlessly. "It was worst for my mother. I think she was secretly afraid that the charges might have been true.''

"You mean she suspected he had stolen those gems from the Smithsonian show?"

Maggie shrugged. "The evidence was so strong. And the stress and uncertainty crippled her. She was already sick with emphysema. Worry simply hurried things along.''

"What about you? How did you deal with the uncertainty?''

"In my mind there was never a question of his guilt. It doesn't make sense that my father could suddenly become a cold-blooded thief. He was smart enough to know he couldn't cheat two governments out of a fortune in gems, especially gems that could never be sold or displayed. The Cullinan IV and the Star of Lahore could never be on public display in a museum. As for selling them—even a weekend rock hound would recognize those stones on sight. There is simply no way they could have been resold without attracting instant attention.''

"Unless they were somehow changed," Jared mused. "Recut, perhaps.''

"Recut?" Maggie stared at him. "You must be mad. Would you repaint the *Mona-Lisa*? Add facial details or body tattoos to Michelangelo's *David*?''

"You might not and I might not, but for some people owning such extraordinary jewels might be worth *any* price. And they might have no intention of showing them again in public. There are plenty of stolen Old Master paintings hanging on the walls of private estates, believe me.''

"And you think my father would be part of that? That he took the gems away somewhere so he could sell them for a private collection?'' Her voice was raw with pain and fury. "If so you're a fool. Jewels were his passion, his very soul. When museums had questions, they came to see my father and he always had the right answers. I suppose some people would call his love an obsession, but his skill demanded total focus and commitment. He would never have destroyed the things he loved.''

And what about his lonely daughter and ailing wife? Jared wondered if Daniel Kincade had loved them half as well as his cold, perfect jewels. How much time did a man with an obsession like that have left for his family?

Maybe there were debts that Maggie didn't know about, causing money pressures that had forced her father to the breaking point. A deeper check on Daniel Kincade's finances over the last years of his life could reveal something. Next on the list would be finding out exactly who had paid the wife's medical bills. Questions led to more questions, Jared had learned. If you were lucky, the right question could unzip all the answers.

Of course, it could also get you killed.

"It was just a supposition, Maggie. I'm not saying your father was involved."

"No? It sounded that way to me." She bit back a flat, angry sound. "Maybe you think I'm all set to try the same thing here. Come to think of it, that's a perfect idea. Why don't I sneak upstairs right now? I'm certain the viscount and his wife must have a hoard of jewels that would be irresistible to a greedy little thief like me." Her voice was ragged, her body stiff. "After all, it must run in the family. Like father like daughter." Her voice broke as she spun toward the door.

Jared caught her midway, his hands gentle but inflexible. "Do you think I believe that, Maggie?"

"I don't have a clue what you believe. Now let me go."

"Not until we have this out in the open."

She jerked at his chest, shoving blindly. "I don't want to talk about it, not any more. Nothing ever changes. Not now, not ever."

"Stop fighting me, damn it." He ducked under her fist, then circled her wrist and trapped her with his body against a bookcase of polished mahogany.

"Let me go, Jared. I won't be interrogated." There was panic in her voice. Jared felt its gray chill bleeding through her rigid body.

He stared at her wide eyes, watching her face go pale. Despite all his careful control, the link seized him completely and Jared felt a relentless sense of disorientation, as if the room was right, but he was *wrong*.

They'd been here before, he thought. They had argued here before, just like this. Colors spun before his eyes, dancing like tiny suns reflected in the abbey's moat.

He spoke then. It was a stranger's voice that framed a stranger's words. "I'm trying to help you, will you but see it."

She made a muffled sound. "All I want is to leave."

"You cannot." The words came low and hoarse, almost without Jared's knowledge. He was overwhelmed, sensing other days, other arguments that had brought equal pain.

Break the link, he thought. *But you can't. Not with each breath driving you deeper, locking you to Maggie and her churning emotions.*

"I know that police car wasn't requested by Lord Draycott last night." Her voice was raw. "You knew it too. I saw it in your face."

Jared took her shoulders and turned her slowly. The woman saw too much, he thought grimly. She always had. It had been her greatest danger.

He frowned. Where had *that* come from?

His hands tightened as he tried to still her angry struggling, and the movement sent the sheet unraveling about his waist. Then it caught between their bodies and slowly pooled onto the floor.

She barely seemed to notice, straining against his grip. But Jared noticed, every nerve from neck to knee springing to angry, painful awareness.

He didn't want to feel the soft silk of her skin at his wrist. He didn't want to know the warm slide of her breath at his naked shoulder. But he did, and the excruciating clarity was compounded by the hunger rising through him, thick and hot. What he couldn't understand, couldn't accept, was that his need felt somehow . . .

Familiar.

He stared at her pale face, straining to understand the chaos of his emotions. And in that second, with a furious slam of color and texture, Jared knew exactly how she would taste, how she would move beneath him in her na-

kedness. Locked against her, he watched the raw images
burn to life with erotic clarity.

Her thighs as they strained against pale damask.

Her neck encircled with a delicate chain of silver and
pearls.

Her face as he made the pleasure rise and break within
her.

Cursing, he released her and stumbled back, unable to
breathe for the force of the searing visions. Even without
physical contact, the memories held, flooding him with new
sensations.

"Jared, talk to me." Her hand brushed his neck. Instantly
the force of contact swept him deeper. He saw a woman in
peach silk with lace at each elbow. He felt the rich splendor
of nights in a biting wind and her hands digging at his
chest, the only warmth or meaning in a world gone mad.

God, how he had loved her. How he had fought for her,
only to watch her ripped from his fingers.

His fault, all of it.

"Jared, what's wrong?"

His hands were clammy as he pulled away. *Wrong?
Everything was wrong. His body was wrong and the room
was wrong. Most of all, loving her was wrong.*

Because loving her had killed her. Someplace in a past
he could neither name nor understand they had touched like
this before. As lovers. There was no doubt left in his mind.

Something lay cold in his throat, and Jared knew it was
fear. For the past that had not left them and the danger still
to come.

Chapter 20

STEADY, MACNEILL.

This has an extraordinarily weird feel, even for someone like you, whose experiences of confinement and torture have created a new definition for the word.

But Jared knew his odd gift didn't extend to seeing fragments of the past. He took a gravelly breath and felt as if he'd chewed tar. "Maggie, something's going on here."

She brushed at her hair with shaky fingers. "What's going on is that you're trying to keep me a prisoner. You're trapping me, giving me orders. Just like *before*."

So she felt it too, Jared thought. He said nothing, letting her final words hang with ugly clarity.

She took a harsh breath. "I didn't mean that."

"I think you did." He felt his jaw, hard like the iron bars of his cage in the jungle hills. The link was tight, electric, snapping all around him. He had never felt more alive, or more out of control, and he wouldn't stop until there were answers. "In fact, I think you meant it as much as you've ever meant anything."

"No." She raised her hand as if blocking a blow. "I couldn't." She gnawed at her lip. "There's no sense to it. Why did I say *before*? There isn't any before." She managed a laugh. "The word just slipped out, that's all. I was angry and it slipped out. It didn't mean a thing." She repeated the words firmly.

Trying to make herself believe it, Jared thought. *And not succeeding.*

He knew exactly what she was feeling. Anger, confusion.

Oily waves of fear. He was feeling all those things himself. "It didn't just slip out and it wasn't an accident, Maggie. You were seeing things. Feeling things. With me."

Her face went starkly pale. "How do you *do* that? Stay out of my mind." She shook her head. "Except that's impossible, isn't it, Jared?"

He didn't move. The tar taste filled his throat and chest until he could barely breathe.

"Isn't it, Jared?" Her hands were two tight fists, and she was shaking. "Tell me."

How could he tell her what he was still struggling to understand? What a whole battery of experts couldn't agree on despite four thick boxes full of detailed psychological reports?

How could he tell her that he was either a borderline madman or a cruel joke of nature, produced by human barbarity?

"What is it you're asking, Maggie? Can I read your thoughts? Can I slip inside your head and eavesdrop whenever I want? The answer is no."

Not whenever he wanted. The link worked best during physical contact—and during times of stress. About that, Jared hadn't lied. But God help him, he wouldn't tell her the full truth either. He doubted she would believe it if he did.

She crossed her arms, searching his face and sorting his words for truth or lies. She had always been too quick, too sharp. And it had killed her.

Jared's body locked.

Killed her.

He saw the words. Heard them.

Sweat touched his brow. Regret, fury, desolate loss— they pounded him now in cruel waves of sight and remembering.

"Jared, what's wrong?"

"You'd—better go." Maybe with her gone, this tormenting link would snap and the bleak images would fade with it.

"But you're . . ." Her gaze ran along his body. She pulled her gaze back to his face, flushing deeply.

"Naked?"

"Upset," she snapped.

"It will go away." He turned, keenly aware of the effect her presence was having on his hardening body.

"Then I'll go. But I see patterns. It's what I'm good at. And if you need something, anything . . ." She let the thought trail away.

"I won't."

As the door closed behind her, Jared saw it for the lie it was. A woman like Maggie Kincade could make a man forget nightmares with a single smile, and her touch could banish a dozen fire-breathing dragons.

Jared knew that with absolute certainty.

He knew because she'd done it for him once, long before.

His hands had stopped shaking by the time he dialed the phone. Five minutes had given him time to toss on worn jeans and calm down somewhat.

The receptionist was brisk and professional. "Dr. Freed's office. May I help you?" Cold and detached. Used to dealing with neurotics, suicides, and kooks, Jared thought. A bloody sort of job to have.

"Jared MacNeill. I need to speak with him."

There was a moment's hesitation. Papers rustled. "I'm afraid he's unavailable, Commander MacNeill."

"Who's on to cover for him? From the official ministry list?" Jared added grimly.

There was clear protocol for a case like his. Miles of it. With the security aspect factored in, he couldn't speak to just anyone. Not with the things he knew.

More paper rustled. "That would be Dr. McNamara."

Jared's hands tightened.

Elizabeth Hanson McNamara. Four years of neurology at Royal Edinburgh Infirmary. Two years at Mass General, followed by more specialty training at Johns Hopkins. A woman who loved being in control and hated her patients quite passionately.

Jared had seen all that in a brief five-minute interview

and a lingering handshake. He could have lived with that—
but not with the rest of what he'd sensed.

That Dr. Elizabeth McNamara was keeping secrets from
both her current lovers, one a high-level attaché to the
prime minister and the other the wife of the Danish am-
bassador. She was also feeling undue personal interest in
her newest patient.

Interest that was patently sexual.

Jared had thought *his* mind was a wreck. Then he'd
stared into the darkness of hers. One appointment had been
more than enough for him.

"Commander MacNeill, would you like her number?
She can call up your case file if you'd like."

"No, that won't be necessary."

"Is there a specific problem? I'm sure Dr. McNamara—"

"No problem. I'll try Dr. Freed next week."

He hung up before there were any more questions. Every
instinct warned against further contact with this woman,
although she was one of the team of three medical experts
assigned to oversee his case after his return from Asia. Next
week he would try the others, and until then he would nav-
igate this particular storm on his own. His sensitivity was
growing, enhanced by every moment of contact with Maggie, and even that he could deal with. What he couldn't
deal with was the possibility of failing her.

He'd failed himself in Thailand and he'd failed his partner, but Jared would remove himself from the game before
he failed Maggie. And it was a game, he sensed. A very
deadly game.

He held his hands rigid before him and watched them
shake. His shoulders bunched, refusing to relax. It was a
play-by-play encounter, with a madman in control. If Maggie or her father had something important, there were
easier, more direct ways to claim it. But their enemy wasn't
taking the direct approach. He was taking his bloody time,
studying Maggie and letting her fear build. Jared sensed
that he needed to know she was afraid of him.

Then and only then would his game move to its deadly
conclusion.

Jared forced his hands to stillness. He did the same

to his turbulent thoughts—or at least he tried.

Maggie Kincade didn't need a confidante with an unraveling hold on reality, he thought grimly. She didn't even need an inventive lover. What she needed was a protector.

For now, he was the only one available.

A half-eaten grapefruit lay next to an untouched scone on Maggie's plate. She stared at both, not really seeing either.

She had no appetite, and she probably looked like the walking dead. Not surprising, given her restless sleep and upsetting encounter with Jared. She had woken twice, startled by the creaking of wood and the cry of the wind while her heart pounded.

Dreams, she told herself. Images caused by high stress and an artist's overactive imagination. Staring out at the moat, blanketed with sunlight, she almost believed it. When she finished her tea, she rose briskly, determined not to wait for Jared. He had made it clear that he wasn't interested in her help with whatever problem was bothering him, and his refusal hurt her.

Forget it, she thought. He probably already has.

Sunlight played over the tiny leaded panes. Rainbows cascaded from the acres of crystal displayed along the great hunt table. The sight reminded Maggie that she was inside one of the most famous houses in England. Chessa or Faith would be unflappable, absolutely at ease and confident. So why couldn't she do the same?

Footsteps echoed behind her. She spun around, one hand to her chest. "Marston, you frightened me."

The abbey butler was immaculate in black worsted waistcoat and jacket. Only the electric blue running shoes left Maggie blinking.

"I am sorry if I disturbed you. I did knock, but you seemed rather . . . absorbed."

"I was thinking about this house. It must take a whole battalion of people to wash the crystal after a party, and I don't even want to think about the windows."

The butler smiled faintly. "Entertaining does pose certain challenges, but nothing that has proved insurmountable. Of course, the days of weekend shooting parties for two hundred are over. Some would say just as well.''

''Two hundred?'' Maggie shook her head. ''Sounds like unfair odds against the poor pheasants, if you ask me.''

Marston refilled her teacup, his expression unreadable. ''I suppose the world was a different place then. In my grandfather's time it was nothing to bag a hundred deer and half as many pheasants. I believe that two of your presidents enjoyed doing just that.''

''Touché.''

''Certainly no offense was meant,'' Marston said calmly.

''And none was taken. It's just that . . . this house is so overwhelming. Every corner hides an Old Master painting or what I'm certain are priceless Chinese porcelains. I keep expecting to pass a Van Gogh or two.''

''That would be the small canvas in the Long Gallery,'' Marston murmured.

''A real, honest-to-goodness Van Gogh?'' Maggie gave a shaky laugh. ''This isn't the kind of place where I feel comfortable.''

Marston's brow climbed slightly. ''I would expect that you fit in superbly in any company or any environment. I would venture to say that it is one of your many skills. If you will forgive the familiarity.''

Maggie saw the faint smile he wasn't trying to hide. ''That's probably the nicest thing anyone's ever said to me, Marston. And if this is your way of being familiar, the thought of your formal treatment terrifies me.''

''Absolutely killing,'' he agreed. ''Or so I'm told.''

''You probably tyrannize the viscount and his wife shamelessly.''

''I?'' Again the brow rose. ''That would be most improper. I hope I am never improper in any of my duties, although an occasional bit of guidance is in order.''

Maggie chuckled. ''So you don't deny it.''

''I wouldn't dream of it.'' Deftly, Marston arranged a handful of freshly cut roses in a silver vase. ''Will Commander MacNeill be taking you to tour the abbey today?''

Abruptly Maggie's smile faded. ''I have no idea. Why did you call him commander?''

"Once a Royal Marine, always a Royal Marine. He was one of the most decorated in his company, I believe."

Maggie digested this bit of information, frowning. "Why did he leave active duty?"

The butler paid intense attention to the placement of his last rose. "I do not believe I have an answer to that, miss."

"Something happened, I know it. Sometimes when he looks at me, I get the strangest sense that he can—"

"In that case, you'd better ask *me* that question." Jared stood on the threshold, clad in well-worn flannels and a perfectly cut charcoal turtleneck. On him, they looked elegant, informal, beautifully tailored in their simplicity.

Heat jackknifed all the way to Maggie's toes. He didn't look like a soldier. In fact, he could have been in movies. He had the unflinching calm that pumped-up male stars strained to achieve and generally failed.

Maggie decided to tell him that one day. She was certain it would annoy him. But first she wanted answers. "You were in the Royal Marines?"

"I was."

"And you left?"

"I did."

"Why?"

"For several reasons."

She tried to read his eyes and failed. "Gee, don't overwhelm me with answers here, MacNeill. Just give one or two for starters."

"I needed to spend more time at home."

"Where's home?" Maggie zeroed in on the opening.

"To the north."

"That's a huge help. North *where?* North of London? North of Manchester? North of—"

"Edinburgh. Near Skye." He said the words slowly, and Maggie realized how little he was in the habit of talking about personal things.

"That's an island off the coast of Scotland, isn't it?"

"It was the last time I checked."

Behind them Marston swept the last cut stems into a bundle of waxed paper, then cleared his throat. "Would you care for luncheon now, Commander?"

"None for me. Ms. Kincade has eaten?"

"Rather too lightly, in my opinion."

"I'll see what I can do about it if you'll part with some of those strawberries you grow out in the conservatory."

Marston tapped his jaw. "Along with clotted cream and perhaps some chocolate shavings?"

Jared grinned. "Be still my beating heart."

Marston murmured something that sounded like "scoundrel" and disappeared.

"I think I can speak for myself," Maggie said stiffly. "And I'm completely full."

He studied her face. Yet again Maggie had the uncomfortable feeling that he was sifting through her secrets. "Bad night?" he said softly.

Maggie wasn't going to discuss her disturbing dreams. "You still owe me answers, remember?"

He filled a fragile cup with Darjeeling tea and studied her over the rim. The lines at his mouth gave Maggie the idea that his night had been almost as bad as hers.

"What kind of answers?"

"If your home is near Skye, why don't you have one of those incomprehensible accents? You know, like Mel Gibson in *Braveheart*."

"Ach, the puir lad had na half the sound of the Isles in his voice. Na fine coaching will bring the Gaelic where it is na born to blood and bone." The words rolled rich and smooth off Jared's tongue. " 'Tis this sound ye were wishing, lass?"

Maggie couldn't suppress a laugh. "Round one to you. How can you make it come and go like that?"

Jared frowned down at the half-filled teacup. "We moved often when I was young. My father was in the Royal Navy and his postings took us one year to the south of France, one year to New Guinea and Australia. I suppose I learned how to blend in as self-preservation."

Maggie gnawed at her lip, considering her next question.

"Don't," Jared said softly.

"Don't what?"

"Do that." His eyes locked on her mouth.

"You mean this?" Maggie rolled her lip against her teeth.

"God." The word was both curse and plea. "Stop," Jared said roughly.

Maggie stared, not comprehending. Then she felt a slow, hot wave of color sweep her face. "You mean . . ." Her eyes flickered along his chest and grazed his thighs. "It makes you—"

"Precisely." His voice was very dry.

"But I'm not trying to—you know." She broke off with an embarrassed cough.

"No, I can see that."

Maggie shrugged. "I have a mirror, and I have a perfectly good memory. If I were the kind of leggy blond that men follow with their eyes, then I might believe you. But no. I'm far too old for fairy tales."

He stared at her, cup in hand, then muttered a soft curse. "Who's been at you, Maggie Kincade? Give me the bastard's name."

"No one," she snapped. "Or maybe everyone. And this conversation is over, since you keep lobbing all the questions back to me." She stood up and tossed down her napkin, wondering why it was suddenly so hard to breathe. Maybe it was his face, half in sun and half in shadows. Or maybe it was the way his eyes tracked her slightest movement. "Stop staring at me. And while you're at it, stop doing that other sneaky thing you do."

"Enjoy the sight of your smile? Savor the way sunlight touches your hair?"

Her flush deepened. "You know exactly what I mean. I'm talking about how you watch me. How you slip down into my head and—well, *see* things." Her hands tightened to fists. "Go ahead and deny it."

"Do you want me to deny it?"

"All I want is the truth."

He pushed slowly to his feet. "The truth could be more complicated than you or I like, Maggie. It might even carry a certain amount of danger. Are you prepared for that?"

He was deadly serious, she realized. "Why?" she said, from suddenly dry lips.

"Because answers always cost. Haven't you learned that by now? You shape beauty in silver and platinum. You ask questions until the outlines come, and then you chase the dreams and pay the price afterward when your shoulders ache and your fingers are cut until they bleed."

How could he know these things? How could he see what she had always hidden so well? "I don't know what you're talking about."

"Don't you?" His hand opened on her cheek. She felt the slow brush of his skin. She closed her eyes as longing rose in her, keen and sweet.

There had been other men. There had been other moments of wanting.

But none like this.

Never with all her nerves in a melting rush and her hands shaking. "You didn't answer my question," she rasped.

"You didn't answer mine."

Maggie managed a shrug. "Sometimes I pay. Sometimes my fingers hurt. It's no more than I expect."

His hand opened, tracing her cheek. "If I looked, I could find the scars. One from a soldering iron. One from a wire cutter that snapped." His eyes narrowed. "And right now your neck hurts." His palm slid beneath her hair, massaging knots of tension that Maggie hadn't even been aware of until that moment.

A sigh escaped her lips. "There ought to be a law against you, MacNeill." His hands moved in silence, and Maggie felt each movement pull her deeper. With a great effort, she managed to hold her body stiff. "Not that a law would change anything. The women of the world would simply ignore it."

"I'm not interested in the women of the world."

One eye cracked open. "You're not?"

"Only in one of them. Someone who argues as easily as she breathes. Someone with hair the color of warm honey."

She swallowed hard and fought for levity. "L-lucky girl."

"I don't think she sees it that way."

"She probably has her reasons." She gave up the fight, leaning into his body and sighing with pleasure as he massaged her stiff shoulder. Without quite knowing how, she found her head settled on his shoulder and her hands at his waist while her body fast turned into gelatin. "This woman—this *hypothetical* woman," she corrected quickly, "maybe she feels out of her league."

His hands framed her spine and worked slowly downward. "There are only two of us here, Maggie. There's no league and no one is playing referee."

"I am. It's something else I'm good at. It's destroyed at least two good relationships."

"Want to tell me about them?" His voice was deceptively calm, but when Maggie looked into his eyes, she saw their sudden intensity. Was it jealousy or simple curiosity?

"No, I don't think so."

His hands were pure, potent magic. Maggie knew it was dangerous to let him slip past her guard this way—but she couldn't quite remember why.

"Talk, Maggie."

She drew a long breath. "There's really nothing to tell."

"Try." His thumb skimmed the base of her spine and feathered upward.

"Aaaaa." Logic skittered out the window. "The first?"

"The first," Jared said grimly.

"He was smart, funny. Gorgeous. All the things that fascinated me."

"How did you meet?"

"At the sea lion exhibit at the Monterey Aquarium. He was seven and I was five."

Jared's lips curved. "Hot date by the kelp bed?"

"You'd better believe it. He told me about his pet rock collection and I showed him my favorite quartz geode. It was love at first sight. Real *coup de foudre* stuff." She tilted her head, giving him better access to her shoulders. "Then his nanny showed up and it was back to the highrise in Pacific Heights. Two ships passing in the night."

"What happened to him?"

"I hear he's got his own computer company in Sausalito and he's worth about a zillion dollars. I guess he traded in his pet rocks for silicon chips."

"Smart fellow. Now tell me about number two."

She stiffened. "Him?"

"Him."

"There's not much to tell. He was a conceptual artist who specialized in making virtual eco-statements."

"I beg your pardon?"

"Juilliard grad. He wrote experimental music to accompany live footage of polar weather patterns and posted them on the Web. It wasn't until months later that I realized his music sounded like John Cage's. *Exactly* like John Cage's, in fact. He stole it note for note."

"Nasty surprise."

"Not half as bad as discovering that he was stealing my platinum wire and hocking it for music equipment."

"Ouch."

Maggie sighed. "It was definitely a dark day at Red Rock."

Jared's fingers broadened their mesmerizing span. "What happened?"

"He packed his amplifiers and left. He assured me I had a huge father fixation and no man would ever work out for me. In his case, he was right. Oh, *there*." She wriggled with pleasure. "I'll kill for more of that."

Jared suppressed a groan. The sort of possibilities flooding his mind had nothing to do with muscular therapy. They were dark, earthy, and largely involved pinning her to the bed and keeping her there for a century or so. Knowing that they were unforgivable did nothing to stop their heat or their inventiveness.

He wanted Maggie Kincade, needed her fiercely. He was also picking up enough of her thoughts to register her spiking pulse and elemental female response. But taking advantage of that knowledge was completely out of the question.

"Who came next?"

She stiffened against his chest. "Next?"

"Number three. After the pet rocks and the virtual eco-statements."

"No one."

She was lying. Even without his senses on overdrive Jared would have recognized the signs.

"No sophisticated jewelry dealer from Paris?"

Maggie shook her head.

"How about an emerald mine owner from Brazil? Someone with deep pockets and perfect moves."

"No."

"Then maybe—"

"No. *No.*" With an angry sound, Maggie pulled away. "There was nobody else who counts, Jared, so forget it." She put her hand on the windowsill and stared stiffly out over the sunny green lawns.

A thousand miles away, Jared thought. He could sense the weight that had settled over her. She was cold. Uncomfortable. Angry.

And perhaps a bit frightened.

"Maggie—"

"No, Jared. Don't ask."

"I won't. On one condition."

She waited.

"Remember what you said before to me. If you ever feel like talking, come and find me."

He saw the stiffness in the set of her shoulders and the tilt of her head. "I won't feel like it." When she turned, her eyes were shadowed with memories and regrets. "But thanks just the same. Now do I get the tour or not?"

"Patience." Jared moved toward her, drawn by the pain still shadowing her eyes.

"I never was very good at patience. And I'm not answering any more questions, I warn you."

"No questions."

"Then what's wrong? What's so important that it can't wait?"

"This," Jared said softly. "Only this."

He bent his head, cradled her cheeks, and kissed her.

Chapter 21

A KISS, MAGGIE THOUGHT.

Two mouths. Four lips. At most a sigh and the brush of restless tongues. Nothing mind-shattering or earth-shaking there.

Except the heat of it started in her toes and shimmered up through her legs, while Jared held her carefully, as if they were both poised on the razor edge of some monumental discovery.

Maggie swallowed. She wasn't ready for that sort of discovery. "Jared—"

He stilled her with the pad of one thumb, then followed with the warm friction of his mouth. Maggie closed her eyes, forgetting her uncertainty. Forgetting her name. As his tongue feathered her lips, she made a lost sound and eased against him, trembling.

"Maggie?"

"*Umm.*"

"I think we might be starting something here." His voice was thick. "Is that what you want?"

She heard dimly, as if from a great distance. Why was he talking when there was so much pure sensation to explore instead? So much sweet, elemental lust.

She smiled at that. Maggie Kincade wallowing in hedonism. Reveling in lust with a man she barely knew.

He gave a soft laugh as he slid his fingers into her hair. "Why are you smiling?"

"Me. This." Her arms inched around his neck. "Incredible."

"Mr. Eco-statement didn't make you feel incredible?"

She slid her mouth against him in a slow, sensual *no*. His hands opened over her back, easing beneath lace and linen to find the heated skin beneath.

"I'll take that for a negative," he muttered.

"Right again." She felt his short, jerky breath against her mouth. "Jared?"

"Skin," he said hoarsely. "I need skin." He found the ridge of her spine and worked upward, bone by bone. "You're shaking, Maggie."

She was doing a lot more than shake, Maggie thought. She was dissolving slowly. She clutched at the front of his sweater and tugged upward, sighing as she found his chest. At the first wary touch of her hands, he cursed.

Imagine Maggie Kincade making a man curse.

She eased onto her toes and nuzzled the ridge of his jaw, working slowly to his earlobe. She had a haunting image of shoving off those form-fitting clothes and nuzzling every inch of him.

Jared's hands locked. He said something low and hard.

"Gaelic?"

He nodded.

"What did it mean?"

"You don't want to know." He tilted her head and stared into her eyes. "A moment ago I said we'd started something. I was wrong, Maggie. We've already gone beyond starting. Like it or not."

"I did. Like it, I mean." She swallowed. "I'm not used to being so—overwhelmed."

She'd expected speed and a swift, sudden move for the bedroom. Instead he raised her hand and surprised her again, kissing her open palm with distracting thoroughness.

"You make it too easy to do the wrong thing." A pulse beat at his temple as he traced her inner wrist. "It doesn't take a palm reader to know this can't work, not for long enough to matter. You're worth more than a day or a week, Maggie."

Her hand closed slowly. "What are you trying to say, Jared?"

"That two things could happen right now. One, you slap my face and kick me out of here."

"Hardly polite of me."

"Two, you walk away and pretend this never happened."

Maggie ran her hand slowly over his forehead. "I was never good at pretending."

"Maggie, there are reasons." His eyes darkened. "I don't—"

Behind them the door creaked. Marston cleared his throat, looking uncomfortable. "I am very sorry to intrude, but there is an overseas telephone call for you, Commander. Two faxes have also arrived from the viscount in London. I suppose the strawberries will have to wait."

"A lot of things will have to wait, I'm afraid."

Jared took his time letting go of Maggie's hand. His gaze remained locked on her face.

Maggie spoke, her voice stiff. "You see it's bad timing, Marston."

Jared tensed. "Maggie, let me explain."

"There's no need. You're right as usual, Commander. Don't let me keep you."

"Damn it, Maggie—"

She walked past him to the door, never looking back.

Damn the man.

Maggie sat on the sunny slope above the moat, pulling silver wire into exquisite serpentine links to complete a choker for her antique cameo. With every move, sunlight swept the metal curves, scattering light over her hands and face, but she barely noticed.

Damn me for wanting him.

Her fingers slipped, and the wire gouged a deep welt across her palm. She stared at blood welling like garnets across her skin. It wasn't like her to be awkward or clumsy with her tools.

She closed her eyes, trying to push Jared out of her mind. Instead came a flood of memories. The first hot slide of his mouth. The first slow brush of his fingers.

Today would definitely be a bad day for soldering. The

way her hands were shaking, she would probably set her clothes on fire.

He had his reasons for saying what he did.

The problem was that the reasons didn't make her feel any better.

Calm down.

She tried hard, watching the moat bubble past weathered stones of granite that had probably been quarried ten centuries ago. Even the hedges at the abbey were three hundred years old, so Marston had told her.

Something pushed at her foot, and Maggie smiled to see Max rolling ecstatically in the grass, stubby tail twitching. "So, big guy, what do you suggest? Do you want to help me knock him down and rough him up?"

Barking, Max nudged her hand with his soft, wet nose.

"You just don't have the killer instinct, do you?"

Neither did she, Maggie admitted. Jared had been right. They'd been on a reckless course, and it shamed Maggie to think that he had pulled away, not her. She winced at the sobering awareness of how out of control she had been.

Point taken. Next time she'd be a mature, reasoning adult and keep her emotions firmly under control.

Max barked, then suddenly stiffened, his eyes fixed on the stone bridge over the moat. A low growl spilled from his throat.

"What is it, Max?"

The dog stood frozen, his teeth bared. A bird soared over the roof. Somewhere in the distance a train whistled sadly over the wealden hills.

And then as swiftly as he had tensed, Max was once more himself, racing in circles over the lawn to chase his tail through a bar of sunlight.

"Crazy dog. Must be something about this old house." Maggie shivered as something stirred at the back of her mind. On her first night here she had felt an overpowering attraction to this very spot, where the moat whispered beneath the old bridge. Her fingers clenched on the grass as a blind, unreasoning fear settled over her. "Stop it," she said sharply.

Max stopped running and eyed her warily.

"Not you. Go on and play."

Maggie stared blindly at her unfinished choker, forgotten on the ground, and wondered if the Draycotts listened for ghostly steps in the moonlight or laughter from shadowed hallways.

Her shoulders ached and her neck throbbed. She reached up to massage the knotted muscles, but it only made her remember the heat in Jared's thorough, patient hands.

His slow inventive kiss.

"Enough." Angrily, she tossed down her tools and strode to the edge of the moat, where a pair of swans cut a silver path across the water. It was a place out of dreams, a house whose beauty was so sharp that it became almost painful. Age and history had left their mark on every weathered stone, but the love and pride of generations of Draycotts lay equally clear.

She turned to find Marston crossing the lawn, his running shoes glowing in the sunlight.

"I hope I am not disturbing your work, Ms. Kincade."

"No problem. I wasn't getting much done. Watching Max is more fun than working." She stared up at the gray walls and the yards of gleaming glass. "Don't you feel strange here, Marston? Last night I had the *definite* feeling one of those old suits of armor was about to climb down off the walls and follow me upstairs."

"A not unusual sensation." He studied the high parapets, stark in the sunlight. "It is a house of power and secrets, to be sure. I recall that my father swore he saw someone step down from a portrait in the Long Gallery on Boxing Day." His mouth curved slightly. "My mother swears it was merely the result of his overindulgence in Scottish whisky."

A ghost in the portrait. The hairs on Maggie's neck rose at the image. "I suppose you've heard a lot of legends like that about the abbey."

"More than I can count."

"And what about you, Marston? Have *you* seen a gray, ephemeral shape drifting down from the paintings?"

"Draycott Abbey holds many secrets, Ms. Kincade. They are part of the house's great allure."

"Then you have?"

He looked out over the moat and down to the wooded hills. "When the sky is black and the wind is high off the weald, I have heard sounds. Twelve bells and one more. I have even sensed that I was not entirely alone." He shrugged. "Probably no more than my overactive imagination fueled by my great love for this place. But I digress most disgracefully. Your cousin from Sussex just phoned."

"Faith?"

The butler nodded. "She requested that you return her call at your leisure."

"I'll go right now. Come on, Max." With a high bark, the dog raced toward her, his long ears flopping. Maggie cast a look back at her silver and pliers. "Is it safe to leave these things out here?"

"I believe so," Marston said dryly. "There has not been a simple burglary at the abbey for three hundred years."

Only much later did his odd choice of words strike Maggie.

Simple burglary.

What other kind was there?

"Maggie, where the heck are you? Why didn't you *tell* me you'd gone to the abbey? I tried your hotel and got no answer, and I was going out of my mind dreaming up disaster scenarios."

Leave it to her cousin to track her down, Maggie thought with wry affection. "I'm fine, Faith. I meant to call, but things have been a little rushed."

"Is something going on, Maggie? You sound funny. Distant, I guess. Or tired." Maggie's cousin spoke in a husky rush, allowing no time for a response. Faith Kincade approached a conversation like everything else in her life: with careful planning and a breakneck pace of execution that permitted no deviations and no delays.

"Maggie, there *is* something wrong. Why don't you answer?"

"Because I can't fit a word in, as usual. And I'm fine, Faith."

"Then why did you leave London? When I couldn't

track you down, I called Chessa in New York. She told me
to try Lord Draycott.''

Maggie pushed back a damask curtain at the window of
the sunny first-floor study. Max was curled on the floor
beside her, half asleep. "I'm here working. At least I'm
trying to. This house is rather . . . overwhelming.''

"Forget overwhelming. I'd give my firstborn for a private tour of those phenomenal gardens,'' Faith wailed.
"Pure medieval. No clumsy Victorian renovations there.''

"You don't *have* a firstborn, Faith. Or have you been
holding out on us?''

Faith's dry sniff was very loud. "As if I have time for
a meaningful relationship, with six topiary centerpieces to
finish by next week. I don't even have time for an *un-
meaningful* relationship. When I was in school they never
told me that perennials and herb gardens could be hell on
a person's love life.''

"And you're enjoying every second of it,'' Maggie said
astutely.

"You bet I am. I've got topsoil up to my elbows and
hazel twigs in my hair and I've never been happier. Why
just yesterday—'' She stopped. "This call isn't about *me*,''
she said sternly. "What's going on? You wouldn't have
left London earlier than planned without an ironclad reason,
not with the Etruscan jewelry show opening this week.
What gives?''

Maggie tried to avoid an out-and-out lie. "I wanted to
try out some new ideas before the exhibition.'' *The exhibition I probably won't be in,* she thought darkly. "When
Lord Draycott asked if I'd like to stay here for the week, I
jumped at the chance.''

"And miss the Etruscan exhibit?''

"We're not exactly on Mars here, you know. I'll get
back to London before the month is out.''

Maggie heard the rhythmic tap of her cousin's slender
fingers on the phone. "You're lying. It's a *man*, isn't it?
After all these years you've gone and fallen in love. Oh,
this is perfect! Is he English, American? How did you meet
him?''

"There's no man, Faith.''

"You don't have to hide anything from me, Maggie."

"I'm *not* hiding anything. There is *no* affair—meaningful or any other sort. I'm here to work and that's it."

"He's married, is that it? Something complicated and terribly tragic—a sick wife that he can't bear to leave." Faith gave a noisy sigh. "Don't worry, I won't say a word to Chessa."

"Faith, I am *not* having an affair with a married man."

Movement across the room made her turn. Jared braced one shoulder on the door frame, studying her. Maggie wondered just how long he had been listening. "Hold on, Faith," she said, covering the phone. "Did you want to speak to me about something?"

"Actually, I came to give you the official tour, but there's no hurry. Go ahead and finish your call."

With you listening? Not a chance. She uncovered the phone. "I'd better go, Faith. I'll speak to you tomorrow after things are more settled."

"That was *him*, wasn't it?" Faith crowed with triumph. "Tell him the secret's safe with me. If he needs a good lawyer, I have the name of someone very reliable in Tunbridge."

Maggie rolled her eyes. Once her cousin had an idea in her mind, there was no shaking it free without major surgery. "Faith—dear, sweet Faith—you are *completely* off target this time."

Jared suddenly stiffened. He pushed away from the threshold, then strode past Maggie toward the window.

"Look, Faith, I have to go."

"But—"

"Talk to you tomorrow." Maggie put down the phone. "What's wrong"

He shook his head, rubbing his neck as if it hurt. "Something . . . someone. Odd, I can't feel it now." He made an angry sound and closed his eyes, his fingers opening slowly on the window, almost as if he was trying to feel something written there.

Which made almost as much sense as a ghost stepping out of a portrait, Maggie thought irritably.

Suddenly his shoulders tensed. "*Got* you. Out past the

moat.'' He raced for the door, his hand already digging beneath his jacket. Maggie could have sworn she saw the dull outline of a gun as he pounded down the hall. She was about to go out after him when Marston panted up the rear hall, a large box in his hands.

''The strangest morning in a decade,'' he muttered. ''First my line rings every two minutes. Then this package arrives. Ah, Ms. Kincade, I have something for you. But why was Commander MacNeill racing toward the moat?''

''He said something was wrong.'' Maggie glanced at the bulky package. ''That's not mine. I'm not expecting any deliveries.''

Marston's hands tightened imperceptibly on the box. ''In that case, I believe we will hold this for the commander.''

''Is there a return address?''

Marston smoothed the wrinkled paper. ''Middle Earth Designs. Does that mean anything to you?''

Faith. Dear, sweet Faith.

''It's my cousin's landscape design company in Sussex. She must have meant it as a surprise.''

The butler continued to stare down at the box. ''I believe we should wait.''

''Why?''

''Because I told him that all packages had to be cleared through me.'' Jared's hair was windblown, and his eyes glinted with menace.

Maggie blocked his way as he reached for the box. ''No. Not until you tell me why you charged outside just now.''

''I thought I saw someone by the bridge. I was mistaken.'' His words were clipped. ''It was just that great gray cat chasing butterflies in the sunlight.'' Jared took the box in a careful grip. ''When did it arrive?''

''Just a few moments ago, Commander.'' Marston's forehead creased with concern. ''I would have brought it sooner but there were a dozen calls on my personal line.''

''What sort of calls?'' Jared asked softly.

''Misdials. When I picked up, the line was dead.''

''How many times?''

''Ten. Maybe twelve.'' Marston's brow rose. ''You don't think—''

Jared cut him off, lifting the box to a polished oak side table. "Middle Earth Designs?"

"That's my cousin's company in Sussex. There's nothing to get upset about," Maggie said sharply. "Faith loves surprises. She's always sending unexpected gifts to her friends."

"Call her back," Jared said flatly.

It took a heartbeat for his quiet order to sink in. "You think it's some sort of . . . trick?"

Jared bent to examine the paper. He traced each edge carefully, then sniffed the bottom.

"Look, Jared, you're taking this all out of proportion."

"Call her." This time there was no ignoring the snap of a command in his voice. "Ask her if she sent you anything for delivery today."

"Oh, all right. Then she'll be positive I've gone off the deep end," Maggie grumbled, lifting the phone on a nearby pedestal table and dialing her cousin's number.

"Middle Earth Designs. How can I—"

"Faith?" Maggie spoke quickly, so her cousin wouldn't hear the worry in her voice. "Sorry to bother you, but did you send me a package? A large box, about 10 by 20."

"I was going to send you some roses tomorrow. In fact, I just cut them a minute ago. But today—no."

Something heavy settled in Maggie's chest. She stared at the anonymous, impersonal box. "It's from him," she whispered. "He knows I'm here. He knows Faith and Chessa, too. Oh, God, he knows everything about me."

"Maggie, what in heaven's name is going on? *Maggie, talk to me.*" Maggie's hands shook as Jared took the receiver.

"Your cousin will call you back in a little while."

"Who *is* this? I want to talk to Maggie."

"Shortly. I'm sorry, but I have to ring off now." Cool. Implacable.

Professional, Maggie thought.

Because now it was his world and his business. He was assessing a threat, estimating a counteroffensive. Dear sweet God, what had she gotten herself into?

"Sit down." Jared pushed her gently into a chair.

She smelled the sharp tang of whisky as he pressed a tumbler into her hands. "He *knows*, Jared. *He* was out there by the moat, wasn't he?"

"We don't know that," he said flatly. "Drink this."

With utter detachment Maggie raised the heavy crystal tumbler. Jared opened his fingers over hers and guided the glass to her mouth. "All of it."

She coughed at the hot bite of the spirits, then finished the inch left in the glass, determined not to fall apart. "What happens now, Jared? He's gotten in—but why?"

"As a test. Or maybe as a demonstration of his power." Frowning, he pulled out a cellular phone and spoke softly. "Izzy? I want backup on every phone here. That's right, all three numbers. And I want a printout on all incoming calls, with name and location. I know that's illegal, but you know a dozen ways around that. I saw what you did with that switch last month in Paris, remember?" He paced tensely, the phone close to his mouth. "Fine, do it that way. Just make it quick." He studied the box on the table. "And check on a courier company called Lion Express. That's right, like the animal. Send everything to my computer. Nothing more via phone, understood?"

Jared rang off and pocketed the small phone. "New rules," he said tersely. "All packages or deliveries go through me, Marston."

"Very good, Commander."

Jared touched the box carefully. "And I'm giving you both notice that from now on the phone lines will be monitored constantly, so if there's something you'd rather not have overheard you'd better not say it. Marston, be sure to alert the Draycotts about this."

Maggie let out a breath. "I suppose there's no other choice."

Jared studied the taped edge of the package. "An explosives team will be arriving from Hastings within the hour. Meanwhile, I'm taking this outside for a closer look." Jared looked at the butler. "Marston, if anything happens, you're to get Maggie out and Nicholas down here pronto. He'll handle the next step."

"What do you mean?" Maggie started after him as he

carried the box toward the front door. "You don't really think that might be some kind of explosive."

He moved past her. "Don't follow me, Maggie."

"But you'll need tests and an X ray, won't you?"

"I have some equipment in the old conservatory." He gave a dry laugh. "If that goes up, Nicholas would thank me."

"You can't do this, Jared."

He turned, his gaze meeting hers squarely. "It's what I'm paid to do, Maggie. It's my job. This won't be the first time."

If he'd meant to reassure her, he failed completely. Maggie envisioned him crouched by other packages, sweating as he listened for telltale clicking or the smell of chemical explosives.

"Wait for help," she whispered.

"There's no time. I have to determine if this is real or not. If it's carrying a timer, we don't have the luxury of a delay." He gave Marston a hard look. "*Both* of you stay here. And keep Max inside. Is that understood?"

Marston nodded. "Understood, Commander."

Maggie blinked at the sudden flood of sunlight through the open door. What if there was a bomb? What if she never saw him again? "Jared, I—"

The door closed. She started after him, but Marston gripped her arm with surprising strength. "I'm afraid I cannot allow you to go out, Ms. Kincade, much as I would like to join you there." He turned and appeared to be listening intently.

There was only birdsong. Only a silence that was suddenly threatening.

"Stubborn man," Marston muttered. "Unfortunately he is right about this. It is his job and we must leave him to it," he said grimly. "What we need now is a strong cup of Darjeeling laced with whisky—especially since I have a damned good view of the conservatory from the kitchen window. Are you coming?"

Maggie nodded, shaken by the anger and worry in his eyes. She had no way of knowing that it was the first time the sober butler had broken form and cursed before a guest in twenty-six years of exacting service at the abbey.

Chapter 22

MARSTON PACED BEFORE THE OPEN WINDOW AS THE SEC-onds crawled past.

"He's done this before?" Maggie asked tensely.

"Many times. It was his specialty. Greece, Hong Kong, the Falklands." He slanted another glance toward the conservatory. "And Thailand, of course."

"I can't think about it." Maggie cradled her teacup, barely noticing how the heat burned her palms. "Did any of the bombs go off?"

"Once," Marston said. "Only once."

The cup lurched. "What happened?"

Marston continued to stare out at the old conservatory. "I believe you'd better ask Commander MacNeill." Behind him the phone rang, shrill in the silence.

After a brief hesitation, Marston raised the receiver. "Marston here." He nodded slowly. "I'm afraid he is not available. Izzy, you say? Yes, I'll tell him that you phoned. I'm sure he will be glad to know the work is finished." Marston's gaze wandered to the shadows at the far side of the moat. "When do I expect him? Soon, I hope. Very, very soon."

The butler hung up slowly. "That was the commander's colleague. The phone work is complete. I don't believe we've had listening devices here since 1990, when the queen—" He drummed his fingers against the glass.

"Marston?" Maggie swallowed. "What if he . . ." She couldn't finish.

"No one will die here at the abbey while I'm on duty."

He strode to a high cabinet and pulled open a narrow drawer, his expression resolute as he removed a small automatic pistol and slid a clip into place. "I would appreciate it if you stayed here and watched the conservatory, Ms. Kincade. I believe I will make a round of the house." His jaw hardened. "Just in case."

Beyond the moat and the Witch's Pool sunlight curled around a holly hedge. Without warning the wind dropped and clouds slid before the sun, shadowing the lawns.

A voice boomed out of the shadows. "Just let me have the blackguard within my reach. I'll teach him to intrude!" A hint of white lace slid into view, followed by shoulders draped in black satin. "The utter audacity to bring an object of harm here to my abbey. I *won't* have it, by heaven!"

At his feet the holly stirred, and a gray form ghosted into view. The great cat jumped to the stone bridge and meowed.

"Where, Gideon? In a truck just leaving the estate?"

The cat's tail flicked side to side.

"Too late?" Adrian Draycott spun about, staring to the south where the gravel drive twisted away, lost in a row of oak trees. "I'll set a bolt of lightning on the bounder if he sets foot on abbey soil ever again."

The cat's ears pricked forward, suddenly alert.

"He's going to open the box? The bloody fool. Expert or not, Commander MacNeill will require our help." Adrian rubbed a spectral hand across his jaw. "Thank the saints that the viscount and his family are nowhere about."

A mass of holly flew down in a rain of dark leaves as he swung about. "Trouble, always trouble," he muttered. "A pack of fools, these mortals be."

The lace at his cuffs fluttered, then melted into the stone wall, followed an instant later by the length of Adrian's tall form. "Are you coming, Gideon?" The words boomed from empty space. "I will need your help, my friend."

In answer the cat took a delicate leap across the stone bridge, then raced over the lawn toward the old conservatory.

*　　*　　*

Jared touched the heavy paper carefully.

He had dealt with explosives often in Europe and the Middle East, places where schoolchildren grew up familiar with names like Semtex and C-4. Over long months of duty he had developed the distance and objectivity to confront each assignment as if it were a simple exercise with no effect on the safety of himself or others.

But now, sweating amid the ferns in the abbey's conservatory, Jared found his objectivity fraying.

He had already called in full backup, of course. A municipal security team would bring metal containers to house the package until the firing mechanism could be disrupted and the device detonated harmlessly. Meanwhile, Jared had constructed a makeshift barrier of heavy iron lawn furniture and two solid metal gardening tables.

Not foolproof, but it was a start.

The waiting turned into a torment. With every brush of his fingers on the box he felt the sullen link tighten. The slightest touch brought an onslaught of cold emotion, marking state of mind of whoever had wrapped and delivered the box.

The courier service named on the box did not exist, Jared sensed. Lion Express would appear on no corporate index or directory, in spite of Izzy's relentless searching, and Jared refused to sit by and wait for disaster to strike.

Gently he slid a specially adapted stethoscope against the nondescript brown wrapper.

Silence.

Patiently he tried every inch, and each time he was met with utter stillness. The mechanism might be digital, triggered by silicon chips and microcircuits. It could also be chemically or magnetically triggered, the sort of thing that was increasingly popular in the Far East.

Jared lifted a black metal box with a long probe and ran the boom carefully over the brown paper, listening for an electronic hum or a burst of static indicating the presence of a wireless transmitter that could trigger a detonation from a distance. Each pass came up clear.

So far the box was clean, yet Jared's senses were screaming. Both experience and his singular intuition warned of close risk. His first priority was safety, and that meant taking no chances. The basic rule of explosives was to presume detonation capability until proven otherwise. He struggled for controlled objectivity, trying to forget that in one second the conservatory and a sizeable section of the abbey could be turned into flying debris.

Sweat dotted his forehead as he sprayed the top of the box and watched the paper glisten, then turn translucent. There was no trace of the oily stains that chemical explosives might leave. There was no network of wires or structural tubing visible beneath the paper.

Whoever had sent this package was playing with them, making this some hellish test. Jared opened and closed his fingers, fighting to stay calm, though any second could bring a deafening blast and an acrid wall of smoke as circuits and wires clicked to their deadly purpose.

With a silent curse he called up habits learned over years of exacting training. *Forget everything but technique. Use your eyes and ears as if your life depends on them because it bloody well does.* He almost smiled at the memory of the barrel-chested demolitions instructor from Leeds who had cursed and goaded him through his first year of specialized training.

And don't bloody well forget to breathe.

He forced a stream of air into his lungs and studied the box.

Not heavy, but that meant nothing. These days detonators could weigh less than five pounds and triggers even less.

No indication of motion or sound. Again, equally inconclusive.

What he needed was a topflight CAT scanner and an X-ray machine, along with the newest disruptive devices, but he had none of them.

What he did have was his singular gift.

Summoning all his energy he focused deep, past the brown paper, past the scrawled lettering and the cardboard. Tightening his concentration, he probed the heart of the box.

The contact shimmered, and images churned into his head. Lonely seacoast. The muted sound of a foghorn.

Scrub pines bunched along a place of utter isolation.

Jared shifted, driving his focus deeper into the cold cardboard and rough paper. There he found anger, cunning, and the premeditation of a keen mind, but no active bomb that he could sense. Fear, not death, was the sender's intent. Fear was meant to grow, feeding on itself, until Jared and Maggie watched empty corners and jousted with terrifying shadows of their own invention.

While a stranger laughed. And waited.

Out of the corner of his eye, Jared saw something move beyond a dwarf orange tree dotted with white blossoms. He was reaching for his Browning Hi-Power pistol when a gray shape ghosted through a row of ferns and brushed against his ankle.

"This is no place for you, my friend. You'd best be gone."

The cat's tail flicked once. He jumped onto a broad oak table jammed with ceramic pots and watering cans.

Jared scowled. "Go on, blast it. Out with you. This is no time for showmanship, damn it." Jared felt his blood freeze as the gray body shot forward, dislodging a watering can. With nightmare clarity, he saw the heavy pewter topple toward the box on the table.

He dove headfirst. Brackish water sprayed over him, soaking the box. Every muscle tensed as he struck the floor and waited for the deafening crack that would be the last thing he would ever hear.

As water dripped over the paper, the box seemed to deteriorate, collapsing inward with a liquid hiss. Jared rose, grabbed the cat, and leaped beyond the protective barrier.

There was no deafening explosion. Water trickled down his cheeks and hands, the only sound in the room. Then the cat gave a low cry and squirmed free of Jared's fingers.

In one leap he was on top of the box, which crumpled to a damp shell.

"Someone very special must be watching over you," Jared said softly as he pushed himself to his feet, feeling an almost painful awareness of everything around him, from the exquisite lace of a foxtail fern to a dust mote that danced through the thick sunlight. The scent of orange blossoms and the rich smell of potting soil filled his lungs, making him feel almost giddy. It was over, he realized. Something had changed. Perhaps the water had offset some delicate balance inside the box.

He tugged at the wet paper, assailed by a pungent, bittersweet scent as he tore away the last fold. All that was left inside were long streaks mounded against the cardboard, interlaced in perfect squares.

Jared stared. He had seen lines like those before. The embassy bombing in Greece? The attack on a British school in Malaysia?

The image eluded him.

He sniffed the drying white squares. Crystals of some sort. Sugar, Jared realized. But *why*?

The cat pressed closer, inquisitive and unafraid. Jared ran a hand over the sleek fur while he studied the patterns in the crumpled paper. Could they possibly be simple circuits made of sugar mixed with some organic, conductive material? Or was he dealing with a biohazard hidden in that innocuous sugar?

Jared knelt by the box, feeling no further sense of threat. The paper was cold, inert beneath his fingers. "Somehow I think this was all meant to manipulate us. This madman has a timecard filled out, and he's watching us squirm. He's careful and I suspect he's also deranged."

The cat swatted the box disdainfully, then hissed as a pool of melted sugar ran toward his foot.

"Watch that." Jared pulled the cat away from the box. "No telling what's mixed with that sugar without a complete set of tests."

The cat stepped delicately across the stream of melted sugar, then turned to look at Jared.

The pattern on the brown paper drifted in and out of Jared's vision, a puzzle that should have carried meaning. There was no doubt that he'd seen those careful squares before.

Hong Kong, he realized. Six years earlier, when the explosive device of a criminal Triad group was confiscated following a string of bomb threats in public buildings. Was the same madman at work here?

Jared thought not. This was personal, a message of power and a declaration of ultimate knowledge of Jared's past, just as the Middle Earth address was to show knowledge of Maggie's family and where she could be hurt most.

Jared swore grimly. He watched water trickle down the sodden box, streaking the address until the black letters blurred. Nothing had been a coincidence, and nothing that had happened so far could be dismissed lightly.

He stared at the blurred address, seeing parts of letters and lines.

Lion Express. The box's message finally clicked into place.

Daniel Kincade. Daniel . . . in the lion's den.

I'm here for Daniel Kincade, the box was meant to say. *I'm here and I'm waiting.*

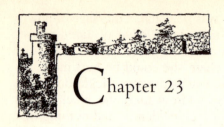

Chapter 23

MAGGIE PACED BESIDE THE HEAVY LEADED WINDOWS. There was no movement in the conservatory or beyond the trees. The moat rippled and the roses swayed, but there was no sign of Jared.

Her hand tightened on the sill. She tried not to think of him crouching by the box, testing for the presence of explosives, tensed for a blast.

Her fault. Hers and her father's.

Tears pricked at her eyes, and she rubbed them away angrily. The game had gone on long enough. She refused to allow any more danger to the innocent people around her. She would leave tomorrow. Back in the States, she could track down some of her father's old friends and . . .

And *what?*

Maggie took a hard breath as something nudged her hand. She looked down to see the gray cat padding delicately over the windowsill. His keen amber eyes burned, full of a restless intelligence.

"What am I going to do?" she whispered. "I've brought this danger to all of them."

The cat's tail arched with feline grace. He sat on the sill, staring down toward the conservatory almost as if he could read the course of her thoughts.

"Ridiculous," Maggie whispered. "Ghosts don't drift out of old paintings and cats don't pull thoughts out of people's minds. Not even very clever cats like you."

The gray ears pricked forward. He pushed to all fours, meowing loudly.

Against all logic or sense, Maggie leaned closer. "What is it?"

The great animal did not move, body tense, ears erect.

A board creaked, and she spun around, her fingers locked around a heavy crystal decanter. Marston should have returned, but there had been no sign of him, and she was taking no chances. "Who's there? Come out now," she rasped.

Wind brushed her face, and the curtains rippled in a sudden current. Maggie had the sense that she was being watched.

Nerves, she told herself. Too much imagination. Suddenly voices boomed along the front stairs. Maggie followed the sound, crossing the broad marble foyer. Through the open door to the front salon she saw Jared with one arm braced on a marble mantel, his body rigid. Across the room a man in a black vest and military fatigues paced with an arrogance that was nearly palpable. A hydrogen bomb wouldn't have drawn their attention from what appeared to be an old and familiar argument.

"Still fouling up, are you, MacNeill? What's the body count this time? Or have you stopped keeping score?"

Jared's fingers tightened on the gray stone. "What are you doing here, Cox? I specifically requested you *not* be assigned to this call."

The man in black drove a gloved finger against Jared's chest. "There *was* no one else. And you know I'm still the best."

"The threat has been immobilized."

"Is that a professional opinion?" The man named Cox smiled thinly. "I guess your mind really did go unscrewed in that box in Thailand."

Jared's hands locked. "I believe that's enough."

"Is it? You said the threat had been immobilized in Kowloon, too, didn't you? Look what a botch-up that was. Seventeen dead and a score more wounded."

Jared stared at the streaked marble as if it might be hiding an answer to some vast and insoluble problem. "You're wrong as usual. It was six dead, seven wounded."

"And *most* of them were ours. Good men doing a job

you weren't fit to oversee. You make me bloody sick.''

"Take it outside, Cox. Take your team with you. Tell your superior he'll have a complete report in triplicate waiting on his desk tomorrow.''

Cox's ruddy face tightened. "He'd better. Otherwise there'll be a lot more men here asking questions, and you might just get roughed up in the process. No one's forgotten Kowloon.''

"Leave Kowloon out of it,'' Jared said harshly. "You wanted Daphne and she didn't want you. Why don't you grow up and put it behind you?'' From the cold way Jared spoke, Maggie knew he had said the same words before.

"You wish,'' the man beside him snarled. "*You wish*. She was finished with you, you bloody Scot. She was going to turn Crown evidence.''

Jared shook his head. "And you believed her, because her hands were beyond magic and her skin was like golden pearls and she could do things that made you forget your own name. Don't be a fool. Daphne Ling had a whole scrapbook full of men wrapped around her finger before she was even fifteen. It was what she was raised and trained for, and the Triads *always* collect on their investments. Especially the human kind.'' He sounded tired suddenly, as if the story and its outcome belonged to someone else and he had heard it once too often. "Forget about Daphne. It's the best thing you can do for yourself.''

"Like *hell* I will. She was going to break off with her husband and the Triads.''

Jared laughed softly. "*No one* breaks with the Triad. They've made criminal loyalty a high art form in Asia, and you're either one hundred percent with them or you're one hundred percent dead. Daphne had become accustomed to the style of life that narcotics, gambling, and prostitution provided for her. What could you give her on a common soldier's pay?''

Cox reached for the pistol holstered beneath his arm. "She *loved* me, damn it. She was going to have my baby,'' he snarled, pain and rage tightening his voice. "And you couldn't stand it so you set her up, wiping out half a dozen innocent people in the process.''

"I didn't set the bomb that took Daphne's life," Jared said tightly. "I didn't oversee the final dismantling either."

"But *you* gave the assessment. *You* set the m.o." Cox's finger stabbed into the air. "And *you* killed her, MacNeill."

"Stop thinking with your hormones and read the files. The evidence backs me up."

"I don't give a bloody damn about files or evidence. We both know how easily papers can be changed."

Maggie inched into the shadows, understanding enough to see that two men had been betrayed by a clever woman. Was this the source of the pain that filled Jared's eyes when he thought no one was watching?

Jared paced to the window. "Do us both a favor and go home, Cox. Otherwise tell me what you really want here."

"What I *want* is Daphne and the heat of her unforgettable body. Since I can't have that I'll settle for revenge. You're going to pay for Kowloon. I'm going to see you dragged through the mud."

"Better men have tried, Cox. Better men have failed."

"Maybe you should have stayed in that box. Another year might have made you almost human."

Jared pushed away from the fireplace. "Good-bye."

"Don't walk away from me, MacNeill. I'm not finished here."

Maggie saw him pull the gun from its holster and level it at Jared's back.

She crossed the foyer, lunged for a silver vase full of roses, and spun around, tossing the contents into the officer's ruddy face.

The pistol jerked violently as water trickled down Cox's cheeks. Two red roses fell, quivering against his shoulders.

"Attractive, Cox." A tall man in black fatigues and a padded vest moved quietly past Maggie, then halted in a stiff military posture. Maggie recognized him from the police station in London. "You've work to finish outside. And you'll holster that weapon before I remove you from duty permanently."

Cox snapped a salute, while the roses continued their slow slide down his vest. "Yes, sir."

"Outside. Finish the inspection detail. And clean off those bloody roses."

"*Sir.*" Cox's boots made wet, sucking noises as he crossed the room, leaving a trail of muddy footprints across the priceless old Peking carpet. Then he was gone.

The white-haired officer strode toward Jared. "Good to see you again, MacNeill." He stretched out his hand, then gestured at the bandaged palm. "I won't shake, if you don't mind. Took a bloody sliver in training last week. Sorry about Cox. The man always was a hothead. I apologize for any unpleasantness." The officer turned to Maggie. "Am I permitted an introduction?"

Jared seemed to hesitate. "This is Margaret Kincade. Her jewelry has been selected for Lord Draycott's first exhibition. Maggie, this is Major Hugh Preston, Royal Marines."

The thin, craggy face creased in a smile. "Call me Hugh, please." He studied Maggie thoughtfully. "Exhibition? I suppose that would be the Abbey Jewels event. I saw something about it in a memo last week, but all this paperwork makes it impossible to remember anything." He started to hold out his hand, then shrugged. "A bloody nuisance, this thing. It's a pleasure, Ms. Kincade." He turned crisply. "Well then, I'll be off. We've the package safely contained now, and the first reports should be coming in within the hour. Some new chemistry, by the look of it. Possibly a new toxic agent."

Jared gave no answer.

The older man seemed to consider his next words carefully. "Sorry to hear about Thailand. Those people should have been shot." He took a hard breath. "Anytime you consider coming back, let me know."

"I won't."

"Ah, well, too bad. Could have used you last month in that sweep up near Manchester." He nodded to Maggie. "A pleasure, Ms. Kincade. Good day to you." His boots tapped with military precision across the foyer and out to the front door. Then sirens keened, breaking the stillness.

"Aren't you going to ask?" Jared followed her to the window and traced the stiff line of her jaw.

Maggie swallowed. "She must have been a special woman."

"Special isn't the word," Jared said harshly. "Tormented. Brilliant. Insatiable. But not *special*." His hand anchored her shoulder. "Turn around, Maggie. Look at me." She turned, almost against his chest, almost close enough to be swallowed up by the strange restlessness in his eyes. "What else do you want to know?"

All of it, she wanted to say. But the controlled tension in Jared's body warned her that he was struggling with bitter memories, and Maggie was afraid the wrong question would hurt them both.

"It's not easy to remember. It's even harder to talk about. Still, you have a right to answers." His hands tightened, then slid into her hair. "Ask me."

Tell me about Thailand. Tell me about that box the officer mentioned. She swallowed. "Tell me about your job in Hong Kong."

She felt tension lance through him again. "Antiterrorism. There was a flood of panic at the thought of millions of hostiles held back by flimsy wooden gates and checkpoints. If the Chinese government chose to move in, there was no way we could have stopped them. But in the end they didn't. Instead there was a constant stream of isolated incidents. Most of it was criminal, part of the endless infighting of rival Triad gangs staking out a power base." He made a tight, angry sound. "That's where Daphne Ling came in. She was Triad through and through, even though Cox still refuses to believe it. Her husband was a very highly placed 'dragon,' and I have no doubt it was his idea to see how many government agents Daphne could sink her lovely claws into."

"Did she succeed? With you, I mean?" Maggie whispered, already hating this woman she had never seen.

"She tried. I think it amused her at first when she failed. Then she was not amused. I can't go into all the details, I can tell you that she became a useful source for our own misinformation to the Triads."

"You mean you fed her false information?"

"The information she received was . . . reworded." Jared

shrugged. "Don't waste your sympathy on Daphne. She knew *exactly* what she was doing."

"What about that man Cox? Didn't he know those things, too?"

Jared shifted restlessly. "He saw the evidence. Right up to the end, he argued that she was telling the truth." When Maggie hesitated, his hands tightened. "Go on and ask. I don't want lies between us. I'll tell you what I can, even if it's less than what you want."

"What happened that day in Kowloon?"

"It was a setup. The bomb was planted by the Triads to make the British look like cold-blooded killers. The ruse might have worked if we hadn't managed to move most of the Chinese civilians out of the way. When it was over, Daphne showed up and swore that the Triads had ordered her death. Cox put her inside a truck with the second bomb disposal crew and told her it was the one place she would be safe. But someone had stashed a little gift in her handbag." Jared took a harsh breath. "They detonated the bomb right outside the National Bank of China, so it looked like British work. Cox saw the reports, but he refuses to believe them. He says I missed the second bomb—and that I did it on purpose. Now you see why the Chinese say keep your friends close and your enemies closer."

Horror left Maggie silent. So much calculation and betrayal. The lines of Jared's Chinese book slid through her head: *All warfare is based on deception.* "You wouldn't do something like that."

"No," he said. "But try explaining that to Cox."

"Is Daphne Ling why you left the service?"

"That—and other things."

Maggie tilted her head. "What other things?"

Something moved in his eyes. The story of Kowloon had been savage and cold, but Maggie sensed that there was worse to come.

She had to know the rest of it. If there were shadows, she meant to share them with this brooding, honorable man. "Marston said you'd been posted all over the world. He mentioned Thailand."

Jared's hands tensed in her hair. "I was there. Three and a half years."

The sirens were gone now. The abbey lay quiet around them, hiding the secrets of its own restless past.

"Was that your last posting?"

"It was." Maggie felt him drawing away from her. Already he was back in some crowded Asian street or stifling jungle.

Maggie understood the spell of the past. She wondered if Jared had ever truly released that part of his. "Tell me what happened."

"Do you really want to know, Maggie?"

She nodded, frightened by his detachment, as if he was considering a stranger's past, rather than his own.

"You think you do, but you don't." His voice was cold and controlled.

"Let me decide that."

"What's there to say?" He moved one hand to the window, his face cast into shadow. "I made a mistake. I was caught. Nothing original about the story."

"There's more," Maggie said softly. She locked her arms at her chest, frozen by the physical and emotional distance that lay between them, measured out in silence and unanswered questions. "So where does that leave us, Jared?"

"I'm trying, Maggie. God knows, I don't want to keep you out. In so many ways you're just what I've needed— a wild wind to storm through my life and knock me flat."

"Hardly a compliment," she muttered.

"But it is. The best kind. I've been forced to change, and it's come at a high price. I've had to question everything around me, but I don't want to question you, Maggie."

"Then don't. Just open your arms and let me in." She stood waiting, suddenly fearless, offering all she had to give to this quiet, restless man who faced death without a second thought, only to close up tight when questioned about his past. "After all, how bad could it be? You haven't been involved in any junk bond scandals, have you?"

"You don't understand," he said harshly, not returning her smile.

"I'm trying to," she whispered. Her hands slid around his waist. "You've just saved my life, Jared. I owe you."

"I don't want your gratitude," he said harshly. His muscles bunched beneath her hands. "I don't want you to do *anything* because you feel obligated."

She read the stormy uncertainty in his eyes, where need waged a hard war with rock-hard principles.

Damn a man with principles, she thought. They both could have died an hour ago. They should be doing more important things than talking.

"People want me to pretend my past didn't happen," he growled. "But like you, I've never been good at pretending. Not much good at forgetting either."

"Then don't try." She opened one hand against his chest, feeling the hard tattoo of his heart beneath her fingers. "Maybe it's time you followed your advice to Cox. Put the past on a shelf, and leave it there while you get on with things, day by day and hour by hour. When you face it again, you might just find that your mountain has turned back into what it was all along—a molehill."

"Is that what you did after your father disappeared?"

"More or less. I did my share of backsliding, but it finally worked."

Jared brought his head down and brushed her hair with his lips. "What are you asking of me?"

Staring into his shadowed face, Maggie came to a grave decision, hoping it was the right one. The woman in her swore it was, but the awkward child and the insecure teenager whispered she was a fool to take such a risk on a man who was still so much a stranger.

"Stop talking, Jared. Stop thinking. Then kiss me."

"Because you're obligated?"

"Does this feel like obligation?" she whispered, fitting her slender body to his and sliding onto her toes to nuzzle his neck.

Jared closed his eyes, fighting desperately for control.

What she felt like was heaven, he thought, touching the pure burn of her spirit. It wasn't a thing he could misread while in such close contact. He knew that she was offering herself freely, without reservations, without guilt, without shame.

Awed, he savored that vibrant light, so much a part of her character. Light was the secret to the power of her unusual designs. How could he share the shadows of his past and the cold certainty of his future with her?

"I want to kiss you. Part of me says I'm a fool not to."

"I like that part," she said. "He gets my vote."

Sunlight pooled around them as Jared cupped the fine line of her cheek. "Understand me, Maggie. I've waited a long time to feel this way. I'm not running away." He smiled tensely. "Not quite. You make me remember myself before Hong Kong. Before Thailand. The old dreams have come drifting back and I was so sure they were all dead. But gut instincts and flaring hormones aren't enough to get us through."

"They'd feel awfully good." She gave a brittle smile. "I'm not all that—practiced in these matters, but I know touching you would be spectacular."

He touched her mouth with his thumb, a feathered caress that left her trembling. He read the need that shimmered through her and its sweet, flaring afterburn. She'd never lied to him, never backed down, and never turned away. He loved her for that as much as everything else.

Love.

The realization slammed down, cold and hard like a winter storm that pounded without warning off the great gray loch where he'd played as a boy. How could he love her? What had he to offer but days of being an oddity, followed by the early death glimpsed with such stark clarity in that box in Thailand and a dozen times since?

It was torture to hold her and not push the sensual edge to its conclusion. Torture to care so much and know she was going to end up hurt, whether he stayed or walked away. Being a gentleman couldn't save her now. They had crossed the faint, tenuous border that marked the edge of friendship and the beginning of intimacy.

Jared wanted her as his lover, wanted that with a force that left him speechless. He wanted the shuddering moments of discovery, thigh to thigh. He could already envision her face suffused with surprise when he drove her up to a pleasure she'd never imagined.

He closed his eyes, forehead to hers as he fought his hardest battle in fifteen years of dangerous work. "Time, Maggie. We both need it. So we can be certain of what we want." He forced his hands to loosen, his face to shift into a smile.

"You've got one week," she said. "Then I put on my war paint and come after you. Trust me, you'll be sorry you made me wait."

"Not one week. Less," he said gravely. "I've got some things to settle with the abbey's security and there will be questions for Nicholas to tackle. Whether he wants to go on with this exhibition, for one."

"Under the circumstances, he probably shouldn't."

Jared brushed the soft fall of hair from her forehead. "You don't know Nicholas. He's as stubborn as a bad-tempered baboon. He'll never let you off the hook." He felt her swift spark of hope, followed immediately by its cruel extinction. "Put it on the shelf, Maggie," Jared said, surprising himself as much as her. "Let's both try. Just for a while."

She shook her head slowly. "I ought to sic Max on you. Make him knock you down and seriously rough you up."

"I'm in terror already. If he globs any more saliva over me, I might cave in completely."

Her hands moved on his. Slowly they opened, and slowly they pulled free. "Go," she whispered. "Take care of your work—and that thinking you talked about. But don't take too long. I've discovered I'm an impatient woman." She took a deep breath and shoved her fingers through her already tousled hair, leaving it a chaos of amber and gold in the sunlight.

Jared almost reached for her then, almost shoved his damnable scruples out the window.

"Don't worry about me," she said, her voice firm. "I'm going to find Max and teach him some killer guard dog moves."

"Lucky dog," Jared said.

"Just you wait, Scotsman. You haven't seen *anything* yet."

Chapter 24

AFTER JARED LEFT, MAGGIE STOOD WATCHING A BAR OF sunlight touch the fragile old carpet. Her hands opened, reaching for something she was almost afraid to define. She couldn't possibly deny the attraction between them, yet they both had secrets, dark corners that they were unwilling to share. What kind of trust could come from secrets?

He was right, she knew, to make them wait. Jared would never knowingly hurt her, but he still had walls to be scaled, serious ones by the look on his face.

Maggie heard a tap on the door.

Nicholas Draycott entered, looking tired and worried. "I've just arrived from London and Jared said I'd find you here. How are you managing?"

"Well enough. But why aren't you shouting at me?" She swallowed. "All I've done is bring you danger. You should toss me out on my backside."

"None of that kind of talk. Whoever is doing this will be stopped." He ran a hand through his hair. "Jared and I are working on several plans to accomplish just that."

Maggie watched sunlight play over the moat. "How can he do what he does?"

"Because it's his job, and he happens to be very good at it."

"Good at nearly getting killed? He took the package out to the conservatory without any hesitation." Her voice shook. "He said you wouldn't mind if *that* went up in smoke."

"He was right. The old conservatory is almost a hazard,

yet I can't bear to have the structure pulled down." He rubbed his neck. "But I didn't come here to talk about architecture. There have been some developments that you ought to know about."

Maggie went very still. "About my father?"

"He hasn't been found."

Her heart pitched. "Not another bomb?"

"No, not that." Nicholas smoothed the surface of an inlaid rosewood table. "First there were the incidents in London, then the phone call made to the local police last night, supposedly by me. Today a similar call was made to the Royal Military Police, warning about a bomb here at the abbey. Someone is mocking us, and I find his sense of humor most distasteful."

"Jared thinks he's playing with us, maybe in a show of power."

"He could be right." Nicholas braced one shoulder against the marble mantel. "Unbalanced or not, this man is damn clever, and so far he's left nothing traceable."

"Don't the police usually keep records of emergency calls?" Maggie asked.

"We've already checked. The first call was actually logged in as coming from my town house in London. The bomb call today was tracked here to the abbey. And I'm not referring to the call Jared made to request backup."

"I don't understand. Did someone break into your home in London?"

"I almost wished they had," Nicholas said grimly. "Then this might have made more sense. There was no break-in and no one else had physical access to our London telephones." He hesitated, drumming his fingers on the polished marble. "But to someone with the right kind of skills, there might have been different access."

"You mean that somehow he made the phone calls *seem* to come from those places even though they didn't?"

Nicholas nodded. "It's difficult, but not impossible. Phone fraud has become a high art form. With a few bits of information and some high-tech equipment, I'm told that the Queen Mother's phone calls could be rerouted to the IRA." He laughed grimly. "And vice versa."

"My God," Maggie whispered. "I thought that only happened in movies."

"I'm afraid not. Technological changes occur every day, codes imbedded and computers given supposedly unbreakable security. Unfortunately, the criminals move just as fast. Sometimes even faster."

"Jared said that the phones were going to be monitored starting today. Won't that help?"

"Up to a point. It might turn up a clue as to how the calls are being rerouted."

A cold bubble seemed to rise and fill Maggie's chest. "For some reason these people are trying to get at me, but this isn't your problem. It would be best if I went back home before things get worse."

"Why?" he said bluntly. "If you leave now, nothing will be solved. Whoever has been following you will simply trail you back to the States."

Maggie turned away to hide the shaking in her hands. "What do they want from me? I have nothing of my father's. I've sold the jewels, and all his papers and documents were with him on that airplane when it crashed. What are they hoping to find?"

"I wish I had an answer. Clearly someone is interested in what you have or what you know."

"I don't *know* anything."

Nicholas closed a hand on her shoulder. "I believe you without question. So does Jared. We're not ready to throw in the towel, I assure you. We've worked hard to promote this event so that it becomes the dazzling opener in what I hope will become a major yearly exhibit. That requires government support, good press, and financial backers. We've been fairly successful so far, but there's been a major snag."

She could barely speak. "What kind of snag?"

"I've had word that certain persons in high places object to Jared's presence. They want him replaced by someone who has active military status."

There was more, Maggie sensed. Far more. "Does this have to do with what happened in Thailand?"

A shutter seemed to fall over Nicholas's face. "What do you know about that?"

"Nothing. He won't say. But that officer named Cox said something about it. He mentioned a box. When I asked Jared, he became utterly distant."

Nicholas made a short, angry gesture. "It's not my story to tell, Maggie. It's his, always and only. He's suffered too much not to have earned that right. Just give him time."

"I'm trying. But what if he's replaced?"

"Then everything changes. The situation may become complicated."

Maggie heard the tension in his voice. "They don't want me in the exhibition. They don't want me here at all, do they? I'm too much a reminder of my father."

His shrug was an eloquent answer.

She turned away as a fish jumped from the moat, sending silver spray through the golden sunlight. So much beauty, she thought.

So much cunning and betrayal.

"I should go home."

"No." Nicholas smothered an oath. "I'll fight this decision every step of the way." His eyes held a dangerous glint. "As it happens, I have a fair bit of clout."

Maggie hadn't any doubt of that. He was a man she wouldn't care to have as an enemy. "I hope you don't regret this. And as I recall, you haven't shown me that necklace yet. I'd like to begin my examination as soon as possible, so I can order specialized materials. You'll want complete period accuracy, I assume."

Nicholas didn't immediately answer. He turned away, straightening a vase beneath the window. "I think the necklace should wait," he said slowly.

"Why?"

"The restoration work will be a major undertaking, and this isn't the best time for you to be worrying about anything but your original designs for the exhibition. I'll need all your finished pieces in three weeks if we're to begin work on the catalogue. Then the display cases will have to be specially designed. I haven't even begun to think about lighting."

He spoke fast and calmly, but Maggie sensed there were key details he wasn't telling her.

"I have seven pieces done already. You'll have the rest on time." *Assuming there's no bomb blast in the gatehouse.*

He gave her a crooked and entirely charming smile. "Hell of a mess, isn't it? Kacey says it's a gift I have, finding trouble."

"I've done my share of helping you."

Marston's sedate footsteps made Maggie turn. The butler cleared his throat. "There is a phone call for you, my lord. Your wife."

Maggie smiled at the light that entered Nicholas's face. "Calling to be certain I haven't forgotten to bring her brushes, no doubt. And she's right, I would have forgotten." He took Maggie's hand in a firm grip. "Let me know if there's anything you need. I've ordered the metals you requested. Meanwhile, Marston knows where everything is. Probably better than I do," he added.

"Quite possibly," the butler said dryly.

Jared hunched forward, tapping at his computer keyboard in the sunny front library. It had taken him a solid half hour to finish a report about the package. The physical remains had already been sent off for analysis, with a list of chemical components expected in twenty-four hours. The re-routed phone calls had a few bureaucrats muttering angrily, and his latest conversation with Nicholas had done nothing to relieve Jared's anxiety.

In Nicholas's words, there was a move afoot to see that Maggie was handled more "professionally." That meant hard questioning and lots of it. Then would come the threats to reveal some of her father's shadier business transactions unless she agreed to full cooperation with a government investigation.

Jared's fist slammed down on the polished table. Pressure wouldn't work against her. It would only close her up tight. Meanwhile, Jared didn't trust her in the care of anyone else, not when so many questions remained.

And if they tried to remove her from his protection?

He had only one option. They would leave the abbey

until Nicholas had a chance to countermand the decision. There were still quiet villages on deserted lochs in Scotland where two people with the right contacts could hide for months.

His next order of business was to check in with Izzy. Jared preferred to communicate via modem, knowing that his computer security was ironclad.

He typed in a password and waited impatiently for the transmission to proceed.

Izzy?

Right here, Mac.

Need answers. All phone lines monitored?

All done. Records available.

Knew you could do it. Any results on that envelope I sent you?

None. Fabric held no hair or skin samples. No luck with metal case either. Absolutely clean.

Just hoping.

Jared watched a frond of asparagus fern shiver at the window. There had to be answers, and the best way to find them was to narrow the choices. Abruptly he remembered Maggie's belief that the stolen gems would be impossible to disguise.

Anything unusual in the gem trades? Volume of jewels being offered for sale or changing hands? Any usual gems being shown for sale or recutting?

Will check. Have contact in Amsterdam who can help.

Good. Give info soonest. Also need financial search. Medical bills for Kincade, Sarah Amelia. Chicago hospital, probably Cook County, within the last year.

What am I looking for?

Jared frowned at the computer. What *was* he looking for? An anonymous donor who had paid the family medical bills? A dummy corporation set up by Daniel Kincade to handle the family's finances after his disappearance? Or was this just another wild-goose chase?

Need total amount of bill and how paid. Name and dates of checks if possible, too.

Gee, Mac, you going into healthcare business?

Not anytime soon. Also need check on real estate or stock purchases by Daniel Kincade, last ten years. Send to usual file, full security.

Got it.

Final request is rundown on express delivery system. Name: Lion Express. Keep a light touch, understood?

Understood. Expect answers tonight.

As Izzy signed off, Jared imagined his associate rubbing his hands in delight over this new challenge. He could ease his way into any computer on the planet—business, private, even secure military systems. Best of all, Izzy had extensive contacts so that he could do most searches legally.

But searches still took time.

Jared sat back and steepled his fingers. He was tired of playing cat and mouse. The fastest plan would be to lure Maggie's pursuers out into the light at a time and place of Jared's choosing. Nicholas had already made some suggestions, but none left Jared comfortable about Maggie's level of safety. Among the possibilities was an invitation-only auction of czarist amber coming up in Paris. If he made certain that Maggie's presence was well publicized, Jared was certain her pursuer would wrangle an invitation, too.

And until then?

Jared sat back, rubbing the knot of tension at his neck. Until then everyone going in and out of the abbey would be personally screened and approved by him. The case of this morning's delivery would *not* be repeated, and Maggie would stay under personal observation at all times by him, Nicholas, or a colleague who was equally reliable and discreet.

The scent of wildflowers caught his attention. He pushed to his feet at the sight of Maggie standing at the door with Max peering expectantly from her arms.

"Sorry if I interrupted." Her hair cascaded over her shoulders, and there was a smudge of charcoal on her cheek. She was wearing a slide of deep blue silk that shimmered every time she moved. Jared wanted to drag her down on the rug and sweep away the silk, then drive them both to delirium.

He closed his hands to keep from reaching for her. "You didn't. I was finished."

"You must be very good at those things." She ran a hand through her hair, leaving it a storm of amber and gold. "I never could get beyond the first help screen."

"All it takes is a bit of practice." There was no mistaking her crackling tension. She was brittle, uncertain, on the edge—and he also knew it would be the last thing she'd ever admit to. "Been working?"

She shrugged. "I tried. All I managed to do was ruin three sheets of silver."

"Get some rest," he said softly.

"I thought maybe . . ." She touched his jaw with the warm curve of her palm. "If you're finished here, I thought you might want to . . ."

He wanted.

Oh, how he wanted. The force of what he read shimmering in her mind left his throat dry and gritty. He considered it, too. Gripping her hand and guiding her upstairs to enjoy a bout of grinding, mindless sex. Except that it would be grounded in what felt damnably like love. The old-fashioned, roses-and-diamonds kind. The kind of love that left a man planning names for his first child.

There lay the problem.

Love was something that demanded more than a night. Love demanded plans and a future Jared was certain he didn't have.

Yet even then, he considered it. Right up until he saw the thick white bandage slanting across her thumb. "You're cut."

"The wire slipped." She shrugged. "It happens."

"Damn it, Maggie—"

"It's *nothing*." She glared at him. "Sometimes I get burned, sometimes I get cut. It's hardly earth-shaking, MacNeill."

He exhaled slowly, fighting a primal need to possess and protect. She was becoming an obsession, and that was all the more reason to give them both some space.

She pulled away stiffly. "Look, forget it. You're obviously busy and I'm tired. I could use a good night's rest. Max will keep me company, won't you, big guy?" She nuzzled the puppy, who barked and buried his nose deep in the soft folds of her sweater.

Exactly where Jared yearned to be.

Somehow he kept his expression cool. "Maybe you can control his drool factor."

"A little puppy drool doesn't hurt a flea, does it, Max?"

Jared started to say something to soften the rejection. But Maggie was already gone, the scent of her perfume lingering like a forgotten summer afternoon.

Killing him with slow, perfect precision.

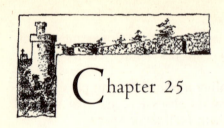

Chapter 25

THREE HOURS LATER THE WOODS AROUND THE ABBEY were silent as the moon pulled from a black ridge. Nothing stirred at the Witch's Pool or the old gatehouse. Only the moat moved, restless in the silver moonlight, reflecting tangled lines of clouds.

A perfect background to his bleak mood, Jared decided. He paused in his nighttime security round, listening to the hundred normal sounds of an old house settling. Breathing, Nicholas called it. The complex noises could be unnerving if you weren't used to them.

The wind sighed over the moat and shook the old casement windows. Somewhere a wall creaked. Jared stared at the somber portraits along the shadowed corridor. He could almost feel their eyes upon him—especially that haughty-faced aristocrat with the sad eyes up in the Long Gallery.

Adrian Draycott was the man's name. According to Nicholas, the eighth viscount Draycott had not been a man to trifle with. The hardy adventurer had fought off vicious *dakhoits* in the Punjab while he'd made some exceedingly clever investments in the East, and with the family fortunes secure, he'd wandered wherever his heart chose: Sardinia, Crete, even to the Americas. But some old sadness had clung to him, and he'd returned to the abbey he'd loved so well. There he had died, leaving behind even more rumors and legends, along with the legacy of his beloved roses, which still graced wall and hedge.

There was more to the story, but Nicholas would never reveal it. Now as Jared stood in the restless silence of night, he felt the lure of those strange legends. In this ancient house he could well believe that ghosts might walk.

Beyond a pair of heavy tapestries, he saw shadows gather across the hall, where Maggie lay sleeping.

He was moving before he knew it. His hand rose to grip the polished frame as he felt a desperate urge to see that she was safe. There was perfect reason to push open the door, check the locked windows and scan the room.

It was purely her safety that drew him.

But he hesitated, trapped in shadows and stillness. Opening that door would be an invasion of her sleep and privacy. It was late and he was in no fit mood for company.

But beneath all Jared's cool logic moved a greater force. The door latch twisted in his hands as he felt a sudden desperation to see her in the moonlight with her hair fanned out over the pillow.

To watch her sleep; see her dream. Just once more.

The door opened.

His feet made no sound on the thick carpet. Moonlight slanted through the windows and dusted the bed where she slept, one hand tugging at the sheets. A fine chain glinted at her wrist, links of beaten silver—her own work, no doubt.

In that endless moment while the house slept around him, Jared felt the orbit of his life pitch sharply. Something fell away from him as he watched her chest rise and fall slowly beneath the sheet, the image of all he had ever wanted and never hoped to find.

Honesty he had never lacked. Wit, perhaps. Sanity even. But never honesty. He accepted the truth of that perilous moment when arguments were put behind him. He moved beyond all he had been and found a dreaming face before him, calm and beautiful beyond his imagining.

He made no move to touch her as he watched the light brush her brow while the curtains drifted in a faint breeze. Odd. The windows were sealed and every door was locked. There was no reason for the gauzy panels to float out beside the French doors to her balcony.

Frowning, he padded to the far wall. All the bolts were thrown, and every window was closed tight. The movement was probably from some tiny crack in the ceiling or a chip in one of the leaded glass panels. There had to be dozens of places where air could creep inside the ancient house.

Moonlight touched his hand as he turned at the window. Jared almost felt its cold weight on his skin. For an instant the room spun and the details changed. Silk walls turned to stone. Plaster ceiling merged to solid oak beams.

Impossible.

Yet Jared knew only too well that nothing was impossible, that normal logic and everyday reality could twist in cruel distortions. His own visions had proved that far too often since his return from the horrors of a sealed box in Thailand.

By cold, hard effort he shoved away the anger. Tonight was not for vague imaginings and restless wishing.

Tonight was for the possible.

He turned away, one hand to his brow. What he needed was a hot shower and a good night's sleep. But first he needed to forget the woman on the bed, the woman whose beauty called to him until his breath caught and his whole body ached.

He looked down, angry to see that his hand was shaking. What power did Maggie Kincade hold over him? Why in this night of all nights did her dreaming eyes call to him with promises of more joy than he could imagine?

He fought to remember she was a client in danger. He told himself what he felt was merely the result of months of solitude and pain, followed by unrelieved celibacy.

But the words didn't work. Wanting filled him, climbing in his chest and blocking even the simple act of taking breath.

I want you, he said silently to the figure on the bed. *I want you more than I can imagine, more than is safe for either of us.*

His hands closed slowly. He drove his fists deep into his pockets and forced himself to look away, to turn back toward the door—and the sadness of his own room, where too many shadows lay in wait.

Somewhere a clock chimed.

He had to go.

It was the moral thing to do. The proper thing to do. But the night was still, and her perfume sweet, and Jared did not move as the low chiming strokes filled the abbey halls.

Ten. Eleven. Twelve.

A few moments more, he thought. To stand so close and imagine being closer still.

Linen rustled in the darkness. "Jared?" Blankets shifted and hit the floor.

He froze at the husky rasp of fear and confusion in her sleepy voice. How would he explain that he only wanted her presence and the scent of her soft skin?

"I was checking the doors." To his irritation, Jared had to clear his throat. "Sorry if I woke you."

She sat up slowly, her eyes wide. Moonlight drifted over the sheer white cambric that hugged her shoulders. "I had the strangest dream. Something about a necklace—only it wasn't a necklace. It became a crown of fire that burned all who touched it. There were voices and horses and someone else, but I don't remember the face." She took a shaky breath. "Was it a dream, or is this beautiful house driving me crazy?"

Jared didn't move, afraid to turn and see her pale skin and the dark hair tumbled around her shoulders. Imagining was hard enough, but *seeing* her would undo all his careful control.

"The abbey is a place for odd dreams." Somehow he made his voice firm, level. "Nicholas says it's a trick of the shadows, something that gives even the most practical visitor a dose of wild imagination. It can shake a person badly."

"It hasn't shaken you."

He shrugged. "I was prepared."

"Why don't you look at me?" Maggie's voice was a thread of sound.

Turn? Face all the things he couldn't have? No, this was the better way. Cool, calm distance and never forgetting this was business. He was a man without a future. The cold vision of his death had made that clear enough. Time and again he had watched his body fall in a pool of blood beside a lichen-covered boulder and a tree with a broken limb, and

Jared had learned young not to doubt the truth of such visions, a gift of his Celtic blood.

He had neither expected the gift nor wanted its terrible weight. Though the power ran long in the MacNeill line, it surfaced ever in the firstborn son, said to be the heritage of a woman who watched all her kin die beneath a Viking's ax. As the berserk invader laughed, she had called down a curse on all her enemies and a cry that no MacNeill should again ever be taken unaware by betrayal. By her prayer the gift was given, always falling to the firstborn male, who was to guard the safety of the line and the drafty stone walls that brooded above a great loch.

But tradition had been broken. After the death of Jared's brother, the gift had moved, falling to a soldier unsuspecting and unprepared where he crouched in a stifling box in an Asian jungle. Had he been home while his brother needed him, would the future have changed? Could Jared have stilled his brother's hand in suicide? Would Grahaeme still stride those high hills, his laughter shaking falcons from their nestings above the gray seas?

Jared closed his eyes, forcing away a leaden wave of guilt. "What if" could drive a man mad more surely than sin, and Jared was already too close to madness.

And to sin.

Linen whispered. Cambric stirred. He sensed her perfume moving in the still air.

"Look at me, Jared. I won't melt. I certainly won't break."

But I might, he thought, his shoulders rigid. *Or I might do something neither of us could forgive while so much is still unsettled.* "Go back to sleep," he said harshly. "I won't disturb you again."

He heard her sudden, sharp breath only inches behind him. He stiffened as her hand settled on his arm.

She was worried, uncertain. He read every nuance of her mind, opened to him in a wash of painful clarity. She wanted to understand. She wanted to comfort him. She wanted—

He closed his eyes at the image of exactly what Maggie wanted to do in that big white bed while their hands met and their skin moved in slick, silent rhythm across the linen sheets. Heat and surrender. Need and yielding.

Jared cursed softly.

But it was no good closing his eyes and pretending he hadn't felt the hot edge of her desire. She herself might sense it only vaguely, but to him the image was painfully clear.

She wanted his hands on her skin. She wanted his body, a warm weight above her. She wanted his laughter and his breathless groan while he brought himself hilt-deep inside her.

"You don't know what you're asking, Maggie."

Her hand didn't move against his arm. "I'm asking to see your face, Jared. I'm asking for . . . answers."

"I told you once that answers take a toll. Usually they make things worse."

"You don't really believe that."

What did he believe? Jared closed his eyes, tried not to notice how her fingers felt against his skin. He tried not to wonder how it would feel if her hand slid to his chest— and then lower. "Whatever you feel is wrong," he said roughly. "Whatever you want is . . . dangerous."

"Beauty always has a price," she said, her voice husky at his ear. "My father taught me that before I was old enough to hold my own soldering iron."

He almost smiled at that. Any other woman would be talking about clothes or houses or career plans, but Maggie spoke reverently about soldering irons. Singular and fierce, she was a woman who would forever fill the lonely corners of a man's heart, if he was wise enough to let her.

Jared froze. How had he come to think of forever? He of all people knew there was no future in such dreams. Not for the last surviving MacNeill of Loch Maree.

But something made him turn. He lost his logic at the sight of the moonlight captured in her hair, falling like silver powder on her cheeks. "Beautiful," he whispered.

"No." Her hand opened and her fingers twined through his. "But what we make between us could be." When he didn't answer, she gave him a crooked smile. "I could use a bit of help here, Commander. I'm not in the habit of propositioning stoic men who look as if I've shocked or disgusted them.''

"Neither shocked nor disgusted.'' Already his body was hardening, all too aware of how close she stood and how little she wore beneath that sheer white slide of cambric. He closed his eyes. "Go back to sleep, Maggie.''

"Is that truly what you want, Jared?''

"It doesn't *matter* what I want. It never has. There is duty. There is honor and repaying old debts. Nothing else counts in the end.''

In the end. In an end that was far too close.

Her palm curved over his jaw. "You're wrong about that.''

Jared felt the heat of her skin and the slide of her fingers. He was drawn to her as to no other woman, linked in a way that felt as old as memory or time itself. In that moment of shimmering contact, he stared deep into her soul.

There he saw perfect forms of platinum and polished amber, all waiting to be completed. He felt the joy she would bring to each creation with her passion.

Too close, he thought, already bending her body closer. She shivered, restless, uncertain, and then completely fearless as his hands slid into her hair.

The fine cambric inched from her shoulder, revealing creamy skin and the curve of one full breast. She whispered his name, the sound blending with the moonlight, rich with all the magic she had yet to realize she possessed.

Jared didn't want to see into her heart. He couldn't bear to know all that she was offering him. Grimly, he fought for distance and sanity. "Maggie, listen to me.''

"I don't want to listen. I don't want to talk,'' she said huskily.

"You *have* to.'' He pulled her to the bed and made her sit. With great focus he smoothed the cambric up, covering the shadowed curves that beckoned still. "Before you touch me again, I need to explain something.''

"Your past doesn't matter, Jared. Not to me.'' Her shoulders were squared, defiance burning in her eyes. "Nothing you can say will shock me or drive me away.''

"Maggie, don't make this any harder.''

"I'll make it as hard as I can. I don't believe a word that officer said. You'd never set a bomb to take someone's life. No one who knew you would suggest such a thing." She crossed her arms, patient and implacable.

"I didn't set the bomb. But after that, things changed. I worked harder and longer. I followed every case and took on the jobs no one else wanted." His hands hardened. "Narcotics among them."

"Work was a distraction. It's perfectly understandable."

"Not a distraction, an obsession. In six months I had more arrests than men twice my age. It was like a sickness, the need to control and cleanse the filth I saw everywhere around me."

"I understand."

"You don't. You *can't*. It's a different universe, Maggie. There are places in Asia where girls of twenty are dead of old age or twisted beyond recognition."

Maggie didn't look away. All he saw in her face was her concern and sympathy. Suddenly Jared needed to shock her, to show her exactly how far apart their lives were. "I was posted to Thailand, to work with an American Drug Enforcement team. Drug lords, crooked cops, nothing shook me. I was relentless, incorruptible, and completely off my head. I fit in perfectly with the cowboys I was assigned to."

"You had good reason to be bitter after what you'd seen. And the things you did were to *protect*, not to harm," she argued fiercely. "How can that be wrong?"

"Sweet God, if only it were so easy. When you push as hard as I did, people always die. Protection was the last thing on my mind." He turned away. "Only getting even counted. Maybe it's just as well that I was stopped when I was."

Jared leaned against the wood bedpost, fighting his way through the blood and shrapnel of dark memories.

"Tell me, Jared."

He drew a harsh breath. *Tell her?*

"Please."

He watched moonlight on the moat and felt like a stranger lost in a different, noisy place. "You can buy anything in Asia, drugs, guns, servants, it's only a matter of finding the price. I stumbled on this particular market by chance when I got lost after an investigation. But they didn't deal in pirated software or rubies smuggled in from Burma. They dealt in babies, Maggie.'' His forehead pressed against the sharp wood as he remembered the stench, the crying. ''For one hundred *baht* you could buy a healthy infant. Four dollars got your pick. The price fell if you bought in quantity, of course. But there was no need for looking because being cute or healthy didn't really matter. It wasn't part of the plan.'' He drew a harsh breath, even now reluctant to put those razorlike memories into words.

''I'm here, Jared. Tell me the rest.''

He heard the din of insects beating at oil lanterns. He smelled the pungent blend of cooking oil, fish, and human fear. The night market was all around him, as real as it had been six years before. ''It didn't matter how they looked. They never even had names, you see, because they were simply a means of concealment for the high-grade powder that would earn millions on a city street in Europe or America. It was brilliant, actually.'' His voice shook, every word drawn out by sheer physical force. ''It was the perfect way to slip through customs. After all, who's going to take a second glance at a sleepy baby beneath a blanket. Except of course by that time, they weren't sleeping, they were dead.''

His hands were locked around the post now. He could barely breathe with the choking memories. Thirty tiny forms. Lifeless. A means to conceal the white powder.

''They used *babies* to hide their drugs?'' Maggie's voice was a wisp of sound as she stared at Jared's rigid back.

''For almost two years. The night I found them was the first bit of bad luck they'd had. I saw to it that they had a lot more.''

Maggie wondered what kind of mind could plan such horror. Surely there had to be a special part of hell reserved for men like that. ''So you hurt them. I'd say you had every right.''

''They became my new obsession. From market to market, day or night, I was always too close. They weren't used to police who didn't play by their rules. When all the attention started hurting the bottom line, they decided I was an annoyance they could do without.''

She touched his locked hands, covering them with her own. ''They hurt you?''

''They tried,'' he said mechanically. ''Twice they nearly cut me down in backstreet ambushes. But that's the bloody thing about dying—when you don't care a *damn*, it never happens.''

Maggie's breath hissed free. She couldn't stand to think of him bleeding and alone in the filth of a noisy alley. ''Thank God,'' she whispered, her hands sliding around his waist. At least she understood the pain in his eyes now.

''But you're wrong. They *did* get me. It just took them a while longer. And I played right into their trap.''

Maggie closed her eyes, afraid to hear—more afraid *not* to hear. She had suspected he carried deep, hidden scars, but she had no idea they would be like this. Her hands locked about his rigid body. ''Tell me.''

''I disrupted their major buying event. We ran the mothers off, then torched the building. No one was hurt, but their operation lost face. A lot of people were angry at the arrogant foreigner who didn't play by any rules. I suppose I was coming to feel I was invincible. In two years I'd only been hit once, and that was just a flesh wound.''

''I'm sorry,'' Maggie said softly.

''Oh, don't be sorry yet. You haven't heard the best.'' He stood stiffly against her hands, but she didn't pull away. ''I found out where their next market was to take place, their biggest yet. I should have wondered when I found all the details so easily. Of course that was part of the plan. I was to be the guest of honor.'' He spoke slowly, and Maggie knew he was back in the horror, part of a nightscape of greed and unimaginable evil.

''We were up north near the Burma border, in real frontier territory. There were already dozens of women waiting when we rumbled in from the jungle.'' He shook his head slowly. ''They'd been told their babies—girls, all of them— were going to be adopted by rich Americans and taken off to the land of golden streets. Who were we to spoil their fantasy?''

''You saved their children,'' Maggie said fiercely. ''If they had known the truth, they would have thanked you.''

''Maybe. No one likes to see their dreams trampled. We soon had a riot on our hands, with a hundred screaming mothers who refused to go away without their adoption receipt—absolutely phony—and their precious one hundred *baht*. That's when the local police showed up. Of course that was part of the plan too,'' he said coldly. ''We had no business disturbing their territory when a big heroin processing lab was barely ten kilometers away. The local police were only too happy to lead us to it.''

Tension gripped Jared's body. ''We closed up and hit the road, and with each kilometer the locals grew more talkative. Suddenly they were our best friends, offering cigarettes and tea. I suppose that's when it began to sink in that this trip might be something more than they suggested. It was twilight and the road had dwindled to a footpath through a wall of jungle when our friends led us over a hill to a scattering of lights. We closed in, guns drawn. I still remember that hellish darkness all around us.'' Jared laughed softly, and Maggie shivered at the sound. ''By then the locals had vanished, and there was no missing the stink of a setup, but of course it was too late. We were heading back to our jeep when the mountain exploded, and the buildings behind us tore apart like straw. The man I was with took twenty bullets through the chest. Then they came for me.''

He waited, his hands twisting over the polished wooden bed frame.

Maggie couldn't hold back a broken sound of fear. She put up a hand, hating the flat impersonality in his voice. ''Jared, *don't*.''

''Don't what?''

''Sound as if you're talking about a stranger, someone who doesn't matter and might not even exist.'' Her hands closed over his shoulders.

He gave no sign at all of noticing. ''You're close there.

By the time they were done with me, I *didn't* exist. I certainly didn't matter.'' He turned slowly, and moonlight hollowed the gaunt lines at his jaw. ''Not surprising, under the circumstances. A year in a box will do that to anyone.''

Chapter 26

SHE ONLY STARED. "A BOX? I'VE HEARD ABOUT THIS BOX, but no one will explain. I don't understand."

"Four corners," he said slowly. "No windows. No door. Food shoved in once a day—if you can call it food."

Maggie stiffened with comprehension. "They held you in a box? But why would the Thai government—"

His laugh was a rumble of bitterness. "Not the Thais, though they were glad enough to see me gone. The police were from Burma—excuse me, the Union of Myanmar. By all means let's be correct in our terms. Wouldn't do to get the name of your jailer wrong, would it?" His hands opened and closed, as if with a will and intention of their own. "Any more questions before we call it a night?"

Only a thousand, she thought, feeling as if they stood on opposite sides of a cold, stormy sea. And she knew she had to hear the rest—for Jared as well as for herself. "Why, Jared? What good were you to them?"

"A fair question. But that part, too, had been carefully arranged. You see, that building on the mountain wasn't a drug lab at all. According to the official reports, it was a nice little village school and we had just incinerated several hundred innocent Burmese children. Definitely a capital offense."

"But they were *lying*," Maggie blurted. "Besides, you weren't in Burma, you were in Thailand."

"I'm afraid not. Up there you don't see border markers, and you sure as hell don't see customs offices on the edge of a mountain. Our friendly Thai police had led us ten kilometers over the border.'' He stared at the pool of moon-light on the carpet as if looking down into hell itself. ''It took the British authorities six months just to find out I was alive and another three to find out what the charges were.''

''How did you survive?'' she whispered.

Dimly, so dimly Jared heard the pain in her voice. But for whom? He struggled to remember the stranger who had knelt in the noisy darkness, dirty and shaking, caught at the very edge of madness. Not him, that creature of torment.

Then one night the sight had come and everything had changed . . .

''Survive? I wrote letters in my mind. I was very careful, every line and word, and I carved a mark on the wall for every stifling day that passed.''

''How did they find you?''

Jared struggled to pull his mind out of the madness, out of that square of darkness. He hadn't said so much to Nicholas or the professional psychiatrists he had been sent to upon his return. He wondered how much they had guessed. ''They found me because of one man who understood. A man who was too stubborn and arrogant to take no for an answer.''

''Nicholas Draycott,'' she whispered.

''A rare man. I can never repay him for his help. So now you know all of it.'' He shrugged, a mixture of moonlight and darkness by the window. ''Rest well. You'll be safe here, I'll see to that.''

''And who,'' Maggie whispered, ''will keep you safe?''

Slowly his big hands uncurled from the wooden post. ''Irrelevant.'' Without another word he started for the door.

''*Who*, Jared? Because you damned well need someone beside you when the memories return.'' Her chin rose in stormy defiance. ''You've tried it alone. Now try it with someone else.''

''There's nothing more to say. The adventures are over, Maggie. The rest is just a performance. There's no one inside to care, no one at all. Don't waste your arguments and your anger on a ghost.''

She caught his shoulders and spun him around. ''Put the

past to rest, you told that officer. Good advice—so why don't you take it yourself?''

Their bodies were chest to chest as she glared up at him, her eyes blazing.

Beautiful, he thought, watching moonlight dust her angry cheeks while emotion poured off her in waves. But the force of her feelings couldn't change the truth. He had a job to finish, perhaps two or three. Then fate would bring him through a misted glen to a lichen-covered boulder and a tree with a broken branch.

There he would find death waiting.

''There's nothing more to find. All the singing's over, Maggie. The clapping's done.''

''I think you're afraid. It's easier to sneak away into the dark than fight for the possibility you might be wrong.'' She stood rigid, her hands opening and closing at her sides. ''That means you've let *them* win, Jared. It means you're still caught in that box.''

''I can see my own death, Maggie. The man who came back can see just about anything, if he puts his sight to it,'' he said harshly. ''Just one little unexpected bonus of a year in hell.''

''See? What do you mean?''

He felt his pulse hammer at his jaw. She had goaded and prodded, and now here he was, ready to blurt out the truth.

And watch her laugh? Worse yet, watch her back away in fear?

Jared realized he'd gone too far to stop now. ''Sight. A vision passed down in my bloodline for fourteen generations. By family legend it passes only to the eldest son, but with my brother's death, it moved to me. At the time I was crouched in the Burma jungle trying hard to remember my name,'' he explained grimly.

Her head rose. Very slowly she touched his cheek. ''What you're saying is you can see the future?''

''No. I sense things. Words that haven't been said. Emotions. Sometimes even secrets. Mostly it comes through touch.''

''Touch.'' She blinked. ''You mean like some kind of psychic?''

"Not *like*." His mouth hardened. "Not that I can control the focus, although I seem to be getting better at that with practice."

Maggie shook her head sharply. "You expect me to believe that you are—that you can . . ."

"Yes," Jared said simply. "Because it's true."

Her eyes narrowed. "In that case, what are you seeing now?"

"Parlor tricks? I think not. Either you believe or you don't," he said coldly. A MacNeill had his pride, and he had already explained more than he should have. God help him, he wouldn't deny what he was, not even for Maggie.

He set his shoulders and looked away, stung by her tense silence. He *wouldn't* beg. Nor would he give another word of explanation. She was the one who'd squeezed and probed until she'd gotten answers. If she didn't like what she heard, it was too bloody bad.

"Fair enough. No parlor tricks and no test questions." Her hand crept up the front of his sweater, then opened over his heart. "I won't ask what you're seeing now or if you can read my mind." She smiled, a mix of challenge and female recklessness as she eased against him.

Instantly he saw.

Dear sweet God, how he saw. The play of hands across heated skin. The surge of blood when clothing fell and no more barriers remained. The clarity of what she was offering made his pulse spike.

His hands tightened on her shoulders. "You're playing with fire, Maggie."

Her smile was smooth and slow. "I thought that was *your* job, Commander. Assessing potential for explosions. Dismantling volatile devices."

His face hardened. "You haven't been listening. It stops here. There aren't going to be any fireworks, Maggie."

"You want to know *your* problem?"

"I'm fairly certain you're going to tell me."

"It's right *here*." Her finger jabbed at his chest. "There's *supposed* to be a heart in here, something that makes you take risks and dream dreams. My father taught me that, Jared. He might have been impossible at business, but he damned well knew how to dream. You've forgotten how to imagine. At least silver can catch the light. At least cold metal reflects the fire of all that's around it and—''

His hands shot down over her wrists. With a low curse, he yanked her against him and sealed her mouth beneath his.

He was tired of arguing.

He'd show her fire if she wanted it, and he'd bloody well make her feel all the dreams locked inside him.

She was sputtering as the bedpost caught her back and held her motionless. Jared closed his eyes and drank in the taste of her mouth. Wanting filled him, blind after so many weeks of denial, and his hands speared down her spine until he found the warm swell of her hips. His mouth twisted on hers, driving and savage. He was amazed at how she trembled, amazed at how much he wanted her to tremble.

Her hand opened at his chest. ''I thought you didn't want this.''

''Oh, I want, Maggie. I want so much it terrifies me.'' He wrapped his hands in the warm silk of her hair and forced her head back. ''You should be running right now. Shaking in fright about what I'm thinking.''

She met his hot gaze square on. ''Should I?''

''Yes. After all I've told you.''

''What have you told me? That you've some sort of un-usual skill. So what? There's nothing so amazing I've seen yet.''

His hands tightened, and he felt the heat snap through him. ''Is it proof you want?''

She didn't back down, didn't relent by the merest inch. ''I do.''

''Then you'll have it,'' he whispered. He snared her wrist. Eyes closed, he nipped the creamy skin.

And slid deeper, swimming down to find the electric flow of her emotions.

In colors they came. Boldest red and flaring blue. Yellows and golds that raced over molten silver, as fine and rich as her singular designs. The force of it left him panting, shocked.

In that same rich flow, Jared found the rest of her secrets.

That she wanted him no matter who or what he was. She had no reservations and no regrets in her love.

Love. The feeling roiled in pinks and bright crimson. Clear to him, though she might not yet have used the word.

"Maggie," he began, his voice harsh. "You stop a man's heart."

Her smile was a curve of aching beauty. "Fine words, Commander. But I've still to see that razzle-dazzle you've made so much of."

She didn't want to talk, no matter how fine the compliments. He saw clear through to her soul now and knew exactly what she wanted. Heat and recklessness. Giving and blind surrender.

She'd have it now.

He bent her back. In one mad sweep her gown went flying and pooled at her feet. And there she stood, wearing a shimmer of white lace at her thighs and nothing else. He saw the glow of her skin, the sweet thrust of her nipples, and the fine flush that covered her cheeks.

"You're staring."

"There's a great deal to stare at," he rasped.

He felt the sudden leap of her pulse and the desire that shot through her body. She opened, hands and heart shifting as she let the reality of her love fill her mind.

"Be sure, Maggie. Be very sure. It's been a while for me," he said bluntly. "For many reasons, once we start there won't be an easy way to turn back."

"I'm tough. I can take it, Scotsman. A few bruises and nail marks won't scare away a Kincade."

His hands tightened. A dark surge of need made him nip at her ear and savor the cool, beautiful line of her upturned chin. He was going to take her places she'd never been. He was going to show her worlds of pleasure that had no name. "You make me feel savage, like some blue-painted ancestor knee-deep in heather and mist."

"Promises, promises." Nearly naked, she stood on her toes and nuzzled his neck with her lips. Then with her tongue.

He cursed at the heat she provoked. His hands moved to her ribs and then closed hard. The past lay heavy around them in the moonlight, and Jared could almost sense the quiet footfalls of restless ghosts.

Warriors slain on desert sands, part of the great Crusades. Reckless adventurers and pirate princes. Draycotts who had given their blood to protect these towering stone walls.

And lovers who whispered in the shadows, bodies urgent with need.

He closed his eyes, fighting free of the house's magic. He had enough magic right now, spilling from his contact with Maggie.

"Anything else dire you insist on telling me? Wives hidden in attics or kinky fetishes I need to know about?" She worked at his shirt, pulling it from his waistband.

"That you're destroying me."

"Destruction is good," she whispered, lips to his hard jaw. "Now let's go for total devastation." Her fingers slid under his shirt and traced the lines of his chest. Jared felt the swirl of her passion and her flare of surprise. She wasn't used to this. No other man had touched her this way, made her shiver this way.

The thought nearly pushed him beyond control. With a groan he trapped the curve of her breast, then tugged one taut crimson crest between his teeth.

Her breath came ragged. She made a broken cry as her nails dug into his chest. Need was a storm in her head, racing through the link to flare in Jared's own mind.

Her breath was puffy. "Jared, I want—"

"I know," he said hoarsely, seeing almost before she did. His hands slid along her hips and eased lower, pushing past the wisp of lace to cup her heat. "Let me feel your wanting, Maggie. Let me have your fire."

There in the shadows and the silence Jared found the tangled curls that hid her wet heat. And in the same moment he parted the sleek folds, goading her deeper into the pleasure that stretched before her like a slender golden rope.

So tight. So hot where she sheathed him. He shattered her control, pulling her nerves tighter until she stretched in an exquisite bowstroke of yearning.

Desire burned. Need sang.

In one more moment Jared knew he would be as lost as

she was. And he wasn't ready for that paradise yet. "Maggie, I—"

"Yes," she said shakily.

His hands slid into her hair as he held her face still, plundering her mouth with a violence he had never expected in himself.

"More," she rasped, digging at his shirt, her legs restless against him.

Jared knew a dark surge of triumph at her need. It was a need he knew perfectly how to assuage. With every second of contact, his knowledge of her wants grew in his mind, cast in exquisitely graphic detail.

She frowned, shoving at his shirt.

Linen flew. Lace tore and struck the floor.

Skin to skin at last.

Their hands met in a sigh of pleasure as moonlight gilded bodies that were almost too taut for bearing. Tongue to tongue, chest to chest, they lost themselves in each other.

She nuzzled his chest, tasted his warm skin and tested the rigid length of him. She goaded the hot muscle trapped within her hand until Jared felt his control shred, and when her lips feathered over him, he tensed, cursing at the unspeakable slam of desire she provoked.

Her tongue was like silk as he gripped her face, pulling her away. "No more," he said harshly. He brought her hands to his chest and sent them in a tangle to the bed. Soft damask whispered as Jared pulled her atop him.

She gave a lost, broken sigh. "You can really feel what I'm thinking?"

His grin was slow, relentless. "Every wicked thought."

A flush stained her face and slid over her chest. "This could get tricky." Her head tilted. "Unless I take the offensive."

She arched slightly, then straddled his rigid heat.

This is what I want, she thought.

And heard his soft curse.

I love you, she thought, and felt him lift her and part her slowly, with infinite care.

"Yes," she whispered. Against his neck, his chest, his mouth.

Worlds collided.

Universes merged, flared, re-formed.

Pleasure surged, tightening every muscle to something bordering pain. Jared let them both feel the pulsing heat, made them both wait until raw sensation nearly overwhelmed all other awareness.

His hand slid between them. "You feel like roses," he whispered, cradling and tantalizing. "Hot, sweet petals. Tonight I'll find how you taste, Maggie."

She closed her eyes while silver streams wrapped around her. Blindly she rose, fingers trembling in his hair as desire bloomed. Jared felt the flare through his own body, felt her wild blinding rush that sent her falling, lost in spirals of wonder.

He drove her up anew, catching her soft cries with his mouth, greedy for the touch and taste of her shocked response. He was the first to make her shudder, he saw. The first to make her feel such blinding sensation.

His eyes closed as her nails dug at his back. He felt her silken contractions, pulling, pulling. She rose against him, her hot breath an erotic claiming.

With a muttered oath Jared pinned her hands to the white bed and took her the final way, driving her with exquisite friction that burned in dark waves of pleasure.

Endless need.

Perfect giving.

The past clung close, shadowed and silent like the great old house. Bodies taut, blood racing, they took and gave, fought and tumbled, learning all the secrets that lovers share. Her sigh echoed his soft groan as skin moved to sheathe heated skin.

He looked at their locked hands—and felt two sets of skin, two sets of bone and sinew. Every place they touched was the same, desire doubled, awareness nearly overwhelming.

When her eyes beckoned, hot and entreating, Jared opened his hands against hers and followed where she drew him, down where her soul waited, calling to his through a timeless spiral of love. The pain of her touch burned more than any wound, but he wore the torment gladly. He closed his eyes, only to find her image even brighter, flaming in his mind, part of his own nerves and synapses through the magic of his strange gift. She twisted, hot and giving beneath him, and her broken sounds of pleasure frayed the last ends of his control.

She locked her hands on his neck and pushed against him urgently. "This is what I want, Jared. Not diamonds. Not silver. You—me. Now."

She let him touch all her secrets, all her churning pleasure.

Lost, he thought.

And didn't care. All his careful plans and strategies vanished like dawn mist off the great loch below his old home. Only the night mattered. Only the radiance of Maggie's passion and the heat that shivered between them.

When he felt the shudder that swept her, he gripped her hips and pushed until there was no deeper to go. Her sleek skin parted to hold him, hot and tight, their bodies linked.

"Jared, I'm dying."

Death. The word held no sting, he found, while her body moved beneath him. He almost laughed with the shock of it. He would thank her. For whatever hours he had left, he would stir her joy and make the days ring with her laughter. "I am too, my heart. But I'll die inside you."

Hot and sweet, she held him.

Hot and sweet, her mind reached out, out, part of a link that had waited here at the abbey for centuries until their return. Gwynna or Maggie, she was the sun of his world. As a warrior he would protect her. As a man, he would honor her with his name.

And as a lover, he would answer joy with joy while the abbey held them in its restless magic.

She gave a broken sigh of pleasure as he pinned her to the bed and filled her with his whole straining length. Breath to breath, their spirits met, battled, fused. Too long denied, skin parted, claimed, clung. Then her legs tightened, and the pleasure of her silken response drove him beyond control.

She arched, surprise in her cry as he took her up again, and then once more while the white damask bedspread whispered and shifted beneath their stormy need.

Her name was on his lips when the hot, rich seed of his warrior line spilled deep inside her and Jared found the shifting pleasure that had so long eluded him.

And there beyond the mists of forgetting, she stood waiting. Somehow he had always known she would.

All I ever dreamed, she thought.

And Jared heard, smiling even in the ragged fury of his final pleasure just before they toppled together into wordless worlds of silver.

The bedspread lay twisted on the floor. The sheets were in a tangle somewhere near the pillows.

"Absolute devastation."

Maggie stretched, expectant and replete. Moonlight lit her tousled hair, and her smile was radiance itself.

"Not quite," he said. "That was just a test, Kincade."

Her hand rose, nuzzling his jaw. "Promises, promises."

He moved, hard again, meeting her heat with a need only grown more fierce in its knowledge.

"You're joking." Her eyes widened. "Aren't you?"

"There's one other thing about MacNeill men. Something I didn't tell you."

Movement, deep and sure.

Hands, locked and straining.

"That's not possible." She gasped as desire rippled, built.

"I was thinking about this when you were driving me crazy with your hands, trying to free Max. I was wishing you were right here, trapped against the linen sheets." His eyes were sin itself.

Just as his hands were heaven.

Maggie sighed. *So was I.*

She heard his low curse in answer. Then pleasure hit her, hot and sweet, and her response slammed back to Jared.

"That was adequate," he said, possessing her with hard, sure strokes. "But this, my beautiful Maggie, this will be spectacular."

Why don't you prove it? she thought. Her laughter broke

into a gasp as joy spun up and passion claimed them yet again.

One by one the stars rose above the moat.

One by one the candles guttered and went out.

Chapter 27

JARED DRIFTED SLOWLY, MOUNTAINS BEFORE HIM AND soft heather beneath his feet. Everywhere there was mist and cool wind, rich with the scent of peat fires. His body shifted, searching for something he could not name.

Something warm.

Something radiant.

Suddenly there were visions of smoky blue eyes. Hair that filled his hands like warm honey. Stretching lazily, he reached out.

And met warm fingers. Pale dawn light on silken skin.

She was even more beautiful when she slept. Her skin glowed with a fine blush, and he saw the delicate tracery of blue veins where her hand lay outstretched beside him.

A storm of emotions filled him, and greatest among them was love, something the Scotsman had been so sure he'd never find or possibly deserve. Smiling, he remembered the places she had taken him in the stillness of midnight. The feelings she had taught him as they'd tumbled over those crisp white sheets.

Every image had his blood rushing, his body hardening. *Again. Now, while she sleeps.*

The desire snapped and growled through him like a wild beast. Somehow Jared caged it, savoring her stillness and the gentle colors of her mind beneath his fingers. She was dreaming of silver and hammered platinum. Bezel-set citrines and Siberian diamonds. He sensed the perfection of form before her, always beckoning, always eluding.

His hands cupped her wrist with infinite tenderness.

Never had he expected that loving someone could be so simple. All he had to do was breathe and the emotion was there, trapping him tight and filling him like sunlight in every cold corner and empty space. Never had he expected that sliding down into someone's mind could be so painless—or so brutally addictive.

Almost without thinking he brought his palm up the creamy ridge of her inner thigh, then groaned as her pleasure flowed back to him, caught in waves of gold and pink. A voice whispered that it was dangerous to linger, to want so much and fall into another's soul so completely.

If so, Jared would consider the price well paid.

Bending down, he skimmed her shoulder, nuzzled her chin, then fit his mouth to hers. Unerring, his fingers moved to coax and tease the hollows that left her dry-mouthed and restless.

To hell with dangerous, he thought as he trapped her breathy sigh of waking just before it slid into a moan of dark pleasure. *I will have her and hold her, enthrall and entice her.*

For as much time as I have left.

"Jared?" Her hands covered his neck, pulling him closer. "You're not wearing anything. You're—"

"I know." He eased between her soft thighs. "Convenient, isn't it?"

"Is this going to be a habit with you?" Her smile was sleepy and entirely radiant as he fit his body to hers, already drawing her up into a wave of pleasure. "If it isn't, I don't want to know."

Someone was breaking bricks on his head.

Or maybe it was on his chest.

With a low oath, Jared struggled up from linen sheets and sated sleep. There were aches in his arms, nail marks on his back, and the tiny print of Maggie's teeth on one shoulder.

All made him feel infinitely smug.

She didn't stir as he smoothed a strand of tousled hair from her cheek. "Maggie," he whispered. "I've got to go."

"Hmmmm."

He traced her cheek, loath to wake her, loath to leave the sunlit joy of her.

"It's morning." He frowned at the bedside clock. "Actually, it's almost afternoon."

She twisted, dragging the pillow around her head. "More silver. Melted. Hot." Her lips curved in sleepy oblivion. "Incredible lines and texture."

Jared was pleased to sense that *he* had more than a little to do with the graphic dream she was having. Smiling, he smoothed the tangled linen from her shoulder. "I'll bring you breakfast. Strawberries and chocolate. Fresh scones with cream. Maybe even some champagne nicked from the abbey's cellar."

Her nose crinkled. She rolled to her side. "Not the jade. Diamonds. Hot and white. Two more facets to go." With an irritable sigh, she dragged the pillow onto her chest. "Need more solder."

Jared realized it was all the soft, intimate farewell he would have from her.

Ten minutes later he stood in the doorway to Marston's kitchen, savoring the smells drifting from the old Aga oven.

The butler slanted one quick glance up from the pastry dough he was kneading on a marble slab. "Good morning, Commander." His eyes narrowed at Jared's tartan attire. "Is there some special occasion that I've missed?"

"None that I know of." Jared ran a hand through his hair. He still wasn't sure what had prompted him to take out the old kilt. Perhaps it was the rich boyhood memories he'd put away since his return from Thailand.

Or maybe he'd simply wanted to watch Maggie's reaction. "Not unless you count the best night of sleep I've had in years."

Busy sampling a steaming scone, Jared missed the crinkle at Marston's eyes and his knowing smile. "I'm delighted to hear it. If you would like to eat in the breakfast room, I'll bring things in directly."

Jared stretched lazily, enjoying the feel of the heavy wool

pleats and the memories they brought of happiness so thick and heavy he could hold it in his hands.

Spring afternoons tramping by byrnes that bubbled over peat-black earth. Summer dawns in a loch so cold it swept your breath right back into your chest.

Why had he been so quick to bury that past? Maybe his boyhood years of traveling with his family had left him a chameleon, far too good at changing to suit whatever environment he was cast into.

If so, he was tired of changing. It was time to peel off the layers and find out whether he liked what he found.

"Don't bother, Marston. I'll take another scone and have my tea outside. I need to check the electronics on that new gate and run a few tests on the outer security. Then I probably have a dozen messages to sort through."

"Very well, Commander, though you leave me with precious little to do."

"Then my next request is a bottle of that superb vintage La Trouvaille Nicholas thinks he can hide in the back of the cellar. Also two glasses to go with it and a basket of strawberries. Dipped in chocolate, if that's manageable."

Marston carefully kept any hint of satisfaction from his face. "It will be quite manageable. Shall I be packing for one or for two?"

Jared's smile was slow and dark. "Two. Definitely two."

The thought made him run through his security checks even faster than usual. With a satisfied smile, he finished examining the last feet of wire he'd laid the day before. All done. Every inch hummed.

Now he had the whole afternoon before him.

They did, he corrected, striding toward the conservatory, wondering how much longer he could manage to stay away from Maggie for form's sake.

Not that he had the slightest doubt he was keeping any secrets from Marston. The old butler had the eyes of a sharpshooter and the discretion of a priest. He also had the soul of a born matchmaker.

"Mac?"

Jared turned, his face creasing in a smile. "Izzy? What are you doing here? What could possibly drag you away from that glossy mainframe you're married to?''

The tall man in carelessly worn blue jeans and a gray sweater could have been a football player or an actor. His lean body held no hint of flab anywhere, and every muscle was perfectly conditioned from the recreational kickboxing that was Izzy's specialty.

Jared was one of the few people who knew that Ishmael Harris Teague was a crack sniper and a seasoned soldier with electronics skills that continued to make him highly attractive to a dozen branches of the military service.

''Call it curiosity. I wanted to get a firsthand look at this house you've had me checking. Very impressive.''

Jared's brow arched. ''The architecture, you mean?''

''No, the ISDN lines.''

Jared laughed, taking his hand in a solid grip. ''Just because Draycott Abbey has a few ghosts and some dusty armor doesn't mean it can't be cutting edge.''

Izzy's handsome mahogany features eased into a smile. ''Ghosts? I've never seen an honest-to-God ghost, though I suppose I'd *be* a ghost if you hadn't saved my tail on that last op outside Rangoon.''

''Just doing my job.''

Izzy slanted a look at Jared's legs. ''I like the skirt.''

''Don't start,'' Jared muttered. ''It's called a *feiladh mor*. A kilt, to philistines like you.''

''Hey, if it walks like a duck and talks like a duck . . .'' Izzy moved nimbly, dodging Jared's right hook.

Jared pulled back with a grin. ''Come in and have some tea. It's probably still hot.''

''Nothing stronger?''

''You don't know Marston's tea.'' Jared strode into the conservatory, brushing a pile of papers and magazines off the sole table. Bracing one hip, he poured a cup of tea from the thermos Marston had prepared. ''Speaking of ducks.''

''What?''

''You. Somebody had to keep an eye on you over there. You were so wet behind the ears that you left a trail of water, my friend. The bad guys saw you coming miles away.''

Izzy smiled broadly, rubbing his neck. "Yeah, you're right. What I didn't know could have filled a library. But you can't say I'm a slow learner."

Jared grinned. "Tell that to the men who had to bang your jeep back into shape every week. You've got to be the worst driver on four continents."

Izzy shrugged good-naturedly. "I'm still God's gift to anything with wings. You ought to see me jockeying a Night Hawk, Mac." Izzy used the old nickname that had come out of their days together in Thailand. They still spoke with the sort of shorthand that came from long hours spent sweating together in dangerous places.

Izzy spread his powerful, dark hands. "Sweet and silent, Mac, my boy. I've still got the magic touch."

Jared turned away.

He remembered all too clearly how he had once seen those broad, competent hands stretched out on a rough bamboo wall while a swaggering Thai drug lord prepared to drive a spike through each palm.

The bastard hadn't succeeded. Jared had seen to that by sweeping into the courtyard and hosing down the area with an HK-37 that took no hostages.

Izzy remembered too. There was a little crinkle in his eye that told Jared enough time had passed that he could look back at the event with detached black humor, an attitude that had kept them both alive during their two-year stint in the drug wars of the Golden Triangle.

"So what gives, Mac? Who is this lady of mystery?"

"You haven't guessed? It's Daniel Kincade's daughter. Have you come up with anything I can use?"

"Maybe. Kincade had no real estate holdings of note, but I thought you'd be interested to know that he was involved in a start-up French electronics company located outside Marseille. Their specialty is miniaturization of microwave communications."

Jared tried to juggle this new information. "Tell me what you know about microwave technology—anything that might relate to gemstones. I suppose that would include lasers, since most are generated through rubies."

"Microwave research is the hot new kid on everybody's

block. Every electronic firm with a staff of more than two has an R & D person working in that area and you don't want to know how many technoids the western nations have slaving over that particular fire.''

Jared tapped at a bag of potting soil. "So it's big enough for someone to get killed over?''

"Godzilla looks like a one-celled organism next to this kind of stuff, Mac.''

"And Daniel Kincade might have been involved with some new technology that required gem material.'' Jared pushed to his feet, frowning. "If so, why hadn't anyone heard about it?''

Izzy shrugged. "These guys aren't your usual computer nerds. The stuff they're juggling is certifiable national security. Some folks are saying that microwave technology will be the *only* technology in the next twenty years, and I happen to believe them.''

Jared gave a silent whistle. "That means Daniel Kincade's work might just have gotten him killed.''

Izzy laughed darkly. "The way I see it, if he was working on cutting-edge stuff, the question wouldn't be *if* someone killed him but which one of a dozen nations arranged to pull the trigger. That's how cutthroat this stuff has become.''

Again Jared felt a kick of surprise. Izzy was no tenderfoot. He was skilled in every branch of electronic technology and an expert at programming. This whole business was turning out to be bigger than Jared had suspected. "Do you still have people guarding Maggie Kincade's cousins?''

"Both are in place. Handpicked. Armed, and highly deadly.''

Jared chuckled at the image. Woe be to any nasty who took on one of Izzy's people. At least he could stop worrying about Maggie's cousins for the time being. "Maybe you can find out what that French company was working on when Kincade disappeared.''

"I'll have a look.''

Jared stared out at the abbey lawns, gold and brilliant green in the early afternoon sun. "What else did you turn up on Kincade?''

"Damned little you don't know already. For a famous man, he kept a low profile. Comfortable house, quiet family, passable credit. But when I was tracking his career I started picking up things."

Jared stopped pacing. "What kind of things?"

"On the surface, it was all perfectly normal. Every year he took routine visits for jewelry buys, but major gem and hardstone sources aren't on your everyday vacation itinerary. Emeralds from Colombia. Rubies from Myanmar. Lapis and nephrite from Afghanistan. Those are the most volatile governments around, Mac. Yet Kincade came and went at will. It seems he knew half the people in those governments on a personal basis."

Jared felt something cold press at his neck. "Are you suggesting Kincade was a spy?"

"Not exactly. Hell, I don't know what I'm suggesting. I'm just presenting patterns, offering possibilities. It's what you asked me to do, remember?"

"So I did." Jared rubbed his neck. Was it actually possible that Maggie's father had used his business as a cover for transporting official secrets? "There's another possibility," he said slowly. "He could have been working for his own government."

Izzy shrugged. "Hard to say. They don't exactly post a little red flag beside the names of their operatives."

"Keep looking, Izzy. If he was on official business, that would change everything."

"Governments don't usually turn on their own operatives."

"No, they don't." Jared put his hand on a leaded glass window while possibilities whirled through his head. "Did you check with our usual government sources?"

"I tried. They swallowed their tongues on this one."

"It's nice to know that *some* things are beyond you, Izzy. Restores my faith in humanity." Jared's smile faded quickly. "Keep at it. And step up surveillance on that Dutch jeweler Maggie went to visit. If he goes running, I want backup and immediate notification. In all your spare time, take a closer look at that French microwave company. The sooner we know what Daniel Kincade was working on before he disappeared, the sooner we can make a guess about who might be trying to track Maggie.''

"Roger, Mac." Izzy headed to the door, then turned. "By the way, give my regards to the lady."

"What lady?"

Izzy gave a slow, cool smile. "The one who's got your glasses fogged up big time. Makes me glad to know even a hard case like you can get KO'd." His eyes narrowed as he glanced over Jared's shoulder. "Speaking of ladies, you'd better brace for impact. Looks like one over there, fully armed and bearing down full throttle. I don't think I'll be staying around for the fallout."

"What do you mean, Izzy? Who—"

"Are *you* the one?" She was twentyish with a storm of carrot-red hair. Dressed in rubber gardening boots and a faded green suede jacket, she was stunning and clearly furious.

"Am I the one what?"

Her hands settled on her hips. "The man my cousin Maggie is having an *affair* with?"

Chapter 28

"AFFAIR?" JARED REPEATED.

"That's right. Unless you want to call it something worse."

Jared stared. The woman was about five feet, four inches tall. Her worn denim pants were streaked with potting soil on both knees, as if she had just come from gardening. Her hands, at least what he could see of them, were mottled with dirt.

Abruptly, her identity clicked in. The cousin with the landscape design firm. But how had she known that he and Maggie were involved? And how had she gotten past Marston? He held out his hand. "You must be Faith, Maggie's cousin. I'm—"

Her hands dug into her hips. "Don't try to charm *me*, Commander MacNeill. I know exactly who you are. I also know my cousin. Maggie's terribly vulnerable with this exhibition coming up, and it wouldn't take much for a clever, unprincipled man to worm past all her defenses. So, are you the man?"

Clearly, Faith Kincade had no problem speaking her mind, but Jared wasn't about to discuss his love life with a complete stranger, even if she was Maggie's relative. "I'm not sure where you got the impression that your cousin and I were involved."

He was still holding out his hand.

She stared at his fingers as if they were dead fish. "Where doesn't matter. And I notice you didn't answer my question."

"Maggie and I are not having an affair." Jared wasn't sure what he would call it, but it wasn't an affair. He wasn't sure any single word would do justice to the feelings he had for Maggie. "And if we were," he continued smoothly, "I certainly wouldn't tell you. Any news would be hers to break."

Her eyes narrowed. "Where's Maggie?"

"Up at the house, I believe. Would you like for me to find her?"

"No!" Faith frowned as she moved restlessly through the room, straightening an asparagus fern and pinching dry leaves off a dwarf orange. "What a mess. Lord Draycott obviously needs help choosing his gardening staff. And you can forget about finding Maggie. She'll murder me if she knows I'm here checking up on her." She gave Jared a sharp, assessing look. "And count on it, I *am* checking up on her. I want to be certain she's not in over her head."

Jared studied her right back. "Are all Kincades so interested in each other's business?"

"Trust me, I'm the least interfering of the lot. Chessa would have pinned you down and wrung out every detail by now, and you wouldn't have known what hit you. Finesse, that's her style. Me, I go right for the jugular."

"I'm very glad to hear it."

"No you aren't, but you're a good liar, Commander."

Jared turned a rusted iron garden chair back onto its feet. "Would you like to sit down while you conduct your interrogation?"

"I don't think so. Something tells me I'd better stay on my feet. Tell me what's going on here?"

At that moment Marston panted up from the courtyard. "Oh, you've met Ms. Kincade, I see. I was going off to find Maggie."

"I skipped out on him," Faith finished, entirely unrepentant. "I wasn't about to give him any time to think up an elaborate story."

"Thank you, Marston. I'll see Ms. Kincade back to the house when we've finished here."

"Very well, Commander."

As soon as Marston left, Faith rounded on Jared. *"Well?*

Exactly what's your interest in my cousin?''

Jared wasn't about to wander into personal matters. ''Some odd things have happened since Maggie arrived in London. I'm trying to find out why.''

''It's her father again, isn't it?''

''Why do you say that?''

''Isn't it always?'' Abruptly Faith turned and clicked her tongue over a sagging camellia. ''Don't you know these things have to be watered on a rotation cycle?'' Frowning, she shoved up her sleeves and dumped the straggling plant on a nearby potting table. ''Anything will thrive in the right soil with proper sun and water.'' She eased the plant from a packed ball of clay and inspected the roots. ''Still intact. In another week it would have been beyond help.'' She tipped soil into the pot, slid in the plant, covered the roots. ''What kind of problems?''

Jared blinked, then realized she was talking about Maggie's situation, not the plant she was repotting. ''We were attacked and nearly run down by a backhoe. Then someone broke into her hotel room in London.'' He decided not to mention the recent bomb incident.

''*What*? She never said a word to me. I'm going to murder her myself,'' Faith muttered, elbow-deep in potting soil.

''She was right not to tell you. The fewer people who know about this the better.''

Faith looked up, anger flaring in her eyes. ''I'm not *anyone*, Commander, I'm her cousin. Maggie and I don't keep secrets from each other.'' Her eyes narrowed. ''You've got professional written all over you. A Scotsman, too. There's nothing like a man in a kilt.'' She measured him some more. ''Why don't you have the accent?''

''We moved a good bit while I was growing up. Now it comes and goes.''

''Or you make it come and go. Very useful when you're romancing the ladies.'' She gave him no time to answer. ''There, it's finished. See that it's watered daily for a week. Standard fertilizer after a month.'' She looked around the room, brushing her hands and leaving another streak of dirt over her chin. ''Unforgivable to let a beautiful old place like this go to ruin.''

"I'll pass on your message to Lord Draycott."

"Don't bother. I'll tell him myself."

Jared had no doubt that she would. He had the firm impression that where any growing thing was concerned, Faith Kincade would be relentless. "Why did you ask if this had to do with Maggie's father?"

"Whenever things went wrong in Maggie's life, her father was usually involved. My uncle was never home—not when it counted." She swept her hair up off her shoulders with a sigh. "Even after he died, the problems didn't stop."

"What kind of problems?"

Her lips pursed. "Are you good at what you do? Can you guarantee you'll keep Maggie safe?"

"I'm good." At one time he had been the very best. But that was before he'd spent fourteen months inside a box buried under two feet of Asian dirt. "I'll be protecting Maggie every minute until this is settled. No one is going to get past me."

"Even if it means risking your own neck?"

"There's no halfway about security. An explosion goes off or it doesn't and there's no way to take a bullet halfway, Ms. Kincade."

"I hope you mean that. Because if anything happens to Maggie—"

Jared heard the break in her voice. "We're doing all we can. Unfortunately, there aren't enough facts for us to be sure of anything right now."

She rubbed her neck, spreading a line of dirt beneath her ear and paying no attention whatsoever. "So what *do* you know, Commander?"

In just a few moments Jared had come to know many things about Faith Kincade. She could be a tigress when her principles or her design skills were called into question. She also appeared to be fiercely loyal to her cousins and prone to meddling when she thought it was necessary. There was an easy way to find out if she had any other information she wasn't telling him.

Jared leaned closer. "You've got some dirt on your neck." Calmly he brushed at the long black smudge and concentrated on Faith Kincade.

He slipped under the irritation and the bravado to find shadows and an old sadness. Another swift brush left Jared with the impression that the source of that sadness was a man, but he probed no deeper, unwilling to uncover secrets that did not involve Maggie.

He stepped back. "Maggie's father is involved."

"We were told her father is dead."

"According to official reports. As you know, his remains were never conclusively identified."

Faith Kincade's dirty fingers drummed restlessly on an overturned terra-cotta pot. "Do *you* believe that he's alive?"

Jared made an impatient movement with his hand. "What I believe is irrelevant. Someone has been watching Maggie, stalking her and harassing her. Either he suspects that Maggie has something of value, or he feels that she is the best way of getting at her father, who they think is still alive."

Faith went pale. "How are you going to stop him?"

"I'm going to stay with her. I'm going to watch her and keep her safe, even when it makes her madder than hell."

Faith turned to pace the small room. "She was so excited about this trip to England." Faith sighed. "Now this."

"What was her father like?"

Faith made a hard, flat sound. "He could be funny and charming. There isn't a stone he couldn't identify or a facet he couldn't make better. But he was reckless and irresponsible with those who loved him most and I'll never forgive him for that."

"You don't appear to have trouble speaking your mind."

Something came and went in her eyes, and then she shrugged. "Don't change the subject. We're talking about Maggie. She has the true Kincade stubbornness, and she wouldn't take a penny from any of us. His debts were *her* responsibility, and she meant to handle them herself."

Jared frowned. "So she sold his inventory, painful or not."

"How did you know that?"

"Because I was there. I saw her do it. An amazing sight, it was." Jared remembered exactly how she'd looked in black silk and gray pearls. It wasn't something a man would ever forget.

Faith eyed him closely. "You must be the one who threw the reporter out the door."

Jared smiled, not saying a word.

"For the record, she hasn't had many men in her life, Commander. She's not like Chessa, our cousin, who must have been through half the New York City phone book. Strictly the *better* half, of course." Faith stared into Jared's eyes, as if trying to probe his mind and heart. "Take care of her, Commander."

"I intend to."

"Good." Her head tilted. A devilish gleam shot through her eyes. "And for the record, I'm glad you two are together."

"I didn't say that—"

"You didn't need to. It's written all over your face. Just treat her right, so I don't have to come back and cripple you for life."

Jared hid a smile. He had to be a foot taller, yet she was issuing the threats. "I'll keep it in mind, Ms. Kincade."

"Faith," she corrected. "Something tells me we're going to be close. Maybe even family. Now I'd better scram. If Maggie finds me interfering, you and I will *both* be in serious trouble."

Her boots squished softly as she padded over the lawn and back toward the drive.

Ten minutes later, Jared looked up and felt his heart kick. Maggie was walking over the grass in blue jeans and a skimpy white shirt, with her hair floating out around her.

His knees went weak at the sight of her.

He tossed down his gloves and crossed the last distance, pulling her into his arms. "Good morning," he said softly, bringing her palm to his mouth.

"It is now. You should have wakened me."

"Impossible. Not unless I had solder and pliers to sell. You were working hard in your sleep."

"Well, I'm not working now." She brought her hands to his chest. "Are you?"

"No," he said huskily, seduced beyond measure by her voice, by the brush of her hands. "Maggie, no matter what happened last night—"

"You think it was a mistake?"

"Never a mistake." He stopped and tried again. "Damn it, there are reasons we shouldn't be involved," he said, trying one last time to be sane while his mind slowly turned into sawdust.

"You don't turn into a werewolf at midnight, do you? Will you dreeenk my blood?"

Even now she could make him forget the darkness and laugh like a blind, love-struck boy.

Jared looked down to see a black blob launched at his foot. The blob barked once, then attacked Maggie's knee with furious exuberance.

"Down, Max."

The puppy gave another high, straining leap.

"Don't yell at him, Jared. He's lonely."

"He's not lonely, he's dangerous." Jared frowned as another gob of puppy saliva covered his shoe. "Down, Max," he ordered. "Go find your own friend. This one's already taken."

Somewhere up the hill a door opened. They heard Marston's call, then a low whistle. Max ran around them once, then streaked off, ears back and tail flapping.

"Who'd have thought Max was such a fair-weather friend?" Maggie said, laughing.

"No, just a realist. He's probably gone off in search of food. He had filet mignon for breakfast today. Marston's spoiling him rotten."

"Prim, proper Marston? Another tough guy with a heart of gold," Maggie whispered, nuzzling Jared's ear.

"Are you suggesting that I . . . "

"Absolutely." Her hands slid around his neck, and she pressed her body against him, tantalizing and slow. "Got a problem with that, MacNeill?"

He tried to think. He tried to breathe. Suddenly complicated brain processes were entirely beyond him. "Problem?" he repeated blankly.

Then he put all his reservations behind him and bent his

head slowly, knowing she expected speed and fury. Instead he brought her racing tenderness and the gentle brush of his palm on the curve of her breast. He was determined to be different, the man she would always remember.

He cupped her face with his palm. "You make me feel savage. Maybe you *should* worry about what happens when the moon rises."

"In that case, I guess I'll be giving blood early this year." She bit gently at his lip. "Or maybe I'll do some conquest of my own."

"No need. You've already seduced, invaded, and conquered completely. I'd given up, Maggie." He trapped her mouth for a hungry kiss that had them both breathless.

No reservations. No regrets.

The sunlight was a drifting, physical presence around them as he caressed the fine line of her cheek. "I've waited too long to feel this way," he whispered.

"What way?"

"Remembering old dreams, dreams I was absolutely certain were dead. Don't ask me why, Maggie. Don't even ask me how. Feeling this way is enough. So I'm damned well going to enjoy it. I'm going to see that you do, too." The words came roughly against her cheek, her brow.

Maggie looked up at him. Her heart took several swift, jerky beats that only intensified the sense that she'd been dunked deep and stripped of air. "Jared, there was something I was supposed to tell you. Nicholas. He's inside—" She closed her eyes. Tried to think. "He said—never mind what he said. Just kiss me."

His eyes glinted like silver sent to the flow point. "That I will," he said roughly. His head bent as he gathered her close. "But you'd better hold on, my love, because it's going to be a hot, bumpy ride."

From his sunny office, Nicholas Draycott stared outside, where two people were silhouetted against the old conservatory. Behind him the door opened and a woman stood outlined in sunlight that clung to her golden hair.

"Nicky, are you in here?"

"Right here, love." Nicholas turned, and as always his heart skipped at the sight of his wife.

"I couldn't find you anywhere." Kacey straightened her husband's lapel and smiled as he tugged her into his arms.

"I told you not to come," Nicholas said tensely. "There have been too many problems down here. I don't want you and Genevieve hurt."

"Your daughter is fine, ensconced on a chair in the kitchen with Marston, singing raucous ballads and eating fresh peanut butter cookies." Her words faded on a sigh as he kissed her thoroughly.

When Kacey could breathe properly, she leaned back and tilted her head. "Is Faith right to be worried about Maggie?"

"Maggie couldn't be in better hands than Jared's."

Kacey looked toward the conservatory. "Literally, it would appear."

"They're adults, Kacey. They've both been hurt, but it's time they came back to join the living." After a last glance outside, he took his wife's hand and led her to the door. "Let's rescue Marston before Genevieve talks him out of our best champagne and all his life's savings. Then you two are heading back to London within the hour."

"Genevieve can be dreadfully persuasive," Kacey said thoughtfully. "What poor male will be able to keep up with her?"

"We have at least two decades for me to get used to the idea of her growing up. With any luck, nunneries will be back in style by then."

Chapter 29

TEXTURES, MAGGIE THOUGHT DREAMILY.

Color and shimmering heat. Metals that melted and flowed beneath her fingers.

Jared was all of that to her.

She realized then exactly how deep she'd fallen for this man of quiet strength and granite honor. There would never be another to show her such worlds, such pleasures, Maggie knew. Sighing, she closed her eyes, her forehead to his chest while she accepted the reality of all he'd come to mean to her.

Planned or not, safe or not, her heart was given. She took a slow breath, wondering if he could read all those thoughts too.

Her eyes opened. "Were you . . . reading me?"

His eyes narrowed. "Every second."

"Irritating man." She smiled slowly and filled her mind, her hands rising to his broad shoulders.

Jared tensed as the images spilled through him in hot, graphic detail.

Her hands on his naked back. Her body as she shed the last of her clothes and eased around him, taking him completely into her heat. No regrets. No limits.

Their lips met, hungry and searching. "See Maggie," she said breathlessly. "See Maggie tear off the man's nice shirt. Even that luscious kilt he's wearing so well." Then she pulled him down for a kiss that had Jared tottering between laughter and curses.

"Oh, Lord, I forgot about Nicholas. He wanted to see

you.'' She eased away and ran a shaky hand through her hair. ''One look at me and he'll know everything.''

''He probably knows already. It's one of his more annoying traits. What he hasn't guessed already, Marston will have told him.'' Jared cradled her face. ''I'll go deal with Nicholas. Why don't you find Marston and track down the champagne and strawberries I asked him for? I'm starved and you must be, too. Then we'll go down to the Witch's Pool.''

Nicholas was pacing in the foyer, his hands deep in his pockets.

''Sorry, I was delayed.'' Jared's smile faded as he took in Nicholas's tension. ''It must be important if you came down from London.''

''Marston just had two phone calls from a Dr. Mac-Namara in London. She was looking for you.''

Jared shrugged. ''She was one of my medical debriefing team. An unpleasant woman.''

''Odd that she'd phone now. Still, we have bigger problems. I had a long visit this morning from a contact in Whitehall. The consensus is that Maggie should be brought in for questioning. All to be done most informally, of course,'' he added in a tone of bitterness.

Jared's fists opened and closed. He wouldn't let them get their claws into Maggie. He knew too well what they were capable of, and she had been hurt enough. ''What set them off?''

''My contact doesn't have any details, and no one will talk to me in an official capacity. Apparently, I've angered the wrong people by refusing to cancel this exhibition.''

''Maggie could fight this,'' Jared said angrily. ''Go public. And with experienced legal advice she could hold off proceedings for weeks.''

''It could be done.'' Nicholas looked away. ''But if she fights them, everything will come out in the press. The media interest would increase even more until they had a frenzy with the story. There would be no hope of the exhibition continuing.'' The viscount's eyes narrowed on the sunny lawn. ''We're proposing direct sponsorship of the

Royal family and participation by all the major cultural branches. The British Museum is very interested, especially if we can corral topflight sponsors. That means security is bound to be a question, and quite legitimately so. But the people handling security happen to be the same ones who want Maggie brought in for questioning. If we don't play, they don't play.''

Jared cursed. "I won't sit by and watch her picked apart. Can't they get their answers without terrifying a young woman with no blame in the matter?''

"Apparently not. Though I'm of the clear opinion that this business goes far beyond the theft her father was accused of.''

"So am I, but I still can't prove it. There might be some new technology involved, something Kincade was working on when he disappeared. Meanwhile, we both know Maggie's not up to a tough interrogation, and I doubt they'll be in any mood for kid gloves.'' Jared ran a finger over the framed map above Nicholas's desk. His gaze fell on the red coves bordering the North Sea. "I'll have to take her away. We'll leave today, before they come looking here.''

"I'm afraid I have to agree.'' Nicholas reached across his desk and searched through a stack of papers. "I've got some contacts prepared for you.''

"How long do we have?''

"Two days, maybe more, but I'd feel better if you were off within the hour. I'll hold them off as long as possible.'' His eyes darkened. "There's something else you should know. I've been looking into that name Maggie used the night she arrived here.''

Jared had almost forgotten. He frowned. "Gina? Glenda?''

"Gwynna.'' Nicholas gently unfolded a yellowing sheet of paper. "I found this old sketch in the library.'' Sunlight danced on an oval face and brilliant eyes. "You remember the necklace we found plastered behind the wall of the wine cellar?'' He pulled a box from his desk and gently opened the lid. Sunlight played over tarnished silver and a dozen bright blue diamonds.

"That's it?''

Nicholas nodded. "It will be spectacular when the settings have been properly cleaned and repaired." He frowned. "But I don't want Maggie to see it yet."

"Why not?"

"Because the abbey records show it was made by the daughter of the fifth viscount, a supercilious man with great influence at court. He was not a pleasant man, by all descriptions. His chief interests in life were politics and securing more wealth than anyone else in England. It seems that he left his daughter entirely on her own here."

"A common enough story."

"True, but she appears to have been remarkable for the standards of the time. She traveled to Venice, ostensibly for the Grand Tour, but in fact she found a master craftsman to teach her metalwork. That would have been no easy trick for a woman in those days."

Jared felt a hard knot forming at his neck. "What happened to her?"

"There were few records after her return. She appears to have made a dozen pieces of jeweled plate for the abbey's household collection and a few items of jewelry for her own use."

"You're not answering my question, Nicholas."

"What happened is she died. Right out there by the moat." Nicholas stared at the restless water. "The records suggest she was harboring a wounded political fugitive at the time. A traitor from north of the Tweed."

"A *Scotsman*?" Jared found he could barely breathe.

"So it seems. A force was sent from London, but she slipped out an hour earlier, seeing him off to safety. I'm afraid she wasn't so lucky herself." Nicholas turned. "She was shot by an advance guard who'd come looking for her fugitive. There was talk that he had a fortune in jewels meant to be carried to France, to purchase support for the Scottish cause."

Each word burned into Jared's head with searing pain. *Jewels. Shot.*

"They found her body on the grass beside the stone bridge," Nicholas said grimly. "It was said that a rose grew up in the exact spot where she fell, its petals streaked with a curious red mark that resembled blood.''

''What was her name?''

''It could all be coincidence, you know. Possibly some sort of mistake. Records weren't always kept so carefully in that era.''

Jared fought to breathe. ''Tell me her *name*.''

Nicholas drew a long breath. ''Gwynna. Lady Gwynna of Draycotte. And I have every reason to believe that she made this necklace. The same necklace that Maggie was trying to find that night she walked in her sleep.''

Upstairs Maggie turned slowly in the sunlight.

She ran a hand through her hair and straightened her simple black chemise beneath a choker of hammered platinum.

Strange to be so happy after so long.

Stranger still to feel at ease *here*.

She turned slowly, studying her face in a small gilt mirror. Would anyone else notice the faint glow of her cheeks? Was her happiness visible? Somehow the abbey no longer seemed to oppress her with its stillness and shadows. Or perhaps she was simply too distracted to notice.

She caught up her tool case and swept a last glance over the Constable landscapes and mahogany end tables. They were *things* now, only things. There was no more menace in their beauty.

She laughed as a black shape shot around the open door and launched its stubby body at her feet. ''So now you remember me, Max. Just like a man to be so fickle.''

Marston panted down the hall and caught the puppy in gentle fingers. ''He got away from me twice, the rascal. I was just going to take him out for a walk when the telephone rang downstairs. The call is for you, a curator from the British Museum.''

Though business was the last thing Maggie wanted to think about, she picked up the phone, while Marston closed the door softly behind her.

''This is Maggie Kincade.'' There was only a soft electric hum. ''Hello?'' she repeated.

She heard a slow indrawn breath, then a soft voice. Perhaps a voice masked behind a cloth.

"You are Maggie Kincade?"

Something stirred the tiny hairs behind her neck. "Yes, that's right. Who is this?"

"Are you alone?" The softness slid away, replaced by tension. "Completely alone?"

Maggie hesitated. "Who *are* you?"

In the background a car door slammed and traffic roared past. *He must be at an outdoor phone box.* Her hands tightened on the phone. "Are you still there?"

"I'm here. I've been here for too long, Maggie, my love." Something rustled across the line, the sound of stiff cloth being pulled free. "Perhaps this sounds clearer."

Maggie stiffened. That soft, rolling voice. The flattened vowels of a Boston boyhood.

But the man who'd spoken that way had died somewhere in a Sumatran jungle, and she had the blackened passport to prove it.

Sweat covered her palms as she gripped the phone tighter. "Who are you? What do you want?"

"To protect you, Maggie. I've always tried to protect you, you must believe that."

She closed her mind, refusing to listen. *"No."*

"I know it's painful. I didn't want the news to come this way, little peach."

Not that name. Not the name that only Daniel Kincade had used.

"I truly wish there was some better way to break this to you, but there isn't. You're in danger, Maggie. It's far bigger than you or I know. Otherwise I would have let them go on thinking I was dead," he said harshly. "No matter how much it hurt."

What about me? she wanted to scream. *How could you let me believe that you were gone?*

She couldn't move, couldn't breathe. He had her father's voice, her father's mannerisms, but was this another trick? "Tell me what you were wearing the day you left," she whispered, trying not to hope.

"Testing me, are you? Good girl. You always were sharp."

"*Tell me.*"

"The gray trousers. They were your mother's favorite, God rest her soul. And along with them the Fair Isle sweater that was your gift. And my ugliest old shoes. The ones with the broken laces."

Anyone could have known, she told herself. Whoever had seen him leave or had been with him on that final flight. But her heart began a noisy, painful pounding. "Then why—"

"I've no more time for questions." Behind him Maggie heard the low moan of a siren. "You've got to hide, Maggie. I'm onto two of them, and soon I'll have the whole dirty network. I'll contact you when it's all over. Until then, go somewhere lonely. Use a different name and spend only cash. No credit cards that can be traced."

"But when—"

"Just listen," the voice said angrily. All the easygoing charm was gone now, stripped away from a voice of steel. "Do as I say. That Scotsman of yours ought to know someplace safe."

He knew that, too? "How did you know—"

"No time, little peach. There never was, was there? I was always coming or going. All my fault."

A thousand questions. A thousand things she had to ask. "Why did you go? Why did they say you stole those jewels?" She hated her voice, soft and broken, the words of a confused child instead of the adult she had become.

"I would have spared you that, Maggie, but they left me no choice. They were too close and I had to disappear. When I did, they saw to it that the jewels vanished too. That marked me as a criminal and they were certain they could run me to ground. But they were wrong. I saw to that. I died instead. It was the only way to protect you, Maggie." He bit off an oath. "Now go away. Go today, as soon as you put down this phone. I haven't much time, and they might be closer than I thought." Somewhere came a tapping sound, like the muted crack of gravel on a window. "Damned thugs."

"Daddy?" It hurt to say the word. It hurt even more to believe it could be true.

"God help us if they trace this call." His voice was muffled from pressing tight against the phone. "Listen, just listen, little peach. Do you still have my ring? Anders said he gave it to you."

"I have it."

"Good. Now here's exactly what you must do. It's the only way you and that Scotsman of yours will stay alive."

Past the framed portraits.

Past the polished silver armor.

Maggie walked blindly, aware that all the questions she'd tried to ignore would not be silenced any longer. What was her father up to? Why had he allowed her to think he was dead all these months?

The memories came then. Her mother at Christmas, crying with shock and pleasure at a necklace of pink pearls that Daniel had made. Her father performing his only magic trick, laughing while he made a cabochon emerald disappear into his fist, then emerge from Maggie's ear.

Don't go, Daddy.

Not long, little peach. Not long at all this time.

Voices came from the corridor, low and tense. Jared and Nicholas, she realized.

"There you are, Maggie. Nicholas was just telling me something, and you ought to hear it too."

Dimly she heard Jared's voice, felt his hand at her shoulder. "He called," she whispered. "He said we were in danger."

"Who called?"

Go away, Maggie. Go today, as soon as you put down this phone.

"My father. At least he said he was my father." Her hands were shaking and her throat felt tight. "God help me, I believe him."

She felt the wall behind her, the cold wood of the desk beneath one hand. Suddenly there were different sounds.

Horses, Maggie thought. Black horses with long manes tossed back in the wind. She heard their angry gait, and she might even have heard the thunder that roared above them.

Or was it the lash of muskets?

Then gray bled over her vision, and she was falling toward the floor.

North they had taken her, north where treeless hills rolled down to meet a leaden sea.

At a thatched roof cottage above the loneliest hill they halted. Their leader freed her hands carefully and helped her down.

"What cause have you for care or comfort now?" she demanded as soon as her mouth was freed. "Your courtesies come too late after the battering I've had for two days."

" 'Twas never meant to harm you, my lady. Only to see you brought here safely."

"Pray forgive me if I have my doubts." She tried for the icy hauteur her titled father had taught her well, despite the bits of grass and twigs clinging to her hair. "A fine establishment. No doubt I shall be delightfully comfortable here."

Something played in the man's eyes. Humor, she thought.

"I await you, my lady." He gestured her forward.

She caught her cloak about her and moved forward, stumbling after so long on horseback. Then the door was thrown open before her. A single candle burned behind, outlining a tall shape.

The candle rose, casting golden light on high cheeks and chiseled nose.

Her heart twisted and pitched in her chest. "No," she whispered.

"You knew me full well last year in Venice, my lady." His voice bore the soft, rolling lilt of the Gaelic Isles, but his eyes were filled with wickedness itself.

"It can't be." She stood, wavering, her vision blurred with tears. "I do not believe what I see."

"Believe," he said huskily.

Then she was caught up in hands that were infinitely gentle.

"Do not look away from me. The vows we made in Venice before God are not to be so easily broken, my sweet Gwynna."

"But how did you find me? When my father came to take me home there was no time. He swept me away before I could send you any word."

"I have my ears," he said. *"And many eyes in England."*

She couldn't breathe. Her heart seemed to slip in her chest. "You've found me," she whispered. *"I did not hope for such a miracle."*

"For you I'll work miracles and more. But I am not your lord, Gwynna. Only your husband. And I would claim your rare skill for my country's use now."

As Jared fought her angry fingers, he picked up bits of broken words, and among them was the name Gwynna. With his hands on hers, the images flowed past, filtered through her dreaming mind. With them came her terror and all her pain.

Had the past waited here for them both, restless within the abbey's silent walls? If so, was this a final chance to bring their sadness to an end?

He felt his friend's hand on his shoulder. "You'd better go, Jared. I've spoken to Marston, and you're to borrow his friend's car, since it's less likely to be spotted. Take the back road through the south wood, so you can avoid the drive. No doubt they'll have it watched."

Jared was glad for the cool, clear instructions. His own mind moved like a clock filled with rust. "We will. And thank you."

"It's for me to thank you." Nicholas looked down at Maggie. "Take care of her. In some way she feels like my own blood kin."

They were halfway to Tunbridge when Maggie came awake in a rush of movement, one hand to the window and the other flung wide.

Jared ducked with a curse and barely avoided the bumper

of an overloaded lorry. "Careful, my love. You'll have us both in a ditch."

She blinked. "Jared? Where are we going?"

"There's been a change of plan." Without taking his gaze from the road, he found her hand and linked his fingers tightly with hers. "They've insisted that Nicholas bring you to London for questioning."

"And they'd do more than *talk*, judging by your face."

"It's likely that it would be unpleasant. Now that your father contacted you, their treatment would be harsh. So they won't find us, not for a while at least."

"I never meant for you to be dragged in like this," she whispered.

"Hush." It was soft, but it was an order just the same. His smile returned as he wove deftly past an aging school bus and two dairy vans. "There's a box behind you that comes courtesy of Marston. Take out everything inside it." There was the faintest lift to Jared's lips. "Then you will kindly put them on."

Twenty minutes later it was done.

Maggie's face was hidden beneath a layer of white greasepaint, with two bright red circles at her cheeks. Her honey hair was caught up beneath a wig of carrot-red yarn, and Jared's change was completed soon after.

An hour later when he slowed for a roundabout near Elstow in Bedfordshire, Jared noticed two police officers leaning intently toward the flow of traffic, checking each car and its occupants against a photograph. No one looked twice at the car with the Elite Party Service sign. Nor did the officers pay the slightest heed to the smiling Raggedy Ann and Andy who waved from the front seat.

Chapter 30

HILLS OF GREEN BORDERED THE TWISTING ROAD. FADING sunlight brushed ruined castles and the foundations of medieval abbeys. Mist crept over the wooded valleys as Jared left the main roads at Sheffield and wound north toward the Border country.

"This isn't right." Maggie's shoulders were hunched and tense. "I should have stayed, Jared. I should fight these people face to face."

"That might be honorable," he agreed. "It would also be madness. Your father didn't underestimate these men, and neither can we."

Maggie made an angry sound. "I'm trying to do the right thing. I just can't decide what it is."

Jared raised her palm to his lips. "Stop worrying. Your father appears to be a man who can handle himself."

"Maybe you shouldn't be so good at that intuition of yours."

"I've never seen anything that you need to be ashamed of, my heart."

"Give it time." Maggie sighed, staring down at their locked fingers, trying to put the worry and uncertainty out of her thoughts. "What does it feel like, this thing you do?"

"Painful sometimes. Intrusive always."

"And right now what do you see?"

"Just a shimmer of images in the back of my mind. Faint colors. Sometimes a ripple of sound, almost like voices in a distant room. I'm finally learning to turn down the volume when I need to.''

Maggie brushed his knuckles with her lips. *I love you*, she thought. *Madly.*

"The volume just spiked," Jared said wryly. His voice deepened. "I love you too, Margaret Elizabeth Kincade. More than madly."

"What happens next?"

"We drive and hope we're not followed."

Maggie took a breath, then let it out slowly. A silver river snaked past the broken wall of a vast abbey, each stone a dark giant in the fading light. "I wish I could trust my father, but I don't. He'd come and go too many times over the years. In some ways he might as well be a stranger. Tell me about this place where we're going. Glenbrae, you called it?"

"It's secluded and full of magic, according to Nicholas. Of course most of Scotland is magical if you have the taste for greenery and mist."

Maggie turned her head at the tremor of longing she heard in Jared's voice. "You miss that, don't you?"

"Sometimes. But there was no longer anything to hold me in the village. Or anywhere else in Scotland."

"What about your family?"

"My parents are both gone. My brother . . ." Jared stared into the dark line of the distant mountains. "My brother died at his own hand. The MacNeill gift was more than he could bear."

Maggie's fingers tightened. *I'm here*, she thought. *For as long as you'll have me. Until forever if you want it.*

His fingers laced with hers. "Forever won't be half long enough."

Warmth swirled through Maggie's heart. "I'll hold you to that, Commander. Now tell me about this beautiful glen."

"Green hills and fine dark woods above a pristine loch. The house is thirteenth century. A traditional Scottish tower house with turnpike stairways and all the usual fortifications."

"Fortifications?"

"Window slits. Gun loops and massive walls, built to hold out rival clans or generally nasty neighbors. Fighting was a way of life back then."

Maggie hid a shudder. "No dungeons, I hope. And no wars now either."

"Only the tourism wars, waged for hard cash. Glenbrae House does well enough in that area, I believe. Nicholas says that visitors come back again and again for its thatched roof and the roses that bloom far into autumn on the mild west coast. Thankfully, the owners are obsessive about period authenticity."

"They're expecting us?"

Jared nodded. "For safety, we'll have to use different names, of course."

"That's what my father said." More deception, Maggie thought. More danger to innocent strangers who shouldn't be involved. She tried to calm her thoughts, knowing Jared would read her clearly. "Do you think he managed to cover our tracks?"

Shadows touched Jared's face. "If not," he said grimly, "we'll know it soon enough."

Hope O'Hara MacLeod stood in the sunlight beneath Glenbrae House's high cantilevered ceiling. On the table in front of her, bows of red raffia twisted around wreaths of holly, and stockings of antique lace lay ready to grace the inn's broad mantel. A fire hissed happily, casting golden light over the walls of her tiny office.

Hope was well pleased with the inn she had made and well pleased with the happiness she had found in this quiet corner of Scotland.

Dozens of guests had stayed beneath Glenbrae House's thatched roof, but her favorites had been Nicholas Draycott and his family. Even now it was hard to believe a year had passed since their visit.

Hope frowned at the phone as static swallowed the voice on the other end of the line. "Hello? Yes, I'm here, Nicholas. And we'll be delighted to receive your two visitors. You say they're arriving tomorrow?"

"Probably late in the day, though I can't be certain."

There was something in his voice that made Hope wait for him to be more specific.

The viscount cleared his throat. "Two people. Will Cameron and Annie, his wife."

Hope repeated the names, marking them in her careful hand in the registry. "Will they have special interests while they're here? Salmon fishing or deer stalking?"

"None of that." His voice tightened. "All they wish is a few weeks of quiet. No telephones, no curiosity. And no people asking questions, I hope."

So that was it.

Hope felt his tension reach across the phone, and she wondered what sort of problems brought the two travelers to Glenbrae. But she had good reason to trust this man completely. "Easy enough to arrange. I'll see that they're put in our quietest room. As it happens, we've no one else here but a pair of retired schoolteachers from Holland." Again the silence hung. "Is there anything else I need to know?"

"A great deal, I should think, but Will Cameron will tell you everything when he arrives. My regards to MacLeod. Tell him I'm counting on some excellent fishing in the spring."

Hope smiled. "He'll be delighted to oblige you."

"He still has that great broadsword hanging in the hall, does he?"

"I'm looking at it now."

"Excellent." On that somewhat obscure comment, the viscount hung up.

Hope was still frowning by the sunny front window when the sword's owner strode into her office. His broad shoulders nearly filled the doorway, and his laughter crackled warmly in the narrow room. "More guests to claim your time, is it? By all the saints, woman, I'm tempted to drag you off to the loch. There I might at least find a minute or two alone with you."

Hope smiled as she always did when Ronan MacLeod looked at her just so, and her heart gave its customary lurch. "But you wouldn't need to drag me, love. I'd come away with you on an instant's notice."

The Scotsman's scarred hands slid into her hair, and he pulled her against him with a fire that amazed her, considering how they had spent the hours before dawn. "I love you, Hope MacLeod. Never doubt this for an instant."

"How could I, when you have such inventive ways of showing me?"

His hand slid lower, curved protectively below her waist. "Have you felt a stirring yet?"

"Impatient man. It will be weeks yet. Maybe even months." Abruptly Hope went still, her eyes very wide.

"What is it?" her husband demanded.

"There." It came again, the faintest hint of tiny feet or restless arms. "He moved, Ronan. Almost as if he heard your voice."

"Or *she*," he corrected. "A heartbreaker with her mother's smile and strange modern ways."

Their hands linked, cradling Hope's softly rounded stomach. "Modern ways that suited *you* well enough, Crusader."

"Aye, so they did. So they *do*."

Hope let her head rest on his shoulder. Already she was sorting through practical questions of linens, silverware, and pastry. There would be flowers to pick, meals to plan. "Blast, I almost forgot about dinner tomorrow. I'll have to tell the Wishwells we won't be able to join them after all."

MacLeod sniffed. "I doubt you need bother." He thought of the three spry sisters who lived in a tiny cottage at the foot of the loch. "They'll find out even before you want them to. That seems to be a particular gift with them."

"Someone's coming."

Morwenna Wishwell bent closer to the window. She was a tiny lady, with white hair and eyes of shocking robin's egg blue. They seemed to dart back and forth across the glen, missing nothing, strikingly young in a face pale and lined with age. She skimmed the misted window with one palm, gazing to the south. "Two of them."

"Who's coming?" Her sister Honoria, plump and red cheeked, rocked in a chair before the fire with a white cat sleeping in her lap.

"Someone important. I can see that." Morwenna Wishwell stroked the silver brooch at her neck. "They are vulnerable." Her lips lifted. "Very much in love, it seems." Once again she smoothed the brooch. "You try, Perpetua."

The tallest of the three, Perpetua Wishwell stared out into the gathering twilight. "I feel it also." There was something oddly compelling in her eyes as they searched the horizon. Beyond the snug cottage an owl called sharply, echoed by the sharp bark of a fox.

Perpetua nodded slowly. "I hear the wind which brings closings after long centuries and a finish to an old mystery. We must be honored this will take place here in our glen." Her lips curved in the ghost of a smile. "But then we are singularly skilled for managing such things. This time we will not need Adrian's assistance."

Morwenna leaned forward. "He's coming to Glenbrae?"

"Not without our summoning."

Morwenna murmured a low phrase, and orange sparks shot in a noisy dance up the chimney.

"Do stop that, Morwenna." Perpetua frowned. "In a moment you'll have the cottage burned down around us."

Morwenna shrugged. "I like to see the sparks, Pet. Besides, I'm cold. Winter's come full well. Can't you hear the wind howling?"

All three fell quiet, listening. Above the wind they heard another sound, low and muffled. It might have been the distant drone of a car traveling fast or it might have been angry voices carried on the gusting air.

"Coming from the south," Perpetua said slowly. "Now, as they did long years before, while danger followed. Two of them I see. But others are soon to come." The fire hissed up in angry sparks and Perpetua sighed. "Come then, my dears. If this danger is real, we have much work to do."

Back and forth the road snaked, past circles of prehistoric stone, gaunt trees, and fallen gravestones. Maggie drowsed, caught in fitful dreams, then awoke to keep Jared company. He drove fast, but not excessively so, forced often to slow for mist or crossing sheep. Just after dawn he pulled to the road's edge and stretched lazily, enjoying a view that had changed little for centuries.

Maggie stood beside him. "It's beautful."

"So it is. I've forgotten how these quiet hills can stir the blood." The sun climbed over the jagged walls of a ruined castle and painted the loch a coppery red. Their hamper was empty, but thanks to Marston's preparations they had eaten extremely well. Maggie had taken the wheel on two occasions, though she found driving on the opposite side of the road a harrowing experience.

From Jared there was never a complaint. He was calm, unflappable.

Professional.

Maggie could only bleed at the thought, for she realized how hard-won all his calm had been. She turned, fitting her body to his. "Tired?"

"A little. But we don't have much farther to go. Two hours or a bit less, I estimate, though the roads may be tricky as we work north."

"In that case, I won't offer to drive."

"I'll manage." He gathered her against him, enjoying how dawn painted her hair with sparks of red and gold. "Worrying again?"

Maggie shook her head. She wouldn't give in to fear. Meanwhile, she was making no attempt to hide the tenderness she felt at Jared's touch.

Not that she would have succeeded, when their hands were linked so tightly.

"I have a bone to pick with you, Commander."

One dark brow rose. "This sounds serious."

"Deadly. As I recall, you once mentioned small cars. Something about performance statistics."

"You tempt me sorely. But when I have you, Maggie love, it will be in a proper bed with a roof over our heads."

What he meant, Maggie thought bleakly, was when they were at Glenbrae. When they were safe from pursuit.

An hour later, as sunlight glinted over glen and byrne, Jared sat forward, pointing down to a slender loch and a

gray stone tower house that beckoned in the distance. "I
believe that's Glenbrae House before us."

The house was older than Maggie had expected, weathered walls rising to a roof of immaculately tended thatch.
To the north, mist drifted past steep cliffs, mirrored in the
dark loch, and the air was heavy with the scent of pine
trees. It was a place of magic, Maggie thought, watching
smoke plume from the high chimney.

She drew a long breath, praying they would be safe here.

Jared stopped the car before a winding stone fence.
"Don't go back and forth over it, Maggie. It's best this
way. It gives Nicholas time to bargain with Whitehall,
while your father does the things he must."

"Do you believe it is really my father?"

"If anyone would know the voice, it's you, my love. He
may also be playing a deeper game than you imagine," he
warned gently.

Maggie squared her shoulders, studying the precise angles of the thatched roof. "I've tried to prepare myself. I
know the truth may be a shock, but I simply want the questions put to rest." She took Jared's arm as he helped her
from the car. "Right now I refuse to think about anything
else but stripping off this ugly wig and washing off this
greasepaint. I doubt that anyone will be looking for us
here." Abruptly her breath caught. "We weren't followed,
were we?"

Jared sent a last glance over the misty hills. "Not a
chance. I would have noticed."

The proprietor of Glenbrae House was waiting for them
as they came up the walk. If Hope MacLeod was surprised
at her visitors' dress, she was careful not to show it. She
spoke with easy friendship as she welcomed them to a cozy
room where firelight glinted off polished wood and colorful
chintz.

"Lunch will be ready shortly. If you prefer to eat upstairs, that will be easily managed. You've had quite a journey, I understand, Mr. Cameron. You might want to clean
up, too."

"Nicholas gave you our names, did he?" Jared stood
tensely.

"He phoned last night to confirm your arrival. He sounded somewhat anxious."

"We were in a rush to get away." Jared gestured at their clothing. "As for this, well, it's rather a long story."

"There's no need to explain, I assure you. My husband will bring in your baggage, but why don't I show you to your room first?" She hesitated. "Lord Draycott said you wanted to be undisturbed."

Jared heard the question in her voice. "We're hoping for privacy, yes." Then with a soft oath, he turned back. "No, that's not the entire truth. You're entitled to know everything. People may be following us, and for reasons too complicated to explain, we don't wish to be found if anyone comes asking."

"So I gathered." Hope considered them, then nodded. "A favor asked by Lord Draycott is a difficult thing to refuse."

"Don't I know it," Jared muttered.

"Put your mind at rest. If the cavalry attacks, my husband will simply beat them off with his broadsword."

Jared's eyes narrowed. "He knows how to handle a broadsword?"

"Amazingly well. Almost like a true native of the Middle Ages." Hope's eyes crinkled at some secret bit of humor. "Now if you'll follow me, your rooms are just up these stairs, and everything's ready for you. I think you'll find the moonlight above the loch superb tonight."

"What were they like?"

Ronan MacLeod paced before the fire, all curiosity, his dark hair windblown from his hike up the glen. To his regret, he'd been caught laying a new section of roof for the Wishwell sisters, and he'd missed meeting the new guests.

"Very nice, for all they arrived in full clown costume. They said they may be followed, Ronan. There could be danger, just as Nicholas hinted."

"If Lord Draycott is involved, they're to be trusted," Ronan MacLeod said with no hint of hesitation. "No one will disturb them here, or I break my vow as a knight of St. Julian.''

Hope rested a soft finger at his lips. ''No more a knight. Now you are a simple twentieth-century man, my love.''

''Not simple, I hope,'' he muttered. ''Were I that, you'd be bored inside a day.''

Hope's head tilted. ''One thing you will never be is boring, my love.'' Her eyes narrowed. ''And unless I'm mistaken, Nicholas Draycott sounded worried. He wanted to be sure that you still had that broadsword in the hall.''

''A mystery,'' her husband said slowly, more curious than ever to see the new arrivals.

Chapter 31

THE BEDROOM WAS HIGH, NESTLED BENEATH THE SLOPING thatch, where it looked out over the whole length of the loch. Candles glinted on the side tables as the last blood-red tinge of sunlight danced off the windows and lit the polished wood floor.

It was a room rich with history, Maggie thought. A place warm with the love of the generations who had lived here.

Maggie awoke locked in Jared's arms. The soft *whoosh* of falling snow brought her fully awake. She tilted her head, peering through the frosted glass pane, and through the haze she saw a pristine world of white and silver, where snow blanketed the glen.

Maggie made out the stone fence and the dark detail of a hedgerow. Farther to the north, something moved toward the loch, a small shape against the snow.

Maggie frowned. It almost resembled a great gray cat, the same animal she had seen at Draycott. Impossible, of course. The abbey was miles away, and no animal could have made that journey.

The linens rustled. A heartbeat later, Jared's strong body moved against her.

She turned slowly. Her hand opened on his chest. *Good morning.*

"That it is. And it's still early." His hand traced her ribs and the gentle curve of her stomach. "Far too early to be up and about."

His mouth moved slowly down her shoulder, skimmed her waist, then nuzzled the tangled caramel curls at her thighs. "Far too early to think of leaving bed," he said hoarsely.

Maggie's laughter caught in a sound of surprise.

Then she thought no more about snow or gray cats or the father who had brought her so much pain.

When Hope answered the knock at the kitchen door an hour after dawn, she had flour up to her elbows and sugar in her hair. Relics of her current baking project—three dozen chocolate scones and a dozen tea cakes.

She found the Wishwell sisters standing on her doorstep.

"Sorry if we're too early." Morwenna Wishwell tugged her shawl closer about her shoulders, her eyes bright with excitement. "We couldn't wait, you see."

"Come in before you freeze."

The three sisters roamed through the warm kitchen. "I do so love the smell of baking scones," Honoria said. "It reminds me of when I was young and a certain dashing clansman from Skye—"

"No reminiscing," Perpetua said briskly. "Remember why we're here."

Honoria flushed. "Of course. It was just the snow, bringing everything back."

Hope intervened, sliding a plate of heated scones before them, then settled in a chair before the fire, rubbing at a streak of flour on her neck.

"And where is the MacLeod this bright morning?" Morwenna asked.

"He's gone up the glen. He heard gunshots in the night, he says." Hope frowned. "I suspect it was nothing beyond the backfire of a car. Sometimes the noise disturbs his sleep."

Perpetua nodded gravely. "He is right to check the hills. Strange things are brewing this day. When does he return?"

"Any time now." Hope sat up straighter, remembering the call from Nicholas Draycott. "Why, is something wrong?"

"Not yet," Perpetua said. "Actually, we've come to offer our cottage to your new guests."

"You've met them?" Hope's eyes widened.

"We saw them arrive yesterday. They seemed a romantic pair, and we wondered if they would like more privacy at our cottage."

"It would be no chore," Morwenna said eagerly. "I'd love to lend a hand here with the cooking, since your young French chef is away visiting her family. And there are all those lovely lace angels to be finished for the Christmas tree. We could all help."

"I don't know." Hope shifted uneasily in her chair. What were the three old sisters about now?

Just then footsteps rang on the path and the door banged open. "What do I find here, a *ceilidh* so early in the morning? Or has the Glenbrae Investment Club decided to meet to ponder some grand new stock acquisition?" Ronan MacLeod stamped into the room, bringing snow and life and crackling vitality. Icy white flakes dotted his hair and shoulders, and his cheeks had a ruddy glow from an hour spent stalking the high hills.

Hope itched to slip into his arms for a kiss, but somehow she resisted, though she suspected her three visitors knew the cost to her willpower.

Perpetua rose to her feet, frowning. "You've been checking the glen, so your wife says. Have you found any poachers in the snow?"

"Not a soul. Any sensible person would be at home enjoying fresh scones with friends before a roaring fire."

Some of the tension seemed to go out of Perpetua's angular face. "Good. The hills will bear watching, even in this snow."

"You mean they might come here this soon?" Morwenna clasped her hands anxiously. "But we thought—"

"Never mind what we thought," Perpetua snapped. " 'Tis of no interest to our friends." She gazed out at the dark face of the loch, as if gathering her thoughts. "The fact is, we've come to offer our cottage to your new arrivals, if they'll have it. It's small, but cozy, and we thought they might like more privacy."

"Oh, did you? And what gave you that thought?" Ronan asked, laughter in his eyes. "Will you tell me it was the same thing that had you checking the loch road last month when those two travelers were stranded in the storm?''

''A bit of coincidence,'' Perpetua said, shrugging.

''Coincidence, do you call it? And what of the load of schoolchildren left stranded by the peat bog when their driver fell weak with the influenza?''

''A lucky guess. We'd been watching the bus from the window and noticed it had stopped moving.''

''Is that a fact?'' Ronan rubbed his jaw. ''For myself, I would have thought you had no view of that stretch of bog from where your cottage lies.''

Perpetua jammed her hands into her pockets. ''It's certain that you're wrong. And you haven't said what you think of our idea.''

Ronan laid a hand on Hope's shoulder. ''I think it best to tell them, my heart. They'll nose out the truth soon enough.''

''Tell us what?'' Morwenna studied them, all curiosity.

Hope sighed. ''It seems that our guests may be in some danger.''

''Danger?'' Honoria pushed to her feet in a whoosh of beautifully muted tartan. ''Then they *must* come down to the cottage. It's much harder to find than Glenbrae. Besides, who would think to look for them there?''

Ronan's eyes narrowed, searching her face.

''Trust us,'' Perpetua said. ''It will be *much* better for them there.'' She made a slight gesture with her hand. ''And who knows, an early storm might cut the glen off from the outside altogether.''

Morwenna drew a sharp breath. ''Pet, do you really think—''

''What I think is that they must leave immediately. We've plenty of food set aside,'' Perpetua continued briskly, ''and it would be a pleasure for us to come here to Glenbrae House. Don't try to pretend that this isn't your busiest time of year, with Christmas on the way.''

Hope made an uncertain sound. ''It seems wrong. They've just arrived here as our guests, after all.''

''It could be that our friends are right.'' Ronan rubbed his jaw. ''Searchers would come here first as the obvious choice. That would give us time to send them about their business.''

Morwenna gave a lilting laugh. ''With your broadsword raised, I hope. I do so love it when you swing it through the air and sunlight catches on the blade. You always had a rare gift with the sword, MacLeod of Glenbrae.''

Hope frowned. ''I can't just ask a pair of guests to leave.''

''You'd like us to *leave*?'' Maggie and Jared stood staring at them in dismay from the hallway. ''Is something wrong?'' Jared asked.

Hope shot to her feet. ''Nothing of the sort. I trust that you slept well. We didn't want to wake you after your long drive. I'll have breakfast directly, if you'd like to sit in the breakfast room before the fire.''

''No, my love,'' Ronan said quietly. ''I think it better if our guests sit here while we discuss this matter over hot scones and tea.'' He looked at the unsmiling man behind Maggie. ''You will be Will Cameron?'' His eyes narrowed. ''Fine wool though it is, that is no Cameron sett you wear.''

''No, it is not,'' Jared said stiffly. ''I fear we have brought danger to your house.'' He held out his hand. ''I am Jared MacNeill.'' The two men shook hands, and as they did, Jared seemed to stiffen, his eyes intent on MacLeod's face.

But before he could speak, Morwenna was guiding him to a chair before the fire, with Maggie beside him. ''You see,'' she said quickly, ''it was all *our* idea. We thought you might like more privacy, so we offered the use of our cottage. We're beyond this side of the loch, you see, and not at all visible from the main road. Since we understand you're in some . . . difficulty, we hope you'll accept our offer.''

Jared rubbed his neck and glanced at Maggie. ''But we couldn't put you out of your home.''

''Nonsense,'' Perpetua said briskly. ''We've been yearning to get our hands on the Christmas decorations for months now, and this will give us a fine excuse.''

Maggie looked at Jared. ''It might work,'' he said slowly.

"Then you'll come and have a look." Perpetua filled their cups with steaming tea. "But not until you finish these lovely scones that Hope has made, and with them a nice cup of Darjeeling. I believe the mist will have lifted by then."

Honoria nodded. "Yes, the mist definitely will have lifted," she said firmly.

The little cottage was nestled into the curve of the high hills, as cozy as Perpetua Wishwell had promised. Long oak beams ran the length of the snug kitchen above the cheerful snap of a fire, and copper pots glittered on a wall filled with potted herbs.

Tartans lit every corner, and at the top of the stairs, a large guest bedroom perfectly suited to their needs overlooked the cliffs to the north.

Maggie stood in the doorway and listened to the gentle whistle of the wind around the eaves. "It's lovely," she admitted, running a hand over the thick down comforter. "The furniture looks very old."

"Positively ancient," Morwenna confided. "In fact it's—"

Honoria cleared her throat. "We've already prepared food. The pantry is full of stews and fresh bread, so you'll be snug here with no need to go out for anything."

A fluffy white cat jumped to the bed and brushed against Maggie's palm, purring loudly.

"Don't worry about Chloe. She generally keeps to herself, don't you, my love?" The cat moved to Perpetua and gave a low meow, then leaped to the floor and raced down the corridor.

"Is everything settled then?" Perpetua asked briskly. "I think it would be the answer to your problem. No one is likely to seek you up here."

Jared laid one hand on the marble mantel. There was energy here, energy such as he had never felt before. It was a quiet, timeless force, like moonlight on a field in winter. When he had shaken hands with Morwenna Wishwell, he had had a brief flash of noise in his head, like the pounding rush of a waterfall. Even now as he studied the room he had the impression of colors and faint movement at the corner of his eyes.

But no amount of focusing could bring the images any closer.

Maggie took Jared's hand. "It would be nice here. And it would be secluded."

Jared nodded. "If you're certain it will be no inconvenience."

"Not a bit." Perpetua smiled broadly. "We'll collect our things and be off right now, if that suits you." She turned to the window. "Chloe? Where *has* that cat gone?" Below her, on a granite boulder flecked with snow, she made out a dark shape.

A great gray cat, body tense, ears alert.

Morwenna crowded close beside her. "It's *Gideon*," she whispered. "I'd know his head anywhere."

"Hush," Morwenna muttered.

"But if Gideon is here, there is danger. Adrian would never have sent him otherwise."

"*Hush,*" Perpetua commanded. "We'll be finished here in but a moment." She turned swiftly. "There's plenty of peat set by for the fire. I fancy that you know how to handle the peat, Commander MacNeill."

Jared nodded. He had learned to stack the peats well as a boy. "That I can."

"Then we'll be off."

Jared watched her bustle through the passage, all energy and effort in spite of her obvious age. The three ladies were unusual, that much was certain. So was the broad-shouldered MacLeod. When Jared had shaken his hand, there had been a wave of dizziness, almost as if time or space had been displaced.

Another mystery, Jared thought. Mystery seemed to suit this quiet glen.

He turned at a quick tapping by the door.

"It's Hamish Lennox," Morwenna said. "Come in, child, and warm yourself."

"Yes, ma'am," the boy said politely. "The missus at the great house, her that's wed to the MacLeod, sent me down. 'Tis a call that is waiting for the mister. Come all the way south from a proper English viscount," he added triumphantly, stamping snow from his feet.

"I'd better go up. I'll bring our bags back when I come," Jared said to Maggie. "Meanwhile, why don't you stay here and get settled?"

"Perfect," Honoria announced. "Morwenna will stay to help you. For myself, I'm going to join Perpetua outside and see what's become of that cat."

"Can't I come too?" Morwenna asked plaintively. "If it *was* Gideon, I want to—"

"You'll be needed here. Come along, Hamish." Speaking softly, Honoria led the young boy outside.

The fire sparked pleasantly. Somewhere came the sharp bark of a fox.

"Why don't you sit here by the fire?" Morwenna said after a moment. "Just you rest in this great chair." She tucked a soft length of tartan around Maggie's legs. "There now, that will be better. You've not a shred of worry in the world, my dear. You'll be quite safe here. We will all see to that."

Dimly, Maggie heard the lilting words and wondered if she had misunderstood. Then her head slanted back against the soft cushions as she drowsed in the warm glow of the fire.

Safe, she thought.

Journey's end.

And as she fell asleep she didn't hear the door open. Nor did she hear Morwenna's light footsteps cross the gravel path.

"So you're from the north, are you?" Perpetua asked Jared as they crunched through the snow toward the great house. "What part would that be?"

"Kinlochewe." His eyes darkened. "I'm afraid I'm the last of my line."

"A great pity, that. But you've a look of health and strength about you. I've no doubt that lady by the fire will give you fine sons and a daughter or two."

Jared struggled with the odd sense that he was being probed, read as clearly as he had done to others. "Have you lived here long?'' he asked, avoiding more questions.

''Some people say we're as old as those gray cliffs up there. We stay by our choice. This glen holds a special magic for us. A man Highland-born like yourself would understand that sort of hold well.''

Jared understood perfectly, crunching through the new fallen snow while the wind sent white flakes in a giddy dance about his shoulders. This *was* a place of beauty and magic. He realized he would be sorry to leave it.

''Are you certain about loaning us your cottage?''

''Of course we are. If not, we wouldn't have offered. Few besides us have ever slept there, you know. Now go on with you and see to your telephone call. I'm going to have a look about for that irritating cat.''

But there was a searching look on her face as she watched him vanish inside Glenbrae House. A moment later a gray shape streaked toward her over the fresh white snow.

''So here you are, Gideon. Trouble afoot, no doubt. Just like that rogue Adrian not to come himself.''

The cat's tail flicked sharply.

''Three of them already?'' Perpetua's eyes hardened as she stared south to the loch road. ''In that case we'd better hurry.''

''You found them?'' He pulled on a pair of leather gloves and holstered his pistol, each movement careful and precise. ''Go to the car. I'll join you there in ten minutes, after I alert the others.''

He put down the phone, staring out at the snow, thinking about old plans and a new world that was to come.

Thinking about the price of disloyalty.

And he smiled.

Chapter 32

"Yes, we're here, Nicholas. There were no glitches, and no one seems to have followed us." Standing in Glenbrae House's quiet library, Jared watched snow whisper against the windows. "Anything new there?"

"I had visitors from London here this morning. They were stunned to find Maggie gone, and you with her. They made a point of conveying the message that she had twenty-four hours to return. After that, they will take full action to find her."

Jared paced, telephone in hand. "They're not to be underestimated."

"I agree. And I'm certain that whatever they are investigating extends beyond Daniel Kincade's jewel theft."

"Have there been any more messages from him?"

"None. Izzy called a while ago with the routing on Kincade's call here to the abbey. It was placed from a phone box in London, so no leads there."

Jared hadn't really expected any. Daniel Kincade was too canny to be trapped by a single phone call. "Any other news I should know?"

"You had another phone call this morning from Dr. McNamara's office in London. She sounded quite urgent, something about a new medication she wanted to prescribe."

"She's one of the government medical team. No doubt my instability will be fully documented in their files. A perfect excuse to have me removed from the picture."

"But this new medication—"

"If Dr. McNamara phones again, tell her I'm unavailable." Jared's face hardened. "We're moving to a small cottage up the loch, someplace far less accessible. I'm only surprised that the Wishwells offered it to us."

"The three old sisters? Don't tell me they're meddling already?"

"They're been quite helpful, actually, though there's something odd about them."

"Enjoy your stay in the cottage. Just keep in mind that the government search will now begin in earnest."

"They're bound to put considerable pressure on you to tell them where we went."

Nicholas laughed grimly. "I'm having a pleasant time concocting the answers I'm going to give them. In fact, I already have a complete itinerary mapped out for you. South America, I think. Then maybe a small town in North Africa. I even think you might make a stop in Sri Lanka."

Jared laughed dryly. "I'm glad you're on *my* side."

"So you should be. I'll phone Hope and Ronan if I have any news. I won't try your cellular phone, just in case it can be traced. Meanwhile, *stay put.*"

As Jared was putting down the phone, Ronan MacLeod walked in with two suitcases. "I brought these down. I'll take them out to the car while you finish in here."

By the time Jared joined MacLeod outside, storm clouds were piling across the cliffs. "More snow coming, do you think?"

"So it appears. Exactly what Perpetua Wishwell predicted. The woman is almost always right about such things." Ronan finished stowing the last suitcase in Jared's trunk. "There's an old storage shed behind the Wishwells' cottage where you can leave your car. No need to alert any strangers to your presence."

Jared slid behind the wheel while MacLeod settled in the other seat. "Tell me something," Jared said slowly. "Was there a gray cat sitting on the fence when we left, or was I imagining it?"

"No cat that I noticed." MacLeod glanced out at the swirling landscape of white. "Not much of anything to be seen now, I'm afraid."

There was a sharp prickling between Jared's shoulders. There *had* been a cat, he was certain of it. The impossible thing was that the cat looked exactly like the great gray creature he had seen at Draycott Abbey.

He shoved the thought from his mind, concentrating on the narrow road. "Have you lived at Glenbrae long?"

"It seems like centuries. Of course, when I met Hope, it was over for me in an instant." His lips curved. "I expect it must have been like that with you and Maggie."

"There are problems."

"Problems always have solutions. Meanwhile, you're among friends here."

Halfway to the loch road, a brown car emerged over the hill. "Someone you know?" Jared asked softly.

Ronan's eyes narrowed. "No one from Glenbrae. I can count the cars on one hand." His voice tightened, "Could it be someone you want to avoid?"

Jared was taking no chances. He turned the wheel sharply, pulling onto a narrow gravel road that skirted the loch. Behind them a horn blasted shrilly. The brown car roared alongside and cut across the snowy road.

A white-haired figure in black military uniform shoved open the door, waving briskly. "Commander MacNeill, thank heaven I found you."

"Preston?" Jared stared at his old superior officer. "What are *you* doing here in Scotland?"

"Long story, MacNeill. Took me hours in this damnable weather. But I've had some information about the box delivered to the abbey. It was some entirely new chemical explosive, and I wanted to discuss it with you privately." His eyes flickered to MacLeod. "If that's possible."

"But why—"

Jared stiffened as a gun barrel brushed his neck, and Preston slid in behind him. "No more questions. You've put us to a great deal of trouble, you know."

MacLeod was already twisting in his seat when his door was flung open and he was gripped from behind by a man in a black jumpsuit. There was a short, tense struggle. Then a brutal kick to the forehead left MacLeod sprawled unconscious in the snow.

Preston's eyes narrowed. "First you'll give me the weapon in your shoulder holster."

Jared hesitated, then complied.

Preston smiled thinly, "And now the backup weapon which is no doubt hidden in your boot. I worked with you in Asia, remember?"

Jared bit back a curse. But with Preston's weapon jabbing his neck, he had no choice but to turn over his smaller pistol.

Preston gave a curt nod.

"That must be the cottage up ahead. We watched you come here this morning."

So they knew that, too. Grimly, Jared played out possible scenarios. "You'll be looking for Maggie, of course."

"Of course," Preston said coldly.

"She's not here. She went over to the village with the innkeeper to pick up some supplies."

"Don't insult my intelligence, Commander. We've had you two in sight since the moment you left the abbey. The costumes were an amusing twist, I must admit. That should keep the bureaucrats off your trail for a few more days. By then, the problem will be irrelevant." Preston laughed softly, wedging the pistol under Jared's jaw. "Drive to the cottage. I have a few questions to ask the daughter of Daniel Kincade."

Somewhere a door creaked open. The wind gave a shrill cry, racing down the glen. Maggie turned from the window with a start. "Morwenna?"

There was no answer.

"Jared?"

Fire crackled beside her in the silent cottage. No one moved outside in the snow. Maggie rubbed her hands, strangely chilled at being here alone. Where were the Wishwells and the others?

She turned and saw a shadow cross the doorway. Fear turned to surprise and her eyes narrowed. "Anders?" He looked far more tired than the last time she had seen him in London. His beard was bushy and untended, and there were dark circles under his heavy glasses. "Why are you here?"

He moved forward uncertainly, hands locked at his waist. "For many reasons."

"I don't understand. How did you find me here in Scotland?"

Suddenly fear left Maggie frozen. *Was Anders one of her father's enemies?* Had he coldly betrayed his oldest friend, then followed her here for some dark purpose only he knew?

Regret played across his gaunt face. "I know you don't understand," he said. "That is also my fault."

"*You* betrayed him?"

"I suppose in a way I did. Daniel Kincade died so that I could live." His voice changed as he spoke. The heavy accent vanished, leaving only the lengthened vowels of a Boston boyhood, and each word clawed at Maggie's memory.

Recognition came to her in a cruel rush. Tears burned her eyes as she struggled to her feet. "No," she whispered. "You're Anders. You *have* to be."

"Perhaps I've played my role so long that I forget who I am, my love."

"You're *not* my father," she rasped. "I don't believe it."

But she saw the small signs of familiarity now. How could she not have noticed them before?

Only because she'd thought him dead.

On their evening in London, she'd seen exactly what she'd expected to see: an old man who was much changed by age and stress. Maggie had put any other differences down to her own perceptions, altered by maturity and the passage of years.

She stared at him blindly. Her father. Not dead at all.

Her breath caught as she struggled with the need to run to him. Struggled with the urge to shout and accuse in anger. "You let me believe you were gone," she choked out; voicing the thoughts left her bleeding inside. "You left me to fight the accusations and cry over your grave while they hounded us and called you a thief and a coward. And I did,'' she choked out. ''Month after month. Because I *be-lieved* in you.''

''This was the safest way, Maggie.'' Daniel Kincade rubbed his eyes. ''This was the only way.'' Slowly, gently, he knelt before her and took her hands. ''Anders knew he had a heart condition which left him little time. I'd spoken to him of my danger, and he made the offer to let me assume his identity. He'd planned a visit to a clinic in Singapore, but as he'd suspected, he didn't survive the month. And I took his place, just as we'd planned, after arranging my death in that flight over Sumatra.''

''But there were more bodies found in the wreckage. What happened to them? You didn't—''

''Kill them?'' He shook his head grimly.

''There are ways, my love.'' Her father touched her face gently, as if he was afraid she might disappear. ''That bit of jungle isn't the easiest area to search, and the local teams had almost no equipment. Thanks to incessant rains and two mudslides, their evidence was nearly useless. I'd planned it that way, of course.''

Something warm dropped onto Maggie's hand. She realized it was a tear. Whether hers or her father's she could not say.

He was alive. He was here.

And he hadn't trusted her with the truth.

Her throat tightened, burning painfully. ''But why? Was it all some great trick?''

''I'm sorry, Maggie. God help me, I wish I could have done things a different way. But these men have no morals and a frightening bond of loyalty. An enemy to one of them is an enemy to *all* of them. My death was the only way to keep you safe.''

She pulled away from him, struggling to understand. He must have planned his disappearance for months. What could possibly require such secrecy and betrayal? ''What do they want from you?''

''What men have always wanted. Power, information. Control over other men.'' He caught her hands, frowning at the red welt along her palm. ''This is new?''

She nodded, mute.

"You've got to be more careful. I've always warned you to be careful, and you never listened."

Nothing had changed, Maggie thought. Her father was still the genius, still teaching, badgering, and controlling her.

Except that now he'd put her life and a dozen others into danger. At that moment Maggie stiffened, seeing Daniel Kincade exactly as he was—a passionate man with great weaknesses.

His eyes narrowed. "What's wrong?"

"It doesn't matter."

"You have the ring I gave you in London?"

Maggie nodded slowly.

"You studied the facets, I take it?"

She frowned. "They were badly formed. I couldn't understand why Anders—or *you*—would have called it beautiful. For some reason there was an extra row of facets just above the crown."

He nodded. "And another row at the base. Too small for beauty, but for my purpose they were perfect. It's all about light, Maggie." His hands closed urgently. "If a focused beam is sent through those rows of facets at the proper angle, the light is distorted."

"Distorted how?"

"A complete shift. Over time it can disrupt all nearby electromagnetic fields. Do you understand what that means?"

"No radios. No televisions."

"That and a thousand other things. I'd only been able to produce a limited area of distortion, and I needed a different facet arrangement to broaden the angle. I'd been working on the project for quite a while. Do you understand what I'm telling you, Maggie? It would be the ultimate power, a means to shut down all communication equipment. Do you realize the advantage that would give an attacking army in war?"

Maggie's whole body felt stiff and cold. She pushed away, locking her arms over her waist. "Who *are* you?" she whispered. "All you talk about is war and power and control. I don't know you. I see now that I never did."

His hands tightened. "My design work was real enough. I loved the jewels and their history. But I always wanted to see more, to understand everything. That's how I was recruited twenty-five years ago, because I was smart and tough and curious. I used all my friendships and my contacts, and I won't apologize for it," he said coldly. "I believe in everything I did and the country I did it for."

"And just what country was that?" Maggie whispered.

"You can ask me such a question?" His body stiffened sharply. "You think I would betray my government?"

"I don't know anything about you. How could I when you never told me the truth?"

"You've got to understand," he said urgently. "All my research was kept secret, closely monitored by a military team. But things began to change. The reports I wrote were taken away unread, and the chain of command changed. I was ordered to report to one man, one of a group who believed they had the exclusive right to create their own private army. They meant to use my discoveries to help them do it. I played along at first, hoping for a look at their complete network. It is staggering, Maggie. They have believers in a dozen continents and a dozen armies, and their loyalty borders on madness." He made an impatient sound, achingly like the sound she had heard him make on a dozen occasions when he was inspecting a flawed stone or a carelessly formed setting.

That single sound told Maggie more than hours of explanations. This was the father she remembered, a man always quick to criticize a competitor's work. The same father who had never had time for his lonely daughter.

"I couldn't take the chance of telling you, Maggie. The less you knew, the safer you would stay. I believed that then and I believe it now."

She tried to harden her heart. She tried to hate him for the cold-blooded decisions he had made. "Then why are you here?"

"Because I need the ring. I knew they were watching me in London, and I couldn't chance it falling into the wrong hands. And when you appeared, I gave it to you. I knew the Scotsman would keep you safe. Otherwise, I'd never have taken such a risk. In case they found me, I wanted to be certain you would have the stones, Maggie. Perhaps someday you would unlock the full value of all I'd discovered.'' He pulled off his glasses and bent forward urgently. "It's in the stones, little peach. The power is in the cut. The right facets and gem material can do things no man can imagine.''

The stones.

Of course, that was the reason. If not for them she might never have known he was still alive. But Maggie couldn't care about stones and their powers. She could only care about the man. "How did you change your face?'' she whispered, seeing all that was familiar blurred over all that was different.

"Surgery. Exercises. Cosmetic implants. It's not as difficult as you might imagine. I had access to a criminal world which specializes in such things, remember? The trick was in seeing that my real identity was never revealed to those who did the surgical corrections. Then I had to make the exchange exactly at the moment Anders died. Everyone was astounded at his miraculous recovery, I can assure you. Now enough about the past,'' he said grimly. "I have very little time before their brotherhood traces me here. I have five names of those in London who are active at high levels, but I'm going to need the ring when I take my evidence to the authorities. It will be crucial to making my case believable.''

Gently Maggie pulled a silken string from beneath her sweater. On the end hung the ring that her father, as Anders, had given her that rainy night in London. "Take it. It's yours anyway.''

His hands closed over hers almost angrily. "No, I told you the truth. It was meant to be yours. Everything I had was meant to be yours. It broke my heart when you sold my last stones, but you were wonderful. From what I've heard, you did a splendid job.''

"Don't,'' she said brokenly, not wanting to remember. She knew nothing of the shadow world he inhabited, and she wanted to remember her father as he had been, flawed but generous. Not this cold-eyed stranger with impossible tales of conspiracy and revenge.

"I love you, Maggie, and I loved your mother. My profession had nothing to do with that. But each year the jobs grew longer, the game more complex."

"A game? Is *that* what it was to you?" She stared at him, furious and shaken. "All those months you were gone and all the days that we missed you were simply a game?"

He shook his head. "I considered it an honor to complete the work I was given. I won't see everything I've discovered fall into the hands of madmen."

"You came back too late. I've gotten over you, Daddy. I don't think I want you back, not like this." The words burned in her throat, driven by pride and betrayal. "I can't afford the damage you always seem to cause."

Snow swirled at the window as they stared at one another. In the sudden, trembling silence, Maggie heard a soft cough, followed by a knock at the door.

"Morwenna, is that you?"

With a whoosh, the door opened, letting in a sprinkling of snow. "Oh, I beg your pardon. I wasn't sure that anyone was here." A small woman in a bright yellow ski parka stood on the steps, her shoulders covered with snow. "We're lost. We were looking for Glenbrae House, but we must have taken the wrong road. You see, we've just driven up from Manchester and we couldn't see anything in the snow."

Maggie forced her voice to be level and calm. "If you want Glenbrae House, you need to take the next road down the hill."

Abruptly something moved out in the snow. A gray form shot past the woman's feet, and she cried out, stumbling against the doorway.

Daniel Kincade rose slowly. "Are you all right?"

"I think so. Whatever it was, is gone now." Snow drifted down over the loch as the woman sat up shakily. Her hand brushed at her temple. "It's my head."

"Let me help you." Daniel Kincade caught her arm and helped her to a chair. "You haven't hurt yourself, I hope."

Her hands closed on his arm, and a dreamy, expectant

look filled her smooth features, "No, I'm fine now," she said. "Lovely, in fact." Her fingers splayed open, working gently across his arm. "I'll just rest here another moment if I may. I'd like to catch my breath, if that's all right with you."

"Of course," Maggie said.

But her father eased his hand from beneath the woman's fingers. "You say you drove up from Manchester? There was bad weather all along that route. I heard that the roads were closed," he said slowly.

Then he took a step back.

"Did you indeed?" The woman's green eyes narrowed. "A slip on my part. I should have said we came in by boat. I wasn't expecting you to notice. I was certain that your reunion with your daughter would distract you."

His hand dove to his pocket, but her own was faster. Sunlight played over a small pistol as she circled the room carefully. "And now that we've established your identity at last, we'll wait for the others. They have a great many questions to ask you, Mr. Kincade. While we wait, you'll kindly step away from your daughter."

"No." Kincade moved with surprising speed for a man of his age, blocking Maggie with his body.

The woman seemed entirely devoid of interest. "It's quite pointless, I assure you. Neither of you will be going anywhere."

"No, *you've* made the mistake," Kincade said grimly. "You don't dare to shoot me. Without what I have in my head, you and your ugly group of misfits are powerless."

"Again, you err. Everything you know is now mine. All the details of the facet angles. All the important contacts in your government, and the names of our group whom you've discovered." She smiled slowly. "I have an unusual gift, you see. Through physical contact, I can register thoughts and emotions. With practice I've become quite good, I assure you."

Maggie took a sharp breath. This cold description fit a gift she knew full well. But was there some connection between Jared and this woman?

"Yes, Ms. Kincade, I was certain that you would recognize the skill. Commander MacNeill is similarly gifted, though his abilities came from physical trauma, while mine came from careful chemical enhancements. His gift is far less reliable, I might add.'' Her pistol angled up, pointed directly at Daniel's chest. ''So don't overestimate your value to us, and don't assume that because I'm a woman, I won't act effectively. If you take one more step, I'll drop you cold.''

Outside a car labored over the rocky hillside.

''Excellent.'' The woman smoothed the fur at the collar of her parka. ''Exactly on schedule. As a psychiatrist, I value punctuality.'' She smiled, a gesture of cool, striking beauty. ''And I find I'm quite looking forward to seeing Commander MacNeill again.''

''What are you doing *here*?'' Perpetua glared at Morwenna, who was clambering over the drifting snow.

''I've come to tell you that I found Gideon. He was down by the loch.'' She smiled calmly. ''And to tell you that Maggie's father arrived. I let him go inside so they could talk.'' She clucked her tongue. ''So many questions she must have after all these months. And they won't have much time. He was trying to explain, saying something about a ring when the woman came.''

Perpetua stiffened, one foot on a snowdrift. ''*What* woman?''

''One in a yellow parka. From London, I expect, considering that accent.''

''You let her pass?''

Morwenna's face fell. ''You mean I should have stopped her? You said only to watch for *men*, Pet. I never thought that . . .''

Perpetua was already moving over the snow, her movements remarkably swift for a woman of such advanced age.

Chapter 33

A CAR GRUMBLED IN THE DISTANCE.

Daniel Kincade lunged to the side and grabbed the woman's wrist.

"Bloody fool," the psychiatrist snarled. Her pistol shook as she squeezed out two shots that left red stains blooming across Daniel Kincade's chest.

Maggie reached out blindly. "Stop or you'll kill him."

The Englishwoman scowled. "He's gone ashen. He must be going into shock." She felt his wrist for a pulse, then bent closer, frowning. "He's hiding something."

She shoved Daniel onto his back and dug at his shirt and coat.

Beneath Daniel's hand, Maggie saw her precious ring. Maybe she could distract the woman before she realized exactly what Daniel had dropped.

She stumbled to her feet. "I'm going for a doctor. A *real* doctor."

Instantly, the pistol swung up toward Maggie. "That would be a very bad idea, Ms. Kincade. At one time, you had use to us as bait to find your father. I urged Preston to rummage through your bags and leave that camisole with a note. Delivering that box to the abbey was my second idea. With enough pressure on you, we knew that your father would eventually emerge from hiding to help you. Now your usefulness is over, and there is no reason I shouldn't shoot you here and now."

"I don't care. I'm still going for a doctor."

Daniel Kincade shuddered, then gave a loud groan. "Don't, Maggie."

"Prop him up," the psychiatrist snapped as her pistol leveled on Maggie. "And don't do anything stupid."

Carefully, Maggie maneuvered Daniel forward, resting his back against a chair. "How do you feel?"

"Lousy. I'm sorry, love. I'd hoped to spare you this." His body shook with a savage cough. "Meet the people who plan to save the world—and kill everyone who defies them in the process." He glared up at the psychiatrist. "If they have their way, everyone will be remade in their likeness."

"Not if," the psychiatrist muttered. "*When.* Any truly advanced society demands loyalty."

"Loyalty to what?" Daniel asked.

"To superior minds. Decisions have been left to the others long enough."

"You can't succeed," the bleeding man said grimly. "No matter how many of you there are, there will always be *more* of us."

The woman's voice was cool and detached as she tossed a roll of white fabric to Maggie. "Bandage his chest. We don't want him to die yet."

"It makes no difference. I'll tell you nothing."

The woman in the parka smiled. "With your daughter as a hostage? Oh, I think you'll tell us everything we want to know, Mr. Kincade."

"Animals, that's what you are."

"Professionals," she corrected. "Just as you were. And in our hands, social inefficiency and incompetence will soon be brought to an end."

Kincade hunched forward, dragging an arm across his chest. "Where I come from, it's called democracy, lady."

The psychiatrist ran a hand over the thick fur at her collar. "Inefficiency cannot be tolerated. The world's resources are growing too limited for that. Meanwhile, the population must be contained and controlled. You will find that out soon enough."

Outside the motor grew louder. Maggie inched closer to her father and slid her fingers into his.

The door swung open.

Jared appeared. Preston was one step behind him, his gun leveled.

Jared bit back an oath when he realized the identity of the woman in the yellow parka. Revulsion filled him as a dozen puzzle pieces slipped into place. As the official psychiatrist, no doubt Elizabeth McNamara knew every detail of his medical files.

He prayed that she hadn't yet discovered the full extent of his gift.

He made a calculated decision to let the shock show on his face, fueling her sense of superiority. "Dr. McNamara? You're part of this?" He made his turn slow and dramatic, every inch of movement carefully planned. Preston was still too close for a parry, but the time to act would soon come.

"Of course. We've known of Nicholas Draycott's grand plans for some time now, and his invitation to Ms. Kincade helped us immeasurably. Her presence offered us perfect bait for her father."

He stiffened at the sight of Maggie with her hand on a bearded man with blood spreading over his chest. He recognized him as the Dutchman Maggie had met in London, but Jared had a sharp suspicion the man was not what he seemed.

Maggie's father?

Proof came in Maggie's pale, tight features as she hovered over the wounded man.

"My God, what's happened here? Jared feigned confusion until he could assess the situation. He had to find out how much the others knew.

"Meet Anders van Leiden." The woman laughed in a way that was completely devoid of humor. "Or at least the man who looks like Anders van Leiden. But of course, he is actually Daniel Kincade, presumed dead in Northern Sumatra but very much alive."

Kincade struggled upright. He coughed hoarsely, one hand to his chest, his face gray and his hands shaking. Jared had no doubt that his wound was serious. He wanted to push past Preston to Maggie, but he couldn't risk any provocation while the odds were still in Preston's favor. One wrong move could get Maggie shot.

"He needs a doctor," Jared said tightly.

"So it would appear." Preston stepped inside and kicked the door shut, never taking his gaze from Jared's back. "If you want your daughter to live, Kincade, you'll tell us where your stones are."

"Stones?"

"The ones you were working on when you vanished. We have your reports and the eyewitness accounts of your two lab assistants. In fact, they told us everything they knew before we shot them."

The words seemed to make Daniel Kincade collapse in on himself. "You killed Sanders? Amy Masterson, too?"

Preston shrugged. "They knew the dangers."

"Not from their own side." Kincade grimaced as fresh blood dripped onto his open hand. "You bastard."

"I believe you had better start talking," Preston said icily. "That is, if you wish to stay alive long enough to help your daughter."

"Release Maggie and the Scotsman. Then I'll talk," Kincade said weakly.

Jared watched and waited, knowing there would come a moment when he could act. When people wanted something as badly as McNamara and Preston did, when they turned into zealots blinded by greed for power, they made grave mistakes. Those mistakes would multiply the closer they came to their goal.

Preston's head tilted slightly. "Give us something first." His lips curved in an unpleasant smile. "As a sign of good faith, shall we say?"

"You don't think I keep the bloody stones *with* me, do you?"

"Of course not, Mr. Kincade." Preston's eyes glinted. "After all, you've eluded us for over a year, so your intelligence is not in question." He glanced down at his watch. "You have sixty seconds to tell me something I want to hear."

Jared saw the wounded man shudder and run a hand across his sweaty forehead, then look at Maggie, the pain clear in his eyes. When he spoke, the words seemed to be torn from him. "I've gone beyond my early blueprints. Last month I finished a new prototype."

Preston hunched forward eagerly. "Where is it?"

"I'll tell you everything once you've let my daughter go."

"That would be impossible," Preston said.

Maggie looked wildly at Jared, pain and shock filling her eyes. Jared shook his head tightly. All they could do now was contain their impatience and wait.

"That's my price, Preston. The stones no longer matter to me. All I want is my daughter's safety."

Maggie gripped his shoulder. "You can't trust him. You've seen what they're like."

With an angry sound Elizabeth McNamara moved closer to Preston. "There's no need to bargain with him. Kincade is irrelevant. Let's get on with business." She crossed to stand beside Kincade and pressed one hand roughly to his forehead. Her eyes fluttered, then opened on a gleam of cold satisfaction. "I told you I could do it."

"Such impatience, my dear." Preston gave a soft sigh.

"Kill him. We can make our own prototype with what I've just pulled out of his head."

Jared felt a stab of revulsion as he realized what he was seeing. She moved with the confidence of someone who could scan a mind with touch, but how was it possible? And exactly how much did Elizabeth McNamara know about him?

Bile rose in his throat, and he did not have to feign his anger. "What is she talking about?"

"I should think it was obvious, Commander. Your Dr. McNamara has a unique skill, the same one you acquired in that box in Thailand."

"I don't believe it."

Preston shrugged. "What you believe is of little interest to me."

Jared tried to dismiss this as a desperate bluff by Preston, but the smug smile on Elizabeth McNamara's lips told him otherwise. Her skills could have given them access to every sort of government secret. No doubt she had also made it her business to follow every detail of the activities at Draycott Abbey and the continuing search for Daniel Kincade.

Preston looked at Maggie's father. "Those refaceted stones of his would save us a great deal of time. The sooner we can move to our final phase, the better."

"There's no need for that," the doctor hissed. "I know the angles of dispersal and which stones make a superior medium. I also know about the warehouse space he leased outside Cheltenham. That's where he's keeping his newest prototype."

"You're wrong," Daniel said.

But Jared knew it was a lie. One look at Preston's face showed that he knew it, too. The doctor's skill was painfully clear.

"She is very seldom wrong, Mr. Kincade. It's part of the reason Elizabeth is so valuable to us. Now, my dear, you will sheathe your weapon. All command decisions come from me."

But her Browning did not fall. "Why are we wasting time? Give me the Scotsman, and with his skills we can read anyone. I already have a dozen experiments I mean to run on him."

"Experiments?" Maggie whispered. "What kind of animals *are* you?"

"Very successful animals," the doctor said coldly. "Before I'm done with Jared MacNeill, I'll know every synapse inside that extraordinary brain of his." Her eyes glinted, possessed with a strange heat. "We will have no need for you or your father, I assure you."

She didn't notice Preston turn until it was too late.

His military pistol coughed out a bullet to her shoulder. There was no emotion in his eyes as he watched her jerk sharply, then crumple to the floor beside Daniel Kincade, moaning.

"A pity," he murmured. "She was convinced she could not be replaced, but the same technique that produced her skill has produced a dozen others, and their abilities have already surpassed hers. She was also showing a personal interest in you, Commander, and that was becoming most troublesome." His mouth hardened. "The new leadership will not include women, of course. Their skills are unreliable. Elizabeth will soon discover that. Meanwhile, her wound is not fatal, but I trust it will teach her that it is always unwise to disobey my orders.''

He targeted his pistol on Maggie. ''And now, Kincade, I want answers. Otherwise, your lovely daughter will lose the front of her cranium.''

Jared's muscles tensed as he prepared to launch himself at Preston. With luck, he could knock the officer's gun off kilter before Preston could fire.

''Pointless to try, Commander. You couldn't possibly reach me in time. Ms. Kincade's skull will be gone before you've taken a single step.''

''No more.'' Kincade gave a broken cough. ''I'll tell you whatever you want, Preston. Damn it, I'll *tell* you.''

Jared saw his chance and took it. ''No.'' He moved in front of Maggie. ''Kincade might lie, but I won't. And I have the skill to read him.''

After a moment Preston nodded. ''Do it. But remember— one misstep and the woman dies.''

Jared crouched beside Kincade, frowning at the red stain that now covered the entire front of his shirt. He took a hard breath, then ran a hand across the man's forehead.

Instantly pain chewed up his arm to his chest. Kincade's wound was grave, his pain nearly overwhelming. He didn't have much time left, Jared realized. ''He's in bad shape.''

''Then you'd better work fast.''

Jared slid down, sorting through the chaotic emotions of a father reunited with his daughter and his fear for her safety. He picked up a ruined building and tables filled with books and electronic equipment. The workshop in Cheltenham, no doubt.

''What do you see?''

''Don't bother to block me, Kincade. It won't work.'' As Jared spoke, he turned slightly, cutting off Preston's view. As his hand moved over Kincade's face, he had a sharp image of a ring with five faceted stones. These were what Preston wanted, Jared realized. He glanced sidelong at Kincade's lower pocket and sensed that was where the ring was hidden.

The old man blinked quickly in assent.

Jared pushed to his feet. "Kincade lied. He brought three of the faceted stones with him. They aren't far away."

"Where?" Preston snapped.

"What happens to Elizabeth McNamara?" Jared touched the woman's clammy forehead, steeling himself against an icy flood of names, dates, and plans. "She needs medical care, too."

"As soon as I have those stones."

"I'll tell you when Maggie's in the car."

Maggie's face was set with determination. "I won't leave without my father."

Kincade pushed to one elbow, every breath straining. "Go, little peach. This is the last gift I can give you, and I hope it will be the most valuable. *Go.*" He gave a harsh cough and then his eyes sank shut.

"Do as he says, Maggie." Jared gave her a steadying look and prayed she would understand. She had to. The odds were getting worse fast.

Trust me.

Maggie nodded, then rose shakily and moved to the door with stiff, angry steps.

"Nothing happens until she reaches the car," Jared said tensely. "I'll be watching."

"Jared, you can't—"

In the same instant, Jared shoved Maggie through the open door, out into the swirling snow, then whirled to face Preston. Greed would make him delay firing until the last second, Jared knew. That would give him precious seconds to maneuver.

"I'll kill her," Preston rasped, leaping toward the door.

But Jared was outside one stride before him. "Not while I'm here, you won't."

Their shoulders met, strained. Flesh met flesh and in that instant Jared saw other details that hadn't surfaced in the psychiatrist's mind: a trail of dead on four continents. A secluded farmhouse where twelve men had met to decide the fate of the world they would carve apart between them. Finally he saw the rest of Preston's plan.

After all useful information had been squeezed free, Jared would be bound and gagged in the car they had driven from the abbey. Then he would be sent to the bottom of the loch, with Maggie beside him.

From the corner of his eye Jared saw movements against the stark landscape. A gray shape perched on top of a rocky outcrop. Other figures huddled nearby, almost obscured by the heavy veil of snow.

"Get back," Preston snapped. A bullet exploded into the snow inches from Maggie's foot. "Otherwise the next one lands in her stomach, and that's a damned painful way for anyone to go. But I'll see to it that you die first, Commander."

Dimly, Jared heard Maggie cry out at the sound of gunfire. She was nearly at the car, her face white. He felt a wave of relief as she slid behind the wheel, slammed the door and locked it.

At least she would be safe for the moment, while he dealt with Preston. And it had to be fast, if he hoped to save Daniel Kincade's life.

"I need those stones," Preston hissed. He was out the door now, circling warily in the snow. "Give me answers, MacNeill, or I won't hesitate to take you down. I have a chopper expected any moment, and I've sent my man to be sure they find us here."

"Stop." Behind them came a groan. Kincade stood braced in the doorway, his face ashen. "I h-had to hide them," he muttered, his voice reedy. "Couldn't take chances until after I disappeared." His eyes seemed to glaze.

Jared knew the old man didn't have much time. "The stones are hidden in his car," he said to Preston. "He's wrapped them in canvas and jammed them beneath one of the tires."

"Where did he leave the car?"

Jared frowned as he saw Kincade struggle to stay upright. He was losing blood fast, and every minute was precious. Their only hope was to keep Preston guessing. "He left his car behind a hedgerow near the northern entrance to the village. The stones are there." In a flat voice, Jared gave

Preston the detailed location. "But you'll have one hell of a time finding the stones in this snow."

Preston lurched forward. "That will be your job, Commander." He gestured angrily with his gun. "The chopper has a medical team and they can take care of Kincade, but first you'll drive us back to the village. If you don't find the stones, I'll kill you and Kincade's daughter myself. Her father will be going with us—for obvious reasons. Now move."

Jared assessed his choices and decided he had none. Grimly, he helped Kincade to his feet, all but carrying him to Preston's car.

"Hurry." Preston gave him a sharp push. "We've spent too many years establishing our network to fail now, with success so close." He gave Jared another jab, but this time his uncovered wrist slammed against Jared's neck.

Even as he struggled to keep Kincade's heavy body upright, Jared felt the burst of contact bring an instant rush of images.

Jungle.

The rumble of distant explosives.

The sound of marching soldiers.

Realization struck him with deadly force. "It was you, Preston? My God, you and your infernal network were behind the explosion in Thailand?"

"I wondered when you'd fit the pieces together." Preston smiled smugly. "We had a successful network in Thailand, and the money was crucial to our growth. Too bad you couldn't be swayed to join us. But of course, the local police were delighted to see the last of you since you complicated their business arrangements. When new contacts in Myanmar needed an English prisoner for a political campaign, you were the obvious choice."

Jared fought back fury. He had been traded off without a second thought, part of a mad grab for power? "What about the bomb outside the Bank of China? Was that one of yours?"

"It suited our ends. Things were growing entirely too peaceful in Asia. The communists hadn't attacked as the population feared, and we needed fresh discord. In times of chaos, civilians inevitably seek out those who are equipped to deal with death and destruction, which is *us*. The soldiers whose names are always forgotten. The ones who do the dirty jobs for pittance pay.'' Preston's jaw worked hard. ''But no more, by God. Now open the car door and get Kincade inside.''

Wind swooped down from the cliffs as Jared moved through the blinding world of white. Even Preston was shoved back for an instant by the unpredictable gusts.

Jared knew he would have to act swiftly. Once they were in the car, he would have no more chances. As he touched the door, wind whipped snow around his shoulders, leaving him blinded. In that instant the ghost of an idea took shape.

He tugged forcefully on the door, feigning irritation, then turned to Preston. ''I'll have to go around. The door is locked.''

''Make it fast,'' Preston growled. ''The chopper will be here in less than fifteen minutes.''

Jared leaned Kincade against the car and crossed to open the front door. Kincade's eyes fluttered as Jared eased him into the seat.

''M-Maggie?'' he rasped.

''Fine.''

''My pocket—take the stones,'' the old man rasped. ''It's too late for me now. Whatever happens, Preston and his kind must never have them.'' He produced a small canvas bag, which Jared slid into his pocket. Then he straightened the old man in the seat, in the process sliding the door latch down until it locked.

''What's taking you so long?'' Preston was only feet from the car, his face set in a mask of anger. As he spoke, something streaked over the snow and darted between his feet. He spun hard, cursing, and a line of bullets bit into the white slope.

A cat—or what looked like a cat, Jared thought.

And with Preston occupied . . .

He sprinted forward, ignoring the rain of gunfire in the drifts around him. With luck, he could lead Preston out of range, on toward the steep rocks to the north.

''You can't escape.'' Preston stumbled through the snow.

Two more bullets hissed toward Jared's back. A bullet dug fire across his right thigh, but even then he didn't stop. Snow whipped around him, leaving the world a veil of white, and he prayed that he could keep his sense of direction. But even then he heard Preston gaining on him.

With barely a break in stride, Jared tossed his heavy coat down into the swirling snow and kept on running.

"You never could learn to play the game properly, MacNeill. Too bad, since you might have been an asset in the new world we are creating." Preston stopped with a hiss, eyes narrowed on the shape stretched before him beneath the swirling flakes. He shoved snow out of his eyes, laughing in triumph. "But you chose the wrong side. And now you'll die for that."

He was still laughing when he sent a bullet through the dark shape at close range.

But there was no lurch of muscle, no groan of shock and pain. Cursing, he kicked at the shape, which tangled around he feet. Jared lunged at him from behind, knocking his pistol into a drift.

Though ten years older, Preston was in peak condition. He burned with the fervor of a zealot, twisting and dodging, but Jared was fighting for the woman he loved, not for abstractions, power or governments. With every breath, he drew a strength that surged beyond normal limits.

He parried once, slammed Preston to the side, and gripped his neck. "Do you know what it's like to be crouched in a box in searing heat?" he rasped. "Have you heard the screams of tortured men around you and smelled the sweat of their fear? You will, Preston. Right now there is a special box being made for you and your kind in hell."

With a cry of rage, the rogue officer twisted free and slammed his boot into Jared's bleeding thigh. Gasping, Jared stumbled sideways, blinded by the impact. Over the whine of the wind he heard the drone of engines and the whir of blades.

Preston sprang forward, searching for his fallen weapon while Jared struggled to clear his vision. Through a haze of pain, he saw Preston dive forward toward the snow, his head thrown back in triumph.

But before the Englishman could reach his goal, a cat sprang from the skeletal bough of a pine tree with claws bared, knocking the officer off stride and away from his gun. Snow gusted around them as the engine roar grew louder and the dark blades of a military helicopter whined overhead, moving north.

Preston followed, snaking past huge boulders and a row of skeletal trees. As Jared followed, he heard the restless slap of water somewhere to his right. He could not allow Preston to reach the helicopter and his flight to freedom. Hurtling over the rocky slope, he closed the gap as the ground fell away into a hollow ringed by trees. In the center stood a gray boulder covered with lichens. Above it was a snow-covered tree with a forked, broken branch.

The same tree.

The same rock that Jared had seen in a dozen nightmare visions.

For Jared, the world seemed to snap into two images, one white with snow, the other dream-like, the core of too many nightmares. He tried to shake off a sense of unreality, frozen at the familiarity of the scene, knowing his own death hung close enough to touch.

A tall figure loomed out of the blanketing white. ''I'll tend to Kincade and his daughter, man.'' Ronan MacLeod glared at the retreating aircraft. ''You had best go after the others.''

A pistol cracked.

Jared squinted into the white wall of snow, driven almost horizontal by the wind. Blindly, he stumbled forward, only to stop as he felt his boots sink deep into a layer of peat. From a boyhood spent beside loch and glen, he knew the deadly significance of the soggy marsh that hissed and rippled beneath him. But a city-born Englishman like Preston was not so lucky.

Desperately the officer struggled on, hands flung forward as the helicopter circled overhead. In clumsy strides, he crossed the edge of the peat bog, then clambered up a rocky slope that rose up out of sight in the banked clouds.

Preston was nearly at the top when the helicopter returned, circling sharply. Caught in a gust, he plunged sideways, unable to find his footing in the ice and snow.

"Preston, wait." Jared felt his words snatched away by the wind.

Too late.

The English officer cried out as his body toppled forward off the sharp ridge, then catapulted out through space. The wind amplified his cry of terror in agonizing waves as his feet thrashed vainly. Then he plunged down to meet his icy death in the waters of the loch rippling far below.

Maggie squinted into the driving snow. Fighting a wave of dread, she stumbled over the white slope, following Jared's ragged tracks.

As soon as Preston had disappeared, she had gone to her father in the car. He was now in the capable hands of Perpetua Wishwell, who assured her that he would not be lost to her for a long while yet. Hope MacLeod had already gone to fetch the local doctor from Glenbrae, and her husband was expected back any moment.

But Maggie couldn't forget Jared's grim certainty of his death, and that forewarning drove her over the snow with wind and gravel clawing at her face. Preston's fallen gun was a reassuring weight, dug from the snow and now shoved inside her coat pocket.

A shrill cry carried on the wind, bringing a new sense of dread. With tears blurring her vision, she clambered on toward a small clearing where snow drifted around a weathered boulder. Nearby stood a tree with a broken branch.

No, Maggie's mind screamed. She could not let Jared's nightmares turn real. She refused to lose him in this bleak place he had seen in so many dreams.

Metal blades beat over her head, and a dark shape loomed from the turbid gray clouds. At the same moment, Maggie saw the flash of Jared's bright plaid. She struggled up the slope to his side while the helicopter hovered low. When Maggie saw the blood that stained the snow beneath him, she gave a broken cry.

Closing her eyes, she shoved him forward and covered him with her body, shielding him in blind refusal to allow fate to take him from her. Somehow she would cheat his grim visions. She would hold him and cover him with her body if she had to.

She'd had a few visions of her own lately. Primal and deep, they whispered that Jared had belonged to her in far more than a single lifetime. This time she would not lose him.

She crouched above him, tightening her grip on his shoulders, refusing to surrender to fear and madmen. Preston and his followers would never harm him again. Ronan MacLeod would follow shortly, and after him would come a score of villagers from Glenbrae. She had only to keep Jared safe until they arrived.

Jared rolled, his eyes narrowed against the wind, taking her with him, away from the surging blades into the shelter of the lichen-covered rock and the tree with a broken limb. Hard hands gripped her; a broad chest rose before her. She heard his voice, and its smoky tones plunged deep into her soul. "Stop fighting me, woman."

"They won't get you. Not again. Preston can shoot me, but I won't move."

"Forget about Hugh Preston," Jared growled. "He's fallen to the loch and he's beyond any human help now."

He struggled to rise as the helicopter pitched, whirling snow up in sheets.

"No," Maggie cried. "You have to get away. I'm of no use to them, but they want you. Just go, while you still can." She pushed him away toward the cottage as the aircraft door opened and a man in a jumpsuit leaped to the ground. Grimly, Maggie shoved past Jared and raised Preston's pistol in a desperate grip.

The man in the jumpsuit halted. "Dear sweet lord, what's been going on here?"

Snow swirled over Nicholas Draycott's dark hair and anxious face as he stared from Maggie to Jared. "Jared, is that you? If so, perhaps you'll tell me why Maggie is holding a gun." His eyes narrowed on the snow. "And why you're bleeding like a pig."

Maggie spun with a gasp. "Dear God, there's so much blood. Here, lean on me."

"My dearest love, I'll survive," Jared muttered with a hint of a smile.

Maggie swallowed hard. "Hope MacLeod went for a doctor. They should be back very soon." She turned her cheek to Jared's chest, breathing raggedly. "I thought Preston—I thought you—"

"Nay, love."

"Don't talk. Just keep your strength until we reach the cottage. It isn't far. Maybe we can commandeer that helicopter of Lord Draycott's."

"There's no need for—"

"No more talking." Maggie gripped him tightly. "I won't let you waste your energy. Your leg—"

Jared stopped her with a kiss that could have seared a platinum plate. Long and slow, he drove his lips over hers, sealing out everything but the wild race of their hearts.

She pulled away with a broken sound. "Can you walk? We need to hurry."

"Later." He opened his freezing hands to cradle her face. "I need something else first."

Behind them Nicholas Draycott cleared his throat. "I could swear I saw a cat racing over that slope. Perhaps it was some kind of mirage."

"It was a cat," Jared answered, never looking up from Maggie's face. "Damned good timing he had, too. If it weren't impossible, I'd almost say he was kin to that great creature I saw in your conservatory." He touched Maggie's chin. "Odd, what imagination does in this kind of a storm."

"Perhaps it's blood loss," Nicholas said grimly. "We have a physician with us. Let's have him look at your leg."

"Later," Jared repeated. "Send him down to check on Maggie's father first."

"But how—" Nicholas gave an exasperated sigh as Jared pulled Maggie closer and slid his hands into her hair.

"Stubborn, impossible man," she whispered. "We need to hurry." But her answering kiss took the sting from her words. When her head rose, her cheeks were wet with tears. "What in the world am I going to do with you?"

"Love me," Jared said hoarsely, brushing snow from her

cheeks. "Today. Tomorrow. Forever. That's all I want in life."

Maggie leaned closer as the wind snapped around them and gave a shaky laugh. "Max is going to be very jealous."

She thought she heard Jared mumble something about puppy farms before his lips closed hard over hers.

Chapter 34

Outside Glenbrae House the snow fell on, silent and thick. Clouds billowed low and white wedges grew against the leaded window, while a dozen people gathered around the roaring fire in the comfortable kitchen.

Morwenna Wishwell filled another steaming mug with tea and splashed in a generous amount of whisky, managing to slosh water over the table and both shoes in the process.

"Do watch that boiling water, Morwenna, lest we have you in to see the doctor next." Perpetua took her cup and set it safely away from harm on the table. "But you're not drinking your tea, Ms. Kincade."

Maggie was huddled before the fire, weighed down by four tartan blankets. Her fingers finally had sensation again, but her shivering had yet to cease.

"Tea?" She pulled her eyes from the closed door across the hall. "Yes, that would be lovely."

Hope MacLeod put a hand on her shoulder. "What Perpetua means, my dear, is that you should have some of the tea you're holding in your hands. It will warm you up in no time, especially if there's as much whisky in it as I think there is."

Maggie looked down, frowning. A cup was cradled between her fingers, and steam tumbled up into her face. She took a drink, wincing as the fiery spirits seared the lining of her throat.

"Takes a bit of growing used to," Perpetua said, nodding gravely. "Try it slowly next time."

But Maggie didn't hear, her eyes locked on the door

where Jared was sequestered with Glenbrae's octogenarian doctor.

"There's no reason to fret, my dear. Your man is sound enough."

Fret? Maggie stared at the door, willing it to open. She wasn't fretting, she was terrified. She'd thought of nothing but Jared since their return from the grisly incidents by the loch.

"Do you think he'll lose the leg?" she whispered.

"Nay, lass. The wound was never so deep as that." Frowning, Ronan poured another bit of whisky in her tea. "The best thing for you would be to have another drink of tea. He'll not want to see you pale as oatmeal, and anxiously expecting his death."

With a wan smile Maggie took another sip, her eyes going wide as the potent spirits bit at her throat.

Hope lifted the bottle from her husband's fingers. "I don't think she'll be needing any more of this."

"But her color's gone flat," he whispered.

"She'll be fine once she sees Jared," his wife answered firmly.

"Maybe the doctor needs blood for a transfusion." Maggie turned her cup blindly as tears burned at her eyes. "Maybe he—"

Ronan gripped her shoulder. "MacNeill will need none of that." He studied her intently. "Though perhaps he will need other things."

"I'll gladly give him anything," she whispered.

The door creaked open. "Ms. Kincade?" The doctor peered owlishly around the kitchen as Maggie stood up. "There you are. Right this way with you."

"But I'm fine, truly. Just a little cold. And sometimes my throat—"

He tilted her face, peering into her eyes. "Open your mouth and say ahh."

"But I'm not—" The wooden tongue depressor cut off her protest.

"Very good," the doctor muttered. "No sign of inflammation. Now let's have your hand." Her wrist was caught, turned, probed. The doctor stared at his watch, ticking off silent seconds. "Excellent," he said finally. "A fine, normal pulse. You're fit as a horse, young woman."

"But what about Jared? Will he—"

Over the doctor's shoulder she saw Jared hobbling toward her. Beneath his kilt a thick strip of gauze covered his lower thigh. "I'll be fine, woman. As I told you before, it was just a scratch."

"Not entirely," the doctor countered.

"Close enough." Jared took Maggie's hand and pulled her toward the table.

Maggie looked nowhere but at his lined face, oblivious to the quiet visitors. "You're too pale. Too tired."

"So, my love, are you." Jared pulled her into the chair beside him.

"I told her she should drink all of her tea, but she didn't." Morwenna slid a cup into Jared's hands. "That same advice holds for you."

Absently he took a drink, then passed the steaming cup to Maggie. "Your turn. Finish the rest of it." His eyes narrowed. "I think you're going to need it."

"Why?"

"The tea first."

Maggie took a swift swallow, then burst into raw coughing as the whisky hit home.

Jared held her shoulders until the spasm passed, then took her palm in his. "I've something to say to you, Margaret Kincade. Something I've never said nor even wished to say before." He eyed the teacup and took a swift gulp, then brought her palm to his lips for a slow kiss that had Maggie's pulse climbing.

Ronan cleared his throat. "We'll be leaving now. I'd best have a look to check that our prisoners are secure out in the storage shed. Nicholas Draycott's people from Edinburgh should be here soon."

"I don't mind if you stay," Jared said. "I don't mind if everyone hears." He didn't take his eyes from Maggie's face. "I love you, Maggie Kincade. I never thought I would or could, but you've turned me inside out, with no hope of ever going back to what I was."

Her hand tightened. "Jared, you don't have to—"

"No, don't argue." He muttered something in Gaelic, then held out a hand to MacLeod. A moment later the whisky bottle hit his fingers, and he downed a tidy amount, flinching only slightly.

"Listen to me, Maggie." Jared's throat was tight and his pulse was ragged. Damn and blast, who would have thought a simple question could be so hard in the asking? His throat felt raw, and if she turned him down, he'd go straight out to the loch and shoot himself.

He cleared his throat. "I've had my reasons for holding back these words, my heart, even when you slid beneath all my shadows. Your touch changed me. What we found together changed me. But up until today, one thing wouldn't change." His hands tightened. "I'd seen my own death out there in the snow, Maggie. A dozen times in Thailand I lived through every cold detail."

Perpetua Wishwell frowned, stroking her amber brooch and murmuring softly.

But Maggie saw nothing but Jared's beloved face and determined eyes.

Jared took a harsh breath. "I saw every detail. The blood on the snow. The tree with a broken branch and the MacNeill tartan fallen against the ground. It might have been me—probably would have been me, had luck and good friends not stood on my side." He shoved a hand through his dark hair. "It appears that I won't be dying here today after all."

A tear streaked down Maggie's cheek. Silently, Jared bent on one knee before her and brushed the salty bead away with his thumb. "I *couldn't* offer you a future before this, Maggie, but now I can. And I'm asking now. Hoping." *Dying*, he thought. His hand opened over her cheek. "Would you marry me, *mo chridhe*? No man could love you more than I do."

All movement stilled. Silence wrapped around every corner of the room.

"M-marry you?" Maggie's heart did a painful jackknife. He hadn't thought this through. He'd nearly died out by the loch, after all. She swallowed hard. "You don't have to say this. It's been a long day and a vicious week."

"There's no one else for me, Maggie. Nothing else I could ever want more than this." He pulled away from her, his eyes hard and dark. "I won't say there haven't been women who've touched me, women I've admired."

"Jared, you can stop now. You don't really—"

"I can and do. Not one of them touched me as you did from the second I saw you. When I slipped into your mind that day, Maggie, I was lost. Trapped in colors and light, caught in all your passion and dreams. I was jealous of the man who'd find your fire, but I didn't dare to hope he could be me." Jared's hands clenched. "Tell me yes, Maggie. I know you best, *mo chridhe*. I've seen all the way to your soul every time we touch."

Behind Jared, footsteps rustled up the stairs, but neither he nor Maggie noticed. Maggie straightened her shoulders. Doing the right thing had never seemed so hard before. She knew her face was pale and her voice reedy. Suddenly the whoosh of the snow at the window seemed very loud.

"If something's wrong, tell me." His eyes darkened. "I won't believe there's someone else. I'd have felt him in your mind."

"Not that." She started to reach out to him, then remembered his singular gift. Closing her hands tightly, she turned away. "The answer is no, Jared," she said mechanically.

The silence stretched, lethal and taut. Hope, Ronan, and the Wishwells were nowhere to be seen. Only snow moved, whispering at the windows.

"Talk to me, Maggie." Jared frowned, reaching out for her hands.

"Don't," she whispered hoarsely.

"Why?"

"Because we have to resolve this without your touch. Because I don't want you in my head," she said desperately.

"Then tell me in words."

Behind Maggie, Hope MacLeod tiptoed past. On her way to the stairs, she gave Jared a swift thumbs-up.

The smell of pine needles and juniper lingered in the quiet air. "Why, Maggie?"

She stood stiffly, gripping the marble mantel, now covered with a length of coiling green holly. "Because it's a bad idea. Because," she said flatly, "you'll only regret it."

"Never."

"You will. Any man would."

Jared started to curse, to haul her into his arms and block the words, but reason held him still. He was too wise a man not to recognize her pain. She'd listened to his bleak story once, and now he'd do the same for her. He'd be civilized and listen for hours.

Then he'd handcuff her to his bed until he changed her mind.

He crossed his arms at his chest as Perpetua Wishwell moved past in the hallway, her hands full of pillows. She gave him a reassuring nod before disappearing up the broad stairs. "I'm listening."

Maggie was pacing now, hands locked at her waist. "It's not about you, Jared. Don't take this personally."

"It's rather hard not to."

Maggie paced to the window, turned sharply, then cut back to the opposite wall, her eyes dark with conflicting emotions. "It's like melting solder and metal. When they bond, if you're careful, they stop being two elements and create something entirely new."

Jared kept his voice level, trying to follow her. "That's good, isn't it?"

"Sometimes it is. It all depends on how you plan to use them and how they'll work together." She took a harsh breath. "It's me that's the problem. Me, not you, Jared. I don't know how to say this any other way."

Jared felt as if a steel fist had torn out his heart.

She doesn't love you, fool. She can't take the kind of life you'd give her. She needs crowds, excitement, people. With the danger past, she must have realized that clearly.

His jaw hardened. "What part of you is the problem?" he asked roughly. "Your eyes? Your hair? That unbelievable mouth of yours?"

"All of me." No smile. No quick look. Only a crushing tone of sadness in her voice.

"Oh? And what is it that's so terrible about all of you?"

"You've had so much pain already, Jared. I can't bear the thought that I'd bring you more." Her eyes, blurred with tears, rose slowly to his face. "And I would. Not because I don't love you, but because I love you too much."

The air seemed to shimmer. Jared felt a burning in his throat as he saw her hand rise, then fall to her side. What he said next would be infinitely important to their future, and he chose his words carefully. "I see. You love me," he repeated slowly. "And that's why you can't marry me."

Maggie nodded, shoving at one wet cheek. "You need someone beautiful and normal in your life. Someone wonderfully calm, with an impeccable background and solid social standing."

Understanding hit Jared in a flood. So that was it. Not the lack of love, but something else entirely. "This is because of your father. Because of the rumors and the scandal."

Her hands tightened. "What's happened here made me see all the loose threads. It's not over, Jared. There will be more police. More reporters and more frenzy. I can't put you through that after—"

He moved in a blur of speed before she could say another bleak word. Ignoring the burn at his thigh, he gripped her hand and pulled her down onto his lap. "Did it ever strike you, woman, that normal is the *last* thing I want or need? That calm and impeccable would drive me mad before one week had passed?"

"That's only now." Her chin rose stubbornly. "Later you'd change your mind when the doorbell didn't stop ringing. When you couldn't walk down a street without a thousand questions shouted at you."

His finger traced her lower lip, sending fresh heat spearing through his body. "Gentle Maggie. Stubborn, impossible Maggie who I love beyond all describing."

"You can't. I won't let you. You were the one who told me every question had a price. So answer this question, because it may save you a great deal of pain later: can you ever rest, wondering if my father did more than he said? I don't think I can," she whispered. "Even if I could, the reporters wouldn't let me. For them the story will never be over."

Jared felt her anxiety bleed over him, a storm of reds and leaden grays. Yet in the middle of those warring colors he felt the fierce, shining flame of her love. White hot, it filled him, seared him, enveloped him. She was determined to protect him, he realized, even when protection was the last thing he wanted. "Stop giving me reasons why we can't be happy."

"No." She turned her head away, her shoulders set. "I shouldn't be touching you. Touching you makes me want you, and then I lose all sanity."

Images shimmered through her mind and left Jared's body hardening. She wanted his hands, his laugh, the hot weight of his body as he filled her. She wanted him with a hunger that bordered on pain.

Jared cleared his throat. "The hue and cry will soon be forgotten. Nicholas Draycott will see to that."

"Just like that?"

"He's a very persuasive man, my dear. Especially when something personal is at stake."

Maggie frowned down at his sweater. "They won't forget back in New York."

"Then we'll go to ground for a few months. We'll sail to Tahiti and backpack through Bali. No one will have the slightest interest in two lovesick, sunburned tourists who can't keep their hands off each other." His mouth curved. "Speaking for myself, of course."

She gave a wistful smile. "You make it sound so easy."

"It is easy."

Footsteps tapped through the hall. "Jared's right, my dear. There are hundreds of places where you'd be unrecognized. One of them isn't a day's drive from here, where green hills skirt a silver loch. Right here." Morwenna Wishwell opened a heavy book and thrust it into Maggie's hands. "You can see it here. A lovely house overlooking the sea. Sheep everywhere and a fine Neolithic hill fort." Her keen eyes swept Jared's shocked face and twinkled. "That man of yours will tell you all about it."

She was gone before Maggie could look up from the

book. "It's beautiful," she whispered, peering down at the blue-green hills ringing a loch dotted with wooded islands. "Isolated, too. It would make a lovely place to stay. I wonder who lives there?"

Jared watched the hills and water blur before his eyes. He remembered the sounds of falcons and the wind singing over the cliffs. He remembered a grand house that had once been filled with laughter. "You like it?"

"It's breathtaking. Just the place to be alone."

"I suppose I might speak to the owner." Memories surged. Laughter that had turned to silence, silence to aching sadness.

Maggie twisted eagerly. "Do you know him?"

"That I do. Very well, in fact."

"Do you think he might consider it? Not that I'm agreeing to anything," she added hastily. Even then her eyes didn't leave the open pages of the book.

"He might," Jared murmured. "With the right inducement."

"You mean money." She gnawed at her lower lip. "Well I haven't very much, and I won't let you go managing this on your own," she said firmly.

"In that case, we'll have to find some other inducement," he said gravely. "Something a man simply can't do without. Something that will set him on his ear."

"Cufflinks. Maybe a matching watch." Maggie shifted again. Muscles that Jared didn't know existed slammed to agonizing arousal. "Maybe a ring for a woman. Is he married?"

"Not yet. The poor man never finished his proposal. I believe the woman in question left him without two clear thoughts in his head," Jared muttered, trying to find a more comfortable position.

And failing grandly.

"Besides," he continued, "I think he would like something more lasting than jewelry. Something he can wake up with in the morning and go to sleep with at night."

She frowned. "A dog? You want us to give him Max?"

Jared would have laughed if he hadn't been in such pain. "What he wants, Maggie, is you. Beside him at dawn.

Wrapped around him at midnight. All your laughter and your smiles.''

She looked down at the book, then looked back at him. "You mean . . ." She caught a breath. "*You* own this place?''

"Every stone and tree. Will you mind living inside drafty old granite walls half of the year?''

"But you can't—I didn't—" Her mouth closed. "Why didn't you tell me?''

"Because I was hedging my bets, in case you didn't like old, isolated castles. And I don't want to take any chances. I want your elbow gouging my ribs and your hair on my pillow when I wake. I want that impossible mouth of yours all over me when I slip into bed at night.'' He smiled. "Or any other time we choose.'' He took her hand. "Will you marry me very soon?'' he said roughly. "I can maybe manage to wait a week.'' She blinked away her tears, and his heart crumbled. "Then again, maybe I can't.''

"What if I hurt your leg? Muss your hair and straighten your tie?'' She gave a little sigh and eased her mouth against his, lingering, tasting.

Affirming.

Answering him with her heart.

Intractable Scotsman. How can I say no?

"Say the words,'' Jared said hoarsely. "I want to be sure I've got them right.''

"Yes, I will. I do.'' Her mouth tightened. "But Jared, what if my father—''

He pulled her to her feet. "Forget the bloody man. Izzy has already flown up to be on hand to watch over him in the hospital in Edinburgh. Until then, I've more important secrets to unravel.'' He swept her into his arms.

"But your leg—''

"I can manage well enough,'' he said hoarsely.

They were halfway up the stairs when Morwenna Wishwell crept into the study and lit an oil lamp in an exquisite crystal holder. Light danced over the mahogany table and brushed the miniature manger of carved figures that looked very, very old. Nearby hung a simple tin angel that spun and dipped in the quiet air.

Upstairs in the bedroom, silver candles sparkled on every table. "How did you ..." Maggie smiled. "The Wishwells, of course. Aided and abetted by Hope and Ronan. You knew about this?"

"Not a clue." Jared cupped her cheek. "I suppose they decided I needed all the help I could get since I was clearly making a hash of my first marriage proposal."

"You managed quite well, as I recall."

His eyes narrowed, and he skimmed the curve of her breast. "I hope you're sure," he said darkly. "I'm not about to give you time to change your mind."

"Well, I thought we could—"

In one twisting movement, he planted her on the bed and trapped her beneath his powerful body. Even then, her concern was for him.

"Jared, be careful. Your leg—you can't possibly—"

The great bed creaked. Chest to thigh, their bodies met, wooed, clung.

Maggie's protests fell away in a soft hiss of surprise. "I guess you can after all," she said as he pinned her to the soft linen sheets, raining kisses over her neck and shoulders.

Her hips moved. His thighs tensed. Jared swallowed as he looked at her flushed face and radiant eyes, then the pale length of her body. Most of his brain dissolved in that moment. He decided he'd better get used to the sensation, since it seemed to occur every time they touched.

Fabric rustled.

Lace fled.

Skin to skin. Heat that goaded heat with unbearable pleasure. "Tell me again," he said hoarsely. "Say you'll marry me very soon."

"I will."

Her nails gently raked his naked chest. "Stop distracting me," he muttered. "I'm trying to impress you."

"I'm impressed."

"Entice you," he rasped. "Overwhelm you."

"In that case, you probably won't like this." Her palms skimmed his ribs and eased lower, wrapped around his hot, aroused length.

"Damn it, Maggie." He twisted, cupping her soft hips and finding the taut swell of her breast with his mouth. Stroke by stroke, he claimed her, enchanted her, until she arched against him, lost in textures of pleasure while his hands traced the perfect path of her fantasies.

She made a soft, broken sound of pleasure.

Oh, there. And there.

Smiling, Jared complied.

"Stop that," she gasped. "It's cheating for you to read my mind."

"Guilty, I'm afraid. But what man could resist?" His fingers eased deeper, coaxing waves of pleasure and intoxicating heat.

He felt the colors rise at the same moment she did. Rich and heavy, they shuddered across to him wherever their bodies touched. Jared stiffened as her climax broke, slamming over them both in perfect synchrony.

With a gasp, Maggie fell against him. "Jared, no. I wanted—"

"I know, my love. And you'll have it." His hands tightened on her hips. Sleek skin parted as the sheets fell forgotten to the polished floor.

She moved against him, soft and yielding. The joy shimmered and built anew, and her eyes were dazed with desire when she pulled him against her. "I do," she whispered. "I will." She wrapped her legs around him, torturing them both with the perfect gift of all the ways she meant to love him. "Starting right now."

"God help us both," Jared muttered. He made a silent vow to share this blinding radiance with her for at least the next hundred years or so. "We MacNeills are very longlived, I warn you."

Maggie sighed as his thighs flexed. He speared deep, merging his heat with hers. "Did I ever tell you—about my grandmother?"

His mouth crooked. "Very notorious, was she?"

Each new thrust sent Maggie's heart spinning. "Terribly. Left her husband and ran off to join a traveling circus in France when she was a spry seventy-two. My father said she had a string of men who would have given every franc for one night with her.''

"So Kincade women don't like to be bored." His eyes darkened. "I'll bear that in mind.''

"Something tells me—" she gasped as his hands sent pleasure between their locked bodies "—that boredom won't be a problem. If I were bored, it would be hard to miss." She shuddered. "Under the circumstances.''

"Exquisitely hard." Jared's body tightened. He poured out praise in rough words of Gaelic, moving deep, so close that their very souls brushed. He wooed her, possessed her, until their skin was slick and their breathing labored.

He groaned when he felt her tighten sleekly around him.

Beautiful, he thought. Fearless and passionate in body, mind, and spirit. All those he had touched, and all had claimed him in equal measure.

He blinked when she twisted with sudden determination and was surprised to find himself turned, caught beneath her sleek thighs. "You're hurt, Commander. I think you need some help," she said in a silky whisper.

"Help with what?''

She moved. The other half of his brain blew cleanly away.

"Oh, that," he said hoarsely.

"You're staring, MacNeill.''

"Most men would." His voice was thick as he met her sweet heat with muscles pushed beyond every endurance.

Hold me here, she thought. *Fill all of me.*

Her unspoken words were the final goad.

Jared drove deep while pleasure coursed between them and joy bound them in blinding waves of color. He would give her diamonds, he swore. He would give her jade and pearls and laughter, along with his name.

But first this. First the pleasure beyond any she'd ever known.

The castle and its green hills could wait.

Nicholas Draycott's grand exhibition would wait.

Now he meant to love her as no other man could. In the candlelight he gave his soul to hers, lost in worlds of platinum and silver. There old curses fell to rest, and ancient fears were healed. Home was here, he realized, anywhere that he could see Maggie's blinding smile. The years seemed to fall away at the realization.

The man in box 225 was finally free to walk out of years of shadows.

He shuddered as she kissed the silver scars along his shoulders with infinite tenderness. Her mouth was sweet, but her thoughts were even sweeter.

"Take me," she whispered. "There's nothing I want more."

No words left.

No memories that mattered now.

Nothing to do but follow her, down into the rippling light, down toward paradise found. Her pleasure grew, wave by dark wave, and Jared speared home, hard and deep. She moaned his name and his hands dug into her hips as pleasure raced and snapped.

Maggie gave a broken gasp as he muttered a phrase of dark praise, then spilled his hot seed deep within her, joined now in ways neither had yet imagined or understood.

Downstairs sparks gleamed around the crystal lamp, spinning up in flecks of gold and rippling purple. Snow hissed against Glenbrae House's tiny leaded windows, and the whole house took up the glow, filled with a joy that had waited too many cold centuries for this night of perfect completion.

Epilogue

IT STOOD AT THE FOOT OF STARK WOODS, A TWISTING mass of pink sandstone towers with slate turrets and eighteenth-century battlements, the home of generations of MacNeill warriors. History hung in every corner, from the clipped yew hedges to the narrow overhung tower windows.

Destroyed half a dozen times by fire, rival clans, and English attack, the house was an architectural hodgepodge with three different roofs and an imposing Victorian wing. Rugged and grand, it dominated a lane of beech trees that twisted down to the loch.

Jared stood, Maggie's hand clasped in his as he stared at the home of his birth for the first time in almost two years. The huge oak door was well oiled and opened at a single touch. He peered into the gloom of the front hall, expecting the smell of must and mold.

But there was none. Even without direct light, he could see that the floors were well polished. As they climbed the great turnpike stairs up the tower into sunlight, he saw that there was no hint of disuse anywhere.

Lochmohr House had been well attended by the staff in his absence. Though Jared had turned his back on his legacy, clearly other, more sober minds had prevailed.

At the top of the stairs sunlight spilled over parquet floors, pristine as the day Jared had left for Thailand. Beneath Jared's arm, Max yipped sharply, pleading to be set free to explore the intriguing shadows of this new place. Jared set him carefully on his feet, smiling. "Mind you don't go far, wretch. You might not care to meet one of my ill-tempered ancestors making his ghostly rounds."

"Is the house truly haunted?" Maggie demanded.

Jared shrugged. As a boy he'd heard footsteps in empty rooms and doors close when no mortal hands were present. "I suppose that depends. My mother thought there were ghosts here. My father swore there weren't. The jury is still out on that particular question."

Maggie laughed, drawing his hand through hers. "I wouldn't mind a dashing Highlander seeking me out in some dark corridor with conquest on his mind."

"Good," Jared muttered. "That's exactly what I intend to do."

Maggie's eyes took on an answering gleam as he pulled her to him and cradled her face. "Bored yet?" he whispered.

"Nowhere close."

"I'm vastly pleased to hear it, *mo chridhe*." Sunlight spilled through the great tower, casting flecks of amber and gold through her tousled hair. She wore a simple sweater of heather gray and above it a single linked chain of beaten silver.

The necklace, Jared thought, was almost as exquisite as her smile.

"Are you certain you'd consider staying here?" he said uncertainly. "It's an hour to the village and there will be no end of work to bring this place truly into the twentieth century."

Decidedly ironic, he thought. The job would be done when the rest of the world was entering the twenty-first century.

"I couldn't think of a better home." Her voice filled with emotion. "It's like walking back in time." She ran a hand over the six-foot-thick stone windowsill and brushed the velvet curtains. Above her head Jared's ancestors glared down in silent splendor from dimly lit canvases.

Atmospheric or not, living here would have its problems. It was only proper that Jared warn her of them. ''There will be no running out for milk at midnight. Everything will have to be thought through and ordered in advance. The phone service often breaks down in stormy weather, and the chimneys are inclined to smoke.''

How bleak it sounded, enumerated that way. Perhaps it was wrong of him to even think about staying here.

Of course, they would soon be heading off for Draycott Abbey, and after that would come the weeks of preparation for Maggie's exhibition.

But first would come a wedding in full splendor at the abbey's nearest church.

Maggie caught his face and slanted it down to hers. ''As a very wise man once said to me, I've never wanted anything else more.'' With their bodies touching, she could not hope to deceive him, and Jared read the full truth shimmering in her mind.

Her passion, as always, left him awed.

For an hour they rambled through the old house, beneath the Great Hall's heavy beams, across an ocean of Oriental carpets to a drawing room that was vintage Victorian. In a different wing of the house, a weathered tower climbed up to overlook the wave-tossed sound. There Maggie stood in the sunlight, with Jared's arms around her.

As she looked far out to sea, the room seemed to blur.

Images spun through her head, and the silence suddenly took on sound.

From the cold north they came, ten men on fleet horses. Gwynna watched them atop the abbey's granite parapets while her heart raced like thunder in her chest.

She told herself there was no need for fear.

The man she loved was safe at the coast by now, or even midway to France. Far too late for the Queen's soldiers to catch him—or the jewels sewn in the lining of his rough cloak.

Jewels that would stir a kingdom and raise an army for the north.

But for armies and crowns, Gwynna of Draycotte cared little. 'Twas only the man she remembered as lightning clawed over the abbey walls. Only the man on his way to safety across the gray, churning sea.

Tears streaked down her face.

She shoved them away with knuckled hands. No tears when he was safe, carried where his duty called. No tears when she felt his gift stirring inside her, where his babe grew even now.

"Someday," she whispered to the stormy wind and felt the word snatched away in the same breath. In truth one day she would cross the water and bring him his child.

Her eyes closed. She was lost in the joy of imagining when a single horse and rider pounded out of the night.

She knew that horse.

Equally well Gwynna of Draycotte knew that rider.

"No," she cried. "Not here." Her hands closed on the cold stone. Why did he return when they bayed like hunting dogs at his heels?

Down the abbey's winding steps she raced, awkward in her haste. Through the shadowed marble halls, so long devoid of joy or laughter, while the house lay silent around her. She cared not for what her father wished, or even for her country. Not when her heart strained to different paces.

His horse stood spent and sweating by the moat, and boots rang over the stone bridge. Then his arms, strong and warm. His kisses like spring rain on face and hair and neck.

"No more could I leave than breathe," he whispered hoarsely. "Another ship will do fair for my passage."

"No," she said, desperate in her fear. "Even one more hour may be too late."

The shot rang out before she'd finished, smoke pluming from the musket of a soldier atop the hill. There was a burst of fire at her shoulder and a buzzing in her head.

"Too late," she tried to say. "Be gone." The pain

clawed into her head and became a snarling darkness.
"Now."
    Her hands reached out to broken dreams and empty air.
The man she loved caught her as she fell.
Fell.
Fell.

"Maggie? Talk to me, damn it."

Cursing, Jared pulled her to his chest. Her face was pale as death, her breathing nearly imperceptible. As before, she'd slipped away from him without any warning.

He thought her eyes would never open.

He was steeled to race for the hospital when she shuddered and blinked.

She stared up at him, disoriented. "MacNeill?" she whispered.

"Right here. What is it, love?"

A breath hissed from her lungs. "A dream. Maybe something more. I'm not sure." She gripped his broad shoulders, desperate to feel his heat instead of the clinging cold of the place where she had been lost. "Sorry," she said raggedly. "I don't know what happened . . ." She sat up awkwardly.

Jared pulled her back against his chest. "You'll stay right here until you catch your breath."

As he spoke, images churned through Maggie's head, dim and cold. Slowly, with Jared's arms around her, they retreated.

Back to a past that finally closed its doors to her.

As they touched, Jared felt the final ripple and sensed when her nightmare was truly gone.

She gave a muffled laugh. "Is this how you mean to treat me? Bullying me at every possible turn?"

Jared's hands were still shaking as he pulled a thick tartan around her shoulders. "You've done too much this week. First the wedding plans and then that exhibition. I won't have Nicholas run you ragged, friend or not."

She put a gentle finger on his lips. "No one runs me ragged except myself," she said firmly.

"You're not sleeping half enough."

"I want you to be proud of me."

"Sweet heavens protect us, I couldn't be prouder or I'd explode. Nor, I expect, could that beaming father of yours." Jared glared down at her. "I don't want you collapsing at our wedding."

Maggie's lips curved in a wicked smile that made his heart skip a beat. "That would give them something to talk about, wouldn't it? *'Criminal's daughter overcome by honorable offer.'*"

"He's no criminal. Now he's a hero." His fingers slid into her hair. "You're certain you're feeling better?"

She nodded, her head slanted against his shoulder. "Have you noticed how beautifully everything has been kept? Someone has been taking very good care of Lochmohr House for you, my love."

He'd noticed, of course. He should have realized that the fact wouldn't escape her keen eye either.

"I think they knew you'd change your mind and return. I think they want to show you that they need you here."

By the time they made their way down the great turnpike stair, her color had returned. As Jared pushed open the front door he caught the scent of pipe smoke.

A dozen hampers lined the stone steps.

A folded pile of tartans, fresh from the process of waulking.

A jar of preserves wrapped in red ribbons.

A carved walking stick of preserved bog wood.

A crate of home-smoked salmon from the loch.

Welcome back, it all meant. Jared touched one of the plaids and nearly stumbled beneath a wave of strong, warming emotions.

An old man sat on the stone bench beneath the beech drive, puffing at a homemade pipe. His craggy features curved in a smile as he stared at Jared and Maggie, then came slowly to his feet and said a phrase of soft Gaelic.

Welcome home, MacNeill of Lochmohr.

Gravely Jared thanked him for the wish.

"She is the one you will marry?"

"As God will have it."

"A fine choice. She will bring the light to this grand house again and the sound of laughter." The old man's eyes narrowed. "I think she will bring the necklace home too, even after all these years."

Jared went very still. The memory of the tarnished stones hidden in the abbey's wine cellar teased his mind.

"You mind well that long ago another MacNeill rode from this loch," the old man said in the soft tones of a man recounting a beloved tale passed down from mouth to mouth. "He'd gathered the riches of a county, hoping to raise French aid and money for troops against a coming English attack."

The sense of history weighed on Jared's shoulders.

Or perhaps it was destiny.

The old man puffed slowly on his pipe. "But it might have been just a story. Every generation makes its own legends. Clear it is that you two will make your share." His aged body stood strong and tall in the wind. "I'll be off to the village now. A thousand questions they'll have about the laird and his wife to be." He frowned, then slowly held out his hand to Jared.

Both men knew the significance of the gesture.

Both men remembered their meeting months before in the village.

Jared, gaunt and mute, newly returned from the hells of his jungle captivity. He had been unable to bear any touch when the MacNeill gift lay new upon him. He had rejected the handshake then.

He would not do so again.

Without a word he reached out and gripped the old fingers tightly. A granite wave of affection surged through him in response.

Welcome home, MacNeill of Lochmohr. These old stones have waited for you.

Snow danced through the air, dotting Maggie's hair and cheeks. As the old man wound his way back down the hill, Jared caught Maggie tight, breathless with immeasurable happiness. It was only then that he felt the difference. A new, shimmering light played through her.

Almost the sense of a different consciousness wrapped around her.

Gently his hand fell, opening over her waist.

Again it came, subtle and elusive. Something burned at Jared's eyes as he realized what he was touching.

The miracle of life.

The next MacNeill, fragile cells already stirring beneath his hand. Still too soon for any medical tests, but not too soon for the gentle probe of Jared's gift. He would tell her soon, but not yet.

Not until they were in a private spot, where he could show her all the joy her gift had brought him.

He took her hand. Together they walked beneath the towering beeches. Happiness left no room for words as the snow fell, soft and silent and very beautiful.

"She's beautiful. I told you she would be beautiful." Faith Kincade blinked back tears as she watched Maggie enter the church, clad in a dress of antique Battenburg lace and a veil of seed pearls.

"Of course she's beautiful. She's radiantly in love," Chessa Kincade whispered, her own voice suspiciously watery. "With a man like *that*, who could blame her."

Organ music swelled, and Faith made a muffled sound, caught between laughter and tears. "I absolutely *swore* I wouldn't cry."

Chessa linked their arms, "It's a wedding. You're entitled to a few tears."

Neither spoke as Maggie moved past, pale but radiant on the arm of her beaming father, who looked surprisingly hale for a man who had reappeared from his own death.

Only the family and the authorities knew the real story. Everyone else had been told the carefully prepared tale of how Daniel Kincade had plunged from the sky and lain unconscious for months in a remote jungle village until a search team stumbled on him only weeks before.

The theft charges had been dropped. Government sources explained the whole business was a grave mistake. Now they were calling Daniel Kincade a hero instead.

As the music swelled, Faith watched the man in black velvet and splendid MacNeill plaid who waited for Maggie at the altar, his joy shimmering, nearly tangible. No one could have smiled harder than Ishmael Harris Teague, his best man, magnificent in a tailored black jacket.

In that crowded church, Faith felt the hand of fate at work, almost as if Jared and Maggie had been pulled here through twisting paths over long, circuitous years of trouble and pain.

Beyond the front steps came muffled curses.

Faith hid a smile. Another reporter being thrown out, no doubt. That would make the sixth today.

Nicholas Draycott possessed an admirable security force. Currently, they circled the church, taking silent pleasure in ejecting any and all reporters who would have marred the day's joy.

In truth the media had had a field day with the news of Daniel Kincade's return. His recognition as a hero only stirred the furor about the abbey's upcoming exhibition. Even now the display cases gleamed in splendor, filled with exquisite treasures of Maggie's creation. Daniel had walked through the night before, nearly reduced to tears. "She's better than I ever was. Do you see the detail on that platinum and the faceting on those diamonds?" he'd demanded, to anyone within hearing range.

Faith knew the pleasure he took in giving away his daughter in marriage to a man he could admire completely. She also suspected that Daniel was enjoying the media's frenzied attention. She was only surprised that Maggie seemed to accept the attention, too.

Of course, having a man like Jared MacNeill nearby for protection had to make acceptance a great deal easier.

As the radiant bride joined her groom at the altar, Faith swallowed a sob.

She *never* cried. She'd fallen down a ravine, been bitten by a snake, and broken her arm in three places. Even *then* she hadn't cried.

"Oh, Lord, it isn't fair. I promised I wouldn't cry."

But today, in a quiet church in a quiet corner of the

English coast, Faith's tears spilled free. It would be a day of many firsts, she decided.

She gave up with a sigh, beyond all help as she dug in her beaded bag and found a linen handkerchief.

By then, Chessa was crying nearly as hard as she was.

Author's Note

HAVE YOU DEVELOPED A TASTE FOR PLATINUM AND TANzanite? White Siberian diamonds and South Sea pearls? Maggie makes it all look so easy.

The craft of jewelry-making is long and time-honored. One of Maggie's favorite books on the subject is Tim McCreight's *Jewelry: Fundamentals of Metalsmithing* (Madison, Wisconsin: Hand Books Press, 1997). Bending, cutting, casting and cold joining—they are all here, presented with pictures of some of the most striking, innovative jewelry being made today.

Maggie would be proud to have her architectural pieces included!

If you are fascinated by amber, that magical and beautiful substance composed of ancient plant resins, be sure to look for David Graham's *Amber: Window to the Past* (New York: Harry N. Abrams, Inc., 1996). The art—and the science—of this rare material is endlessly intriguing. (Remember *Jurassic Park?*)

For a current look at the immense creativity to be seen in jewelry work today, try *Ornament: The Art of Personal Adornment* and *Lapidary Journal.* Both will have you scouting your local jewelry supply store to try your own hand.

The rise of Asian crime families is, unfortunately, more than a matter of fiction. Triads—secret organizations dating back to Chinese resistance movements against the Manchu invaders—now control the flow of heroin out of Hong

Kong, assisted by thriving branches in Laos, Burma, Thailand, and a dozen Western countries. Family loyalty and an unbroken tradition of silence to outsiders makes Triad activity difficult to understand, track, and control. One of the best books on the subject is Gerald Posner's *Warlords of Crime* (New York: Penguin Books, 1988). A word of advice: Don't start this book late at night, or you might have trouble sleeping.

For all those who have written to ask about stories for Adrian and Nicholas: These have already been written. Nicholas's story appeared in the Avon Books' anthology *Haunting Love Stories*, while Adrian's appeared in the *Bewitching Love Stories* anthology, also published by Avon Books. Unfortunately, both books are currently out of print, but watch my website for more details.

There are now six other books in the Draycott Abbey series: (in order of publication) *Hour of the Rose, Bridge of Dreams, Bride of the Mist, Key to Forever, Season of Wishes*, and *Christmas Knight*. These are all available for order by mail directly from Avon Books by calling 1-800-762-0779. Each story is a haunting mix of danger, romance, and high-handed interference by Adrian and Gideon.

Enjoy!

After seven years of writing about the beautiful abbey, I have yet to come close to revealing all its secrets. Adrian and Gideon still manage to amaze me, and the inscrutable Marston has abilities I am only beginning to suspect. Nicholas and Kacey, of course, remain one of my favorite couples. I hope they have all brought you a shiver of magic and a touch of pure romance.

I hope that you have also enjoyed meeting the irrepressible Kincade cousins. For more information, drop by my website at *www.christinaskye.com*. You'll find excerpts of past and future books, reader contests, historical recipes, and frequent updates on life at magical Draycott Abbey.

While you're there, take the haunted abbey tour. Adrian and Gideon will be waiting for you!

Of course, I can't **wait** to hear what you think of Maggie and Jared. You can write to me at:

15730 North Pima Road
#D4
Suite 313
Scottsdale, Arizona 85260

Now I'm back to work.

As you've probably guessed, Faith and Chessa are next in line to have their own books. Though they don't know it yet, both are about to run headlong into gorgeous, irritating, and truly amazing men—along with the mystery of a lifetime.

All I can say is—sparks *will* fly!

With warmest wishes,

Christina Skye

P.S. Don't forget to send me e-mail on line at:
talktochristina@christinaskye.com.
I'd love to hear from you!